THE
IRON
RANGE

A WALTER HUDSON MYSTERY

CHARLES AYER

outskirts
press

Outskirts Press, Inc.
http://www.outskirtspress.com

ISBN: 978-1-4787-8962-8

Library of Congress Control Number: 2017910721

PRINTED IN THE UNITED STATES OF AMERICA

ACKNOWLEDGMENTS

Once again, I'd like to thank the entire team at Outskirts Press. I never dreamed that I would publish four novels in my life, and it would have remained just that, a dream, without Outskirts. In particular, I'd like to give a big shout out to Lisa Jones, a constant source of guidance and support.

Thanks also to my sisters, Susan Ayer and Becky Lennahan, my brother, John and his wife, Jan, and my dear friend Andrea Yalof for their patience and valuable advice.

In particular, I would like to express my profound gratitude to my beautiful daughter, Kimberley Broad. In addition to thoroughly reviewing my manuscript, she told me what I needed to hear whether I wanted to hear it or not. No matter what else this book is, it is better for her efforts.

Finally, my apologies to Trinity Episcopal Church in lower Manhattan. I played fast and loose with the interior layout of that beautiful building to suit the needs of my story. I hope Alexander Hamilton doesn't mind too much.

This one is for my Mother
Dawn Farrar Ayer

ALSO BY CHARLES AYER

Dutch River
Placid Hollow
A Deadly Light

1

SHE LAY ON THE SIDEWALK as if she had merely paused for a nap and would soon get up and be on her way, thought Detective Lieutenant Walter Hudson, as he stared down at the body lying on the sidewalk outside the entrance to Penn Station in midtown Manhattan on an unusually warm, sunny May afternoon. The woman's expression was peaceful, as if she'd been spared the knowledge of what had been done to her, and her final thoughts had been pleasant ones. She clearly was not young, but her skin was smooth, her makeup undisturbed. Her rich dark hair was still in place, fluttering lightly in the gentle spring breeze, adding to the disconcerting impression that she was still alive.

Except, of course, for the small bullet hole in the back of the light sweater she was wearing. But it was small, small enough, thought Hudson, for the average passerby perhaps to miss it.

The doctor from the Medical Examiner's office had already pronounced the woman dead and cleared the body for removal, but there was still work to be done. Police photographers took pictures from all conceivable angles, and a small team of crime scene investigators scoured the area for evidence.

Not helping matters was the wolf pack of reporters, cameras and videocams in tow, that had predictably appeared seemingly out of nowhere, as well as the customary gaggle of gawkers. But this was New York, and the people crowding the sidewalks on this mild Friday afternoon were New Yorkers. They all had places to go and things to do. And, anyway, a dead body wasn't exactly a novelty for most of them; so they largely just skirted the cops and the cameras and went about their business.

"What have we got, Eduardo?" said Lieutenant Hudson to the man standing next to him. Hudson towered over Detective Eduardo Sanchez, even though Sanchez was six feet tall. Both men were powerfully built, each weighing close to 240 pounds. At six-foot-four, Hudson was still trim at that weight, but Sanchez's girth had expanded over the years due to a steady diet of loaded fried egg breakfast sandwiches from a local bodega and frequent lunches of Doubles with bacon and cheese from his lunchtime destination of choice, Wendy's, all carefully concealed from his tiny wife, Angelina, who couldn't understand how her husband kept gaining weight eating the healthy diet she served him at home. Hudson liked and respected Sanchez, and he was glad to have the young detective with him.

"Hard to tell, Lieutenant," said Sanchez, grimacing. "We'll have to wait for the autopsy and crime lab results, but it looks like she died from a single, well-placed shot in the back at close range from a small caliber pistol, possibly a .22, based on the fact that there's no exit wound. Judging from the location of the entrance wound, I'd guess the bullet went straight through her heart and killed her almost instantly, which would explain the lack of blood."

"Any witnesses?"

"If there were, they didn't hang around. You know how it is, sir. And anyway, this is a busy time of day around here, not to mention that the whole thing smells like a professional hit. The murder weapon probably had a silencer on it, but I'm not sure it would've mattered. I'm willing to bet nobody noticed anything until the body was on the sidewalk and people had to step around it, and by that time whoever shot her had just blended back into the crowd."

"You're probably right," said Hudson, tugging at his collar. He could never find shirts that fit his nineteen-inch neck right, and it itched. "Any ID?"

"Yeah. There was no driver's license, but there was a photo ID in her bag that looks like it was an access badge from where she worked, and there were also a couple of business cards. The woman's name is Stephanie Marie French, and her address is one of those fancy places in the East Village that no one can buy because they're never for sale at any price. Looks like she was an employee at a place called Barstow & Company, located on Maiden Lane downtown."

"No driver's license, huh?"

"No," said Sanchez, "but, y'know, she was a New Yorker. A lot of New Yorkers don't have driver's licenses."

"What kind of outfit is Barstow & Company, I wonder?"

"No idea, but Maiden Lane's in the financial district, right?"

"Down there somewhere," said Hudson. It wasn't like he spent a lot of time on Wall Street, but they'd find out soon enough. "The question is, if she worked downtown, and she lived in the East Village, what was she doing outside Penn Station at two o'clock on a Friday afternoon?"

"I don't know," said Sanchez, "unless it had something to do with this." He held up a small, black oblong case.

"What's that?"

"It's a violin case."

"And how would you know that, Eduardo?"

"Because Angelina used to play violin in high school, and I used to carry it around for her. And the woman was carrying sheet music in the bag she was carrying."

"What kind of music?"

"How should I know? The only thing I know about music is I can't play it."

"Same here. Have you already had the case dusted for prints?"

"Yeah, sure."

"Okay, why don't we open it and take a quick look before the crime scene guys take it away."

"Right here?" said Sanchez, looking around as the cameramen and reporters, people with notoriously short attention spans, shifted their focus from the body to the two cops and the instrument case.

"Right here," said Hudson, a cop who'd long ago learned to ignore New York's relentless press.

Sanchez placed the case on the hood of a nearby patrol car and carefully undid the fasteners that held it shut. He opened it up and gazed in. There, cradled in rich, red velvet was a violin, and fastened into the top of the case was a bow.

Walter Hudson was not a sophisticated man, but he recognized beauty when he was staring at it. He gazed at it in silence.

"Well?" said Sanchez.

"Well, perhaps she was on her way to a performance or a rehearsal," said Hudson, carefully closing the case. "All I know is, I'm willing to bet that this violin is worth one hell of a lot of money, and we'd better make sure the crime scene guys know that. The fact that the shooter didn't take it tells me that whatever this was all about, it wasn't a robbery."

"You don't have to worry about the violin, Lieutenant," said a young uniformed cop as he reached for the case. "We know all about the expensive musical instruments people carry around with them in this city. If you collected them all in one place you could trade them for the Yankees. We'll take good care of it."

"I think we're done here," said another uniformed officer who'd been kneeling near the body.

"Did you find anything that'll help us?" said Hudson, looking at the men and envying them their uniforms. Most detectives couldn't wait to trade their uniforms for mufti, but not Hudson. He liked looking like a cop, and the collars fit better.

"Not really," said the cop, "but I bet Detective Sanchez is right: It was a small caliber bullet at close range. We'll find out more when we get the autopsy results and do residue testing on the victim's clothing. And I gotta think it was instantly fatal. It looks like she fell where she was shot, and nothing here says to me there was a struggle or that she tried to move."

"No evidence around the body?"

"Chrissakes, sir, this is Seventh Avenue. There's so much shit on this sidewalk, it'll be almost impossible to separate out anything related to the crime, even if there is something here. But we vacuumed up around the body anyway just, y'know, in case."

"Okay, you can take her away," said Hudson. He turned to walk back to the Midtown South precinct house, which was only a short walk away. Sanchez followed, and a few minutes later they were both sitting in Hudson's tiny cubicle in the detectives' squad room.

"So, what do you think, sir?" said Sanchez.

"I think this is going to be nothing but trouble," said Hudson, tugging his tie off and unbuttoning the top button of his shirt.

"What makes you think that?"

"Judging from her address, the way she was dressed, the way she was made up, and from the instrument that she was carrying, not to mention the fact that she was employed in the financial district, I'm willing to bet that she was well-educated, well-off, and well-known. There's going to be a lot of pressure on us to solve her murder, and solve it fast. And we've got nothing to go on." And I've got Captain Amato to deal with, he thought. But that was his problem, not Eduardo's.

"That's never stopped you before, sir." Eduardo hesitated for just a second, then said, "You heard from Captain Amato yet?"

Walter should have known that Eduardo would read his mind. Not that it was tough to figure out, he thought. The tension between Walter and his boss had descended like a London fog over the detectives' squad room in the past couple of weeks as their relationship, never great, had gone from bad to poisonous for reasons that Walter couldn't fathom.

"Not yet, but I'm sure I will. So let's get out of here while the getting's good," said Hudson, standing up and stretching his large frame. "Something tells me that we're not going to have a day off for a while. Let's go home and enjoy the evening while we can."

"Sounds good to me, sir," said Sanchez, his stomach starting to rumble.

"So, Eduardo."

"Yessir?"

"Was she good?"

"What're you talking about?"

"You know, was Angelina any good on the violin?"

Eduardo Sanchez gave his boss a long, puzzled stare.

"Geez sir," he finally said, "you sure know how to bust a guy's balls, don't you."

They were both smiling as they left the building, but Walter Hudson was haunted by the image of the beautiful woman lying on the sidewalk, as if she were asleep.

2

"**S**O YOU'VE HEARD OF HER?" said Walter Hudson to his wife, Sarah.

They were sitting in the living room of the small home they'd recently purchased after Sarah had unexpectedly inherited a small fortune along with a farm in the tiny village of Dutch River in upstate New York from a great-uncle. They could have afforded a larger home in a pricier neighborhood, but they both loved the Queens village of Fresh Meadows, especially the area around St. John's University where they'd found this house. Besides, they were modest people, and it suited their needs. They'd dined on one of Sarah's signature casseroles, the kitchen was cleaned up, and their three children were all in bed. It was ten o'clock, and they finally had some time to themselves.

"More than heard of her," said Sarah, settling herself onto the sofa, a large mug of hot tea in her hand. "I've worked with her."

"You're kidding," said Hudson, looking at his wife in surprise, as he usually did. He and Sarah had been married for fifteen years and been constant companions for almost twenty, but Walter Hudson never tired of looking at her. She still wore her thick, dark hair long, and her luminous brown eyes, along with her constantly active mind, animated her pretty face, making it lovely.

"No," said Sarah, taking a sip of her tea. "You know I've gotten active in an organization called SafeWays. It operates shelters and counseling for abused women and refugees from the sex trade."

"And you've also been pretty generous to it," said Walter, taking a large drink of his first good cup of coffee of the day. The coffee at the precinct house was a burnt, bitter, vile brew whose only virtue was that it kept him alert.

"*We've* been generous to it, Walter. You know the rule: Whatever I inherited from Great-Uncle Armin is ours, not mine."

"I know that, Sarah. It was just a slip of the tongue." It was a subject far more sensitive to Sarah than it was to him, and he had to stop tripping over it.

"It's just important to me, that's all. You're cop's pay has always been our money, and it's the same with whatever I have."

Walter didn't reply, hoping to get back on the subject.

"So, anyway," said Sarah, her point made, "that's how I got to know Stephanie French. She founded SafeWays, and she still runs it. And she's also been generous to it. I mean, really generous."

"How generous?"

"Like, eight figures generous."

Walter counted zeroes in his head. Ten million dollars at a minimum. So the woman was rich.

"What can you tell me about her?"

"Not much, really. When I say I know her, I mean that I've met her at a couple of fundraising events, and I've spoken to her briefly a few times. She was very friendly, and she seemed like a really modest person despite her money and success, and her looks. The woman was drop dead gorgeous with a figure to match. She could've been a model."

"What about her professional life?"

"All I know is she worked for Barstow & Company, and she managed a couple of their largest investment funds. She wasn't the kind of person who talked a lot about herself."

"You've heard of Barstow & Company?"

"Of course I've heard of it. Who hasn't?"

"I haven't."

"I meant people in the investment world," said Sarah, blushing slightly. It turned out that Sarah had an aptitude for money and investing that hadn't been apparent while they'd been living from month to month on his cop's pay, but which had manifested itself almost immediately after she'd inherited her great-uncle's considerable estate. She now managed all of their money and investments, which was fine with Walter.

"So it's a big company?" said Walter, not at all insulted. He was one of the finest detectives in the NYPD, and his reputation extended into the Police Commissioner's and the Mayor's offices. He was what he was: a cop's cop, and money didn't interest him in the least.

"One of the biggest, right up there with the likes of Goldman Sachs and JP Morgan."

"What do they do?"

"They're an investment bank. They raise capital for their clients, provide investment advice, and help clients with mergers and acquisitions, that kind of thing. They also operate funds where their clients can invest their money."

"Doesn't sound like any bank I know."

"No. You can't open up a checking account with them, and they won't give you a car loan or a mortgage for your house. That's a commercial or a savings and loan bank. They're completely different things."

"And they manage a lot of money."

"You can't count that high. They earn their revenue, billions of it, mostly from fees they collect for managing their clients' money."

"When Stephanie was killed she was carrying a violin with her. Do you know anything about that?"

"No. Actually it surprises me."

"Why?"

"I just figured between the job she had and her charitable activities she wouldn't have time for much else in her life."

"Do you know if she was she married?"

"No, she wasn't. She never was, and she had no children. I had no reason to know that except it came out in a couple of informal talks she gave at SafeWays fundraisers."

"Then I'm assuming," said Walter, "that you don't have any idea who might have wanted to kill her."

"Not a clue," said Sarah, "but I can only imagine that anyone that wealthy and that successful didn't get where they got without making enemies along the way, no matter how admirable they seemed."

"You're right about that," said Walter who, as a homicide detective in the richest city in the world, had seen more than his fair share of what people were capable of doing when money was at stake.

"I guess this means that the kids and I aren't going to be seeing much of you for a while."

"I don't know yet, Sarah," said Walter, putting his empty coffee cup down and sighing. "But from what you just told me, I won't be surprised if I hear from Commissioner Donahue and even Mayor Kaplan on this one."

"At least you get along with both of them."

"They're both fine people, don't get me wrong, but you know how it goes. I get along with them as long as I'm solving their high-profile murders. Once I stop doing that, I'm forgotten. I'm not complaining; it just is what it is, that's all."

"And if what I've been reading in the newspapers is anywhere near accurate, Mayor Kaplan is in the political fight of her life."

"Yeah, can you believe it?" said Walter. "I'm no Democrat, but Deborah Kaplan is the finest mayor this city has ever had, at least in my lifetime. I can't believe she might lose the Democratic primary to that shit Harold Manlius."

"I know. He comes across as such a phony, at least to me. But he's a rich phony, so a lot of people are falling for his line."

"All I can tell you as a cop is that Deborah Kaplan has done an amazing job helping us get the crime rate down in this city, especially considering the mess she inherited."

"Are the Republicans even going to put anybody on the ballot this year?"

"Does it matter?" said Walter who, as a New York City Republican, considered himself an endangered species.

"Well, a lot can change between now and November," said Sarah.

"From your mouth to God's ear. But with the way Manlius has been bashing the NYPD, the last thing Mayor Kaplan needs right now is an unsolved murder of a high-profile woman committed right out in the open. So my dear friends Commissioner Donahue and Mayor Kaplan will roast me alive and serve me up on a skewer if I don't solve it, and quick."

"But no pressure."

"Right."

"Do you think Levi might be able to help you?" said Sarah.

"He's going to be the first person I talk to in the morning."

"But tomorrow's Saturday, and we're going to the Mets game," said Sarah. Walter and Sarah, both lifelong residents of Queens, were loyal New York Mets fans. One of the few luxuries they'd allowed themselves after they'd received their newfound wealth was season tickets to CitiField for the whole family.

"Oh, sweetheart, I don't think there's going to be much to call weekends for a while. But you should take the kids. I don't want my job to get in the way of our indoctrination program."

"No doubt about that," said Sarah, yawning. She leaned over and rested her head on her big husband's shoulder. "Don't wear yourself out, okay?"

"Honey," said Walter, pulling Sarah closer, "the only person on this earth who wears me out is you. Not that I'm complaining."

"So you won't mind if I keep trying?" said Sarah, kissing him lightly on the lips.

"Not a bit," said Walter, taking his wife in his arms and lifting her as if she weighed nothing as he rose from the sofa.

"Are you thinking you might need some help getting your mind off your work tonight?"

"Something like that," said Walter, heading for the bedroom.

"Well, I'll give it my best shot."

"That's all I can ask, sweetheart. That's all I can ask."

3

DEPUTY COMMISSIONER LEVITICUS WELLES and Detective Lieutenant Walter Hudson were a decidedly odd couple.

Welles was close to normal height, but he was dwarfed by the big cop; and his slender frame, thin, graying hair clipped short, and gold-rimmed glasses that magnified his eyes gave him a decidedly bookish appearance.

But Leviticus Welles was a man to be reckoned with. Only a few short years ago he had been just another middle-aged casualty of the Great Recession: a salesman clinging to a job he detested after a long stretch of unemployment, and recovering from a marriage that had collapsed under the weight of his failure.

But then he had stumbled across a body in an alleyway near the Empire State Building on his way to a sales call, and he had been unwittingly drawn into the most important case of then Sergeant Walter Hudson's career, the *Points of Light* case. With Welles's assistance, Walter Hudson had not only solved the case but also saved the city from disaster in the process, and both men had landed directly on the radar screens of both Police Commissioner Sean Michael Patrick Donahue and Mayor Deborah Kaplan.

That recognition, as well as his early background in military intelligence, had led Welles to a job in the NYPD Intelligence division, and the rest was history. He had finally, in his early fifties, found his calling, and his rapid ascent through the ranks was NYPD legend. He was now Deputy Commissioner of the division and, except for the Commissioner himself, was undoubtedly the most recognizable cop in New York.

But Levi was not one to forget friends, and the respect that he and Lieutenant Hudson had developed for each other during the *Points of Light* case had blossomed into an enduring friendship. In the process, Sarah Hudson and Welles's second wife, Julie Remy, whom he had met during the case, had also become close friends. They socialized often and made occasional trips up to the Hudsons' farm in Dutch River together.

But business was business, and as they sat down early on Saturday morning in a small café just around the corner from the townhouse on Wooster Street in SoHo in lower Manhattan that Levi and Julie called "home," they both knew that this wasn't going to be a social call. They both ordered large coffees, and Walter, who had been born hungry, ordered a *pain au chocolat* as well. It was another beautiful spring morning in New York, but neither of the men noticed.

"Thanks for coming all the way down here," said Levi, taking a sip of his coffee.

"No problem," said Lieutenant Hudson after swallowing half of the *pain au chocolat* in one bite. "The kids had me up anyway. I didn't even have to set my alarm."

"Everybody doing okay?"

"Fine," said Hudson. "The kids are growing like weeds, and Sarah's up to her neck in volunteer work. It's amazing how fast you make new friends once you have a little money."

"I know the feeling," said Levi.

"And how about you and Julie? That photo in the *Post* must not have made her too happy."

"Ah," said Levi, "I blame myself. The *Post* is completely in the tank for Manlius, and a picture of Julie and me basking in the sun on a yacht in the Aegean fits right into Manlius's narrative. We should have been more careful. Actually, we were lucky. If the *paparazzi* had gotten there five minutes sooner, they would have gotten a real eyeful."

Levi smiled at the memory. Walter, a bashful man, said nothing.

"But despite all that, Julie and I are both fine. Julie just got another promotion at the UN embassy, which is great, but it means that she's going to be travelling more."

"Perhaps we can all head up to the farm together for a long weekend whenever you're both free. All the folks up there keep asking after you guys."

"That sounds great," said Levi, "but I'm afraid we're going to have to solve the murder of Stephanie French first, or Commissioner Donahue and Mayor Kaplan will have our heads."

"Or some other part of our anatomies. At least then we'll have plenty of time for picking apples on the farm."

"Picking apples doesn't sound so bad right now."

"No, it doesn't," said Hudson, polishing off the last of his pastry. "So what do you know about Stephanie French? Sarah told me enough about her to get me interested, but not much to help me start a murder investigation."

"It's kind of a complicated picture, Walter. There's a lot we know, and there's a lot we don't know, and all of it is probably relevant to your investigation."

"Let's start with the stuff we know," said Hudson.

"The most important thing we know is that yesterday morning Stephanie French was elected President and Chief Executive Officer of Barstow & Company."

"Wow," said Walter, "Sarah told me she had a big job there, but I didn't know it was that big."

"Neither did anyone else. Or only a very few."

"What do you mean?" said Hudson. "I would've thought that something like that would have been all over the business press."

"It was going to be, but not until Monday."

"I don't get it. Why not?"

"I don't know, and apparently no one does outside of the members of Barstow's Board of Directors."

"So how did you find out about it?"

"Let's just say we know people who know people who are on the Barstow Board."

"No disrespect to your department, Levi, but if you have people who know people then there are other outfits who have people who know people."

"I assume you're talking about the media?"

"Those are the first people who come to mind, yes. How did they expect to keep this under wraps for the weekend?"

"The Barstow Board probably didn't have a lot to worry about from the press, Walter."

"But why not? Restraint isn't something you'd normally expect from reporters, at least the ones you and I know," said Hudson.

"The financial press is a little more disciplined than the floggers at the *Post*," said Welles, "and it was a Friday. Most of the financial press take the weekend off, at least under normal circumstances. It probably would have worked, at least before the poor woman was murdered. Now this is too much of a story. I looked online, and it's already on all of the business network websites, as well as *WSJ.com* and *NYTimes.com*. Heaven help us when the *Daily News* and the *New York Post* get wind of it, which should be any minute now."

"And that's when we'll really start to feel the heat from the Commissioner's and the Mayor's offices."

"I'm afraid so," said Welles.

"Well, somebody knows why they were keeping the whole thing under wraps, even if we don't," said Lieutenant Hudson.

"And we'll find whoever that is."

"But Levi," said Hudson, putting down his empty coffee cup, "you said there was also stuff you don't know."

"And that's the funny thing," said Levi, also putting down his cup. A waiter came over and gave them both a refill, and Walter asked for another *pain au chocolat*. "I'll have one of them, too," said Levi to the young man. "There's only so much a man can resist."

"You were saying?" said Walter after the waiter had placed the pastries on the table.

"Her past seems to have a lot of gaps in it."

"That's odd. Usually when a person is that successful their past is pretty much of an open book."

"It usually is," said Levi, "and maybe it is in her case, too. My guys have just barely started to search, and we have to give them a chance. But like you said, with a person as high profile as Stephanie French usually all you have to do is look on Wikipedia to get a pretty thorough bio."

"What kinds of things are missing?"

"Pretty much everything before she graduated from Columbia University twenty-five years ago. I mean, we know that she graduated from East Island High School out on Long Island in 1987, but before that, things are pretty cloudy. We haven't been able to get any of her early schooling records, and we haven't dug up a birth certificate yet, but I'm sure that won't take much time. That'll help us fill in her family background."

"Are her parents are still alive?"

"We can't find any parents, and we don't have any information on any possible siblings, either, but I'm sure all that will be available in her personnel records at Barstow," said Levi just as his iPhone buzzed. He stared at it for a few seconds then looked up at Walter.

"What is it?" said Walter.

"Well, it looks like you'll get first crack at finding out," said Levi.

"What do you mean?"

"We just found out through back channels that the Barstow Board of

Directors is holding an emergency meeting at nine o'clock this morning at their headquarters downtown."

Walter looked quickly at his watch. It was eight forty-five.

"I'll never get there before the meeting starts," he said, starting to stand.

"No need," said Levi, waving Hudson back to his chair. "In fact, it's probably better if you wait until the meeting's ended. I'm willing to bet that a lot is going to happen at that meeting, and you're going to want to find out exactly what."

"You're probably right," said Walter, sitting back down.

"In the meantime, I'm going to head into my office and see what else my team has been able to dig up."

"Maybe it would be a good idea to circle back together sometime later in the day."

"I'll tell you what," said Levi, "why don't you and Sarah stop by our place tonight? You and I can talk shop in private for a while, and then we can all have a meal together and do some catching up."

"That sounds great," said Walter. "What do you say we stop over around six?"

"Perfect," said Levi, rising to leave. "You coming along?"

"I'm going to stay here for a few minutes and give Eduardo a call," said Hudson, pulling out his cell phone. "He's back at the precinct house reviewing the evidence. I want to check in and see how he's doing."

"Okay, see you later," said Levi as he walked out of the shop.

Walter pulled out his phone, but before he started dialing he waved the waiter over and ordered another pastry and a refill on his coffee. Investigating a murder was hungry work, and he had to make sure that he kept his energy up. Strictly business, he told himself.

⸻⟨⟩⸻

"PRETTY MUCH NOTHING, Lieutenant," said Detective Eduardo Sanchez. "We got the results of the autopsy, but there's no surprises. She was killed by a .22 short at extremely close range. The bullet pierced her left ventricle before it lodged between a couple of her ribs. Other than the bullet wound, the coroner said that she was in perfect physical condition, said she would've lived to a hundred."

"At least we recovered the bullet," said Hudson, still sitting in the café, finishing off the last of his coffee and pastry.

"Yeah, we did, and it was in excellent condition. We've already sent it over to the lab to see if we have any matches in the system. They've expedited the analysis, so we should know soon."

"Nothing else?"

"Nah. The search of her bag and the violin case turned up nothing of any use, at least not yet. There was a wallet in there with forty-five bucks and a couple of credit cards in it."

"Run the credit cards for any recent activity."

"Already done, sir. Nothing unusual."

"She own a car?"

"No, but there's nothing surprising about that. A lot of New Yorkers don't have one. And remember, we didn't find a driver's license in her purse. That doesn't mean she doesn't have one, but I'd be surprised."

"Was there a phone?"

"Yeah, there was, but it's one of those iPhones that locks up forever if you take too many tries to unlock it, so we left it alone."

"I'll ask the people at Barstow if they know what the password might have been. I'm heading down there in a few minutes to talk to their Board of Directors."

"Lucky you," said Sanchez.

"Anything else?"

"Nah, the residue that the guys vacuumed up from around the body was just your typical New York sidewalk shit. Nothing of any use."

"Not a lot to go on," said Hudson, letting out a sigh.

"Oh, there was one other thing," said Sanchez, "but I don't know what it has to do with anything."

"I'll take anything you've got at this point, Eduardo."

"The coroner said Ms. French had a tattoo on her left, you know, hip. Said it looked like good work to him, and that it had been there a long time."

"What's a 'you know' hip, Eduardo?"

"You know."

"Yeah, I know. You just don't want Angelina sending you off to Confession for thinking impure thoughts."

"Damn right," said Eduardo, not laughing.

"Did he tell you what it was?"

"Yeah," said Sanchez, clearly relieved to be moving on, "he says it was some kind of musical thing. Just a second." Hudson could hear the sound of rustling paper on the other end of the line. "He said it was a 'G-Clef' symbol, whatever that is."

"You got me," said Hudson, "but I guess it means that she's been a musician for a long time."

"Yeah, for all the good that does us."

"Okay Eduardo, thanks. Give me a call when you hear back from the ballistics guys on that bullet."

"Yessir. Oh, and sir?"

"Yes, Eduardo?"

"I just thought that you might want to know that Captain Amato's been sniffing around, sir."

"You mean he actually showed up at the precinct house on a Saturday morning?"

"Of course not, sir. He just phoned in and asked how things were going."

"And what did you tell him?"

"I told him that the investigation was in its very preliminary stages, sir."

"Nothing else?"

"No, sir. He asked after you, but I said you were in the field investigating leads."

Lieutenant Hudson knew what Amato was up to. He was dying to put in a personal call to Commissioner Donahue to tell him that he was in charge and on top of the case, although that was the furthest thing from the truth. Captain Eugene Amato never wanted to be in charge of anything. Responsibility carried too much downside, and he was too lazy to stay on top of any case, no matter what its importance. Eugene Amato's only ambition was his own ambition, and he was only interested in one thing: his career. Hudson despised him for that, and in truth, so did Commissioner Donahue. And now, for reasons he failed to understand, their relationship, never good, had completely disintegrated, and Walter knew he had to be more careful than ever.

"Did he ask me to call him?"

"I do not recall him specifically saying that, sir."

"Good," said Hudson emphatically.

"What's up with you guys these days?"

"When I know, I'll tell you."

They hung up and Walter looked at his watch. Nine-fifteen. He had no idea how long board of directors meetings lasted, so he figured he'd better get himself downtown. At least it wasn't a long ride from SoHo.

He left the café and hailed a cab. He'd have to put Captain Amato out of his mind, at least for now.

4

"OKAY BOYS AND GIRLS, it's time to sit down and get to work," said Owen Morning, non-executive Chairman of the Board of Directors of Barstow & Company. He was a natty little man in his mid-sixties, dressed as usual in an Italian silk suit that fit his slight frame perfectly, a blue, hand-stitched cotton shirt with a spread collar, and a silk bowtie from his collection that numbered in the hundreds. His silver hair was still thick and wavy, and his small moustache was clipped and short. He would have been a handsome man if his perpetual, bright smile had not revealed unnaturally white, large, capped teeth that made him look like a frisky pinto.

As non-executive chairman, Morning had no day-to-day responsibilities at the company. In fact, his sole role was to chair Board meetings. The Board had wanted to hand the Chairman's title to their new CEO, but the SEC was currently frowning upon the practice and the roles had been split three years ago, a move that had angered the retired CEO and founder of the company, Bryce Barstow, a man who was used to getting his way. So Owen Morning was paid a small fortune simply to chair these infrequent meetings. He had a lot to smile about.

"Oh, please, Owen," said Olivia Chase, Barstow's Senior Vice President and Chief Investment Officer, in a voice that betrayed a lifetime addiction to tobacco. She also served as Vice Chairman of the Board, stoutly refusing to change the title to "Chairwoman" or merely "Chair," a title she found dehumanizing. "Can't you please address us a little more appropriately? It's belittling and inappropriate, especially on such a somber occasion." Olivia Chase was the daughter, granddaughter, and great-granddaughter of bankers, but she'd come up the hard way. There had been no place for women in the financial industry when she'd started out as a floor trader forty years earlier, no matter what her family background, and her lined face bore the scars of her battles. Her bottled brown hair sat on her head like a helmet, making her face look even more worn. She was slightly younger than Owen Morning but looked a decade older.

"I apologize, dear Olivia," said Morning, sounding not at all chastised. "You are correct, of course. Ladies and gentlemen, please take your seats. Time's a'wasting, and I'm sure you all have other commitments to get to."

"I'll have you know I just missed my tee time with the Lieutenant Governor at Winged Foot," growled General Counsel Hollings Harkin. At forty-five he was the youngest member of the Board, but his open-collared, pink, button-down shirt, khaki slacks, and J. Press blazer with the Yale crest on the breast pocket made him look more like a superannuated sophomore than a youthful executive.

"How *will* the State function?" said Barbara Grunewald, a woman of a certain age, uncertain hair color, and heavily applied mascara that did little to disguise her sagging features. Like the rest of the members of the Board, Grunewald was an outside director, possessing no executive role at Barstow itself. She was currently the president of Brentwood College, an elite women's college in upstate New York, where she had been a tenured professor of English Literature for the two decades prior to her appointment to the presidency, a fact that she wanted no one to forget.

In the past, outside directorships of corporate boards had been little more than a feather in one's professional cap whose responsibilities bore little relationship to their compensation. But shareholder lawsuits and new SEC oversight had brought an end to all that, and now outside directors took their jobs seriously and carried expensive directors' liability just in case.

"Enough, enough," said Morning, suddenly serious, rapping his knuckles on the table. "I hereby call this meeting of the Barstow & Company Board of Directors to order. As the first order of business, we will observe a moment of silence in memory of our friend, colleague, and Chief Executive Officer, Stephanie French, who died so tragically yesterday afternoon."

Hollings Harkin looked toward Morning and started to say something, but a sharp look from Olivia Chase shut him up. The room was uncharacteristically silent.

"There," said Morning, after a few, brief seconds. "Now, I believe our next order of business is to elect a Chief Executive Officer to replace poor Stephanie."

"I'm not even sure that she ever became our CEO," said Harkin.

"Oh, cut the crap, Hollings," said Olivia Chase. "She was duly elected, by us, right here. She may only have been our CEO for a few hours, but she was in fact our CEO."

"But…" said Harkin.

"'But' nothing, Hollings," said Chase. "We all know you didn't want her, and we all know why, but the facts are the facts."

"I don't know what you're talking about," said Harkin.

"Oh, yes, you do. The only reason our selection yesterday wasn't unanimous was because you insisted on voting against her. And you voted against her because you couldn't stand the fact that she was smarter, more capable, and harder working than you. She earned more money for this firm than you, or anyone else in the firm's history for that matter, ever did. And she made your dick shrivel every time you got within ten feet of her."

"My God, woman, have you no decency?" exploded Harkin, his face mottling, his eyes popping.

"Look at you," said Chase, smiling. "It's shriveling right now, just at the thought of her, isn't it?"

"Olivia, please," said Owen Morning, "we have too much to do to engage in this type of pettiness."

"We most surely do," said Barbara Grunewald. "As the Bard would have said…"

"Dear Barbara," said Morning, "The Bard is not a member of this Board, and I'm sure that he would not have wanted this meeting to extend into tomorrow, and tomorrow, and tomorrow any more than the rest of us do. So let's move on." He looked at Grunewald with a self-satisfied smile while she desperately tried to come back with a suitable rejoinder, but none was forthcoming.

"Good," he said. "Now, do I hear any suggestions for a successor to Stephanie French?"

"We had two other solid candidates that we considered yesterday," said Allen Cromwell, another outside director, "April Barstow and Seth Stone. Perhaps the best thing to do would be to reconsider those two." Cromwell was a former three-term United States Senator from Connecticut. He had accomplished nothing of note in his life prior to his election to the Senate other than drain his mother's fortune, and nothing at all during his long tenure; but his rich voice and distinguished appearance had made him one of the most recognizable figures in Congress. He also had a gold-plated list of connections in Washington, D.C., which was all that had mattered to the management of Barstow & Company when they'd elected him to the Board.

"Discussion?" said Owen Morning.

"I think we made a courageous decision yesterday by electing a woman to be CEO," said Barbara Grunewald. "It would be a step backward to elect a man, don't you think?"

"No, I don't 'think,'" said Olivia Chase. "We didn't elect Stephanie French to the job because she was a woman, and it would be an insult to her memory even to imply that we did. We elected her because she was by far the most qualified person for the job, and we should do the same thing now."

"But can't we have it both ways?" said Allen Cromwell. "I think all of us would agree that April Barstow would have made a magnificent choice. She is both highly qualified and a woman." He glanced over at Barbara Grunewald, who gave him an approving nod in return.

"I believe Senator Cromwell has made a brilliant suggestion," said Grunewald.

"Well, I don't," said Olivia Chase.

"Really, Olivia," said Grunewald, "I just don't understand you."

"Of course you don't, Barbara," said Chase. "You've spent too many years on that intellect-free campus of yours to understand rational thought."

"Please, please," said Morning. "Let's try to be polite or we'll never get out of here. Now, Professor Grunewald, why don't you tell us why you would support April Barstow."

"Point of order," said Hollings Harkin.

"Yes, Hollings?" said Morning, trying not to sound peeved.

"I believe that according to *Robert's Rules of Order* the names should be placed in nomination prior to discussion."

"Hollings," said Morning before Olivia had a chance to break in, "you may have a point. But this is a highly unusual situation and right now we're just trying to talk things out among us. We will surely get back to Mr. Robert in due time. Now, Professor Grunewald."

Harkin stared down at his yellow legal pad in a sulk, but Morning ignored him.

"I believe," said Grunewald slowly, casting a cautious glance at Olivia Chase, "that April Barstow has demonstrated over a distinguished twenty-five year career here at Barstow & Company that she possesses the intellect, industry experience, and maturity necessary to run this company successfully. Frankly, I thought she should have been our choice yesterday, and I see no reason why she should not be our unanimous choice today. To paraphrase the Bard, I believe the crown would rest easily on her head. And yes, I believe it is vitally important for this company to have a woman sitting in the CEO's office." She glared at Olivia Chase but quickly looked away.

"Hear, hear," said ex-Senator Cromwell.

"Well this isn't a coronation, thank God," said Olivia Chase in a tone that made both Cromwell and Grunewald wince, "and all those words sound really nice, only not a single one of them applies to April Barstow, except for the fact that she's a woman, which, I will repeat, is irrelevant."

"Why don't you elaborate," said Morning, "but politely, please, Olivia."

"I'd be more than happy to," began Olivia in the most reasonable tone she could muster. "Some of you may be surprised to know that I genuinely like April Barstow. When she first came on board here her father asked me to mentor her, and I agreed. Even twenty-five years ago this industry was considered no place for a woman, even the daughter of the firm's founder and chairman, and I was eager to help her. But frankly, it was a constant source of frustration."

"But she moved up through the ranks so rapidly," said Cromwell, "how could it have been frustrating? I would have thought it would be a source of satisfaction for you."

"Well, you're wrong," said Chase, "so let me finish."

"Fine, fine," said Cromwell, shrinking back into his seat.

"Every step of the way, poor April proved to have an inadequate grasp of this industry. We rotated her through Fixed Income, Equities, Private Investing, even Mergers and Acquisitions, but she never mastered any of them."

"Then why was she promoted so rapidly?" said Edward Rauch, the former CEO of a highly successful software company and probably the richest and smartest outside director on the Board. "I thought Barstow & Company was a meritocracy."

"It is," said Olivia. "It certainly was in Stephanie French's case. But human nature is what it is, Ed, and I was told in no uncertain terms that it was my responsibility to make sure that April didn't fail. So I did the only thing I could do: I kept on moving her around, hoping that we'd finally find a place where she could truly excel. Frankly, we weren't promoting her as much as we were kicking her upstairs."

"What was the problem?" said Rauch.

"It wasn't for lack of trying, I'll give her that. And she never once even hinted that she felt any privilege because she was the boss's daughter. She worked her butt off everywhere she went."

"Then what was it?"

"She just didn't have it, Ed. That's the only way I know how to say it. I'm sure you've seen the same thing in your business. All the great attitude and all the hard work in the world don't count unless you've got the brains and the aptitude. April is a lovely woman, and she's bright in her own way, but she just doesn't have what this industry demands."

"All I will say," said Barbara Grunewald, "is that your assessment is far from unanimous. April Barstow attended Brentwood College and is one of our most distinguished alumnae. In fact, she took a course in Shakespeare's tragedies from me when I was still a young assistant professor, and I will never forget her touching readings of Ophelia."

"If Ophelia had been able to calculate an internal rate of return I might be impressed," said Olivia.

"Are you saying, then," said Rauch, "that we allowed a person to rise up through the ranks of this company and become a candidate for CEO whose only real qualification was that she was her father's daughter?"

"As painful as it is for me to say it, yes," said Olivia.

"Well, then," said Morning. "What about Seth Stone?"

"As I recall," said former senator Cromwell, "he didn't receive a single vote in the final tally, or in any of the preliminary votes. I don't know why we were considering him in the first place. Where I come from, votes count."

"Where you come from-"

"Olivia, please," said Morning, thinking he should demand a raise.

"I just think," said Barbara Grunewald, "that we can do better than name a white male to the position. I feel it would be such a step backward."

"I guess it's fortunate," said Morning, "that you weren't around when your Bard was running the Globe Theater."

"Who is this 'Bard' you keep referring to?" said Cromwell, a puzzled expression creasing his handsome face.

"Oh, dear," said Grunewald.

"Let's move on," said Morning.

"Yes, let's," said Olivia Chase. "I'll start."

"Surprise, surprise," mumbled Hollings Harkin.

"Seth Stone," said Olivia, ignoring Harkin, "is the 'yin' to April Barstow's 'yang.' He's one of the smartest people I've ever seen walk through the door of this company in all my years here, and every promotion he's gotten he earned through brains and just plain hard work."

"Then what's the problem?" said Ed Rauch. "I know during our discussions yesterday it came out that, for all his brains and hard work, his actual contribution to the bottom line of the company didn't even come close to Stephanie French's."

"Nobody's contributions to the bottom line came close to Stephanie's, so don't judge him on that basis," said Olivia.

"But still, there was a problem."

"The problem," said Olivia, "is that he's an abrasive pain in the ass. He didn't get along with his own colleagues or his management. Hell, even his clients hated him. He's also probably the most nakedly ambitious person who's ever worked here, and if you're that ambitious you'd better be damn charming, and you'd better keep it to yourself. I should know."

"I've never known ambition to be a liability in this industry," said Rauch.

"I guess that's a tribute to how ambitious he is," said Olivia. "And like I said, he utterly lacks the subtlety, social skills, or charm to temper it."

"I guess I don't understand how he survived this long," said Rauch. "It sounds like he should have been shown the door years ago."

"Because, as I'm sure you know," said Olivia, "in the business world it's always a tough decision to get rid of the really smart ones. You can't do anything to improve a mediocre mind, but we always tell ourselves that if someone is as talented as Seth Stone, then we just have to keep working on his interpersonal skills. But with Seth, it never seemed to work. He's just as arrogant and difficult today as he was the day he walked in the door, and I can't imagine him as the outward face of this company."

"And," said Harkin, "I was told that when he learned that Stephanie had been named the next CEO, he stormed out of the building using not so polite language about Stephanie, this company, and us. I guess he apologized for it later, but I'm not sure we can risk placing a person with so little self control in charge of this company."

"Well, there's a history there," said Olivia. "I thought he'd put that all behind him, but maybe not."

"What's that supposed to mean?" said Ed Rauch.

"Is it really worth dredging up if we're not going to choose him, which I assume we aren't going to do?" said Morning.

"You're right, Owen," said Olivia, "it's water under the bridge. Let's leave it alone."

"Then what do we do?" said Cromwell, the puzzled expression returning to his face.

"May I suggest," said Morning, "that we punt."

"Punt?" said Cromwell.

"Allen," said Morning, "you spent eighteen years in the United States Senate. I'm sure you understand the term. I think we all know what we have to do."

"Oh, Owen, are you sure?" said Olivia.

"Do we really have any other choice?" said Morning.

Of course we do, thought Olivia, but she said, "I guess not."

Hollings Harkin was sitting forward to say something when there was a knock on the boardroom door. The members of the Board stared at each other for a few brief seconds before Morning spoke up.

"Come in?" he said. The door opened a few inches, and a young woman reluctantly poked her head through the narrow opening.

"Yes, Marcia?" said Owen Morning to his personal secretary. "I thought I was clear that we were not to be disturbed for any reason."

"I'm so sorry, Mr. Morning," said the young woman, reddening, "but I thought you might want to know that there is someone waiting for you."

"Waiting for me?" said Morning.

"Actually, sir, he said that he was waiting for all of you."

"And who is this person?"

"He said that he's Detective Lieutenant Walter Hudson of the NYPD, sir."

5

BRYCE BARSTOW HUNG UP THE PHONE and sat back in the comfortable leather chair by the fireplace in his personal study. The large space on the third floor of his 5th Avenue triplex that overlooked Central Park was a pastiche of muted browns, the rich leather furniture melting into the wood paneling and darkly stained oak floors. But the bright sunlight from the overhead skylights and floor-to-ceiling windows, along with the colorful paintings that April had helped him pick out lent the room an almost cheery aspect.

It would have been cheery on this morning no matter what the weather, thought Barstow as he rose and walked, with only a barely perceptible limp, he thought, to the wet bar on the other side of the room. It was only eleven o'clock in the morning, but though he was no longer a heavy drinker by any standard, he decided that it was a perfect occasion for a Bloody Mary.

And why not, he thought as he mixed his drink and stood at the windows that looked out at the magnificent view of Manhattan Island that spread out before him like a conquered kingdom. Why not?

He hadn't made them beg, but he had made them ask, twice. They would have begged him if he'd made them, but he'd learned long ago not to alienate anyone unless it was absolutely necessary. And, besides, he still needed them, at least for a short while longer, until he left on his own terms, not theirs. Unlike the last time.

Of course, they had all hidden behind that foolish company rule mandating a retirement age of seventy for the CEO, but he had always assumed that the rule was not meant for him, that it would be waived in his case as soon as he indicated that he'd decided to stay on beyond that milestone. He'd founded the company, damn it, and he'd built it into what it was today: one of the most powerful financial conglomerates on earth. But of course, he now owned only a small fraction of its outstanding shares, and he'd been barred from voting when the motion to waive the retirement age had been put to a vote.

As he'd tried so desperately to convince the members of his Board, *his* Board, the minor physical limitations that he now lived with in no way diminished his ability to lead the company he had founded and led for so long; and he had no desire, nor could he see any reason, to step down. But they wouldn't hear it. They'd all insisted that the minor stroke he'd suffered earlier in the year had been more severe than it was, that it had affected more than his physical abilities. They'd refused to understand that the embarrassing gaffe he'd made during the last earnings call had been a minor mistake that anyone of any age could have made.

He looked in the mirror on the near wall and saw the same man he'd always seen looking back. His once dark hair had long ago gone to pewter, but it was still thick and wavy, a lion's mane. His tall frame was still erect and lean, his skin unlined and ruddy from countless rounds of golf and days spent sailing on Long Island Sound. Of course, there was that slight but annoying sagging of one side of his mouth, he couldn't deny it, and one eye no longer blinked as much as the other, but those minor symptoms were barely noticeable and indicated nothing. How could anyone look at him and doubt that he still possessed the power, the personal magnetism, and the intellectual acuity that had made him, and his company, what they were?

But there had been that interminable silence during the earnings call as everyone had stared at him.

Of course, inevitably, it had been Stephanie French who'd stepped in and filled the silence with her strong, confident voice, her unquestioned command of the data, her profound analysis of not just the company's performance but of the state of the industry, government policy, and the global economy as well. It was showing off, was all it was. Everyone knew that he, Bryce Barstow, had the same command of the data, the same deep understanding of the global environment that he'd possessed for over forty years. There was no reason to be forced to prove it four times a year at those meaningless dog and pony shows. Results were what mattered, and he'd been delivering results for longer than most of those wet-behind-the-ears analysts had been alive.

The last year, he acknowledged, had been a bit of a disappointment, with earnings down across all business segments. But even great companies have down years now and then. No one bats a thousand, not in this industry. But no, they'd insisted that the bad year had been due to his poor judgment, even before the stroke, and that the company had almost lost key clients because of it. Only Stephanie French's intervention, they had insisted, had prevented those key losses.

And that was the real heart of the matter. The Board hadn't wanted to get rid of him as much as they'd wanted to hand his job, his company, to Stephanie French. He was just fine, as sound as a dollar as they used to say, and everybody knew that. But Stephanie, beautiful, glamorous Stephanie, was the one they wanted to be the poster girl for the company. It was all optics, as if the leadership of Barstow & Company should boil down to a glamour contest.

It hadn't helped that the funds under her management had posted impressive double-digit gains during the previous year, as they did every year, despite strong market headwinds.

He'd known twenty-five years ago that hiring her had been a tragic mistake, that it was just a matter of time before the magnitude of that mistake would reveal itself.

But April had wanted him to hire her friend, had told him that he'd never regret it. She'd told him how, without Stephanie's support, she never would have made it through graduate school at Columbia, a program that Stephanie herself had sailed through at the top of her class, all the while studying the violin at Juilliard.

But now that was all behind him. He'd won. All that was left was the final victory that was now within his grasp, all but inevitable.

Bryce Barstow silently toasted himself as he sat back in his chair.

He reached for the phone to call April and give her the good news, but he thought better of it. April would be in no mood for good news. She'd all but physically collapsed when she heard the news of Stephanie's murder, and her grief was as genuine as his was not. Besides, he was tired, awfully tired. He'd have to make sure to get proper rest and conserve his energy. He couldn't avoid any more embarrassing slip-ups, not now that he was so close.

Yes, he'd wait, but not long. He would have to sit her down and explain to her that, despite the tragic circumstances, his dream, their dream, was now on the verge of coming true. She'd get over Stephanie.

Everyone would. It was just a matter of time.

6

"YOU MUST UNDERSTAND, CAPTAIN, that as non-executive chairman, I have little insight into the day-to-day dynamics of Barstow & Company."

"Thanks for the promotion, Mr. Morning, but it's 'Lieutenant,'" said Walter Hudson to the grinning little man sitting opposite him. He assumed that the man was lying to him, but he assumed that about everyone he spoke to at this stage of a murder investigation.

Twenty of his cubicles at the Midtown South Precinct House would have fit into this office, thought Hudson, as he let his eyes wander around the room. Not that he cared. His cubicle was adequate for his needs, and, besides, he spent as little time in it as possible. Time spent there was time wasted as far as he was concerned. He was only doing his job when he was out in the field. Besides, his cubicle was where Amato could find him, where he had no excuse for not picking up his phone, as he routinely did when he was out in the field.

But this office was no detective's cubicle.

The desk at one end of the room was not the massive pile of timber that Hudson would have expected it to be, but it was impressive nonetheless. His wife would have told him that it was a Louis Quinze piece that predated the French Revolution. Hudson himself didn't possess that kind of knowledge, but he could tell that it was a masterpiece of the woodworker's art.

It was also just the right size for the man now seated opposite him at the other end of the room. He would have looked like a child sitting behind Walter's image of the typical, mammoth corporate chairman's desk. The furniture they were currently sitting in, too, was not what Walter would have expected. He'd been in enough aeries of the high and mighty to know that their tastes usually ran to leather, and lots of it. This furniture though, the two sofas and two chairs arranged around an unstained oak and glass table, was upholstered in a bright floral pattern. It all seemed incongruous to Walter, as did the bright-eyed, dapper elf of a man sitting opposite him who would have reminded him of a poodle if it hadn't been for the large, equine teeth that gleamed from his mouth every time he smiled, which was often. But Walter knew that it was always a serious mistake to prejudge anyone based on appearances, so he brushed those thoughts aside.

"I'm sorry, Lieutenant," said Owen Morning, grinning once again, "but I don't know what else I can tell you. As we all explained to you in the boardroom, bringing Bryce Barstow back as interim CEO seemed like the only logical thing to do under the tragic, and unexpected, circumstances."

"Mr. Morning," said Walter, "I'm not exactly an expert on corporate governance, and I don't mean to sound skeptical, but I know that corporations the size and complexity of Barstow & Company have very detailed succession plans. I assume that Mr. Barstow's retirement decision had been communicated to the Board well in advance and that Ms. French had long ago been identified as his successor." Hudson wasn't quite sure why he'd decided to take this tack, but there had been something off about the atmosphere in the boardroom when he'd sat down with the entire board. Hudson often relied on his instincts, and they rarely betrayed him. He also knew that he seldom learned anything from speaking to people in large groups: they tended to fall back on each other, and stonewalling was always easier when questions could be deflected around a room like so many billiard balls off the cushions. So he'd dismissed the other members of the board with the exception of Olivia Chase, Hollings Harkin, and Owen Morning after collecting their contact information. He was going to speak to the three of them one at a time, despite the howling from Hollings Harkin. He'd be last.

"Well, of course - " said Owen Morning.

"And I'd also assume that you would have had a succession plan for Ms. French."

"That would be correct," said Morning, but Hudson already knew the man was lying. He didn't know what Owen Morning had been good enough at in his life to wind up in an office like this, but dissembling was clearly not one of his strong suits.

"Are you sure?" said Hudson, leaning his large frame toward the little man.

"Look, Lieutenant, maybe I'm not the person you should be talking to. As I've said, as the non-executive chairman I have almost nothing to do with the day-to-day operations of the company, and since I'm rarely here, I'm not the one to opine about the internal dynamics that led to all the recent changes."

"Are you saying that perhaps Bryce Barstow didn't retire voluntarily, that perhaps his departure was more sudden than you would like people to think?"

"Lieutenant, I would never…"

"What other 'dynamics' would you be talking about?"

"Perhaps I shouldn't have phrased it as I did."

"Was Stephanie French a surprise candidate?"

"Well, I don't know why anyone should have been surprised at Stephanie's selection."

"That doesn't quite answer my question."

"I don't know what you want me to say, Lieutenant."

"Did you perhaps think that you might have been in line for the job?"

"Me?" said Morning, laughing. It was, thought Hudson, the first genuine reaction he'd gotten out of the man all morning.

"Why not?"

"I thought I'd made this clear, but apparently I failed. I am neither a long time employee of Barstow & Company, nor am I a veteran of this industry."

"Then why are you Chairman, non-executive or otherwise?"

"As you may or may not know, Lieutenant, after the financial crisis and the Great Recession, the government began to take a close interest in the operations and management of large financial enterprises like Barstow & Company, which led to a great deal of regulatory reform."

"You mean like Dodd-Frank?" said Hudson.

"Yes," said Morning, an ironic smile crossing his face, making him look like Mr. Ed after he'd won an argument with Wilbur, "and isn't that rich."

"Sir?"

"Never mind. Suffice it to say that a great deal of pressure was put on Barstow & Company and many other firms like it to separate the roles of Chairman and CEO."

"Before that, was Bryce Barstow both Chairman and CEO?"

"Of course he was. He was the founder of the firm and an industry legend to boot. There had never been any real thought to separating the offices before the crash."

"Okay, but why were you named to the job?"

"Lieutenant, I am a lifelong academic and government bureaucrat. I taught economics at NYU for many years, and I served a term at the Federal Reserve Bank of New York. My only claim to fame is that I wrote a very popular, at least by academic standards, textbook on the Federal Reserve System, which is still the standard text at most colleges in the country. I am, in a word, a respected name in the world of economics."

"And you also have a great deal of respect in government circles, I'm guessing."

"Precisely."

"And you never had any expectation of being named CEO?"

"I believe," said Morning, betraying only a little impatience, "that I have already answered that question."

"Did Barstow & Company ever need a bailout from the government during the Great Recession?" said Hudson, sensing a dry well and wanting to move on.

"It most certainly did not."

"Why not?"

Another smile, though this one showing no trace of irony, lit the small man's face.

"That," he said, "is a remarkably relevant question."

"How's that?" said Hudson.

"Because Stephanie French saved this company from utter destruction, that's why."

"And how did she do that?"

"Lieutenant, we are now treading in waters that are over my head. I wasn't even associated with Barstow & Company at the time, and I believe that question can be more appropriately directed to people more knowledgeable than I."

"Perhaps so," said Hudson. He had to move on, and he'd have to sift out the truth from the fiction in Owen Morning's tale later. "Thank you very much for your help, Mr. Morning. You can feel free to leave."

Normally people all but ran out of the room when Hudson dismissed them, but to his surprise, Morning hesitated, a reproachful expression on his face that reminded Hudson of a dog who'd just been blamed for something the cat had done.

"I'm so sorry, Mr. Morning," he said, suddenly realizing his mistake. "Will you be needing your office for the rest of the day?"

"No, Lieutenant, not at all," said Morning, his expression brightening.

"If you would like to use it for further interviews I will be more than glad to inform my secretary that I have placed it at your disposal for as long as you require it."

"I really appreciate that, Mr. Morning. Thank you."

"Not at all, Lieutenant, not at all," said a smiling Owen Morning. He shook Hudson's hand and left the office with a bounce in his step.

People are funny, thought Hudson. But he was a busy man, and he let the thought drop.

"HUDSON."

"Hey, Lieutenant, Eduardo here."

"You got anything for me yet?" said Hudson, sitting at the Louis Quinze desk in Owen Morning's office, a Bluetooth device stuck in his ear. He hated the damn things, but at least it freed up both his hands. The chair was a little small for his large frame, but he found it surprisingly comfortable.

"We got the ballistics results back on the bullet that killed Stephanie French."

"That was fast," said Walter.

"I think they got a call from, you know, high up."

"That's what I was afraid of."

"Anyway, as soon as the docs extracted the bullet they handed it over to the ballistics guys."

"And?"

"First of all, it was like we guessed. It was a .22 caliber bullet fired at point blank range, a short round, so it was fired by pistol."

"I don't think we ever believed that it was fired by a rifle."

"These days, Lieutenant, you never know. These pros, they're so good they could carry a specially altered rifle around with them all day, and you'd never notice."

"Yeah, maybe. But what makes you think that this was a professional hit?"

"Because that bullet was fired by the same pistol that was involved in three other murders in the last twelve months, all of them mob related."

"All of them unsolved, I'm guessing."

"Of course."

"Leaving us nowhere."

"Maybe, Lieutenant, but maybe not. The three other murders all went down in the middle of a turf war between two rival gangs."

"Which ones?"

"One of them is called the 'Zorros.'"

"You mean, like, after the TV show?"

"No, sir. The word 'zorro' means 'fox' in Spanish. The gang's been around in uptown Manhattan since I was living there as a kid. They tried to recruit me and my brothers."

"What are they into?"

"The usual: drugs, prostitution, protection, and generally terrorizing everybody into shutting up about it all."

"And what about the other gang?" said Hudson, jotting down notes on a small notepad and pen he'd found in a desk drawer.

"It's more of an organization than a gang, sir, but not one I know anything about," said Sanchez. "It's run by some guy I never heard of named Tommassino Fornaio, who supposedly controls all the organized crime in New York State outside of the five boroughs."

"I've heard of the guy. He's a mobster for sure, but he comes across like a successful business executive. His wife is gorgeous. Both of their kids went to Harvard, and one of them is a legislative aide in the governor's office. He and his wife have set up a nonprofit foundation together, which never seems to have trouble raising funds, and they've both been photographed in public with the mayor and the governor."

"But he's still a thug."

"Damn right, and one of the toughest."

"I guess the Zorros didn't get that memo, because they decided they wanted to expand into his territory," said Eduardo.

"Whose side is our shooter on?"

"He's on the Fornaio side. It seems that all of the dead bodies piling up in the war are Zorros, and from what I hear, they've just about called it quits. I talked to an organized crime guy uptown and he says the Zorros have been beaten so bad they might have to disband."

"What a shame," said Hudson, "you must be heartbroken."

"Yeah, heartbroken. How's things going on your end, Lieutenant?"

"Interesting is all I can say right now."

"Interesting how?"

"It just seems that these guys are putting a story together that they want to sell to me, but it doesn't ring true. I've only interviewed one of the Board members so far, but I've got a couple more sitting here cooling their heels that I want to talk to before they have a chance to coordinate their stories. The others I'll chase down in the next couple of days if they start looking interesting."

"What do you want me to do in the meantime?"

"First, get a warrant to search Ms. French's apartment. Then talk to the detectives who investigated the other murders that were committed with the same weapon, and talk some more to the Organized Crime Division guys. See if they have any guesses who might have pulled the trigger."

"But I'm guessing, Lieutenant, that even if we find out who this guy is, he's not the guy we're actually looking for."

"That's my guess too, but it's hard to tell right now. It's sad to think, but Ms. French might have been a random victim of a stray bullet at the tail end of a gang war. Except, from what I've heard, Fornaio never brings his mob business to Manhattan, so I think the guy who pulled that trigger had hired on with someone else. I want the real murderer, the person who paid him. But we'll have to be careful, Eduardo, because there are a lot of people, people way above us, who are going to want this murder tied up with a bow and solved real quick."

"Yeah, and you know this shooter's probably got a rap sheet as long as your arm anyway."

"Right, so if we catch him they'll just pitch him into Rikers and throw away the key."

"And tell us to move on."

"Damn right," said Hudson. He hung up, yanked the Bluetooth out of his ear, and pitched it onto the desk. He was still muttering to himself when there was a knock on the office door.

⊷⊶

"I'M NOT SAYING that I don't want to help, Lieutenant. I'm just saying that I'm a very busy man."

"I understand that, Mr. Harkin," said Lieutenant Hudson, trying to keep his visceral dislike of the man sitting across from him from being too obvious. After his interview with Owen Morning, Hudson had decided to interview Harkin next despite his desire to annoy the guy by making him wait. He was beginning to think that his most productive interview might be with Olivia Chase, the longtime company and industry veteran, and he wanted to have as much background as possible going into that discussion. Besides, there were more ways to give a guy like Hollings Harkin the business than just making him sit and fume. "I'm just trying to figure out what could be more important than trying to help solve the murder of a woman who was the Chief Executive Officer of this corporation, and who had been a colleague of yours for over a decade before she became your boss."

"She was never my… "

"But she was, wasn't she?" said Hudson. "That somehow bother you?"

"Of course not. Why should it have bothered me?"

"I don't know. You tell me."

"I just got finished telling you," said Harkin, reddening, "that it didn't bother me. So please stop insinuating that it did."

"Then why don't you tell me how you *did* feel about it?"

"Feelings had nothing to do with it, Lieutenant. I'm a professional and so is…was…Stephanie French. That's where it began, and that's where it ended."

"But you voted against her, didn't you? You kept the vote from being unanimous."

"That was simply a professional assessment of mine. It was nothing personal."

"But it's my understanding that in situations like this, it's routine to go back to the 'nay' voters and ask them to change their votes, so that the decision can be presented to the public as a unanimous one. Are you saying that wasn't the case here?"

"No, I am not saying that."

"So you were asked to reconsider, a routine request under the circumstances, and you refused. Why?"

"Because I am a man of principle. It would have been hypocritical for me to change my vote, a vote based on principle, simply for appearances. Others may engage in that kind of behavior, but not I."

"What did you have against Stephanie French?"

"I didn't have anything 'against' her, Lieutenant. That makes it sound personal, which it was not. I simply didn't think she was the right person for the job, that's all."

"But Owen Morning seemed to think that she was single-handedly responsible for saving the company in the wake of the Great Recession."

"Owen Morning has a right to his own opinions, but he wasn't even employed by the company at the time, and he certainly, no matter what his other qualifications may be, is no industry expert."

"But neither are you. You're a lawyer, and you'd only been with the company a couple of years when the crisis hit. Stephanie French probably saved your job, along with the jobs of thousands of others."

"You seem to be forgetting, Lieutenant, that at the time of the financial crisis, Bryce Barstow, a real giant in the industry, was the Chairman and CEO of the company which bears his name, not Stephanie French. It was his brilliant, visionary leadership that saved this company, and no one else's."

"Then why did Owen Morning say what he did?"

"You're asking me to speculate, Lieutenant, and I don't speculate."

"You seem to be a great admirer of Bryce Barstow."

"Of course I am. Who wouldn't be?"

"How about the other members of the Board who decided it was time for him to leave?"

"It was Bryce Barstow himself who decided that it was time for him to retire. He made the call, and he set the date. I don't think you will find anyone on the Board who will contradict me on that."

"Are you sure, Mr. Harkin?" said Hudson. He was guessing, operating on a hunch, but it was working. He could see the shift in Harkin's posture, the change in his expression. He didn't know what Hudson knew, and it was unnerving him.

"Lieutenant," said Harkin after a nervous pause, "I can only recount to you my understanding of the situation. Anyone who tells you anything differently would be hard pressed to prove it."

"That sounds a little less positive, Mr. Harkin."

"If it does it shouldn't."

"Okay," said Hudson, knowing that he'd scored a point but wanting to move on. "Let me ask you something else. Did you ever entertain any hopes of one day becoming CEO yourself?"

"What a ridiculous notion. Of course not. I am an attorney, my father was an attorney, and my grandfather and great-grandfather were attorneys. That's what I was trained to be and all I ever aspired to be."

"And you all went to Yale?"

"What makes you think I went to Yale?"

"You did, right?"

"Alright, yes, but how did you know?"

"The two last names usually give it away for me. And before Yale you went to Groton?"

"Saint Paul's, if you must know," said Harkin, beginning to look nettled.

"And your father, and grandfather, and great-grandfather before you? The same?"

"Of course."

"And you are Hollings Harkin IV?"

"The Fifth, actually. Great-great grandfather founded the name and the family fortune, but it was in shipping, not the law."

"And were you the first to leave the family firm?"

"How have you heard of the family firm?" said Harkin, a look of incredulity spreading across his face.

"There is one, right?"

"Yes, of course. Harkin, Porter & Smith, one of the most respected law firms in New York, and a Harkin has sat in the Senior Partner's office since its founding."

"Until now."

"What do you mean?"

"Isn't that obvious? You left, Mr. Harkin. Why?"

"No, Lieutenant, it's not obvious. I left because Bryce Barstow badly needed a general counsel he could rely on, and he came to Dad, my father, for a recommendation. He recommended me, and we all wholeheartedly agreed."

"Your father and Bryce Barstow knew each other?"

"Of course. They went to Saint Paul's and Yale together, and the Firm has been providing legal counsel to Barstow & Company since its founding."

"So what's not obvious?"

"What?"

"You said that it's not obvious that your family law firm would now have a non-family senior partner. What did you mean?"

"Lieutenant, is all this really relevant to your investigation?"

"I don't know yet. I won't know until I get the answers to my questions."

"If you must know, it was never finally decided that I would not eventually return to the Firm. My father's commitment was to Bryce Barstow. It was personal."

"But you're probably going to stay here."

"Lieutenant, you continue to amaze me. Why on earth would you ever say that?"

"It just seems to me that you wouldn't have taken Stephanie French's election to the CEO's job so personally if you didn't think you were committed to the company for the long term, that's all."

"Lieutenant, as I have told you repeatedly, my decision not to vote for Stephanie French to become the CEO of Barstow & Company was a principled, professional decision based solely on objective criteria."

Perhaps, thought Detective Lieutenant Walter Hudson as he rose from his chair in a gesture of dismissal, but I didn't hear any.

Hollings Harkin hurried out the door. Hudson took pleasure in knowing that he'd at least made the man miss another tee time.

———

IT WAS only two in the afternoon, but Olivia Chase looked like a woman who needed a drink, thought Hudson, as they entered the small, dimly lit pub on the corner of Maiden Lane and Water Street that was only a short stroll from Barstow & Company's corporate headquarters. It was a stroll, Hudson gathered, that Olivia Chase took often. Even Police Commissioner Sean Michael Patrick Donahue didn't start drinking this early, at least not on work days. But Chase had announced that, "this is a discussion that will go better over a drink," so Walter had followed her over to this small watering hole. It was called "The Stray Dog," and a sign hanging out over the entrance depicted just that. It looked like it had been a part of this neighborhood since the Dutch controlled the city and called it Niew Amsterdam. It reminded him of the pubs of his youth, and Walter couldn't help but like the place, despite the hour.

"I'll have a lite beer," he said to the waitress who approached them before they'd had a chance to sit down. The place was empty except for the two of them, and the waitress was clearly anxious for some tip-producing activity. Walter thought he'd noticed her eyes light up when she spotted Olivia, but he might have been imagining it in the dim light.

"He'll have a double Jack Daniels on the rocks, and the usual for me, Kate," said Olivia, as she led them over to a small table in a corner hidden from the rest of the bar like she was on autopilot. It was clearly what the

Germans would have called her *stammtisch*, her permanent table, and her expression was proprietary as she took her seat.

Kate clearly knew her customer, and the drinks arrived fast. Olivia Chase's "usual" turned out to be an enormous martini with three olives on a toothpick. Chase then surprised Hudson by taking a pack of unfiltered Camel cigarettes out of her purse and lighting one up as Kate deftly slipped an ashtray onto the table.

"You know that smoking in here is against the law, right?" said Hudson.

"What's your point?" said Chase, taking a drag and inhaling it deeply.

"Ms. Chase, I'm a cop."

"You most certainly are. But you look like a bright young man, so I'll assume that you've got the good sense to keep your mouth shut about it, just like the folks who run this place."

Hudson thought of the cigars that Commissioner Donahue frequently smoked in his hideaway at One Police Plaza. What's good for the goose is good for the gander, he decided.

"Fine," he said.

"Nectar of the gods," said Chase, after taking a large swig of her drink and emitting a satisfied sigh. "Now, let's get down to business. What do you want from me?"

"Ms. Chase…, uh, is that how I should address you?"

"I'm single, always have been, but what I see looking back at me in the mirror in the morning isn't a 'Miss,' so that'll be fine."

"Thank you," said Hudson. He was starting to like this hard-looking woman. "Right now, I'm just trying to gather background information on the victim, Stephanie French. There doesn't seem to be much known about her personal life, and since you've worked with her for so long, I was hoping you might be of some help."

"On the assumption that murder victims often are either related to or know their killer."

"Yes, that's right."

"Well, you're shit out of luck in the family department, that much I can tell you."

"Why is that?"

"Because Stephanie French didn't have any, that's why."

"Ms. Chase, everybody has parents."

"Lieutenant, I understand biology. All I'm saying is that, to my knowledge, no one ever met her parents, and no one ever heard her mention them, even in passing. Same goes for siblings, cousins, you name it."

Which didn't eliminate them as suspects as far as Hudson was concerned.

"Were you close to her?"

"No."

"Frankly, Ms. Chase, that surprises me."

"Well goodie for you," said Olivia, stubbing out her cigarette. "What makes you think that we'd have been close?"

"Well, you know, you being a woman and her being a woman. I thought perhaps you would have mentored her, that's all."

"Let me tell you something, Lieutenant," said Olivia, draining her glass as another one magically appeared. She lit another cigarette and stared at Hudson's still full glass. "You gonna drink that?" she said, pointing at the glass with her cigarette.

"I'm sorry, Ms. Chase," said Walter, "it's just that I'm not much of a drinker, that's all."

"You're a big boy," said Olivia, looking him up and down. "If I were you I'd man up. I lose interest pretty fast in people who can't have a polite drink with me."

Walter dutifully took a slug of his Jack Daniels, which he had to admit tasted awfully good, and said, "Now, where were we?"

"You were in the process of insulting me and Stephanie by implying that we should have been close simply because we were both women."

"I was?"

"Lieutenant, I got where I got because I'm damn good at what I do. The best. And every time somebody thinks they're complimenting me by announcing that I was the first woman to do this, or the first woman to do that, they diminish my accomplishments, and they diminish me. I'm not just the best woman; I'm the best. Period."

"I didn't mean to…"

"And the same went for Stephanie French," said Olivia, ignoring Hudson. "She didn't get where she got because she was a woman; she didn't get where she got despite being a woman, and she didn't need any damn mentors. She was simply the best at what she did, and she was named CEO of Barstow & Company for that reason and for that reason only." She took a large swig of her second drink, lit another Camel, and sat back, looking like she'd just scratched an itch.

"Hollings Harkin admitted to me that he not only voted against Ms. French, but that he also refused to change his vote in the end to make her election publicly unanimous. Do you think that was because Ms. French was a woman?"

"I think it was because Hollings Harkin is a pussy."

"Ma'am?"

"Look, Lieutenant, I'm not here to psychoanalyze Hollings Harkin or anyone else for that matter, so let's just move on."

"Okay," said Walter, draining his glass just as another one arrived. If he wasn't careful, he'd be bumming a Camel off of Olivia soon. "One thing I'd like to understand is that, until she was elected CEO, Stephanie French reported directly to you, correct?"

"That is correct," said Olivia, giving the big cop a level gaze.

"But you weren't on the slate of candidates for the CEO's job, even though one of your subordinates was."

"That is also correct."

"How did you feel about that?"

"Do you want my thoughts or do you want my womanly feelings, Lieutenant?"

"Goddammit, Ms. Chase, I would've asked the exact same question, using the exact same words, if you were a man and you know it. I'm trying to solve a murder here, so why don't you just give me a fucking break and answer the goddam question."

If Hudson had expected an angry retort, he would have been disappointed. Instead of firing back with an angry response, Olivia Chase hesitated for a second, and then simply smiled at him, a big, genuine smile that took years off her countenance and made Hudson think for the first time that she had probably been good-looking, even pretty, in her youth.

"Good for you, Lieutenant," she said. "It's an appropriate question under the circumstances, and it deserves a response." She paused to light another cigarette. "I suppose you're wondering if I was angry, or perhaps jealous, because a subordinate was selected over me for the big job. Perhaps you think that I may have been doubly angry because I wasn't even put on the slate of candidates."

"Were you?"

"You're damn right I was." She took a sip of her drink and stared at him silently.

"Would you care to elaborate?"

"Do I have to?" said Olivia.

Hudson took a sip of his drink and stared back at her.

"Okay, fair enough," she finally said, the martinis finally starting to loosen her up. "I put forty years of my life into this job. I mean my entire life. You may find this hard to believe, but when I was a young woman I had men who wanted to marry me. I was a woman of my time, and I always assumed that I'd have a family."

"So why didn't you?"

"When did you realize that your job meant more to you than just a paycheck, Lieutenant? That it was more than just a job?"

"I guess I don't remember."

"Neither do I. All I remember is one day I got to work and I was invited into one of the large meeting rooms where there was a cake and a group of people waiting for me with big smiles on their faces. It was my fortieth birthday, and I hadn't even realized it. All I knew was that the suitors had long since stopped calling; I was past the age where having a family was a realistic consideration, and the only thing in my life that mattered to me a bit was my career. And I knew that the only reward I ever wanted was the top job."

"And you never got it."

"And I never will."

"Do you feel that you were treated unfairly, then?"

"Of course not."

"But why not?"

"Because I am three things that Stephanie French was not: old, ugly and cranky."

"But why should that matter? Like you said, you're the best, shouldn't that be enough?"

"Lieutenant, you have to understand that the CEO of any large corporation these days is a public figure, and the public face of the corporation he, or increasingly she, is leading. There are television appearances, magazine articles, and public speeches. Corporate boards want a leader who is not just capable, but telegenic and appealing as well. I'm just not that person."

"And Stephanie French was."

"Have you seen pictures of her?"

"Yes, I have. She was a beautiful woman."

"And you should've seen her on TV. She was magic, Lieutenant, magic."

"And she was good at her job."

"Not just good at her job; she was the best."

"So why did she report to you?"

"Because Stephanie French managed the Balboa Fund," said Olivia, looking at Hudson like that should have meant something to him.

"I'm sorry, Ms. Chase," he said. "You'll have to explain that to me."

"The Balboa Fund is not only Barstow & Company's flagship fund; it is the largest, most successful mutual fund in the world, and it has been since Stephanie French created it almost twenty years ago. It is the key to Barstow's success, and it made her a celebrity."

"So no one wanted to move her."

"That's right."

"So when Owen Morning told me that Stephanie French had almost single-handedly saved Barstow & Company during the Great Recession, he wasn't exaggerating?"

"Not a bit."

"Hollings Harkin seemed to think that Bryce Barstow deserved the lion's share of the credit."

"That's because Hollings Harkin is an idiot and an ass-kissing little worm to boot."

"Not to put too fine a point on it."

"Sharp edges are more my style, as if you haven't noticed."

"I have only one more question, Ms. Chase, and then I'll leave you be."

"Fire away, Lieutenant."

"It's my understanding that Ms. French was elected CEO on Friday morning, but the Board had deferred the public announcement until Monday morning. Can you tell me why?"

"That's easy," said Olivia. "Stephanie asked us to."

"But why?"

"She didn't say, but I can give you my opinion."

"Go ahead."

"You may or may not know that Stephanie French was a violinist. A fine violinist. She had a series of concerts this weekend with a string quartet she played with often, and she didn't want the news of her promotion to overshadow the recitals."

"I know that she was carrying a violin with her when she was murdered."

"Lieutenant, please," said Olivia, paling, "don't let anything happen to that violin."

"Was it valuable?"

"It was a Stradivarius, one of the finest surviving. It's not just valuable, it's priceless."

"So she was good."

"In addition to everything else that she was, Stephanie French was arguably one of the finest violinists in the world today. She could have held the concert chair of any major orchestra in the world, and she could have had a brilliant solo career if she had chosen."

"But she didn't. Do you know why?"

"As far as I know, Lieutenant, the only person in the world who knew the answer to that question was Stephanie French."

Hudson thanked Olivia Chase and left the bar just as Olivia was ordering herself yet another martini. Saved by the bell, he thought. He didn't know why, but he knew that the last dangling question was important, so important that perhaps the solution to Stephanie French's murder might hang on it.

———⟨⟩———

Olivia Chase stared at her fourth martini, her mind slowing down but still functioning. After the fourth it would finally, mercifully, shut down completely, and Kate would call a cab and help her into it. Dear Kate. Olivia hoped that Kate saw something more in her than the hundred dollar tips she routinely left her, but probably not.

She thought the discussion with Detective Lieutenant Hudson had gone well, but she would have to be careful. They would all have to be careful. She had read about some of his exploits in the newspapers and knew that he was a man to be taken seriously.

She picked up her glass and took a sip of her drink, but she wasn't really tasting it anymore. She felt the tear that ran down her face, but she didn't bother to wipe it away. It would dry on its own. They always did.

7

"**I** THOUGHT she owned the whole building," said Detective Eduardo Sanchez to the doorman who had brought him up to the fifth floor apartment and let him in. "You're telling me she didn't?"

"I don't know what would have given you that idea," said the doorman, whose nametag announced him to be "Edgar." He was a tall, slender man, close to seventy who somehow managed to make himself look distinguished despite the poor fit of his uniform and the too slickly combed gray hair. "She only occupied this floor, and she rented it."

The room they entered apparently served as a living/dining area, with a grouping of a sofa, loveseat and chairs surrounding a coffee table on one side and a dining ensemble on the other. Both areas looked out of small windows onto East Fourth Street, a street that in Eduardo's opinion looked decidedly downscale. The furniture itself looked like it could have come from any decent department store. There was a small television in one corner, but a spectacular looking stereo system against the wall.

"This is a lovely apartment in a very desirable location," said Edgar

"I'm sure it is, Ed," said Eduardo, "but I thought she was some kind of, you know, multi-kabillionaire. I was expecting something bigger and fancier, that's all."

"It's Edgar."

"What?"

"My name. It's 'Edgar,' not 'Ed.'"

"Sure thing," said Sanchez, after a brief pause. Nobody ever tried to call him "Ed," and he had to admit he'd be pissed if they did.

"Of course," said Edgar, moving on without skipping a beat, "I didn't know Ms. French personally, but she always impressed me as a modest woman."

"Did she have any live in help?"

"She didn't have any 'help' at all. As I said, she was a very modest woman."

"But what about when she entertained?"

"She never entertained in her apartment. Of course, I can't speak for her, but it seemed to me that Ms. French worked very hard to separate her private life from her public life. The only guests I ever saw entering her apartment were fellow musicians. They rehearsed here often, as you will soon see. "

"She eat out a lot?" said Sanchez, peering into the kitchen.

"Only for business occasions," said Edgar.

"You mean, she cooked her own food?"

"I know she did only because I used to see her coming in with groceries."

"You gotta be kidding me," said Sanchez, walking into the kitchen and starting to open cupboard doors. To his surprise, they were well stocked with staples and cooking utensils. He opened the refrigerator door and was shocked to see that it was full of fresh produce, eggs, cheeses and meats. "Well, knock me over with a feather," he murmured. He left the kitchen, realizing as he left that he had seen no sign of any alcoholic beverages, and walked down the hallway toward what he presumed to be the bedrooms.

"This apartment contains two bedrooms and two full baths," said Edgar, following him down the hall.

Sanchez walked through the first door, but instead of seeing a room furnished with bedroom furniture he saw a space dominated by a grand piano, music stands and chairs, and bookshelves crammed with sheet music and what looked to be textbooks. He wasn't much of a musician, but judging from the titles, the books were mostly about harmony, music history, and biographies of great musicians.

He looked over at the music stands. The one nearest him had a sheet of music on it bearing the title "Air On The G-String." The composer was listed as J.S. Bach.

"What the..." Sanchez mumbled to himself.

"It's actually quite a famous piece of music," came Edgar's voice from behind him, making him jump.

Sanchez turned and looked at Edgar, who had what seemed to him to be a slight smile on his face.

"It's just that I thought a G-string was a, you know..." said Sanchez, feeling himself reddening.

"It is that, too," said Edgar, "but more importantly it is also the lowest string on a violin. The piece of music you are looking at is an adaptation of a movement from one of Bach's orchestral suites, written so that the violin part can be played entirely on that one string of the violin, the G string, by a solo violin. It was, in fact, Ms. French's signature piece."

"You sound like you know a lot about music, Edgar."

"I taught music in the New York public school system for forty years, and I am also a violinist myself."

"So what are you doing here?"

"I should think that would be obvious to a fellow middle-class New Yorker, Detective Sanchez. My wife and I preferred not to move to a retirement village in some alligator infested Florida swampland after a lifetime of taking the cultural offerings of New York City for granted, so I took this position to augment our finances. It has actually worked out quite well for us."

"Was Ms. French a good violin player? When we found her she'd been carrying a violin with her."

"Dear God," said Edgar, his voice taking on a sense of urgency, "is the violin all right? Is it in safe hands?"

"Yeah, we got it," said Sanchez, "don't worry about it. Why, is it expensive?"

"It's priceless."

"I guess that means she was a good player, right?"

"She was a genius, Detective Sanchez."

"Then I don't get it. Why was she a banker?"

"That's a question many people in the music world asked, I can assure you."

"Huh," said Sanchez. He left the room and walked down the hallway to the second bedroom.

The second bedroom was even more of a surprise to Sanchez than the first, but for entirely different reasons. It was the smaller of the two, and it was furnished utterly simply: a single twin bed, a chest of drawers, a dressing table, and a small desk. Sanchez knew little about furniture, but to his untrained eye it looked of decent quality, but nothing fancy. The walls were bare, with the exception of a simple cross, not the crucifix that Eduardo was used to seeing, above the bed. There were no photographs and no paintings. The walls were painted a simple beige. Edgar, too, was looking about the room with a stunned look on his face.

"Not what you would have expected, huh?" said Sanchez, noticing Edgar's expression.

"Not really. Seems almost monastic, doesn't it?"

"What? Oh. I hadn't thought about it that way, but now that you mention it, yeah, it does."

"I don't make a practice of being a gossip, Detective," said Edgar, "but I've heard that one of Ms. French's nicknames was 'Sister Mary Stephanie.' I'm beginning to understand why."

Eduardo walked over to the closet and opened the door. Based on movies and television shows he'd seen, and occasional glimpses into Angelina's home decorating magazines, he expected to step into a walk-in closet the size of his living room, with countless articles of clothing on the hangers and hundreds of pairs of shoes on the floor. Instead, he found a closet that wasn't much bigger than the one Angelina had at home, and it was hardly full. There were perhaps a dozen business outfits on hangers in different patterns and tones of blue, gray and black. They all appeared to be of extremely high quality, and when Eduardo turned out the jacket of one of them he saw that it bore the label of a London tailor. There was a skirt and a pair of slacks with each suit. Across from the suits hung an array of blouses, mostly in tones of white and cream, with a few in shades of gray, blue and red. A half dozen pairs of shoes sat on the floor, all indistinguishable to Eduardo's eye except the height of the heels.

He walked back over to the chest of drawers and opened the top drawer. It was filled with what looked to be ordinary women's underwear, all of it white and nothing fancy or flimsy. The other drawers contained casual slacks and cotton blouses, and even a couple of pairs of blue jeans.

He was about to close the drawers and move on when he glimpsed what appeared to be a medium-sized plastic bag underneath a stack of cotton tops. He reached in and pulled it out.

"Huh," he said, staring at its contents.

"What is it, Detective?" said Edgar behind him.

"Did Ms. French ever bring any men friends here?"

"I'm assuming you mean a romantic interest?"

"Yeah, someone like that."

"No, Detective, never. As far as I could tell Ms. French had no romantic interests. But of course I could be wrong."

"Did she spend much time away?"

"Very little. She made the occasional business trip, but not as many as you would think. I gathered that she'd arrived at a point in her career where her customers came to her."

"Then I wonder what this is all about?" said Sanchez, more to himself than to Edgar.

"What are you looking at, Detective?"

"Oh, nothing," said Sanchez, quickly replacing the item and closing the drawer. "Where's the bathroom?"

"Through this door over here," said Edgar, giving Eduardo a quizzical expression, but too proud to be nosy.

Sanchez made a quick examination of the medicine cabinet but found nothing unusual: no prescription medications, not even any over-the-counter painkillers or antacids. In particular, he noticed no birth control devices or medications.

He then moved back into the bedroom and started looking through the desk. To his surprise, most of the drawers were empty. The middle drawer contained nothing but stationery and writing implements. In the lower left drawer, which was deeper than the others, he finally found something. It was technically a strongbox, he thought, though the metal wasn't of a particularly heavy gauge, and it was secured only by a simple padlock. He rummaged through the middle drawer again, hoping to find a key, but found none.

"Hey, Edgar," he said, looking back at the man who was still standing in the doorway, "how about giving me a little privacy for a couple of minutes?"

"Of course," said Edgar. He closed the door and Eduardo heard footsteps retreating to the living room.

He reached into his pants pocket and withdrew the small set of lock picks he always carried with him. They didn't work on sophisticated locks, but he was confident they would do the trick on this one. He sat down on the chair and went to work. Sure enough, after only a few seconds of fiddling the lock sprung free, and he opened the lid.

He sifted carefully through the box, not wanting his thick fingers to damage any of its contents. There were only a few items, mostly what looked like tax forms. He found one small piece of paper that looked to him to be a photocopy of a stock certificate for fifty shares of a stock he'd never heard of, although he couldn't be sure because he'd never owned any stock and probably never would.

At the bottom Sanchez finally found a couple of things that could prove to be interesting. The first item was a New York State driver's license. So she had a driver's license after all, he thought, but what good was it doing her in a strongbox? There was also a set of car keys with the "H" logo of Honda Motors embossed on them. A Honda, he thought? Sanchez had nothing against Hondas, Angelina drove one; but this woman was supposedly a billionaire.

And then there was the small slip of paper sitting on the bottom. He picked it up and stared at it.

It was an unremarkable document, one that virtually everyone possessed, and he was about to replace it in the box when he noticed one detail, a detail Sanchez knew Detective Lieutenant Hudson would find intriguing. He closed and relocked the lockbox and replaced it in the drawer, but he slipped that one small piece of paper into the inner pocket of his sports jacket, the one that Angelina thought made him look trimmer.

Who was this woman, Sanchez thought to himself as he walked back down the hallway toward the living room and an awaiting Edgar. She most certainly wasn't what she appeared to be.

Detective Eduardo Sanchez wondered how she had appeared to her murderer.

8

"DUTCH RIVER?" said Sarah Hudson. "You've got to be kidding me. So we were practically neighbors."

"Well," said Walter, "we still don't know if she was actually raised there. But the birth certificate Eduardo found says that she was born in the Albany County Hospital and that her parents were Lydia and Bernard French of Dutch River, New York. I've got a call into Maas & Maas, and I'm hoping Jill Maas will get back to me pretty soon."

"So Maas & Maas are still in business, are they?" said Julie Remy, Levi Welles's wife.

The four were sitting in the living room of Levi and Julie's townhouse on Wooster Street in SoHo, a home Julie had inherited from an Arab sheikh whose family's reputation she'd saved, nearly at the cost of her own life. She was part Algerian on her mother's side, but she got her pale complexion and her wavy, strawberry blond hair that she kept short from her father, an ex-diplomat who'd worked in Paris. She spoke fluent Arabic, French, and English, and the Gulf State embassy she worked for considered her indispensable.

Dinner was in the oven and they were enjoying a cocktail, except for Walter, who was still trying to shake off the effects of his conversation with Olivia Chase. He was nursing a Diet Coke while the others were enjoying martinis, a drink he thought he might never want to look at again.

"They're not just still in business, they're prospering," said Walter. "They've hired two new associate attorneys and a new legal secretary to replace Dot Ferguson. The whole town is thriving since we put it on the map with the Charles Sewall case. I've heard Adam Avery's restaurant is now so busy you have to make reservations a month in advance."

"I'm not surprised," said Julie, "Did you see the review the *New York Times* restaurant critic gave it?"

"He deserved it," said Sarah.

"I thought you said Stephanie French went to East Island High School out on Long Island, Levi," said Walter.

"Yes," said Levi. "We initially got that information from the usual news sources that kept bios on her, and we've since confirmed it with the Alumni Affairs office at Columbia University. They still have her high school transcript on file."

"I wonder when she moved away from Dutch River?" said Sarah.

"I hope we'll be finding that out from the Maases sooner rather than later," said Walter, looking at his watch, "but in the meantime, we've got a lot of other things to consider."

"Why don't we start with your conversations with the members of the Barstow Board of Directors," said Levi.

"May as well," said Walter. "I learned a lot about the way Barstow operates, and I met four people who are genuine suspects."

"But Walter," said Sarah, "these people are all highly respected executives, people who've made it to the top. Are you sure that every single one of them is a potential murderer?"

"Yes, I am, and I'm sure I'm going to meet more potential murderers right inside the walls of Barstow & Company before I'm through."

"I remember reading a long time ago," said Julie, "about a psychology student who did her Ph.D. thesis on the personality profiles of murderers on death row and how they compared with other, presumably normal, people."

"That doesn't sound like it would be that much of a stretch," said Sarah. "Those murderers must have been off-the-charts psychopaths by any measurement. Their personality profiles must have been completely different from the average person."

"You're right," said Julie, "they were completely psychopathic. And you're also right that most of the people the psychologists compared them to, the people we'd consider the 'normal' people in our society – friends, relatives, neighbors, business colleagues - were as normal as we assumed they'd be and weren't at all psychopathic."

"Did they profile any NYPD cops?" said Sarah, giving her husband an impish grin.

"As a matter of fact, yes, they did. And you'll be surprised to learn that, despite all the bad press the police seem to be getting these days, they test out to be overwhelmingly intelligent, rational and compassionate, with a high sense of moral purpose."

"Hah," said Walter, grinning back at his wife.

"They did find, however, a very specific subset of the 'normal' population that profiled almost identically with the death row inmates," said Julie.

"You're not going to tell me…"

"Yes, I am, Walter. They were senior level corporate executives, especially those who made it to the CEO's office."

"You said 'almost identical,'" said Walter. "What were the differences?"

"Actually, there was only one: the death row inmates, the true psychopaths, had the capacity to kill without conscience. The corporate executives didn't possess that trait."

"You mean," said Sarah, "that there's such a thing as killing *with* conscience?"

"Of course there is," said Levi. "Think of crimes of passion that people regret the second after they commit them."

"Or think of the cops," said Walter, "who have to use their weapons in the line of duty. Some of those poor guys never get over it. They spend the rest of their lives replaying the scene in their minds and trying to figure out how they could have avoided pulling the trigger."

"I remember," said Levi, "reading the story of a burglar who broke into the house of an old woman in the middle of the night to steal her television. She was sound asleep when he broke in, but something woke her up, and she came walking down the hall and caught him in the act. He bashed her head in with a lamp, killing her. Then he walked into the kitchen, found a soda and some chips, and sat down in the living room, just a couple of feet from the poor woman's body, and ate his snack and watched television for an hour before taking off with it. He was eventually caught and convicted of first-degree murder. At the sentencing, his attorney asked the guy to make a statement expressing his remorse, anything that might help him avoid the death penalty. But he didn't do it."

"But why?" said Sarah.

"Because he didn't understand the question."

"So what you're saying," said Sarah, "is that high level corporate executives are capable of murder; there's just going to be a little bit of conscience involved."

"Yes," said Levi. "Underneath their bland, polished exteriors they are utterly ruthless people, willing to do almost anything to achieve their goals, and they are unconcerned, even oblivious, to the damage they inflict on others along the way."

"Including murder."

"Including murder. And remember, these are extraordinarily intelligent, resourceful people capable of conceiving and carrying out a long term, complex plan. So if one of the Barstow senior executives *did* murder Stephanie French, Walter's only hope of capturing that person will be to tease that little crumb of remorse burdening their conscience, that one speck of difference that separates them from a death row murderer."

"I hate to interrupt this uplifting conversation," said Julie, "but dinner's ready."

"What did you make, Julie?" said Walter, perking up at the thought of hot food.

"It's a lamb tagine, at least as close as I can come to it in my little New York kitchen."

"Let me at it," said Sarah.

They were all heading to the dining room when Walter's phone rang. He was on the phone only a few brief minutes and said little except for the occasional "Really?" and "You're kidding." When he hung up he saw three faces with puzzled expressions staring at him.

"Who was that?" said Levi.

"It was Jill Maas," said Walter, staring back at them all with an equally puzzled expression on his own face.

"Okay," said Sarah when it became obvious that Walter wasn't going to volunteer any more information. "So?"

"I'm sorry," said Walter, shaking his head, "that was just a little confusing, that's all."

"What did she have to say?" said Levi.

"She said that Lydia and Bernard French in fact live in Dutch River, on a small farm out near the edge of the village. She said that they've lived there ever since they were married fifty-five years ago, and that the farm has belonged to the French family for generations. But to her knowledge they never had any children. She said she spoke to her father, Peter, and he confirmed that."

"Is it possible that the Maases just didn't know about any children?" said Sarah.

"Dutch River is a small town," said Levi. "Everybody knows everybody, and everybody knows everybody else's business. And we've all met the Maases. They've lived in Dutch River all their lives, and there's not much in that town that gets by them."

"But you said Stephanie French graduated from East Island High School out on Long Island, right, Levi?"

"Yes, I did. And I've got hard evidence to confirm it."

"Could it be there's another Stephanie French?" said Julie.

"I'm sure there are plenty of Stephanie Frenches," said Levi. "But why would that birth certificate have been in a strongbox belonging to the Stephanie French whose murder we're investigating?"

"We're obviously missing something here," said Sarah.

"We most certainly are," said Levi, "but I'll be damned if I know what it is."

"Jill also said that I might want to come up and talk to Mr. and Mrs. French personally," said Walter.

"Did she say why?" said Levi.

"No, she didn't. She just said that I might find it useful to my investigation to talk to them."

"What are you going to do?" said Sarah, turning to her husband.

"I guess I'm going to drive up to Dutch River tomorrow morning. At this point it can't hurt. But first, we're all going to sit down and eat whatever smells so good in the kitchen. What did you call it, Julie?"

———

Dinner had been a rich and satisfying affair, and they were all finishing their coffee and pastries purchased fresh from a French bakery around the corner from Sarah and Walter's home in Fresh Meadows when Walter's phone rang again.

"Great," he said, glaring at the Caller ID. He put the phone to his ear.

"Yessir," he said. He said "Yessir" once more and hung up. The call had lasted all of thirty seconds.

"Was that who I'm afraid it was?" said Levi.

"Yes," said Walter, sounding resigned. "It was Commissioner Donahue. He wants to see me at seven o'clock tomorrow morning. He told me to be prompt because he doesn't want to be late for Mass at St. Patrick's."

"At least you won't have to drink his whiskey," said Sarah.

"Oh, I wouldn't bet on that," said Walter.

"Do we even have to ask what he wants to talk about?" said Sarah.

"No you don't," said Walter. "He wants to talk about the Stephanie French case, of course, and he didn't sound happy."

"I'm really sorry about that, Walter," said Levi.

"Oh, you're a lot sorrier than you think."

"What do you mean?"

"He wants to see you, too."

9

H UDSON MANAGED NOT TO CHOKE as he swallowed a large gulp of steaming coffee from the mug NYPD Police Commissioner Sean Michael Patrick Donahue had placed in front of him. Leviticus Welles, who had anticipated that the contents of the mugs would be at least half Bushmills Irish Whiskey, had taken a more conservative sip and managed to keep a more neutral expression on his face. Despite the early morning hour, both men knew they would have to empty their mugs or risk losing face in front of their boss.

They were sitting in the Commissioner's pride and joy, his private hideaway down the hall from his main office in One Police Plaza, a room reconstructed in the image of an old Irish pub from his youth, replete with a hand-carved, polished mahogany bar. The barstools, however, were made of rough-hewn, unfinished oak, and the lucky, or unlucky, few who had been invited into this inner sanctum were said to have "earned their splinters." The shelves behind the bar were well stocked with a wide variety of wines and spirits, and there was beer on tap. But the only beverage anyone was ever served was Commissioner Donahue's mother's milk, Bushmills.

Commissioner Donahue was a huge man, almost as tall as Lieutenant Hudson, with an enormous girth that he carried with a surprising grace and agility. His size, along with his florid complexion, thatch of snow-white hair, and an outsized personality that matched his immense proportions, made him one of the most recognizable public figures in New York.

He'd been good to both Walter and Levi, and both men realized that to a great extent they owed their careers to the Commissioner. But they knew, too, that there was a price to be paid: absolute loyalty and results, along with a capacity to match drinks with their boss and continue to function. Walter had never seen Donahue even the slightest bit tipsy, although he himself usually barely made it home upright after his cocktail hour meetings with the man. Sarah always had a hot pot of coffee waiting for him when he walked through the door.

"So, boys," said Donahue after regaling them with yet another story from his days as a beat cop and refilling his own mug, "you've managed to hook another live one, have you?" There was still the faintest hint of an Irish brogue in his voice, even though he hadn't returned to the country of his birth since he'd arrived in America at the age of seven.

"It's beginning to look like it, sir," said Hudson.

"What have you got so far?"

"Well, sir, so far I've spoken to four of the senior executives at Barstow & Company, and I've come away with four suspects; but I'm sure I'll have more by the time I've finished with my interviews. And it's complicated by the probability that this was a contract killing, so we'll never be able to place the true culprit at the scene of the crime or connect him, or her, with a weapon."

"And from what I've heard, you suspect the shooter is someone who at one time or another has done work for Tommassino Fornaio."

"Yessir."

"And what do you know about Mr. Fornaio?"

"Not much," said Levi. "Since he doesn't engage in any illegal activity inside the five boroughs, at least that we know of, NYPD Intelligence doesn't have the kind of data we'd normally have for mobsters operating within our jurisdiction. Do you have anything that might be helpful, sir?"

"Not a lot," said Donahue, which usually meant "a lot." Walter didn't think there was a man, woman, or child in New York City that the Commissioner didn't know at least something about. "Tommassino Fornaio was born in Sicily a little over sixty years ago and raised on the Lower East Side, before the Chinese absorbed most of Little Italy into Chinatown. He's one of those blond Sicilians, and you'd never know he was anywhere near sixty to look at him."

"We heard his wife is a looker," said Walter.

"Not just a looker," said Donahue. "She's stunning. And more than that, she's elegant, polished, articulate, and charming. Her name is Christina, neé Spagnola."

"Is she some kind of trophy wife?" said Walter.

"Not at all. She and Tommy – that's what he calls himself – grew up together. They were childhood sweethearts, and they got married right after they both graduated from NYU."

"It doesn't exactly sound like he was born into a life of crime," said Levi. "What happened?"

"It's hard to remember, but even forty years ago it was still tough for Italians, especially off-the-boat Sicilians like Tommy, to get the good jobs on Wall Street, the major banks, or the big law firms. That was still the domain of Ivy League WASPs."

"So he took the path that was available to him," said Walter.

"Same as we all do," said Donahue, nodding. "But he was smart enough to get out of town, so perhaps someday he could come back with his reputation intact."

"Which it seems like he's done," said Levi.

"Oh, yes," said Donahue. "He's been able to establish some legitimate businesses here in the city; he's a well known philanthropist; and he hobnobs with the high and mighty, including the Mayor, congressmen, and even yours truly."

"What kind of legitimate businesses does he operate in the city?" said Levi. "I looked through our databases and came up empty."

"He owns at least three luxury auto dealerships, and he also runs a real estate investment firm. All hopelessly buried under layers of shell corporations, of course."

"But he's kept his upstate mob related activity going. Why?" said Hudson.

"He's been slowly backing out of it for years, but it's not something that you wake up one morning and say, 'I quit,' you know. But he'll get there. He and Christina spend more and more of their time at their townhouse in Manhattan and less and less time upstate in Newburgh, where his illegal operations are based."

"What about this shooter that we're looking into?" said Walter. "If Fornaio's backing out of his mob activities, why did he let himself get dragged into a gang war with an outfit like the Zorros?"

"Tommy Fornaio didn't get out of Little Italy by letting himself get pushed around by punks like the Zorros. His instinct is to punch back, and punch back hard. And I wouldn't dignify his little issue with the Zorros with the term 'gang war.' From what I heard, he crushed them in about a week, and now there's one less bunch of uptown thugs that the NYPD has to worry about. And, just so you know, he did not move in to take over their operations."

"Then I guess here's the question," said Walter. "Why would Tommassino Fornaio want Stephanie French dead?"

"Oh," said Donahue, "so he's on your list of suspects too?"

"He kind of has to be, sir. It looks like someone closely connected to his mob operations pulled the trigger. Who else would the guy be taking orders from?"

"I understand why you need to consider him a suspect, Walter, and I strongly encourage you to follow up, but my personal opinion is I doubt it."

"Why?"

"Step back and think about it, son. To my knowledge, Tommassino Fornaio has never committed a single illegal act on the island of Manhattan, or any of the other boroughs, for that matter. On top of that, he and Christina have been major contributors to Stephanie French's favorite charity."

"SafeWays," said Walter, wondering if Sarah had rubbed elbows with the mob boss's elegant wife.

"Yes, SafeWays. In addition, Stephanie and Christina were close socially, and Tommy and Christina are big fans of classical music and attended many of Stephanie's concerts."

"It sounds like he's at least one person we can cross off our suspect list," said Levi. "My guess is the shooter went rogue and was working as a free agent for someone else."

"I think so," said Donahue, "but I've been surprised before in this job, and I'm sure I'll be surprised again."

"I think we should probably still talk to him," said Levi.

"I would. In fact, I'll be seeing him today after Mass at a fundraising brunch that Christina is hosting for Catholic Charities. I'll tell him that you'll be coming to seek his advice and guidance."

"That'll be great sir," said Walter. "Thanks."

"Not at all. Now, what are your next steps, if you don't mind me asking?"

Hudson explained to the Commissioner the odd potential connection between Stephanie French and Dutch River.

"Ah, yes," said Donahue, "I'd forgotten that you're turning into a farmer on us."

"Not quite, sir," said Walter, "but Stephanie French's life before her university days keeps getting cloudier and cloudier, and we're hoping to be able to fill in some holes."

"You're not convinced yet that this was someone inside Barstow & Company bearing a grudge or wanting her job?"

"I still think it's very likely, sir," said Walter, "but you know how it is. I didn't expect to run into so many dead ends looking into the past of someone as prominent as Stephanie French. That always sets alarm bells off in my head."

"As well it should," said Donahue.

"Thanks for your time, sir," said Walter, looking at his watch, "but I know that you have a Mass to get to uptown and we have to get on the road to Dutch River." He and Levi stood to go. More than anything, he wanted to escape before Donahue offered them any more coffee.

"That's true," said Donahue, but Levi detected a rare note of hesitation in his voice.

"Sir?" said Levi after Donahue had sat silent for an uncharacteristically long time.

"Sit down, boys," he said, pouring them each another half mug of "coffee."

"Is there a problem, sir?" said Hudson, feeling the mandatory sip from his mug hit his stomach like hot lead. How did the guy do it, he thought?

Both Levi and Walter knew Sean Michael Patrick Donahue to be a confident man, a man unafraid to act and to speak his mind; but still, he hesitated. He suddenly looked older as an uncharacteristic frown brought lines and creases to his usually smooth, ruddy skin.

"You have both," he finally said, looking both men in the eye, "handled complex cases before, cases that involved powerful people and consequences that would go far beyond the case itself. You have always handled them beautifully, to the credit of both yourselves and this Department."

"Thank you, sir," said Hudson.

"Before you go thanking me, let me tell you that every instinct in my body is telling me that this is going to be another one of those cases."

"What do you mean, sir?" said Levi.

"I mean," said Donahue, all traces of Irish humor drained from his face and voice, "that there may be enormous pressure placed on you, and frankly on me, simply to identify the man who shot the gun and declare the case solved."

"I'm confused, sir," said Walter. "What makes you think that?"

"My stomach, son. My stomach is telling me that Stephanie French's murder is more than just a case of corporate jealousy, and that solving this case could shake the established order of this city to its foundations. And my stomach never lies."

"Are you telling us to back off, sir?" said Walter, unable to keep the bewilderment out of his voice.

"No, I am not, dammit!"

"Then, with all due respect, sir," said Levi, "what *are* you saying?"

"Look," said Donahue after another long pause. "You both know me, and you both know a lot about me. You know that I'm a bachelor and I always have been. I have no wife and no family. The only home I've ever known is this city, and the only family I've ever had are the people living in it, especially the members of the NYPD. I don't just know this city; I feel it. When something's wrong in this town I know it, the way most people know they're getting sick. I feel it in my bones. I feel it under my skin like an itch I can't scratch. I don't know anything more than what I've told you, but I sure as shit know that something about Stephanie French's death is very, very wrong. So I guess what I'm trying to tell you is watch your backs, every minute. Trust no one. Do you understand?"

"Yessir," said the two men simultaneously, both of them wondering if "no one" included the Commissioner himself.

"Good," said Donahue, looking at them like he'd read their minds. "Now, I have to go. I don't want the Cardinal giving me any dirty looks when I take my seat in the pews. And boys?"

"Yessir?"

"You have no time. None."

10

"**Y**OU OKAY TO DRIVE?" said Levi, staring over at Walter from the passenger seat of Walter's BMW 535i.

"I'll make it," said Walter, "I'll have a headache for the rest of the day, but I'll survive." He pulled the sleek car onto the Taconic Parkway, shifting smoothly through the gears of the six-speed manual transmission. He was beginning to enjoy the car, although he didn't drive it with Sarah's abandon. The car, including the stick-shift, had been Sarah's idea, their only real splurge after inheriting her great-uncle's fortune, and she loved to put it through its paces, as attested to by the growing stack of speeding tickets in the glove compartment. Walter had initially called in favors with the state police to get the citations quashed, but after a while it had become embarrassing, and he'd put Sarah on notice that she was on her own. She hadn't paid any attention to him until she'd received a notice along with her most recent ticket that her next citation would result in the suspension of her license.

"What do you think that was all about?" said Levi.

"I'll be damned if I know, but I think he was being straight with us. I think he felt like he had to share what his instincts were telling him. I honestly don't think he was holding back any hard information."

"I don't think so, either. That just wouldn't be like him."

They drove for a few miles in silence. The sky was a little overcast, but the roads were dry, and the exquisite German machine loafed over the hills and around the curves of one of the most scenic highways in America as Walter struggled to keep it within ten miles-per-hour of the speed limit.

"Here's what I think," said Levi, breaking the silence.

"About what?"

"About Commissioner Donahue's 'gut feeling,'" said Levi. He paused to collect his thoughts before continuing. "I think there's no such thing as a gut feeling. I think what they are is an accumulation of a lot of disorganized information that hasn't been integrated into a coherent thought yet. I think that Commissioner Donahue has hundreds, thousands of data points and observations in his brain that he's collected over the years."

"I won't argue with you there. I don't think the man has ever forgotten a thing in his life."

"Right. And I think he's seen things and heard things, maybe over the course of years or even decades, that led him to say what he said. It wasn't an irrational feeling; it was just a lot of data that hasn't been organized into a theory yet."

"Or he really is holding something back on us," said Walter, "despite all his protestations."

"It's not impossible," said Levi, "but I still don't think so."

Walter's headache suddenly got worse as they drove on in silence.

"WALTER! LEVI! It's so good to see you!" said the slender, blond-haired man wearing a white jacket and a smile.

"Good to see you, too, Adam," said Walter, looking a little bewildered as his eyes scanned the crowded restaurant, the eponymous "Avery's."

"Wow," said Levi. "I guess business is looking up for you, Adam."

"It's looking up for the whole town, in case you haven't noticed."

And indeed, they had. When Walter and Sarah, along with Levi and Julie, had first stumbled into Dutch River, it was with the intent to sell off the farm that Sarah had inherited from her great-uncle, Armin Jaeger, as quickly as they could. They were city dwellers to the bone, and, besides, the little town had fallen on hard times, and they had wanted to unload the place while it still held some value.

But there had been more to Dutch River than met the eye, in more ways than one, as Levi and Walter soon discovered that Great-Uncle Armin's apparently natural death had actually been a murder. The notoriety surrounding the case had led to a rebirth in the fortunes of the dying town and, in particular, Adam Avery's once deserted little restaurant. It had received a rave review from the *New York Times*' restaurant critic and now Adam, a hometown boy but a Culinary Institute of America-trained chef, was suddenly a celebrity.

"Where are Julie and Sarah?" said Adam.

"I'm afraid this is strictly a business visit, Adam. We're heading back to the city tonight," said Walter.

"Well, do you at least have time for a bite to eat? It's almost lunchtime."

"We'd love a bite to eat," said Levi, "but it doesn't look like there's any place to sit."

"No problem," said Adam, "follow me."

They followed him down a narrow hallway that had once led only to the restrooms but that now had an unmarked door at the end, which Adam opened.

"Welcome to my latest addition," he said, showing them into a small room, which held only four tables.

"What's this?" said Levi.

"I love all the new success and everything, but I still wanted to have a place where my friends and neighbors could come and share a meal without getting elbowed out of the way by the tourists, so I added this room on. It's my little secret. Please, have a seat. What can I get you?"

"I'll just have a bowl of hot soup and a sandwich," said Walter, still trying to shake off the effects of the morning dose of Bushmills.

"That sounds great," said Levi. "Why don't you make it two."

"Soup and sandwich, coming right up," said Adam. "How does ham and cheese sound?"

"Sounds great," said the two hungry men in unison.

But of course, even soup and sandwiches were something special when they were prepared by Adam, as Walter and Levi rediscovered to their delight when he came back with their meals.

The soup was a vegetable bisque made from all locally grown vegetables that had been delivered to the restaurant that morning, flavored with a delicate blend of herbs fresh from Adam's own herb garden. The "ham and cheese" sandwiches were made from the meat of locally grown pigs, patiently cured on the same local farm, and cheddar cheese from a local dairy, all between thick slices of sourdough bread baked by Adam on the premises.

"I made the mustard myself," said Adam, a little bashfully, "tell me how you like it."

The only sounds that came out of the two men's mouths were unintelligible as they wolfed down the simple but delectable meal.

Just as they were mopping up the last of the soup with the last crumbs of bread, the private door opened, and a short, rotund man in a Village of Dutch River Police uniform entered. His pink face beamed as he walked over to Walter and Levi.

"Bert! How are you?" said Walter, reaching out to shake the man's hand, careful not to grip it too tightly. Bert had a chronically sore wrist that sprained easily.

"Officer Steffus!" said Levi. "It's great to see you."

"It's great to see you guys too," said Officer Bert Steffus. The man had been a miserable failure as a cop when Walter and Levi had first met him, but he'd blossomed when he'd helped them solve Armin Jaeger's murder.

"Well, Bert, are you going to tell these guys your news?" said Adam.

"What's this?" said Walter.

"Well, you know, me and Maura got married a few months back." Walter and Levi had met Maura, an equally chubby farm girl from nearby Kinderhook, when Bert had brought her to Thanksgiving dinner at the farm the previous autumn. They had clearly been smitten with each other, and Walter and Levi had been unsurprised when they'd received the wedding announcement.

"Yes, Bert," said Levi. "We were at the wedding, but we don't expect you to remember that."

"Well, Maura's in, you know," said Bert, turning bright red, "a family way."

"Congratulations, Bert!" said the two men simultaneously. The buttons on Bert's already tight uniform seemed ready to pop as his chubby body swelled with pride.

"Would you guys like a little dessert with your coffee before you go?" said Adam. "You're a little early for the fresh berry season, but I whipped up a bread pudding this morning that you might like."

"I'm not going to turn that down," said Walter.

"I think I'll have to give that a try," said Levi.

"Bert?" said Adam.

"Gosh, Adam, you know I've been trying to trim off a few pounds."

"I know, Bert. I noticed you didn't have cream in your coffee this morning when you ordered that Hungry Man Special. Does that mean you'll pass on the bread pudding?"

Bert's inner struggle was palpable on his face. "Maybe just a small piece," he finally said, "but no cream in my coffee, okay?"

"Good man, Bert," said Adam as he went off to get the desserts.

"What can you tell us about Lydia and Bernard French, Bert?" said Levi.

"Actually, that's why I stopped over. Jill Maas gave me a call and said that I might want to go with you when you go to visit them, if you don't mind."

"Any particular reason?" said Levi.

"I've known Mr. and Mrs. French just about my whole life. They're good people, but they're shy, and Jill thought it would go better if I went along, that's all."

"That would be really helpful," said Levi, as Adam returned with the desserts. He couldn't help noticing that Bert's portion was every bit as big as his and Walter's, but his coffee was virtuously black. Adam had also brought a helping of the bread pudding for himself, and he sat down with them. Adam had been a trusted source of advice and local knowledge during the investigation into Armin Jaeger's murder, and Walter and Levi had no qualms about having him sit in on the discussion.

They dug into the rich, warm dessert that Adam had topped with a drizzle of local maple syrup.

"What can you tell us about them, Bert?" said Walter, between bites.

"They're just plain, quiet people, is all. They live way out on the edge of the village at the end of an unpaved road, so nobody sees them much. I used to deliver staples for their pantry to them when I was a kid. That's how I got to know them. And since I've been a policeman I make it a point to stop by once or twice a month to see how they're doing. They're getting along in years now."

"Does Bernard still work the farm?" said Walter.

"He's leased out the farmland and his dairy cattle to the young farmer who owns the property next to his. He helps out when he can, but it's mostly just puttering. He spends most of his time playing his violin, and Mrs. French spends most of her time baking and sewing."

"He plays the violin?" said Walter.

"Aw, you should hear him, Lieutenant. I don't know much about music, but when he plays that violin of his, it's like an angel singing."

"Do you know if they ever had any children?"

"As far as I know, no, they didn't. Why are you asking?"

"Because the name of the woman whose murder we're investigating is Stephanie French, and we have reason to believe there might be some connection." Both he and Levi trusted Adam and Bert implicitly, but Walter didn't think it was an appropriate time to talk about the birth certificate.

"Gee, you can ask them, but I don't think so."

"'French' is a pretty common last name," said Adam, "especially here in upstate New York. Are you sure you've got the right people? I was born and raised here, too, just like Bert, and I never heard that they had any children."

"Well, that's what we're here to find out," said Levi.

"And time is flying, so we'd better get going," said Walter, standing. "What do we owe you for the lunch, Adam?"

"Don't worry about it," said Adam. "People I invite back here don't pay. I'm making so much out front these days it's embarrassing."

"But not more than you deserve," said Levi.

"Thanks, guys," said Adam as the other men walked out the door.

"BERT, what a lovely surprise," said the small, thin woman in a faded dress who answered Bert's knock. She opened the door and said, "Please, come in."

Walter and Levi had ridden over to the French farm with Bert in his patrol car, and Walter was glad they had when he saw the half-mile long road that led them to it. It was nothing more than a rutted dirt path, and Walter didn't think it was anything the German engineers at BMW had contemplated when they designed their cars.

Standing behind the woman was a thickset man dressed in faded denims and a worn flannel shirt. He had thinning gray hair and wasn't much taller than the woman. They both looked to be in their seventies, but Walter guessed they'd looked like that for decades. Working a small farm will do that, he supposed.

They entered the house and found themselves in a small but immaculate living area furnished with a sofa and two chairs that looked old but rarely used. A large braided rugged covered hardwood floors that looked freshly polished. In one corner sat a small Zenith television that Walter guessed was a black and white, and in the other corner stood a wooden straight-backed Shaker style chair and a music stand. On the floor next to the chair Walter saw a small violin case, practically identical to the one Stephanie French had been carrying at the time of her murder.

"Bernard French," said the man, reaching his hand out to Walter. The hand was thick, dry, and calloused, and the fingers were gnarled. The grip was powerful, and Walter wondered how hands like that could play an instrument as delicate as a violin. "And this is my wife, Lydia." He put one large hand gently on the woman's shoulder as she smiled shyly. It was a pretty smile.

"Thank you for inviting us into your home," said Walter after Bert had introduced everyone.

"It's our pleasure," said Lydia French. "Why don't you all come into the kitchen where it's more comfortable, and we can have some coffee and talk." She led them down a short, narrow hallway that opened up into the kitchen. It was a large, bright room, probably two times the size of the living room. A large table made of rough-hewn maple sat in the middle, surrounded by six chairs, although the table could have accommodated more. Ancient but immaculate appliances and wooden countertops stained by decades of use occupied the perimeter.

"Please, sit down," said Bernard as Lydia busied herself with a pot of coffee, which she placed on the table with a bowl of sugar, a large pitcher of cream, and cups and saucers that looked like they could have been wedding gifts.

"I just made a fresh lemon meringue pie this morning," said Lydia, holding out a pie plate. "Would anybody care for a slice?"

"Why, sure," said Bert, his eyes popping.

"That sounds wonderful," said Walter, not really hungry but wanting to be polite, "but just small slices, please." Bert looked crestfallen.

"Now, Bert," said Lydia, noticing his expression, "you know your friend is right. You know how your bad ankle acts up if you get too heavy, and I don't want to have to let out that uniform for you again. I've just about run out of fabric."

"Yes, ma'am," said Bert, chastised.

They all poured coffee while Lydia served up the pie, the largest slice somehow winding up on Bert's plate.

"So," said Bernard after washing down a large forkful of the pie with a gulp of coffee, "what can we do for you young men?"

"We're here concerning a woman named Stephanie French," said Walter.

Bernard slowly lowered his fork. He and Lydia grew still.

"Yes?" said Bernard after a long silence.

"Mr. and Mrs. French," said Walter, "I don't know if you get much news from New York City."

"Not much," said Bernard.

"Then you probably wouldn't have heard that a woman named Stephanie French was murdered in Midtown Manhattan this past Friday afternoon."

Lydia and Bernard's complexions turned the color of the cream in the pitcher as a low moan escaped from Lydia.

"No, we hadn't heard that," said Bernard, his voice suddenly dry.

"We have learned that a child of yours, a daughter named Stephanie, was born in Albany County Hospital forty-seven years ago, which corresponds with the age of the murdered woman. We also found among her possessions a copy of a birth certificate from Albany County Hospital." Walter withdrew a recent photo of Stephanie French from his pocket and placed it on the table in front of the Frenches. "I am very sorry to have to ask you this, but is this woman your daughter?"

They both stared silently at the photograph.

"No, she is not," said Bernard, as his wife collapsed in his arms and began to sob.

11

"DADDY, I'm just not ready to discuss this yet," said April Barstow, sitting opposite her father in his study, a room she'd always despised. The late afternoon sunshine cast long, hard shadows as it poured through the west facing windows, and she had to try not to hold up her hand to shield her eyes as she gazed at her father, trying to read his expression. A tray with coffee on it sat on the small table between them but remained untouched. "I mean, we haven't even arranged for poor Stephanie's memorial service yet. Frankly, it seems ghoulish."

April Barstow was dressed youthfully in a casual blouse and a pair of designer jeans. She was still a good-looking woman as she approached fifty, and she wore the outfit well. All the disciplined years at the gym, and all the money lavished on her beautician and spa treatments had paid off, and she still turned heads. She resembled her mother much more than her father, at least from what she could tell from the single photograph that was on display in her father's home and the one that she had been allowed to keep for herself after her mother had so suddenly died when April had been only seven. The pictures had frozen her mother in time, and now the woman that gazed out from the photo looked almost young enough to be her daughter, if she'd ever had one.

Not that April had ever spent much time looking at the pictures. Her mother had been a pretty woman: small, slender, and dark-haired, and the photographs had captured her beauty well. But April had never been able to get past the sadness that emanated from the photographs, the same sadness that had emanated from her when she had been alive, the sadness that was April's only lasting impression of her mother. No, it was easier not to look.

Her death had been ruled an accident, "accidental death by drowning," in the family pool at their summer home in the Hamptons. But there had always been whispers of suicide. April had overheard the muted discussions of the high levels of barbiturates found in her system. As she grew to adulthood, April had tried to ask her father about those rumors,

rumors that always remained whispered but never went away. But her father wouldn't speak of them and had eventually commanded her never to raise the subject again. In fact, her father had never mentioned her mother's name, in public or in private, since her death. On the very rare occasions when he had been compelled to speak of her, he referred to her either as "your mother," or "my late wife." His reticence had been ascribed to his inconsolable grief.

Perhaps that had indeed been the case, but young April had never been able to shake the memory of her father leaving for work the day after her mother's death and arriving home late after a business dinner, or the image of him arriving at the memorial service from work in a chauffeured limousine and returning to work in the same limousine as soon as the service had ended.

Many people had wondered over the years why the attractive, successful, often charming April Barstow had never married. It surely wasn't for lack of suitors. But, like her best friend, Stephanie French, she had never been even tempted to make the long walk down the aisle, not on the arm of her father, only to be handed over to a man just like him for all she could know. No. Witnessing her mother's pain had been enough. She had no interest in experiencing it first hand. Anyway, her work had kept her busy enough, and Stephanie had always been there for her. The years had flown by.

"Damn it, April," said her father in a sharp voice that jolted her back to the present, "we don't have time for sentimental nonsense, not now."

Just as we hadn't when Mother died? She wanted to say it, but didn't.

"Stephanie was my dear friend as well as my colleague, Father. It's barely been forty-eight hours since she was murdered. I can't simply discard my grief like an old pair of shoes and move on."

"You can and you must," said Bryce Barstow, his hand chopping the air in typically authoritative Barstow fashion. But April couldn't help noticing the slight slur in his speech, or the thin film of drool in the corner of his mouth that drooped ever slightly. "It's Sunday afternoon, April, and I return to work tomorrow morning. We have a lot of planning to do and precious little time to do it. We have no time to waste on sentimentality."

"I guess I don't understand what you think you're going to accomplish or why you even accepted their invitation. I hope you don't have any plans to remain indefinitely."

"There's no reason I couldn't, damn it. You know how I feel about the way I was treated. There was no call for it. None whatsoever."

"Father, please."

"Oh, don't worry, April. I have no plans to cling to a position where I am clearly no longer wanted. I'm playing a cameo role and I know it."

"Then why did you even accept the offer?"

"For the good of the company that bears my name, that's why."

"And?"

"And what?"

"And to ensure that the next leader of Barstow & Company will also bear that name?"

"I don't know what you mean."

"Which means me, I assume," said April, ignoring her father's feigned ignorance.

"Of course it does! Who else?"

"Anybody else, for crying out loud! How many times do we have to have this conversation, Daddy? I'm not competent to lead Barstow & Company, and the only person in the world who doesn't seem to know that is you."

"That's not true! You had support on the Board, and if Stephanie French hadn't stepped in your way, you would have been named CEO on Friday."

"Daddy," said April, pouring coffee simply to give her hands, which were starting to shake, something to do, "any support I had from the Board was lip service as a nod to you, and I wouldn't have even allowed my name to be placed in nomination if I thought I'd had any chance of actually being chosen. I knew Stephanie was going to be elected, and I knew you wanted to see me nominated, so I let it go. I'm not qualified for the job, and I'm not interested in having it."

"I don't know what you're talking about. You have all the qualifications you need."

"By which I'm assuming you mean that I'm your daughter, and that the only thing I would really have to do as CEO is sit in the office and take instructions from you."

"Of course I'd be available to advise you. Why shouldn't I? And you have a strong team in place to support you."

"Oh, please, Daddy. That 'strong team' is made up completely of your sycophants, with the exception of Olivia Chase, and she's got one foot out the door."

"She's an old hag and I won't miss her, and neither should you."

"She's the hag that carried me on her shoulders for the past twenty-five years. Without her and Stephanie I wouldn't have lasted a month. A good team is only as good as its leader, Daddy, you know that, and I'm simply not qualified. If you really want to do what's best for the company, then you should find the best person to run it, and I'm not that person. And, frankly, neither is anyone else inside the company."

"Hollings Harkin is a good man, but he should be supporting you, not the other way around."

"Hollings Harkin is an ambitious little toady who gives me the creeps. I'll never understand why you hired him, especially knowing his background."

"Hollings Harkin comes from sound stock, and I have no regrets about hiring him."

"If you mean he's an apple who fell from the same tree as his father, I guess I can't argue with you."

"Enough about that!"

"You're right, Daddy. Enough. Look, I know this conversation hasn't gone the way you wanted it to, but I believe it's the way it had to go. I am never going to be the CEO of Barstow & Company. Never. You're just going to have to accept that. And you also have to accept the fact that your days there are over as well. You've been asked to stand in while the Board identifies a new CEO. They do not expect you to make any major decisions, nor will they support you if you try to do so. I'm sorry, Daddy. I know how difficult this must be for you."

April Barstow stretched out a hand to her father, but she'd lost him. He'd turned away from her and gone silent, and she knew from long, sad experience that there would be no reaching him. She also knew that her father was a man who wouldn't take "no" for an answer, and that despite everything she'd said, he was still determined to have his way. As always. The light in the room seemed to dim as she rose to leave.

"Good-bye, Daddy. I'll see you in the morning."

He didn't respond as she left his study.

<hr>

"I guess we're confused," said Leviticus Welles, staring across the table at the so plainly stricken couple.

"You asked me a straightforward question," said Bernard French, "and I gave you a straightforward answer."

"Are you saying that you don't have a daughter named Stephanie?"

"I'm not saying that, no."

"Are you saying that you *do* have a daughter named Stephanie?"

"I haven't said that," said Bernard, "but, yes, we do have a daughter named Stephanie."

"But your daughter and this woman are not the same person."

"I haven't said that either, but that is also correct."

"Was your daughter," said Levi, trying to remain patient with this man who, like so many farmers, could be scrupulously honest without speaking a word of the truth, "the person for whom the birth certificate from Albany County Hospital was issued?"

"Yes."

"But this woman," said Levi, pointing at the picture that Walter Hudson still held in his hand, "was in possession of a copy of that birth certificate."

"Doesn't make her our daughter."

"Bernard, please!" said Lydia, putting her coffee cup down beside her plate of untouched pie. "Enough! These people are trying to solve a murder, and we have to help."

"But we made promises, Lydia!"

"Yes, we did. But, oh, Bernard, how can we not help?" said Lydia, tears welling in her eyes, tears that finally broke down her husband's defenses.

"All right, all right," he said, finishing his last bite of pie and emptying his coffee cup before rising from the table. "I think we ought to take these people for a walk, don't you think, dear?"

"Yes, Bernard," said Lydia after a brief hesitation, "I think we should."

"Where are we going?" said Walter.

"Just follow us," said Bernard.

Walter shrugged his shoulders silently at Levi, and they followed the Frenches out the door.

They walked about a quarter-mile, past the barn and a small field where sprouts of corn were just starting to emerge from the damp spring earth. The air was mild, and the footing was firm, but Bert was noticeably limping by the time they arrived at their destination.

It was a small plot, surrounded by an apple orchard. Many of the headstones were so weatherworn they could no longer be read, but the ones that could be read all had the same word at the top: French.

"Six generations of Frenches," said Bernard.

"But there will never be a seventh," said Lydia.

"What do you mean?" said Detective Hudson.

"The state outlawed family plots like this just after I buried my parents," said Bernard. "They both died young, and I was left with this farm when I was still a teenager. Told us private cemeteries like this were a public health hazard. Made us feel grateful that they weren't going to dig up all the graves and move them."

"Does that mean the two of you won't be able to be buried here?" said Bert.

"No, we won't, Bert. We've had to make separate arrangements."

"That's terrible," said Bert.

"It is what it is, son. After we're gone there'll be nobody left to visit us all here anyway, so it doesn't really matter."

"So you're the last of the Frenches?" said Levi.

"The last hereabouts," said Bert. "We're the last of the direct line that moved down here from Canada a century and a half ago." He stood staring at the stones, in silent communion with his lost family.

"Go on, Bernard," said his wife.

Bernard cleared his throat and then said, "Well, then. I suppose you're wondering why we dragged you out here."

"Take your time," said Levi.

"Time," said Bernard. "Time. Huh." The sound came out as more of a choking noise than a word.

"Do you want me to talk, dear?" said Lydia. Bernard shook his head.

"A little over forty-seven years ago," he said, "just at the end of winter, my dear wife and I became the proud parents of a beautiful little baby girl. We named her Stephanie Marie, Stephanie for my only brother, Stephan, who died in Viet Nam, and Marie after Lydia's mother, a lovely woman.

"She was a tiny little mite, barely five pounds at birth, but she was healthy and she fed well, so they let us take her home after three days in the hospital. And everything was fine, you know? She guzzled down her milk when Lydia would nurse her, and the little thing knew how to load up a diaper, that's for sure.

"And, you know," he said, a faraway look in his eyes, "she was the brightest little thing. After just a few days, she'd look at us like she already knew us.

"And then, on her tenth day in this world, Lydia gave her a nursing right around lunchtime. I changed her diaper, just because I loved to, you know? And we put her down for her nap. She never complained. She was an awfully good little girl."

Bernard suddenly stopped talking. His mouth opened, but nothing came out. Then it closed.

"Bernard went back out to the fields after lunch," said Lydia, quietly placing her hand in his. "I sat down at my sewing machine. I thought I'd make a few summer outfits for little Steph. I guess I must have gotten lost in my work, because I suddenly realized that two hours had gone by, and little Steph had never napped that long before. So I went into the room to check on her.

"I guess I knew she was gone the second I stepped into the room. Everything was so quiet, so still. I ran over and picked her up, but it was too late. There was no pink in her skin anymore, and I'll never forget how cool she felt when I touched her. I ran to the back door and screamed for Bernard. I still had little Steph in my arms. I really don't recall much after that."

"I'm so sorry," said Levi, a man with his own children. The story had shaken him. "What did the doctor say had happened? Crib death?"

"There was no doctor," said Bernard, staring directly at Levi.

"What do you mean?"

"I mean there was no doctor."

"Do you mean that you took her directly to the hospital?" said Levi.

"There was no hospital."

"Then who did you go to?" said Walter. "Who did you report her death to?"

"You don't understand," said Bernard. "They would have taken her away from us. They would have made us incinerate her, or bury her someplace where she'd be all alone. We just couldn't let that happen."

"So, what did you do?" said Walter.

Bernard and Lydia walked over to a near corner of the old graveyard and looked down at a patch of ground where no gravestone stood. The three policemen followed them over and looked down at where the Frenches were staring. There was a small slab of polished granite lying flat against the earth. It was just large enough to contain a crudely chiseled inscription:

Beloved
MCMLXIX

"I made a small coffin out of some scrap wood that I had in the barn. We put her in a pair of flannel pajamas that Lydia had made for her. They were nice and warm, you know? And we put her in the coffin with a little stuffed toy that Lydia had made for her."

"It was a little mouse," said Lydia. "She was so tiny, we called her our little mouse. We didn't want her to be all alone in the coffin."

"And we buried her, right here. There was this scrap of granite in the barn that was left over from my Dad's headstone, so I chiseled that little inscription in. We didn't want to have her name on it, just in case people got nosy some day. Anyway, nothing much else would have fit."

"But I don't understand," said Levi, "people must have known that Lydia was pregnant. How did you explain what happened?"

"Officers," said Bernard, "we live a long way from a paved road. We hardly ever got into town, even in the fair weather, and in winter we're pretty much stuck here, and no one expects to see us until spring. Winter set in early that year, before Lydia was showing, and we hadn't told anyone yet. We were superstitious about that, I guess."

"So no one ever knew."

"That's right."

"I still don't understand," said Walter, "how the Stephanie French who was murdered in New York City last Friday could have had the birth certificate of your daughter. Are you aware of any connection between the two?"

Bernard and Lydia French stood together silently beside the grave of their daughter. Long seconds passed.

"Bernard?" said Lydia, finally.

"Yes, dear," said Bernard. He turned to look at the three officers. "Perhaps we ought to go back inside."

12

THE SILENCE WAS COMFORTING, broken only by the rhythmic tapping of cutlery on china, the rattling of ice in glasses, and the soft sounds of the wait staff as they removed one set of dishes, served the next course, and refilled wine goblets.

At least it was only the three of them now, thought Hollings Harkin V, just him and his parents, sitting at the polished walnut table that could seat twenty in the cavernous dining room of his parents' Park Avenue triplex. The dinners with his morose wife and sullen children in attendance had been nerve-searing tests of emotional will that had blessedly come to an end ten years ago when, to the relief of all involved, the marriage had ended. His custody agreement with his then-young children had stipulated that he would see them one day a month, which had been one day too many as far as both he and the children were concerned. They were both now in college, and he hadn't seen either of them in two years.

His ex-wife, Patricia, had never remarried. Their post-divorce life had been a continuation of the marital grudge match, and Hollings Harkin V had been obliged to use his considerable legal skills over the years in seemingly endless disputes over alimony, child support, and property settlements. But, he concluded, it was better than being married to the bitch. Much better.

Of course, his mother, Gloria Dunnewood Harkin, ruined his peace.

"I guess I don't understand where all of this leaves you, Hollings," she said in the upper class, vaguely English accent that she had so carefully cultivated over the years without ever having visited England. Even at this informal Sunday dinner she was dressed as if for the opera, silver hair piled high, jewelry glittering.

"It's too early to say, Mother, and I'd really prefer not to discuss it right now."

"When *would* you like to discuss it, then?"

"I really don't know, Mother, just not now."

"That's always been one of your weaknesses, dear. You have always been afraid to confront your problems head on."

"Mother, it isn't a matter of confronting my problems."

"Then what is it a matter of?"

He put down his fork and knife. A pity, he thought, since the spring lamb and baby potatoes were delicious. But once again, his mother had cost him his appetite. He picked up his wine goblet, took a drink of the Chateauneuf du Pape that had mated so perfectly with the lamb but that he no longer tasted, and put the goblet carefully back down before replying.

"Mother, the Board hasn't even chosen a replacement for Stephanie French yet. It is extremely difficult for me to consider my options until I know what the new management structure of the company will be."

"And I suppose you have flinched from throwing your own hat into the ring."

"It has nothing to do with 'flinching,' mother," he said, but as usual, the arrow had found home, and they both knew it. "I am an attorney, not a financial expert. I went to Barstow & Company to be their general counsel. I never had any intention of being anything other than that."

"They should just admit their mistake and put Bryce Barstow back in charge. Good man," mumbled Hollings Harkin IV from the far end of the table where he sat, slumped, looking like his son with the air let out. As usual, he had his own bottle of wine in front of him and, as usual, it was already almost empty, despite the three double scotches he'd drunk before dinner.

"Perhaps, Father," said Harkin. "You know how I admire the man, but even I have serious concerns about his ability to lead the company any longer."

"What do you mean?" said his father, his words running together.

"He's in his seventies now and…"

"He's the same age as I am! What does that have to do with anything?"

"Father, please, let me finish. It's not only that he's in his seventies, but, as you must know, he has also developed health problems that are affecting his performance."

"How unusual," said Gloria Harkin, staring pointedly at her husband's wine bottle.

"And what's that supposed to mean?"

"Father, Mother, please."

"At least that French woman is out of the way now," said Gloria.

"Yes, she is. I don't think I would have been able to continue as general counsel with her as chief executive."

"I actually rather admired her," said Gloria.

"Well, I didn't," said Hollings.

"Of course you didn't, dear."

"Have to have a set of balls to run an outfit like Barstow," came the slurred voice from the far end of the table.

"However would you know?"

"Dammit!" said his father, gulping the last of his wine.

"Can we please stay on the subject?" said Hollings.

"Oh, there's a subject?" said Gloria.

"My future, of course, Mother."

"I thought we were avoiding that subject, but please go on."

"I'm just trying to say that even with Stephanie French gone, my future with Barstow & Company is uncertain, and perhaps it's time to discuss other possibilities."

"And what would those be?" said his mother.

"Manuel, I'd like a brandy," said his father.

"I think it's time that we discussed my return to the Firm."

"Really?" said Gloria, making it sound more like a statement than a question.

"Father, before long you'll want to think about stepping down as senior partner, and it's unthinkable to me that anyone but a Harkin should take your place. It would be unprecedented."

The only response from the end of the table was soft snoring, as Manuel carefully removed uneaten food and drink from in front of Harkin's unconscious father.

"Perhaps we should discuss this at another time," said Hollings.

"Perhaps not," said Gloria.

"But don't you think we should wait until Father is, uh, more alert?"

"Why, because his opinion might actually matter?"

"But, Mother…"

"Don't 'but Mother' me. Your father has been a non-entity at that firm for the past five years. He gets there at eleven o'clock when he manages to get there at all. Then he gets hauled off to a luncheon with some old clients who still believe he counts for something. By the time lunch is over, he's so drunk he can hardly walk, whereupon some junior associate is assigned the unhappy task of dumping him in a cab and returning him to me."

"I'm sorry, Mother, I didn't know."

"Well, now you do."

"I think then, it's all the more urgent that I leave Barstow & Company and return to the Firm forthwith."

"I know that you and your father have maintained that happy little fiction ever since you left, but you know as well as I that you will never return to the Firm, not as senior partner and not as janitor."

"But, Mother, surely by now…"

"How many secretaries filed sexual harassment charges against you before we finally had to get you out of there?"

"Mother, I hardly…"

"Lost count, did you? I didn't. It was five. Five, Hollings."

"They were all lying! They set me up! I was the one who was being harassed!"

"Oh, stop it, dear. You have the family disease, plain and simple. You inherited it, either by birth or by example, from your father and his father before him. The only thing that saved them was the times they lived in. You didn't get fired for chasing secretaries around the office in their day. It was rather expected. And wives were expected to raise the children, host all the right parties, and soldier on. But times changed, dear, and your behavior cost you your marriage, and it cost you your place at Harkin, Porter & Smith. Forever."

"That can't be!"

"But it is, dear, it is. And I suppose you began your career at Barstow & Company by exposing Stephanie French, a woman who was clearly on her way to the top, to your questionable charms. In fact, I know you did."

"But Mother, how could you…"

"Because I make it my business to know, damn you! How else do you think this family would have survived?"

"But I never did anything after that."

"Yes, after that I assume that you at least had the wits to take your little show on the road. But the damage was done."

"But Stephanie French is gone now, Mother."

"Yes, she is. How fortunate for you," said Gloria Harkin, giving her son a level gaze.

"What is that supposed to mean, Mother?" said Harkin, unable to hold his mother's gaze.

"It means that this conversation is over. Now, tell Manuel that it's time to get your father to his bed. And tell him not to forget to change his diaper. The odor is starting to ruin my appetite for dessert."

━══ſ๔ᴖᴖ━

Hollings Harkin V stumbled out of his parents' Park Avenue townhouse in his customary state of impotent fury. Perhaps if his mother had just once, just once, treated him like the man he was things would have turned out differently. But that had never happened, and it never would. He didn't know how Dad had put up with it all these years. No wonder the poor man drank the way he did.

But he wasn't going to think about that now. Now, he just needed some relief from the unbearable anxieties of his daily life, from the unceasing pressures that came with being Hollings Harkin V.

Yes, relief.

He thought perhaps Bernadette would be a good choice tonight. She liked the rough stuff. He knew it wasn't an act with her, at least not with him. She said so. She said she loved being with a real man, a man who wasn't afraid to assert himself like a real man should. A man like him. She always told him how much it turned her on, how much *he* turned her on, and he knew she meant every word. That's what he liked about her the most: her sincerity. And she looked like Stephanie. God, he hoped she was available tonight.

He reached into his pocket, withdrew his phone, and dialed the number he knew by heart. The conversation was brief but satisfactory. Bernadette was available. She had, in fact, been sitting by her phone all afternoon hoping that he would call. She told him to hurry; she could barely wait. Nobody can fake that, thought Harkin. He knew the real thing, and this was it. He reached into his pocket and retrieved the blue pill that he always kept handy, just in case. He popped it in his mouth and hurried on his way.

━══ſ๔ᴖᴖ━

The low sun was painting the little village of Dutch River and the distant farms in a palette of warm, luminous yellows and reds by the time Bert dropped Levi and Walter off in front of the law offices of Maas & Maas. Even in town, the mild air smelled of spring planting and the sharp, ripe odors of rebirth, while in the distance the sounds of tractors punctuated the stillness of the rural evening.

Both men were drained, emotionally and physically, after their visit to the French farm. They still had a lot to do before the day ended, but at least they felt that they were making progress. They'd had to wait outside the building for a few minutes because, being Sunday, Jill Maas had been obliged to drive in from her home to meet with them, and they'd given her short notice. But she'd given them both a warm smile along with a brisk handshake when she arrived and immediately led them up to her law offices.

The two men had both worked with the tall lawyer with the flaming red hair before, and they both liked and respected her. Jill Maas had done a great deal to save her little hometown from oblivion, but along the way she had also demonstrated her willingness to stretch the boundaries of the law and the legal code of ethics to the limit when she was sure she was doing the right thing. It was a risky game, but she seemed to play it better than most others.

Business had clearly improved for Jill and her father, Peter, since Levi and Walter had last visited them. The once unoccupied lower floor of the Maas Building now housed two new associates and an additional paralegal; and the conference room on the main floor, once crowded with castoff furniture, now sported a polished conference table with matching chairs and a Keurig coffee machine on a side table.

But despite the prosperity and the mutual respect, they still eyed each other warily. Jill Maas had some questions to answer, and she knew it. Levi and Walter declined coffee as they took seats in the conference room.

"I'm guessing you had an enlightening conversation with the Frenches," said Jill, taking her seat at the head of the table.

"Yes, of course we did," said Hudson, "as you knew we would. I've got to say, Jill, I'm disappointed that you weren't more forthcoming sooner."

"I didn't think it was my story to tell."

"Perhaps it wasn't," said Levi, "but you have your own story to tell, and we need to hear it."

"You're right," said Jill, giving him a curt nod.

"Where do we start?" said Walter.

"At the beginning, as usual," said Jill, brushing her hair back nervously. "I'm probably going to repeat a lot of what the Frenches already told you, but I don't know how else to go about this, so please bear with me." She paused for a moment, staring out the large window at the peaceful evening, then down at her folded hands. Finally, she looked up. "My first involvement with Stephanie French, the one whose murder you are currently investigating, began about fifteen years ago. I was brand new to the practice of law, and Stephanie was In her early thirties. She told me a story about how years before, when she was still a teenager, she'd decided that she needed a new identity."

"Did she say why?" said Walter.

"No, she did not, and I didn't ask."

"Did she ever tell you what her birth name was?"

"No, she did not, and I didn't ask."

"Have you ever subsequently discovered what her birth name was?"

"No, I have not. Lieutenant, we're not going to get anywhere like this. May I please proceed with my story?"

"You're right. Go ahead."

"You've probably heard the story a million times. For any number of reasons, a person wants a change of identity or a second identity, so they hire a person with expertise in these matters who scans databases for social security numbers or birth records of people who died at an age when there was only a very thin record of their existence or none at all. The expert ensures that no one has filed taxes or applied for any benefits under that name or Social Security number. In this case, that person managed to find the birth certificate of Stephanie French, the daughter of the Mr. and Mrs. French you met today. It was a perfect match. Obviously, there had never been a Social Security number registered to that name. The two had been born within months of one another, and, for the reasons you learned today, there was literally no trace of the real Stephanie, so whatever life story the new Stephanie wanted to create she could, with no fear of any inconsistencies popping up."

"But she did all this years before you met her," said Levi.

"Yes."

"Then why did she come to see you?" said Walter.

"I guess it's one of the enduring mysteries of Stephanie. There was no reason for her to make contact with Bernard and Lydia French. None at all. There they were, hidden away in their tiny little farm in this tiny little town; and there she was, living and working in a metropolitan area of sixteen million people. They all could have lived out their lives without the Frenches ever learning that someone had stolen their dead daughter's identity."

"So, why?"

"I'm not sure we'll ever know. When Stephanie first contacted me I asked her, of course. I knew and liked the Frenches, and I didn't want to see them hurt, and I told her that."

"What did she say?"

"She said that she was rising in the worlds of finance and music to a level that she never expected and that she expected to go further, much further. She knew that her personal life would be coming under a great deal of scrutiny, and even though she was pretty sure her tracks were well covered, she didn't want to run the risk that someday the Frenches would find themselves ambushed by a bunch of reporters who would dig up the truth about their real daughter. She said she felt that she at least owed them an explanation."

"Did she ever tell the Frenches why she needed to change her identity?"

"Not to my knowledge, no. She just wanted them to know that their daughter's identity had not been stolen for the wrong reasons and that she hoped that they would be proud of the things that she was accomplishing in their daughter's name."

"Okay," said Walter, "but that all could have been taken care of in one visit. But the Frenches told us that they had developed a friendship, a close friendship, over the years. What was that all about?"

"I guess I'm not sure," said Jill. "I think the easiest answer is that Stephanie and Bernard discovered that they shared a love of the violin."

"It's funny," said Levi, "we couldn't get Bernard to talk about that much."

"He's very shy about his musical ability," said Jill. "He's pretty shy about everything."

"But from everything we know," said Levi, "Stephanie French was a world class violinist. I know that Bert said Bernard was good, but I can't believe that he was much more than a fiddler."

"There you are wrong," said Jill. "I'm not a sophisticated enough music fan to say whether or not Bernard was anywhere near the same level as Stephanie, but he was a remarkable musician. Stephanie told me that it was like discovering Toscanini conducting an elementary school band. Lydia told me that whenever Stephanie came to visit, Bernard and Stephanie would spend at least half the time playing music."

"I guess I'm puzzled," said Walter.

"What about?" said Jill.

"You said that you're not sure you knew why Stephanie revealed herself to the Frenches. But she gave a very plausible explanation. And the musical connection is clearly a reason by itself for maintaining the relationship once they'd met. So what aren't you sure about?"

"I have no reason not to believe that you are correct, Lieutenant."

"What, then?"

"Oh, Lieutenant, I'm wandering off into speculation and gut feelings, and I hate doing that, especially since this is a murder investigation."

"Why don't you let me be the judge of what's useful to me and what's not."

"Okay," said Jill, but still she hesitated before continuing. "I never got to know Stephanie all that well, so I could be completely wrong, but I always got the impression that one of the reasons she sought out the Frenches is that she was looking for a family."

"Do you know if she ever made any reference at all to her birth family?"

"Not to me."

"Well, I guess we're all wandering way out of our areas of expertise by speculating," said Levi.

"I have a couple more questions for you, Jill," said Walter.

"Okay," said Jill, stretching the word out as she eyed Walter warily. She had learned long ago not to underestimate these two men.

"Did you have any continuing relationship with Stephanie once you introduced her to the Frenches?"

"It depends on what you mean by 'relationship.'"

"Let's not play games, Jill," said Walter, his voice taking on an edge.

"I used to meet her at the train station in Albany when she came up."

"Why?"

"Because she didn't own a car in the city, and she didn't want one registered in her name. She wanted to keep her travels as anonymous as possible. So I bought a car for her, a Honda Pilot that's over ten years old now, and put the title in the name of Maas & Maas."

"Why a Honda?" said Walter. "She was rich; she could've had any car she wanted."

"The easy answer is that she didn't want anything that would raise her profile. But I just think that's who Stephanie was. The Pilot is unbelievably reliable. It has a tough suspension and four-wheel drive. That's all she wanted. Stephanie had no use for conspicuous consumption."

"And that was the extent of your interaction with her?"

"Pretty much."

"Are you sure?" said Walter. "Mr. and Mrs. French seemed to indicate that they thought that you had developed a friendship with her independent of your business with them."

"I don't know where they would have gotten that idea."

"Okay," said Levi in his soft voice, "then here's my question: why you?"

"Excuse me?" said Jill.

"Why you? Why, when Stephanie decided that she wanted to contact the Frenches, did she decide to go through you? How had she ever heard of you?"

"Dutch River is a small place, Mr. Welles. It was even smaller back then. Where else would she have gone?"

"Why didn't she go back to the person who'd found the identity for her in the first place?"

"I wouldn't know."

"Or perhaps she did."

"Levi, I was barely ten years old when Stephanie French took on her new identity. What you are suggesting is impossible."

"Perhaps you were too young, but not this firm," said Levi. "I seem to remember you telling us once that you are not only the child of an attorney, but also the grandchild of one. Maas & Maas has been in existence for decades."

"I'm not following you, Levi."

"Of course you are. Stephanie French contacted Maas & Maas because she was directed here by whoever found her new identity for her in the first place, someone with whom your father did business in the past. We need to know who that is."

"Levi…"

"Jill, please."

"I'm sorry, I really can't help you."

"Perhaps we should call your father."

"He can't tell you anything I can't."

"Goddammit, Jill, we don't have time for this. We have a murder case on our hands that's getting colder by the minute. Your client is dead. You have nothing left to protect. It could be critical to our case to find out who helped her change her identity."

"I'm sure you understand," said Jill, tentatively, "that people who undertake these types of activity require confidentiality. I also hope you understand that it would not be in the best interests of this firm for it to be known that we did business with, ah, certain types of individuals."

"Jill, this was all thirty years ago," said Levi.

"That doesn't mean that people still don't require confidentiality."

"So the person who approached you is still alive."

"Yes, and he would still prefer to remain anonymous."

"And how do you know that? Has he been in contact with you?"

"He doesn't have to be. I just know."

"Are you telling us," said Levi, "that you're frightened to tell us?"

"I'm not frightened. I just feel a strong obligation to protect this person's identity. He is someone I admire a great deal, that's all."

"Can you contact this person?"

"Perhaps."

"I'll tell you what then," said Levi. "Lieutenant Hudson and I will leave the room while you contact this person and request permission to divulge his identity. Perhaps he'll be willing to balance his privacy against the need to solve the murder of a woman who didn't deserve to die."

"Stay here," said Jill after a moment's hesitation. "I'm going to go to my office to make some calls." She rose and left.

"What do you think?" said Walter after Jill had closed her office door behind her.

"I think Jill, or her father, dealt with someone with a long reach."

"Yeah, and someone who obviously still has one."

"Walter, are you beginning to think what I'm beginning to think?"

"If I am, I don't want to think about it." Walter rose from his chair and looked out the window at the little town that once again seemed to be the epicenter of enormous events. It was a town he'd come to love but that also seemed to hold more than its fair share of secrets. He turned back to the room as he heard the conference room door open and close.

"Well?" he said to Jill, who stayed rooted by the door, her skin pale, her eyes wide, a small sheet of stationery in her hand. She held the paper out to Walter.

"His name is Tommassino Fornaio, and he wants to see you."

"Any idea where Devon-on-Hudson, New York is?" said Levi, staring at the scrap of paper that Jill Maas had handed him.

"Nope," said Walter. "And I've never heard of a restaurant named 'Cuccina della Torino,' either. I'm just letting the GPS take us there. It seems to be near the Hudson River, though, close to West Point."

"I wonder why we're not meeting him in Newburgh, or in the city? And why are we supposed to use the rear entrance?"

"I don't know. Devon-on-Hudson is pretty close to Newburgh, though, and the restaurant might be one of those places whose customers wouldn't be happy seeing a couple of cops walking through the front door."

"But we're not even in uniform," said Levi.

"I'm trying to remember the last time not wearing my uniform actually fooled anybody, Levi."

Levi looked over at his friend. "You've probably got a point," he said.

⸺◦◦◦⸺

Jill Maas looked out the front window until she saw the two men climb into their car and drive out of town. She respected them both and, more than that, she liked both them and their families enormously. But as she walked back into her office and unlocked the secret drawer hidden away beneath the desktop, she wondered how long that friendship could last now.

The drawer slid out smoothly, and she withdrew the fading manila folder. The folder that had been sealed closed ten years ago and never opened since; the folder that contained only one word on the cover: Stephanie.

Levi and Walter had been right. She and Stephanie French had developed a friendship over the years, and Stephanie had shared much about her life with her. But there were some things that she wouldn't share even with Jill, with no one, and those things she had written down and given to Jill for safekeeping.

Jill had sworn never to open it unless Stephanie gave her express permission to do so. They'd never discussed what Jill should do in the event of Stephanie's death. Like all young people, they rarely contemplated their own demise.

But as she stared at the unopened envelope, she wondered.

How much did she owe to the living, and how much to the dead?

13

"FOR GOD'S SAKE, SETH," said Amanda Stone, as she carefully put down her wineglass and stared at her sulking husband through the fading evening light, "you've just been handed a golden opportunity, a second chance, something very few people get in this life. What are you going to do, just throw it away?" The air was still mild, but the atmosphere was chilly between the two as they sat in next to each other in matching *chaises longues* on the spacious deck looking out on their enormous pool behind their home in Greenwich, Connecticut.

Amanda Noordman Stone's roots in New York City went back to its Dutch founding. Jakob Noordman had sailed to what was then known as Niew Nederland with Peter Minuit, the man who notoriously purchased Manhattan Island from the local natives for twenty-three dollars. Minuit eventually returned to the Netherlands in disgrace, but Jakob Noordman had stayed, becoming a wealthy patroon with enormous landholdings in what is now known as the Bronx. The fortune had only grown over the centuries. Amanda's mother's family, though not nearly as wealthy, traced its roots to a cousin of Queen Mary who may or may not have been distantly in the line of succession to the English throne.

Amanda's family had not approved of her engagement to Seth, a young man who, though possessing a first-class mind, could boast of nothing more than middle-class roots and decidedly boorish behavior. But Amanda's father, Hendrik Noordman, a man whose profligate philandering had only been exceeded by his prodigious drinking, had squandered the family fortune with a series of reckless investments, usually made during whisky-soaked phone calls with his equally inebriated stock broker. He proceeded to die in a spectacular car crash on the way to the family estate in Dutchess County just prior to its repossession and the week before Amanda and Seth's planned nuptials. Police at the scene reported that both Hendrik and his broker, the only other passenger, were found still clutching bottles of single malt Scotch in their dead hands. The family, humbled, couldn't blame Amanda for pinning her hopes, both financial and romantic, on the talented if unpolished young man.

But Amanda, after a quarter-century of dutiful matrimony, felt that she'd been let down on both counts.

No doubt, Seth had done well financially, becoming a multimillionaire after starting out with nothing. They lived a nice life in Greenwich in a large home in a trendy neighborhood with his and her Mercedes SUVs in the driveway and the requisite sailboat moored at the Greenwich Yacht Club. But being a multimillionaire, especially in Greater New York, was not what it used to be, and the life they led, though successful in its own George Babbitt kind of way, was far from meeting Amanda's expectations.

Amanda Stone aspired to more, and she felt that she was about to get it if her stubborn husband didn't once more throw a golden opportunity to the four winds.

"I'm not throwing anything away, and you know it," said Seth Stone, a man who largely resembled his name. He looked far more like the construction workers that his father and both his grandfathers before him had been than an investment banker. In his youth he had been considered ruggedly handsome, but to Amanda's dismay, the formerly rock-hard block of a body which she had found irresistible in her youth was now going to fat, and his once leonine head and face now more resembled that of a gargoyle on a Renaissance cathedral, even as she watched her friends' husbands grow slimmer, sleeker, and more attractive with age.

"Then I assume that you will be marching into Bryce Barstow's office first thing tomorrow morning and demanding that he support you to succeed Stephanie French."

"A lot of good that would do me," said Seth, resting his empty coffee cup on the table between the two chairs. The Stones maintained an expensive wine cellar, which Amanda eagerly featured when they entertained, but Seth rarely drank anything other than coffee and the occasional beer. "Bryce Barstow is an addled old fool, and the only thing he intends to do before he gets thrown out on his ass once again is install his daughter in his place."

"Oh, please, Seth. Bryce Barstow can't possibly believe that April is in any way capable of running that company. Even April and the Board know that. What Bryce Barstow wants doesn't count, but things will go much easier for you if you go into this with his support rather than without it."

"It doesn't really matter what he thinks of April. What matters is what he thinks of me, and that isn't much. And the same goes for the damn Board."

"I simply refuse to believe that, Seth. I still believe that the job would have been yours for the taking if that damn bitch Stephanie hadn't been in the way. And now you've been given a golden opportunity, now that she's been..."

"Now that she's been what?" said Seth, staring at his wife, "put down like a dog at a pound? Eliminated?"

"Now is not the time to be getting all misty about the love of your life, dear."

"Oh, cut the crap, Amanda."

"And what 'crap' would that be, dear? That you weren't foolishly infatuated with that woman all the years that I was bearing and raising your children while you were working ninety-hour weeks side by side with the lovely Stephanie? That you didn't follow her around like a puppy follows its master at social events while I was standing there watching? That you wouldn't have left the children and me in a heartbeat if she'd given you a finger wave? Do you mean that 'crap'?"

"Stephanie and I were barely on speaking terms by the time she died, and you know it."

"That doesn't mean you weren't still hopelessly in love with her, and you know *that*."

"Amanda, this is getting us nowhere."

"There. We finally agree on something. How lovely."

"Look, I want to get the top job as much as you want me to, but I've got a problem."

"Only one?"

"Cut it out, Amanda. You know what I mean. I didn't get a single vote from the Board when Stephanie was elected. They didn't want to have anything to do with me. Jesus, even April got two votes."

"Yes, one from that mindless bimbo Barbara Grunewald and the other from Hollings Harkin, he of the wandering eye and loose zipper. I always wondered if April ever rewarded him for his loyalty. In any event, neither of their votes will count at the next election and you should ignore them. You have to worry about Bryce Barstow and the other members of the Board."

"April isn't like that! She may not be qualified to run Barstow & Company, but she's a lovely, decent woman."

"Oh, dear. Shall I conclude from your heartfelt response that you have refocused your affections on the lovely April to help her deal with her heartbreak and loneliness at the loss of her best chum?"

"You know, Amanda," said Seth, hauling his heavy bulk out of his seat with an effort, "every time I think you can't sink any lower you surprise me one more time. This conversation is over." He turned to go inside.

"Oh no, it is not," said Amanda in an icy, controlled voice that stopped Seth in his tracks. He turned back to her and met her gaze.

"What? Don't you think you've said enough?"

"I haven't even started, dear," said Amanda. "Now you listen to me. I have spent my entire adult life doing everything I possibly could to further your business career, despite the fact that you wouldn't give me a second glance after you met the sainted Stephanie."

"Whatever you did was for your own selfish purposes. Don't try to peddle me that story that you were doing it all for me."

"My motives were hardly important. The fact is that I did it. I supported you when nobody else would, even your beloved Stephanie. You don't know the half of what I've done to make sure that you had every opportunity to climb to the top of Barstow & Company. All I expect from you in return is for you to hold up your end of the deal. I will not allow you to quit on me now. Do you understand?"

"Sometimes you frighten me, Amanda."

"Good. You should be frightened."

Seth retook his seat and sagged in defeat. He could only fight his wife for so long.

"Amanda, look at me."

"Must I?"

"Yes, you must. Look at me, Amanda. What do you see?"

"Let's not play games, Seth. What are you getting at?"

"Do you see someone you'd expect to see on CNBC when you turn on the TV in the morning? Do you see someone who will make people sit up in their seats when he testifies before Congress? Do you see someone who people will put on a short list for Secretary of the Treasury? Because that's the type of person investors expect to see in the CEO's office of Barstow & Company."

"I can't help it if you've let your looks go down the drain. Go back to the gym. Buy some new suits. Get a new hair stylist. These are all things you can correct if you just put your mind to it."

"Do you really think that's what I'm talking about?"

"This is getting tiring, Seth. What's your point?"

"My point is, no matter how qualified you or I think I am to lead Barstow & Company, and no matter how much we both want that, I'm beginning to think that all those folks who wouldn't vote for me are right: I don't have the personality or the temperament for the job. I mean, Jesus, even the clients I make a fortune for can't stand me, and changing my barber or getting a new tailor isn't going to change that. I'm almost fifty years old, Amanda. I am who I am."

"Now you listen to me, Seth Stone. I don't expect to live out my life here in fucking Connecticut cultivating award-winning roses. I want the Manhattan townhouse. I want to host the charity galas. I want to be on the Board of Directors of the Metropolitan Opera. I want all the things I would have had as my birthright if my father, may he roast in hell, hadn't pissed them all away. I have done everything, Seth, everything, to make sure you have the chance to get those things for me. I'm too old to start over. So don't whine, just do it. I don't care if you have to strangle Bryce Barstow in his bed and throw his daughter off a bridge. Do you understand?"

"Yes, Amanda. I understand."

"Good. Now, would you like dessert out here or in the library?"

※

THE PIZZA WAS DELICIOUS, though it wasn't the type of meal that either Walter or Levi would have expected to share with Tommassino Fornaio.

The GPS in the BMW had gotten them to the little town of Devon-on-Hudson easily enough, and the Cuccina della Torino hadn't been difficult to spot, right on Main Street. They'd parked in the back as instructed, and knocked on the only door they'd seen: a metal, windowless affair that looked like a service entrance.

They'd knocked twice and had just about decided that they must have been knocking on the wrong door when it was finally opened by a heavyset man with dark, curly hair, a badly trimmed moustache, and a friendly smile who smelled faintly of rising dough.

"Hi, I'm Anthony," he'd said. "I'm Tommy's nephew. Please, come in."

He'd led them to the main dining room of the restaurant, to the table where the only other patron sat. He'd placed a steaming pizza in front of them, and then quietly disappeared into the kitchen.

"My nephew granted me the favor of closing his restaurant a little early tonight," said the small, trim man with blond hair fading to silver sitting across from them, picking at the small antipasto plate that his nephew had placed in front of him, "so that we could meet in privacy."

Tommassino Fornaio was wearing casual clothes and looked more like a successful insurance agent who'd just returned from a round of golf with wealthy clients than the man who controlled all organized crime in New York State north of the city limits.

"We appreciate that, sir," said Levi.

"So, gentlemen," he said, looking at Levi and Walter with large, clear blue eyes, "my good friend Commissioner Donahue tells me that you may have some questions for me regarding the untimely death of Stephanie French, a woman both my wife and I admired greatly. We were both stunned at the news of her death."

"We actually have more questions than we thought we did," said Walter.

"Well, then," said Fornaio, "why don't we take them one at a time?"

"First," said Walter, after taking a slice of pizza, "as Commissioner Donahue probably told you, we have traced the murder weapon to someone, we don't know who, who we believe is, or was, in your employ in some way."

"Let me stop you right there," said Fornaio in a quiet voice and measured tone. "No one in my employ owned the firearm to which you are referring, and no one in my employ had anything, anything, Lieutenant, to do with the tragic death of Stephanie French. Is that understood?"

"I understand, Mr. Fornaio," said Walter, "but we have pretty solid information that the weapon was used on occasion during some disagreements that may have arisen between a gang called the Zorros and members of your organization. The method of the killing was similar to the method of some of the killings that took place during those disagreements."

"Perhaps," said Fornaio, putting down his fork and patting his lips with a napkin, "you didn't understand me when I spoke. Let me be clear. I have never heard of any organization called the 'Zorros,' and I have no idea what you are talking about when you refer to so-called 'disagreements.'" He turned his attention to Leviticus and said, "I don't know where the NYPD is getting its intelligence these days, but it appears that you have some faulty sources. You might want to check them out, Deputy Commissioner Welles."

"Thank you, we will," said Levi, knowing that this was no time to be getting into an argument like this, and this was no man with whom to be getting into one.

"Good," said Fornaio, turning back to Walter. "Now, Lieutenant, you indicated that you might have another topic of discussion."

"I believe you spoke to an attorney named Jill Maas today," said Walter.

"Yes, I did."

"She seemed to indicate to us that you might have some information regarding Ms. French's identity. As you probably know, it has become apparent to us that Stephanie French is not her birth name. It is vital for us to know as much as we can about her true background in order to solve her murder, and we were hoping you could help us."

"Normally I don't discuss business matters," said Fornaio, pushing his antipasto plate away, "but because of my friendship with and admiration for Ms. French, and my strong desire to help you find her killer, I will tell you what I know, although you will probably find it disappointing."

"Anything would help, sir."

There was a knock on the door, and Anthony Fornaio entered with espressos for everyone and a small plate of pastries. He removed the pizza, which was almost gone anyway.

"That pizza was amazing, Anthony," said Levi. "Thank you."

"*Di nenti*," said Anthony, smiling.

"It means 'you're welcome,' in Sicilian," said Levi, noticing Walter's puzzled expression.

"You understand Sicilian, Mr. Welles?" said Fornaio.

"I'm not fluent, but I can get by," said Levi in perfect Sicilian. "My wife and I visited Sicily for a couple of weeks this past winter, and I managed to pick it up while I was there. The history of that island is amazing."

"Your gift for languages is becoming legendary," said Tommassino, also in perfect Sicilian. "Now I know why. Sicilian is my native tongue and I can't detect an accent. Congratulations."

"*Grazij,*" said Levi.

"Thank you, Anthony," said Fornaio, reverting to English. He took a small sip of his drink, picked up a pastry, and sat back in his chair. He nodded to his nephew in polite dismissal. "I usually don't indulge in sweets," he said, turning back to the two policemen, "but my nephew gets his pastries from a tiny bakery that still operates on the Lower East Side, not far from where I grew up, and I find them irresistible. Please, try one."

Walter picked one up and almost moaned as he took a bite.

"I'm glad you like it," said Tommassino, with a smile that looked genuine. He carefully placed his demitasse cup back on the table, "but back to business. A long time ago, perhaps thirty years now, I received a call from a minor business acquaintance, a man who transacted most of his affairs in midtown Manhattan. He said that a friend of his had contacted him requesting a favor. He told the story of a very young but extremely talented woman who, for reasons known only to her, needed to change her identity. He said that he normally wouldn't get involved in minor matters of this sort, but his acquaintance had been adamant. He said this woman was profoundly gifted and that we would never regret any assistance we could offer her. He said he wouldn't have bothered me, but he thought that a transaction of this nature might better be done outside of New York City.

"Normally, of course, I would have refused. I am a legitimate businessman, and I avoid these types of questionable activities. But I was a young man then, and I had to admit that I was intrigued. So to make a long story short, I was able to obtain a new identity for this woman: Stephanie French."

"Did you ever find out anything about the woman's past, or what made her so intriguing?" said Levi.

"To answer your first question: no. I never found out anything about the woman's true identity. I respect people's privacy, and I never saw any reason to pry into hers. To answer your second question, of course I did, but not until many years later. My wife and I had been invited to a charity event at which the evening's entertainment was to be a performance by a young but highly regarded string quartet. They performed quite a varied program of music, but the featured piece was Bach's 'Air On The G-String,' which is, as you know, a virtuoso piece for the violin. I am no music critic, but it was apparent to me, as it was to everyone in that room who wasn't deaf, that the young violinist was nothing short of extraordinary, perhaps a genius. And her name was Stephanie French. I made a point of introducing myself after the recital, and it was during our conversation that I learned that she was also a rising star at Barstow & Company, a company with which I had some significant investments. She told me of a new fund that she was managing, called the Balboa Fund. I called Barstow & Company the next day and had all my investments transferred over to that fund. I've never regretted it."

"Intriguing, indeed," said Levi.

"Indeed," said Fornaio. "Over the years both my wife and I became good friends with Ms. French. My wife became heavily involved with Stephanie's organization, SafeWays, as has, I have been given to understand, your wife Sarah, Lieutenant."

"Only in a small way," said Walter.

"Still, any participation is important. My wife, Christina, has in fact met Sarah and found her to be an impressive young woman."

"I'm glad to hear that," said Walter, not sure at all if he was glad.

"Did Ms. French ever learn of the assistance you gave her when she was young?" said Levi.

"No, never."

"Are you sure?" said Levi. "Jill Maas apparently knew of your involvement, and it's my understanding that the two women became friendly over the years. Perhaps Jill let something slip."

"Jill Maas is an intelligent woman as well as a fine lawyer," said Fornaio quietly. "I can tell you with absolute assurance that she never would have betrayed that confidence."

Neither of the two policemen doubted his word.

"Do you maintain any contact with the person who originally approached you regarding Stephanie?" said Levi.

"Sadly, that man passed away years ago."

"Did you ever ask him the identity of the man who originally approached him about Stephanie?"

"I have learned, Mr. Welles, that in this life it is wise to ask only those questions to which you truly want an answer. So, no."

"Do you have any idea who would have wanted Stephanie French dead, Mr. Fornaio?" said Walter.

"No, I do not. But I promise you that if I ever find out anything that will assist you in your investigation, I will contact you. Now, gentlemen, if you will excuse me." Tommassino Fornaio rose to leave. He shook hands with Walter and Levi and slipped out the back door without another word.

The two cops drove home in silence.

14

"**M**ANLIUS HAMMERS KAPLAN ON POLICE BUDGET," screamed the headline of the morning's *New York Post*. "*Demands Drastic Cuts Until 'Injustice Stops.'*"

"Jesus, you'd think the election was tomorrow," said Lieutenant Hudson, throwing down the newspaper in disgust. "It's not even June." He and his wife were sitting in their kitchen, the sun pouring through the back window, but neither of them was feeling the warmth.

"What's this guy's gripe, anyway?" said Sarah, pouring a second cup of coffee for both of them. "Wasn't he born rich?"

"Yeah, he was," said Walter, "and then he got a lot richer with a lot of help from the NYPD, which he seems to have conveniently forgotten about."

Harold Manlius had indeed been born rich, and with the help of his father's money had only gotten richer, buying up block after block of abandoned real estate in the South Bronx and Brooklyn and reselling the gentrified properties at astronomic profits. The NYPD had allocated enormous resources at great cost to the formerly crime-riddled properties to keep them safe while they were under redevelopment.

"Maybe Commissioner Donahue should send him a bill," said Sarah.

"Fat chance of that," said Walter. "Every politician in this city is scared to death of the guy."

"But why? He's a seventy-year-old multi-billionaire who's never held political office in his life. He's nothing but a cranky old socialist who doesn't want anyone else to get rich now that he's got his. What makes anybody think he can win?"

"You know this city, Sarah," said Walter, putting down his coffee cup and leaning back in his chair, "you win by running to the left. If your opponent is a Republican, run as a Democrat. If your opponent is a Democrat, run as a Progressive. If your opponent is a Progressive, run as a Socialist; and if your opponent is a Socialist, start quoting from *Das Kapital* and getting weepy about the Rosenbergs and Alger Hiss."

"My goodness, sweetheart," said Sarah, "I think that's the longest speech I ever heard you make."

"It just pisses me off, that's all. Deborah Kaplan is a moderate Democrat, and there's no way she can get to the left of Manlius, even if she wanted to, which she doesn't."

"Are you saying you think he can win?"

"You're damn right I am. You'd think people would've learned after the Mayor Nutting fiasco, but they haven't. New Yorkers are always determined to learn the same lesson over and over."

"At the expense of the NYPD."

"Yes," said Walter, staring again at the headline.

"And how do you think this is going to affect your investigation into Stephanie French's murder?" said Sarah, just as Walter's mobile phone beeped, announcing a new text message. Walter stared at the phone for a few minutes and then looked up.

"I don't know," he said, "but I think I'm about to find out."

"Why? What was the message about?"

"It was from Commissioner Donahue's office. He wants Levi and me there immediately if not sooner."

"That doesn't sound good."

"It gets worse. Mayor Kaplan's going to be there, too." Walter drained his coffee cup and stood to leave.

"Be careful, Walter."

"Don't worry, I will. And I'll tell the mayor you said 'hi.'"

———

FOR ONCE, blessedly, it was just coffee. And for once, they were sitting at a table instead of at the bar.

Commissioner Sean Donahue and Mayor Deborah Kaplan were of an age, both in their mid-fifties, but it was hard to tell when they were seen together. Donahue's thick white hair and wide girth made him look a decade older than the small, trim mayor whose hair was still its original brunette without the assistance of artificial coloring. But they had a professional and personal, though not romantic, relationship that went back decades, and they were clearly comfortable in each other's company.

Walter and Levi had met outside One Police Plaza and had ridden up to the top floor together, where Donahue's administrative assistant had led them past the door to the Commissioner's main office and down a narrow hallway to the non-descript door to which only she and the commissioner possessed a key. Mayor Kaplan had already arrived, and both Levi and Walter got the uncomfortable feeling that they had interrupted a private conversation when they walked through the door.

"Hello, Walter. Hello, Levi," said Mayor Kaplan with genuine warmth as she shook hands with the men without standing. "How's Sarah, and how is that rambunctious little boy of yours, Walter?"

"Sarah is fine and sends you her regards, Madam Mayor," said Walter, astonished as usual with the mayor's politician's gift for remembering names seemingly without effort, "and little Daniel is growing like a weed and still as rambunctious as ever."

"The apple doesn't fall far from the tree, does it?" she said. "And Levi, I just saw Julie last week at Gracie Mansion, where we held a reception for some senior United Nations representatives. Her career seems to be flourishing, and she looks younger every time I see her. I wish she would share her secret with me."

"You and me both, Your Honor," said Levi. "People keep accusing me of marrying a child bride."

"I daresay we've all been accused of worse," said the mayor, "and let's drop this Your Honor and Madam Mayor nonsense. We all know each other too well, and this conversation is too important to be wasting time on useless formalities."

"Yes, ma'am," said Walter and Levi simultaneously. Calling her "Deborah" was just not going to happen, any more than either of them would call the commissioner "Mike."

"Now," said Commissioner Donahue, "I imagine both of you are wondering what this meeting is all about."

"Yes, sir," they both replied.

"I received a call from the North Homicide office at about six o'clock this morning. They'd been called over to Riverside Park, where a body had been found a little before dawn. The officers on the scene surmised that it didn't appear to be a natural death, so they called the homicide guys over."

"And what made them think," said Walter, "that it might have been a murder?"

"Take a look for yourselves," said Donahue, reaching into a briefcase sitting on the floor at his feet and withdrawing a thin manila envelope, which he handed to Walter. The only item in the folder was an 8"x10" color photograph, which Walter laid on the table so that they could all see it.

"Oh," said Levi.

It was a picture of a man, perhaps middle-aged, lying on the leafy ground of the steep hillside that led down to Riverside Drive and the Hudson River. He was wearing a light jacket, jeans, and a pair of running shoes. On the ground beside him, just out of reach of his right hand, was a pistol. A knife with a thick handle, which made Walter think that it was a hunting knife, was buried up to the hilt in the man's chest, just below the sternum. Walter knew that it had pierced the man's heart and that death had come swiftly. And pinned between the man's jacket and the hilt of the knife, like a document pinned to a message board with an enormous thumbtack, was a piece of paper. Something had been written on it, but the angle at which the photo had been taken didn't allow Walter to read it. He and Levi both looked up at the commissioner with a growing sense of dread.

"Any idea what was written on the piece of paper?" said Levi.

"Yes," said Donahue, "but I'm going to need your help, Levi, because it wasn't written in English."

"What did it say?" said Walter, but he and Levi already knew the answer.

"It said, '*di nenti.*' Can you tell me what the hell that means in English, Levi?"

"I take it you've already run that gun through ballistics," said Walter.

"Of course I have," said Commissioner Donahue. "What's the use of being commissioner if you can't throw your weight around now and then? And no wisecracks from you, Deborah."

"Never," said the mayor, smiling.

"And I'm sure the gun matched the weapon that killed Stephanie French," said Walter.

"Yes, it did."

"Was the man carrying any ID?" said Levi.

"Yes, he was," said Donahue, "although we really didn't need it. Our organized crime guys identified the vic on sight, said he'd committed at least three murders with the same weapon and the same MO over the past few years. He'd been charged twice, but all the charges had been conveniently dropped."

"Of course," said Mayor Kaplan.

"What was the guy's name?" said Walter.

"Joseph Hanson, according to the ID," said Donahue, "but I doubt that's the name he started out his life with."

"It sure would've been nice if the guy had been delivered to us alive so we could've braced him," said Walter. "Tommy Fornaio had to know this wasn't going to help us."

"I don't know whether he did or didn't," said Donahue, "but I am sure that any benefit or lack thereof to us was hardly one of his top priorities. Tommy Fornaio, as you know by now, is a charming and polished man, so much so that you tend to forget that he is still a thug."

"And he didn't want anyone left alive who could connect him with the murder of Stephanie French," said Walter.

"That's only part of it," said Donahue. "I'd bet my pension that he had absolutely nothing to do with Stephanie French's murder. I'm sure he knew that he could easily prove he had no connection with that."

"So why kill Hanson?" said Mayor Kaplan.

"Because he is connected with a lot of other criminal activity. If we'd taken Hanson alive, he would've known that he was down for capital murder, and he would have talked for days to us and to the FBI about all of the other jobs that he's done for Tommy over the years, just to avoid a lifetime in prison with no parole."

"And Tommy wouldn't stand for that," said Walter.

"Of course not," said Donahue.

"There's another possibility, you know," said Levi, picking up his empty coffee cup and looking at it like he just noticed it for the first time.

"What would that be, Levi?" said the mayor.

"That whoever hired this guy to murder Stephanie French got to him before Tommy Fornaio did."

"And what makes you think that?" said Donahue.

"Think about it, sir. I agree with everything you said about why Fornaio would've wanted the guy dead, and I'm sure he would have made him dead sooner rather than later, but I also think that he would have made sure to extract the information we needed from him first."

"Why?" said Donahue, his eyes widening with interest.

"Because the sense I got from talking to him is that he wanted to find out who murdered Stephanie just as much as we did."

"But then why was that sign stuck on the poor guy's body?" said Mayor Kaplan. "'*Di*' whatever it was."

"Good point," said Levi. "Of course, I immediately assumed when I first saw it that it was a signal from Fornaio that he'd done it, but now I'm thinking that it was a misdirection play."

"A what?" said Kaplan.

"A misdirection play. It not only takes attention away from the person who really murdered Stephanie, it also makes the whole thing look like a mob hit gone bad, that the real target of the shooting was someone else, not her. It was all just a tragic accident. Case closed, we can all move on."

"But that's bullshit," said Walter.

"Sure it is," said Kaplan, "but it's also pretty damned clever. Whoever thought of it should go into politics."

"But do you think the tabloids will buy it?" said Donahue.

"Sure they will," said Levi. "The tabloids, all the media for that matter, have the attention span of a newborn kitten. They've milked Stephanie French's murder for all it's worth, and now this is their excuse to move on before their readers get bored."

"And if we continue to pursue it, we'll just be playing into Manlius's agenda," said Walter, pointing to the front page of the *New York Post* sitting on the table next to them, the same one he and Sarah had been staring at just a short while ago.

"Yes," said Kaplan. "The NYPD, with the Mayor's full support, of course, wasting the taxpayers' money, stubbornly chasing a case that should be closed. The press will eat it up."

"You're not saying you want us to drop the case, are you?"

"Of course not," said Donahue. "I'm just telling you to be careful, that's all."

"Careful of what, sir?" said Walter.

Instead of answering, Donahue reached over and grabbed the newspaper.

"I'm guessing you didn't get to Page Six this morning, Lieutenant?"

"No, sir. I just saw the front page before you called."

"Well, then, perhaps we should take a look," said Donahue, flipping the pages. Page Six was the *Post's* gossip page, and Donahue opened up to it and laid the paper down on the table between them.

In the middle of the page, in full color, was a photo of Walter in his and Sarah's brand new BMW, driving down Queens Boulevard, windows open to the mild spring air. In the background, three small children sat on the sidewalk huddled around a woman holding a sign in her hands that said "No Money, No Food, No Home." Walter knew that the image had been PhotoShop'd, but that hardly mattered. People don't scour Page Six in search of the truth. Because of his numerous high-profile cases, Walter was easily recognized by thousands of *Post* subscribers. The caption was written in bold capitals. It read: "Solving Crime The NYPD Way: In Style!"

"Careful of *that*," said Commissioner Donahue.

—————

Levi and Walter had just stepped out of One Police Plaza when Levi's phone rang.

"Hello," he said, then stood still and listened for a full minute. "Interesting," he finally said. "Okay, thanks."

"What was that all about?" said Walter.

After Levi told him, Walter pulled out his own phone and retrieved a familiar number from his "Contacts" list.

"Hey, Eduardo," he said into the phone, "I need you to run down-town and follow up on something for me."

15

"WE WILL NOW bring this extraordinary meeting of the Barstow & Company Board of Directors to order," said Owen Morning, rapping his knuckles on the table like a teacher quieting his students. He looked particularly dapper this morning in a navy blue Brioni suit, white cotton shirt with a severely spread collar, and a burgundy bowtie. It was the outfit he intended to wear to his own wake, but he kept that tidbit to himself. His face shone like a polished apple.

"Thank you, Owen," said Bryce Barstow, "now…"

"Please, Bryce," said Morning, "let me continue." He, along with everyone else in the room, had feared that this was going to happen. They'd feared it when they'd decided to reinstall Barstow as temporary CEO on Saturday morning, even though they'd felt it was their only choice.

"Now, see here, Owen," said Barstow, his voice rising, "I'm the Chief Executive Officer of this company, and, in case you've forgotten, mine is the only name on the letterhead. You are, let me remind you, the *non-executive* chairman of *my* company. You've gaveled the meeting to order. You've done your job and we thank you. Now…"

"Bryce, please," said Ed Rauch, sitting up. He was an impressive looking man, and as an independent director and a man who had run his own business for decades, he had never been beholden to Bryce Barstow. He was one of the few people in the room who was not intimidated by the man. "This is a Board of Directors meeting, not one of your staff meetings. Owen is our Chairman, and he will run the meeting. We have an agenda, and we will stick to it."

"Dammit, Ed," said Barstow, his voice becoming even louder.

"But before we get to the agenda, Mr. Chairman," said Rauch, talking over Barstow and pointedly looking directly at Owen Morning, "I believe we need to discuss the propriety of having an unannounced guest in the room."

"What the hell are you talking about?" said Barstow, almost shouting now.

"April," said Morning as softly as he could to April Barstow, who was sitting by herself in a chair against the wall near the door, "I'm very sorry, but I'm sure you understand that guests attend Board meetings only at the express, written invitation of the Board. And given the nature of our discussion this morning, I'm sure you understand that your presence here is inappropriate."

"Now you listen here, Owen," said Barstow, the right corner of his mouth starting to droop, causing his words to slur slightly, "I'm the damn CEO of this company, and I can invite anybody I damn please to our Board meetings, and I don't have to ask anybody's damn permission."

"In fact, you do," said Ed Rauch in a quiet, commanding voice. "Bryce, you know that you were brought back in a transitional role…"

"I know no such thing! I'm the CEO…"

"And as such," said Rauch, ignoring Barstow, "you should give absolute deference to the Board as we continue our crucial task of identifying our next permanent CEO."

"We all know who we're going to choose," said Barstow, "so I don't see the harm in having her attend. In fact, it's important for her to be here so she can get up to speed on all the important issues."

"Bryce, please," said Owen Morning, rapping his knuckles on the table so hard it hurt, "let's get back to the agenda." But he knew he'd lost control of the meeting, and he didn't know how to regain it.

"Mr. Chairman, if I may," came a quiet voice from near the door.

"Yes, Ms. Barstow?" said Morning, barely containing the note of desperation in his voice.

"I would like to apologize," she said, "for being the cause of a disruption in this important meeting."

"April, don't…"

"Dad, let me finish," she said, locking her eyes on her father. "I was somehow given the impression that I had been invited to this meeting. I assumed it was merely to be present for the first few minutes while my father was welcomed back to the company. I apparently either misunderstood or was misled, and I am deeply embarrassed. I will now leave so that you can carry on with your meeting in the privacy you require."

"April!" said her father, but it was too late; she had already left the room and closed the door behind her.

"Why don't we all take a break?" said Owen Morning, just as his admin, Marcia, once again opened the door and poked her head in. "Marcia, how many times must I tell you not to disturb our meetings?"

"I'm so sorry, Mr. Morning, but there's someone waiting in the lobby. He says he wants to speak to Ms. Grunewald."

"You mean 'Professor Grunewald,'" said Hollings Harkin. His evening with Bernadette had left him in a commanding mood. Maybe he should teach Marcia a lesson or two, he thought.

"Thank you so much, Hollings," said Barbara Grunewald, giving him a smile that only further swelled his ego. Perhaps he'd pay another visit to Bernadette tonight, he thought. Yes. She was probably already waiting by the phone for his call. He felt even better.

"Oh, let's just cut the shit," said Morning, peeved. The morning had not gone at all as he had planned. "Who is it and what does he want? We have a meeting to conduct here."

"He says his name is Detective Eduardo Sanchez," said Marcia, quailing, "and he says he needs speak to, ah, Professor Grunewald right away."

WALTER had felt a twinge of regret at sending Eduardo to talk to Barbara Grunewald. It wasn't that he didn't trust the young detective to do a good job; Eduardo had proven to Walter over the years that he was up to just about any task he was assigned. But Walter had personally interviewed all the other members of the Barstow & Company Board, and he was afraid that he had left Eduardo at a disadvantage. So by the time he got back to his cubicle at the Midtown South precinct house, Walter had decided to call Eduardo and tell him to hold off on the interview until he was able to get down to Barstow headquarters and help him out. But just as he was reaching for his phone it rang, seemingly in reproach for not trusting his able colleague to do his job. He picked it up.

"Hudson."

"Hey, Lieutenant," came a cheery voice over the line, "it's Sergeant Lennahan down at the front desk."

"What's up, Sergeant?"

"I got some guy down here, says he wants to see you."

"Who is it?"

"Some guy, says his name is Potter."

"As in 'Harry'?"

"Yeah, but he says his name is 'Clay.'"

"You're kidding."

"I shit you not, Lieutenant."

"I never heard of him. Look, I'm busy, Sergeant. What the hell does this guy want?"

"He says it's about the Stephanie French murder. Says he can fill you in on some of her past."

"Does he have the inside scoop on the next invasion from Mars, too?" The standard request to the public that anyone having any information that may help the NYPD solve Stephanie French's murder should call a specially created hotline number had generated the usual flood of calls from the thousands of cranks and shut-ins desperate for any kind of attention.

"Doesn't look like that kind of guy to me, sir."

"Okay, Sergeant, but if you're wrong I'll make sure you'll be issuing parking tickets on Eighth Avenue for the next month." He was kidding, and they both knew it. Walter had known Sergeant Lennahan for years and trusted his ability to size people up.

"Yessir," said Lennahan, laughing.

It looked like Eduardo was going to be on his own, after all. Just as well, thought Lieutenant Hudson.

—◁═══◊◊═══▷—

"ACTUALLY, I'm more comfortable speaking English," said Eduardo Sanchez to the woman with the ingratiating smile sitting across the table from him. They were sitting in the large Boardroom alone while the others were taking what Owen Morning had decided was a much needed break. In truth, Eduardo still spoke perfect Spanish, but after hearing the woman fracture his beautiful native tongue in just a few brief introductory words, he decided he had no time for Spanish lessons and no patience for condescension. Besides, he needed to understand what the woman was saying. "But thank you for offering."

"You're welcome, Detective," said Barbara Grunewald, "but as a professional educator I implore you not to let go of your roots. Having a cultural identity is so important these days."

I have a cultural identity, he thought; I'm an American. But he let it go.

"Now, Dr. Grunewald," he said, "it is my understanding that you have a long history with April Barstow."

"Yes, I do. She is perhaps the most distinguished alumna in the proud history of Brentwood College, of which I am honored to be the current president. And, in fact, she was a student of mine when I was a young professor."

"So she stood out even as a young student?"

"Oh, heavens yes. Brentwood College has prepared many fine young women for leadership roles in this world, but April was perhaps the finest. And, of course, she was as utterly charming back then as she is now. I recall encouraging her to follow in my footsteps and study English Literature at the graduate level, perhaps even pursue a career in academia. It was my dream that one day I might welcome her back to Brentwood as a faculty member but, of course, greater things were in store for her."

"Did you stay in contact with her after she graduated?"

"Oh, yes. We maintained a lively correspondence. I treasured her letters, and I've kept every single one of them."

"Ma'am, we've obtained a copy of Ms. Barstow's college transcript."

"And how did you manage that, Detective?" said Grunewald, her smile faltering, caught off guard by Eduardo's sudden change in tack.

"It was on file at Barstow & Company," said Sanchez.

"Oh. Of course."

"We couldn't help noticing that Ms. Barstow seemed to be an average student at best, ma'am. Mostly B's, a couple of C's, and two A's, both in the two courses she took from you."

"What are you implying, Detective?"

"I'm not implying anything, ma'am. Her undergraduate record is consistent with her graduate performance at Columbia: average and unremarkable."

"I'm not at all sure I understand what you're getting at, Detective Sanchez."

"It just seems that you saw academic, and maybe personal, qualities in April Barstow that others seemed to have missed."

"The academic world can be cruel and arbitrary, Detective, as I know from long personal experience. I believe my assessment of April is vindicated by the extraordinarily successful life she has lived since her college days. Others can defend their assessments if they are so inclined."

"How well did you know Stephanie French, Dr. Grunewald?"

"Certainly not as well as I know April," said Grunewald. "I knew her largely through our interactions at Board meetings."

"But she wasn't on the Board, was she?"

"No, but she made so many presentations to the Board that she attended practically every meeting."

"What was your assessment of her?"

"I thought she was a fine executive."

"Other people thought she was extraordinary, special."

"Well, of course everyone is entitled to his or her opinion."

"So you didn't think she was extraordinary the way that other people, other Board members, did?"

"I guess it depends on how you define 'extraordinary,' Detective. I know that Ms. French was considered something of a genius in the narrow field of finance, and she was a fine musician."

"But?"

"But she wasn't extraordinary in the same way that April Barstow is, Detective. When April walks into a room she brings electricity with her. And not just electricity. She brings beauty, refinement, and excitement. It's like...well, I just can't describe it."

"Is that why you voted for Ms. Barstow instead of Ms. French for the CEO job?"

"Not at all. I simply thought April Barstow was the most qualified candidate. I did vote, however, to make Ms. French's election unanimous. It's not that I thought the woman was unqualified; I just felt strongly that there was a better choice available."

"The woman," thought Eduardo. Interesting.

"How long have you been President of Brentwood College, Dr. Grunewald?"

"What?" said Grunewald, caught off guard once again by Eduardo's sudden shift in topic. The man is smarter by half than he lets on, she thought, and he's been well trained.

"It's a simple question, ma'am."

"Of course. I'm sorry. I'm afraid recent events have left me somewhat distracted. I have recently celebrated my seventh anniversary as president."

"How would you say the college has been doing under your leadership?"

"Brentwood College continues to be a dynamic academic community where young women can grow and thrive, both intellectually and personally, without the distractions and the aggressive environment sadly found at so many co-educational institutions these days, even the finest among them."

"That's wonderful, ma'am, but how about financially?"

"We are a non-profit college, not a business, Detective."

"I understand that, but you still need money to operate. I know that most private colleges can't survive on just tuition income. They need generous giving from alumni and a healthy endowment to cover operating expenses." In fact, Eduardo Sanchez, a City College graduate, had known none of this before the long phone conversation he'd had with Leviticus Welles on his way downtown.

"Detective, all small private institutions operate in a challenging economic environment, but I think Brentwood College has more than held its own during my tenure."

"But it really hasn't, has it?"

"Detective, what on earth are you talking about?"

"Dr. Grunewald, our research indicates…"

"And whose research would that be, Detective?"

"Ma'am, the NYPD has a first-rate intelligence division."

"And I'm sure it does a fine job of helping you capture criminals, Detective. But private colleges are complex entities, and I can hardly believe that the police are equipped to analyze them."

"You'd be surprised ma'am. May I continue?"

"I doubt you will wait for my permission, Detective. So please, go ahead."

"Thank you, ma'am. Our researchers have discovered that over the past seven years, Brentwood College's endowment has failed to grow. In fact, it is now fifty percent smaller than when you became president."

"Detective, I know this is probably difficult for you to understand, but sometimes a college needs to dig deeply into its financial resources to make the crucial investments necessary to ensure the long-term health of the institution."

"But, Dr. Grunewald, our research indicates that you have been drawing on the principal of the endowment simply to cover operating expenses. Our research has also revealed that alumnae giving has declined significantly in recent years."

"As you can imagine, Detective, many small colleges have struggled in the wake of the Great Recession. Brentwood College is not alone…"

"I'm sorry to interrupt, ma'am, but our research also seems to show that Brentwood College has fallen far behind its peer group in terms of its financial health."

"Damn your research!" said Grunewald, her chin visibly beginning to quiver. The fluorescent overhead lighting suddenly seemed to cast hard shadows on her carefully made up face. "What the hell can this line of questioning possibly have to do with solving Stephanie French's murder?"

"Ma'am, it just seems that having an alumna of your college become CEO of a major corporation could be an enormous financial benefit. It would raise the profile of your college tremendously. April Barstow would be the living symbol of the benefits of a Brentwood College degree."

"What are you saying, Detective Sanchez? Are you saying that I'd commit murder to save my college?"

"I'm just saying, ma'am, that it must have been a big disappointment to you when Stephanie French was named CEO of Barstow & Company instead of April Barstow, especially since you must have thought April had the inside track because of who her father was, that's all."

"I have already made it clear that I would have preferred April Barstow to have gotten the job, and I continue to support her candidacy in light of recent tragic events. But I believe I have made it clear that I have sound reasons for my support that have nothing to do with any financial crisis at Brentwood College that the NYPD seems to have dreamt up."

"In fact, ma'am, we have just this morning spoken to the president of Brentwood College's Foundation Board, a Ms. Buffy Claridge, and she told us that the board had convened an emergency meeting last week, which you attended, to address the college's financial crisis."

"Buffy Claridge has been a disaster ever since I made the mistake of naming her to that job," said Grunewald, her voice becoming a rasp. "I don't believe a word she says and neither should you."

"Sure ma'am."

"Now, Detective, I believe this meeting is over."

"Yes, ma'am," said Detective Eduardo Sanchez, rising to leave.

Barbara Grunewald had turned into an old woman during the course of the interview. Her mascara had cracked and melted in all the wrong places, splotches of bright red lipstick stained her capped teeth, and her entire body seemed to sag.

Sanchez almost felt bad for her.

Professor Barbara Grunewald ran to the ladies' room as soon as Sanchez was out of sight, fearing that she was going to be sick. She felt even sicker as she glimpsed at herself in the mirror.

Why had she told that damn nosy detective about her letters to April? At least April's responses had been dry and harmless, no matter how desperately Barbara had tried to read returned passion into them. And at least she hadn't told him of the copies of her own letters to April that she'd made and kept. She knew she should destroy them all, but she wasn't sure she could make herself do it.

She pulled mascara and lipstick out of her purse and desperately tried to repair the damage as best she could before heading back down the hallway to the boardroom.

She couldn't let April see her this way.

16

DETECTIVE LIEUTENANT WALTER HUDSON WAS NOT HOPEFUL as he stared across his desk at the man sitting in the small chair in his cramped office savoring the station house coffee like it was a premium blend. But then he reminded himself of the day only a few years ago when a disheveled Leviticus Welles had appeared at his desk in a soaking wet, ancient London Fog raincoat. He hadn't been hopeful then, either.

But this man didn't show any signs of being the next Leviticus Welles. He appeared to be in his mid-seventies. A pair of what looked like reading glasses sat atop thinning gray hair, which was badly combed, if at all, and there was a day's worth of silver stubble on one side of his face, as if he'd started the job but forgotten to finish. He wore a 1980s vintage New York Mets jersey that fit tightly over a bulging belly and a pair of khakis with what Walter hoped were paint stains on the front. But his eyes were alert and intelligent, and a constant smile brightened his aging features. You never know, Walter reminded himself.

"This coffee is wonderful, Lieutenant, thank you," said the man.

"You're kidding, right, Mr. Potter?" said Walter. "We use that coffee as an interrogation tool on murder suspects."

"I guess they never worked at a stock brokerage then," said Potter, laughing. It was a nice laugh without a trace of the bitterness he heard so often these days, especially from men of Potter's vintage.

"We seem to have one thing in common, sir."

"What's that, Lieutenant Hudson?"

"We're both Mets fans."

"Oh," said Potter, looking down at his jersey, "I've been a Mets fan since 1962, their first year. It broke my heart when the Dodgers moved to Los Angeles, but being a stockbroker taught me not to cry over spilled milk. And the Mets have given us some good times, haven't they?"

"They sure have," said Hudson. "So what can I do for you Mr. Potter? Clay, right?"

"My full name is Thomas Clayton Potter, Junior, Lieutenant. But everybody called my father 'Tom,' and Clay Potter was, as you can imagine, a catchier name for a salesman, which is what I was for forty-five years."

"But you said you were a stockbroker, right?"

"Yes, I was. Some people sell vacuum cleaners; some people sell cars. I sold stocks. It's all the same game."

"I thought stockbrokers were more like investment advisors," said Walter.

"A lot of people think that, Lieutenant, because that's what the brokerage houses, like the one I worked for, want you to believe. But mostly, the brokerage houses just buy up blocks of a particular stock and tell us brokers to get on the phone with our clients and push it. It's like a car dealership with too many minivans on the lot. The manager tells the salesmen to convince everyone who comes in that what they really need is a minivan, no matter what they came in looking for. But don't get me wrong, Lieutenant. Over time, stocks are a pretty good investment, and I never felt like I was really steering a client in the wrong direction. Firms that do that don't last very long. I wouldn't have done it for forty-five years if I hadn't liked what I was doing."

"Interesting," said Walter, thinking that he'd like Sarah to talk to this guy. "So, anyway, you said that you had some information about Stephanie French's past. Did you work with her in the financial industry when she was younger?"

"No, Lieutenant," said Potter with a chuckle, "Stephanie French was not in the financial industry when I met her."

"Then how did you meet her?"

"I met her at a strip club."

"You met her at a *what?*"

"A strip club. You know…"

"Yeah, yeah, I know. But what the hell was Stephanie French doing at a strip club?"

"She was a stripper, Lieutenant."

—————

"She was a *what?*" said Hudson, putting down the pencil he'd been holding. This guy was probably just another crackpot after all. He'd give Sergeant Lennahan hell for this.

"She was a stripper."

"Mr. Potter, I don't mean to sound skeptical, but from everything I've learned about Stephanie French, the last thing I would expect her to be is a stripper. Perhaps we're talking about a different person."

"We are not talking about a different person, Lieutenant. Look, I know you must think that I'm like a lot of other guys who come to see you, some lonely old goofball who's either losing his marbles or just wants some attention."

"I can't lie to you, Mr. Potter, the thought is crossing my mind."

"Just give me a chance, okay?"

"Okay, but this better be good. When did you meet her?"

"It was about thirty years ago."

"My God, she was what, seventeen years old thirty years ago."

"That sounds about right," said Potter.

"Where was this?"

"I'll get to that."

"Okay."

"I was forty-five years old at the time, and I'd been working on Wall Street for almost twenty-five years by then. Me and the missus were living out in Nassau County, in East Island. We'd had our kids young, and they were both out of the house by then. Thursday nights were bingo nights for the missus, so I told her that I'd just have dinner in town before I came home. I'd always be home by ten or eleven, about the same time she got back from bingo."

"But you weren't going out for dinner."

"Sure I was. I wouldn't lie to the missus. I'd grab a burger at McDonald's and eat it on the train on my way uptown. A man's gotta eat, Lieutenant."

"Okay," said Walter, agreeing with at least that sentiment, "so where was this strip club you're telling me about?"

"It was a place on Ninth Avenue, on the corner of Forty-Fourth Street. A place called the 'Leopard Lounge.'"

"Never heard of it," said Hudson, picking up his pencil to write down the name.

"You're a young man, Lieutenant. This was a while ago."

"So you're saying this place closed down before my time?"

"I wouldn't know. I haven't been there for almost thirty years, but I doubt it's there any longer. I think the online porn business kind of killed most of the strip clubs."

"Okay. Keep going."

"This place was a typical strip joint, you know? It had a stage with a bar around it and chairs where the customers could sit and drink and watch the show. They'd hand cash tips to the girls to get, you know, special attention."

"Which I'm sure they got."

"Don't judge the girls Lieutenant," said Potter, his jovial expression turning serious. "They were just trying to make a living with what they had, that's all. They were good kids."

"Okay, so you sat by the stage and watched the show. Then what?"

"I didn't do that, Lieutenant. Remember, I was in my mid-forties. It was the young guys who showed up in groups from work or wherever who sat at the stage and threw their dollar bills at the girls. You know, bachelor parties, that kind of thing. I just sat at a table in the back and watched the show."

"How long did you do this?"

"A couple of years, I guess. I've got to admit, I liked looking at a pretty girl as much as the next guy, but I was getting pretty tired of the routine. I found myself looking forward to the Big Mac on the train more than going to the show. I guess that's when you know you're getting old, right?"

"I wouldn't know, Mr. Potter," said Walter, not having to use too much imagination to guess what Sarah would do to him if she ever found out that he'd been ogling strippers.

"Some day you will, Lieutenant. But, anyway, like I was saying, I went into the Leopard Lounge one night thinking that it might be my last visit there. But when I got inside there was a commotion going on up at the stage like I'd never heard before. There were so many guys crowded around that at first I couldn't even see what all the hooting was about. But then there was a break in the crowd, just for a second, and I saw her."

"Are you going to tell me it was Stephanie French?"

"Yes, it was Stephanie, although that wasn't what she called herself back then. She just called herself Brittany."

"Brittany what?"

"Just Brittany, Lieutenant. It wasn't her real name. Half the strippers in New York called themselves Brittany, I think."

"So what was the commotion about?"

"She was beautiful, Lieutenant. There were a lot of good-looking strippers at the Leopard Lounge back then, but nobody, I mean nobody, had ever seen the likes of her there or at any other club. The face, the body, I mean she was the whole package. But it wasn't just beauty; it was like she had some, like, gravity field that just drew everyone to her. The Leopard Lounge back then used to have two or three girls on the stage at once, but when Stephanie, you know, Brittany, was on the stage the other girls didn't even bother. Sorry Lieutenant, it's been a long time since I thought of her as anything but 'Stephanie.'"

"No problem. That must have pissed off the other girls. It was taking money out of their, you know, pockets, right?"

"You'd think so, but no. Word spread fast about Stephanie, and pretty soon the crowds at the Leopard had doubled or maybe even tripled. I was even having trouble keeping my table in the back."

"So she was making money for everyone."

"You bet she was."

"And there was no reason for the other girls to be mad at her."

"That's right, Lieutenant, but it was more than that."

"What do you mean?"

"Before I ever even said 'hello' to her, I knew she was the most charming person I had ever met. And you could tell everyone else thought the same thing. She had this smile."

"You mean, like she enjoyed what she was doing?"

"You really never have been to a strip club, have you, Lieutenant?" said Potter, his expression turning incredulous.

"Sorry, but no."

"No matter what men would like to believe, strippers don't enjoy what they're doing. It's a job to them. It's money that they badly need, that's all. Some of them have drug habits; some of them have kids. They need to pay rent and buy groceries. They strip because it's their job, and they do it for the same reason everybody else has a job: to feed the bulldog, that's all."

"So they smile for the same reason the salesladies at Macy's smile."

"In a way, yes, but for the strippers it's more. They know that their customers need to believe that they're having a good time. It's part of the fantasy that keeps the men coming back."

"Then you're saying that all the girls smiled."

"Sure."

"So what was so special about Stephanie's smile?"

"Look, Lieutenant, she was an underage girl stripping at a club in

Hell's Kitchen in Manhattan. There had to be a bad story behind that, right?"

"It's hard to think there wasn't."

"But her smile, her smile seemed to say that somewhere deep inside, she was happy no matter what hell she'd been through that landed her at the Leopard Lounge."

"So, is that it?" said Walter, as if what he'd already heard hadn't turned his murder investigation on its head.

"No, that's just the beginning, Lieutenant."

"You're not telling me…."

Clay Potter hesitated for a few seconds before saying, "Oh, Christ, no Lieutenant."

"Then what?"

"That first night, I was just sitting there minding my own business when she suddenly came over and sat down with me while she was on a break."

"Looking for a tip, I guess?"

"Looking for relief, Lieutenant. She obviously wasn't taken by my good looks, and she certainly didn't need my money after the haul she'd made up on the stage."

"Relief from what, then?"

"From all those young men. They were all begging her to sit down with them and have a drink. There wasn't a single one of them who didn't have some fantasy that they'd somehow get her to come home with them. It had to have been frightening to a young girl. But the manager encouraged the girls to chat the customers up between acts, so she couldn't just hide in the dressing room."

"You were like some sort of refuge for her."

"Something like that."

"So what did you do?"

"I bought her a drink, a Diet Coke, which was apparently all she drank besides water. And we chatted."

"What about?"

"Oh, this and that. She mostly asked me about what I did. She seemed really interested in it, and judging by the way things turned out, I guess she really was. She was awfully smart, and she picked up on stuff as quickly as any college-educated trainee that we had at the firm, that was for sure."

"Did she ever talk about herself?"

"Not really, and I didn't pry, but I could tell right away she wasn't from around here. She talked like the people on that old PBS radio program, *A Prairie Home Companion*, you know? Anyway, the only thing she ever talked about was music, and how much she loved to play the violin. She said she practiced all the time and she hoped that she'd make enough money so that she could start taking lessons again. She said music was what kept her going."

"She said, 'again'?"

"Yes. Why?"

"Because that seems to tell me that, no matter what had brought her to the Leopard Lounge, at one point in her life she'd been able to afford violin lessons, which meant that she came from an educated family, or at least a family that valued education. And violin lessons aren't cheap."

"I didn't think of that back then, but I guess you're right."

"So that was it?"

"Yeah, pretty much. We'd chat, and then when her break was over I'd give her a tip, usually ten bucks or so. Then I'd leave."

"You mean you didn't stay for her next show?"

Clay Potter hesitated once more. "How do I say this, Lieutenant? She was just a teenager, and I knew it. I knew I shouldn't have been sitting there watching her take her clothes off in the first place. But I just couldn't help it. And I loved our little chats. But after that I left."

"Even though you mostly talked about money? It never got personal, right?"

"No, but there's one little tidbit I haven't told you yet."

"What's that?"

"It was actually me who got her started on her career."

"What do you mean?"

"I told you that she found what I did interesting. Well, one night, just a few weeks after I first saw her, I gave her a stock certificate instead of a ten dollar tip."

"A stock certificate for what?"

"For fifty shares of Tesseract Corporation stock."

"You mean *the* Tesseract Corporation?" said Walter. Even he'd heard of the giant Internet firm. "That was a pretty expensive tip."

"Not back then it wasn't. Tesseract was just getting started, and those shares were hardly worth the piece of paper they were printed on. But I had a hunch about it."

"What did Stephanie think? What did she say?"

"It was funny, Lieutenant. She just stared at that worthless piece of paper so hard she almost quivered, like there was something magic about it. She said 'thank you' and ran off to hide it away somewhere before her next show started."

"Did she ever mention it again?"

"Within a couple of months after I gave it to her, Tesseract took off and the stock started to skyrocket. Pretty soon that worthless stock was worth $100 a share. Then the stock split four ways and went back to $100. And over and over. But most of that was long after I'd stopped going to the Leopard, so she never really mentioned Tesseract to me again. Instead, what she wanted to talk to me about was the stock market and investing in general. Before I knew it, she was talking about articles she'd read in the *Wall Street Journal*. That's what she wanted to talk about. And her music, of course."

"I'm guessing that stock gave her enough money to escape the Leopard Lounge."

"Maybe, but I don't think that's why she left."

"What do you mean?"

The old man shifted uncomfortably in his chair, clearly uneasy about what he was about to say. He was quiet for a moment, but Walter didn't push him. "One night," he finally said, "I came in, and there was something different about her."

"You mean, about her attitude?"

"Let me get to that part. What I noticed first was that she had a tattoo that she'd never had before. It was a G-Clef, you know that musical thing, and it was tattooed on her, you know, her derrière. It looked fresh. And let me tell you something else, Lieutenant, it was hard to tell in the dim light of that place, but I was pretty sure she was banged up. And the saddest part was that it was the only time I ever saw her when she wasn't smiling that smile of hers."

"Did you ask her about it?"

"Yeah, I did, but she didn't want to talk about it, so I didn't press it."

"And what was she like the week after that?"

"There was no week after that. I came back a week later, and she wasn't there. Same thing the next week. So I asked the manager, his name was Sandy something, what was up, and he just said she was gone, and he acted a whole lot like he didn't want to talk about it. The crowd was about half what it was when Stephanie was there, and I think he was pissed."

"You never saw her again after that?"

"I actually saw her one more time, but it was years later."

"Did you just bump into her by accident? Did she even recognize you?"

"No, Lieutenant, it was ten years ago. She came to my retirement party."

"You're kidding."

"No kidding. She was already pretty much a celebrity in the financial world by then, and it caused kind of a stir. She only stayed a few minutes. She walked up to me and said she just wanted to thank me for everything I'd done for her. She gave me a little kiss on the cheek and then she left. My boss tried to get me to postpone my retirement after that."

"Wasn't she afraid that you might start talking about how you met her?"

"She knew me better than that, Lieutenant. But more than that, I don't think she cared."

"How could she not have cared? It could have ruined her career."

"Stephanie French was a woman who was fundamentally at peace with herself, Lieutenant. A lot of men saw her at that strip club when she was young, and I'm pretty sure that she knew that one day one of those men might recognize her. But she knew who she was, and she would've dealt with that if she had to. Besides, she was making so much money for Barstow & Company and its clients by that time, I don't think it would've mattered if she spent her lunch hours jogging up and down Wall Street naked."

"That's quite a story, Mr. Potter," said Walter. "I can't tell you how much I appreciate your willingness to come in and talk. And don't worry, I'll never tell your wife about the Leopard Lounge." He'd meant it as a joke, but Clay Potter didn't laugh, and Walter knew that he'd made a mistake.

"I lost the missus a few years back, Lieutenant."

"I'm sorry to hear that, Mr. Potter."

"So am I. She never would've let me out of the house looking like this, you know?"

Walter knew.

"Do you remember anything else about the manager? A last name, maybe?"

"Sorry, Lieutenant, I don't." He hesitated, and Walter suspected that he had something more to say, but at that moment his desk phone rang.

"Shit," he said when he saw the Caller ID. "I'm sorry, Mr. Potter, but it's my boss. I better take it." He stood, thanked the man, and briefly shook his hand.

"No problem," said Clay Potter, looking around. "This isn't what I expected a police station to look like, but I think I can find my own way out." He smiled, then turned and walked out the door, with a little more spring in his step than when he'd walked in, thought Hudson.

As soon as he was off the phone, he called Levi, told him briefly about the Leopard Lounge, and asked if he could perhaps chase down the manager. It was a tall order, but if anyone could do it, Levi could. Walter promised to fill him in on the details later.

17

THE MEMBERS OF THE BARSTOW BOARD had all returned to the boardroom to reconvene their meeting, and Detective Eduardo Sanchez was walking down the hall toward the elevator when he saw April Barstow come around a corner and walk down the hallway in his direction, hugging some folders to her chest, looking like a new student at a big school.

"Hello, Ms. Barstow," he said.

"Hello, it's Detective Sanchez, isn't it?" said April, a tentative smile on her face. It had already been a long morning, and attention from a cop, even a nice looking cop like Eduardo Sanchez, put her on her guard.

"Yes, ma'am. Are you going back to the Board meeting?" said Sanchez, noticing the tentative smile, but thinking it was nice anyway.

"No, Detective, I'm not a member of the Board. I'm just trying to go about my duties, although I have to admit that's not easy under the circumstances. It's hard to believe that Stephanie was – that Stephanie passed away – only three days ago."

"Were you and Stephanie close?"

"Very close, Detective. We were lifetime friends, both personally and professionally. I never would have gotten where I have in my career if it hadn't been for her."

"Do you think you might have a few minutes to talk, ma'am?" Lieutenant Hudson hadn't specifically asked him to interview April Barstow, but he was also learning that detective work often hinged on simply not passing up on unexpected opportunities.

"You mean, about Stephanie?"

"Yes, ma'am."

"Sure, but I'm not sure that I can help you with finding her murderer, if that's what you want to talk about."

"Not at all, ma'am. We're just trying to find out everything we can about her, especially about her past. You never know what little bit of information will help us solve her murder."

"Then why don't we sit down in my office? Would you like some coffee?"

"That sounds great."

They took the elevator down a floor and walked down the hallway to an office suite comprising a space for April's administrative assistant, a young man named Henry, and a large, sunlit corner office for April. April and Eduardo had no sooner sat down at a table near the windows that looked out over a spectacular view of the Upper Bay when Henry brought in a tray with a jug of coffee, cups and saucers, and cream and sugar. He poured a cup for each of them and left quietly.

"Better than the station house coffee," said Eduardo after taking a sip, "thank you." He looked around the office without trying to seem too obvious about it. It was expensively furnished, as he would have expected, and the walls were crowded with photographs of April at different times in her life with a variety of people, most of whom Eduardo didn't recognize: the high and the mighty, the wealthy, several of her and her father, and many of her and Stephanie. He couldn't help notice there was none of a husband or family.

"You're welcome," said April, noticing him scanning the photos. "She was beautiful, wasn't she."

"Yes, she was," said Eduardo, seeing no sense in lying about it.

"If you're looking for family photos you won't find any. I lost my mother when I was quite young; I have no siblings, and I was never married or had any children. And, no, I'm not gay, and no, neither was Stephanie. I think it's odd that men who choose to remain single are called bachelors, while women who choose to remain single are called lesbians, don't you?"

"I've never thought about it, ma'am," said Eduardo, truthfully.

"Then you're a rare man," said April, "but I'll take you at your word."

"Can you tell me, ma'am," said Eduardo, a man who remained happily mystified by all women and was desperate to change the subject, "when you first met Stephanie French?"

"I can tell you the place, the day, and the hour, Detective," said April with a smile that was no longer tentative. "It was Tuesday, September 4, 1990, the day after Labor Day, at 8AM in a lecture hall at the Columbia School of Business. I'm sorry, I don't remember the room number. It was the first day of class at the graduate school for both of us. We bumped into one another walking into the room, literally. We laughed about it and then sat down together. We were fast friends from that moment on."

"What did you have in common that made you friends?"

"Oh, it wasn't anything that we had in common, not at first. You know how it is, Detective. I'm a city girl, but I'd gone to little Brentwood College in upstate New York, and there I was at great big Columbia. It was a bit daunting. And there was Stephanie, who knew all the ropes because she'd gone there as an undergrad. It was nice to meet someone who could help me find my way around."

"And what about Stephanie?"

"You mean, what could glamorous, brilliant Stephanie have seen in me?"

"I didn't say that ma'am, and I didn't mean it."

"I know you didn't, Detective, and I apologize. I don't know why I said that."

"It's okay."

"I think," said April, "that it was just part of Stephanie's nature that she was drawn to people who needed her help. I also think she liked the fact that I wasn't nosy about her past. You know how a lot of people are, especially women: 'Oh, tell me all about you,' and all that. It was pretty clear that Stephanie didn't want to talk about her past any more than I wanted to talk about mine."

"So she never told you where she grew up or anything like that?"

"Not in all the years I knew her, Detective. All Stephanie French ever asked of people was that they take her as she was. Most people couldn't control their curiosity, but I could, and she treasured that. It was the foundation of our friendship."

"And you never talked about your past, either?"

"Well, of course, she inevitably knew more about my past than I did about hers by the simple fact that she worked for my father's firm. But I never invited her over to my parents' house for dinner or anything like that."

"What did you talk about? What did you have in common?"

"We had most of our classes together, so we talked a lot about school, especially since Stephanie gave me so much support. And we also had a love of music in common."

"What do you mean, you know, about the support?"

"Detective, let me be blunt: I was not in Stephanie's league intellectually any more than I was in her league musically. I was accepted at Columbia because my father made an enormous donation to the business school. I had actually been rejected there as an undergraduate, despite the sacks full of money my father had offered to drop at their doorstep. He was furious, but in the end, I was happier. Brentwood was a better fit for me, and they were quite happy to accept Daddy's mountains of lucre."

"But Stephanie was different."

"Stephanie French wasn't just smart, Detective; she was brilliant. She seemed to know everything before it was even taught. I don't think I ever saw her open a textbook unless it was to help me out, and she graduated at the top of our class anyway. And all while she was studying at Juilliard."

"You said you weren't in her league musically, either. Does that mean that you're a musician, too?"

"Not in the way that Stephanie was, but yes. I began piano lessons at the age of four, and I've played ever since. Most people consider me an excellent pianist, but I'm an amateur, and I know it."

"So you and Stephanie didn't play music together?"

"Oh, we played together all the time. It was one of the things that sustained our friendship over the years. I'd go over to her apartment after work, usually once a week, and Stephanie would cook a quick supper for us, and then we'd play into the wee hours. She had the finest pianists in the world begging to accompany her, but she never seemed to mind my limitations. It was just so much like Stephanie." Eduardo thought he saw April's eyes begin to fill up, but she recovered quickly.

"What else did you have in common?" he said.

"Well, we worked together at SafeWays, although I had never accumulated the personal wealth that Stephanie had, so I played a more minor role. But Stephanie treated volunteers at SafeWays the same way she treated everyone else. It truly didn't matter to her whether you donated a dollar or a million dollars. It was the contribution itself that counted, not the size."

"How was she worth so much more than you?" said Sanchez. "Weren't you paid about the same at work?"

"Well, she earned far more than I did in bonus money because of the performance of the Balboa Fund, but it wasn't that."

"Then what was it?"

"She invested her own savings, and, as you can imagine, she did it brilliantly. Her earnings from Barstow & Company were insignificant compared to the wealth she accumulated from her personal investments."

"Okay, but I know that you were both being considered for the CEO's job, so there had to be some sort of competition between you guys over the years, right? How did that affect your friendship?"

"There was never any competition, Detective."

"I'm sorry, I don't get it. You were both being considered for the top job. You both climbed up the same corporate ladder. How could there not have been competition?"

"Because we were never being considered for the same job," said April, shifting in her seat almost as if this was the part she really wanted to talk about.

"But..."

"You have to understand, Detective, that Stephanie spent her entire career dragging me along behind her out of friendship, and I'm embarrassed to admit that I let her do it. Between her and Olivia Chase, they were able to maintain the fiction, the fiction my father wanted to believe, that one day I might be able to succeed him as CEO. But that's what it was: a fiction."

"But two people voted for you, didn't they?"

"Yes, they did. Hollings Harkin and Barbara Grunewald, as I suppose you know."

"Then at least two people thought you were qualified."

"Yes, a sexual predator who loathes women and beats up prostitutes for fun; and Barbara Grunewald, who for all intents and purposes sexually harassed me all through college, and who still hasn't given up. Isn't that rich?"

"What?" said Eduardo, sitting up with a jerk, his eyes widening.

"You mean you weren't aware of Hollings Harkin's little peccadilloes? I guess I'm a little disappointed in the NYPD. I know his father always managed to get the charges dropped, but I figured you folks would have had a record of his arrests somewhere in your archives."

"Did he ever harass you or Stephanie?" said Eduardo, jotting down a note.

"Oh, he wouldn't have bothered me. Daddy saved him when he was thrown out of the family law firm for his shenanigans. He wouldn't dare do anything that would get him on Daddy's sh-, uh, wrong side."

"But why did your father save him?"

"Because Daddy and Number Four, Hollings's father, were old friends. I thought it was disgusting, but my father never fails to disappoint me."

"And what about Stephanie?" said Eduardo, suddenly feeling like he was getting somewhere.

"What about Stephanie?"

"Did Harkin ever, you know, bother her?"

"'Bother' is probably the wrong word. People like Hollings Harkin didn't bother Stephanie; she treated him like a piece of lint she flicked off her jacket. But yes, he attempted to exert his dubious charms on her, early and often."

"He must not have liked being rejected like that."

"Not to get too Freudian, Detective, but 'impotent rage' is the phrase that leaps to mind."

"Do you know if he ever threatened her with violence?"

"No, I don't, but Stephanie never would have talked about that. She was a tiger when it came to protecting other women, but she took care of herself quietly."

"I'm guessing that her becoming CEO, becoming his boss, must not have made him too happy."

"Far be it from me to help you do your job, Detective Sanchez, but I think Hollings Harkin would have preferred to kill Stephanie French than work for her."

Demure, reticent April was turning out to be nothing of the sort, thought Sanchez. Maybe he'd underestimated her. Maybe a lot of people did. He decided to find out how much further he could take her.

"Okay, then how did Stephanie get along with your father?" he said. "I mean, speaking of people who wanted Stephanie out of the way…"

"As difficult as my relationship with my father is, I hesitate to identify him as a murder suspect." But she's going to, thought Eduardo, and she's going to enjoy it. "I'll leave that up to you, if only out of filial duty. I will say, however, that I've never seen Daddy quite so angry as when he was informed of the Board's decision. But to answer your question, Stephanie got along fine with my father over the years, just like she got along with everybody, though I can't say the feeling was ever mutual."

"You're saying your father didn't like Stephanie? I thought he would have at least admired her for all the profit she made for him."

"You clearly don't know my father, Detective," said April, smiling faintly. "As far as my father is concerned, no one has ever earned a penny for Barstow & Company but him."

"Do you think he didn't like her because he saw her as competition for you for the top job?"

"No, I don't think so. You have to understand that it never occurred to my father that I wouldn't get the top job. He just assumed that he'd get his way with the Board the same way he did on everything else."

"Then what was it about Stephanie that he didn't like?"

"I think," said April, hesitating briefly, "that Daddy couldn't tolerate the idea that anyone at Barstow & Company, man or woman, was smarter than he was, and I think he probably recognized that about Stephanie from the day I introduced him to her. But honestly, I'm not sure I'll ever know. All I know is that he never wanted Stephanie to work for Barstow & Company in the first place."

"Then how did she get a job here?"

"Because I begged my father to hire her, that's why."

"But why? Someone with her qualifications must have gotten terrific offers from all kinds of places."

"Of course she did."

"Then, I guess I don't get it."

April Barstow sat silently for a few long moments, looking down at her hands.

"Haven't you been listening to me, Detective?" she said, finally looking up.

"Of course I have, Ms. Barstow."

"Okay, then let me put this as bluntly as I can: I'm not that bright. I was a mediocre student at Brentwood as an undergrad, and I would have flunked out of Columbia if it hadn't been for Stephanie. I knew I was going to fail at Barstow & Company. I didn't want to go to work there, but my father insisted. So I moved heaven and earth to get Stephanie to apply there and to get my father to hire her. It was my only chance not to let my father down."

"So he just basically gave in to you."

"Perhaps. There's a lot about my father that I'll never understand, that I never want to understand. All I know is he never liked her from the start, and no matter what she did, he never changed his opinion."

———※———

"GODDAMMIT, LIEUTENANT, I'm not going to take the hit for this!" said a red-faced Captain Eugene Amato, pointing at the TV screen in his office on the top floor of the Midtown South precinct house. As usual, he was the perfect image of a corporate executive, not a cop:

His sandy-colored hair was carefully barbered, his charcoal gray Brooks Brothers suit impeccably tailored, his white cotton shirt unwrinkled. And Hudson knew that underneath his desk his Johnston & Murphy brogues were polished to a high shine.

"I wouldn't expect you to, sir," said Hudson, trying to remain calm as he watched Harold Manlius's image flicker on the screen.

"What's that supposed to mean?" said Amato, his expression turning wary.

"Nothing sir."

"I take my responsibilities seriously, and I'll take responsibility when I'm responsible!"

"I'm sure you will, sir," said Walter, barely suppressing a smile. He loathed the man, but Eugene Amato was his boss, and Walter had to be careful.

"You better watch it, Hudson. One of these days your drinking buddy in the Commissioner's office isn't going to be there. Not that you'll care, with that rich wife of yours."

Walter knew that Amato was quietly rooting for Harold Manlius to defeat Mayor Deborah Kaplan in the upcoming primary election. Manlius had already promised to fire Commissioner Sean Donahue, and that could only benefit Amato. Donahue thought Amato was a buffoon, and Amato's career was effectively stalled for as long as Donahue remained Commissioner.

"Maybe we should avoid making this personal, sir," said Hudson, giving his boss a level stare. As usual, Amato couldn't maintain eye contact, and they both returned their gazes to the TV.

As much as he detested the man, Hudson had to admit that Harold Manlius was a powerful and impressive presence, both in person and on the television. After forty years in the public eye, his tall, powerful frame, chiseled features, and signature mane of thick, chestnut hair were recognized immediately by almost everyone in the city. His language was often crude, and his message was blunt, but Walter knew that it resonated with a wide swath of the New York City voting public. And now he had the NYPD squarely in his sights.

"The people of this great city, and by "the people" I don't mean the rich capitalists who control Wall Street and Gracie Mansion, I mean you, the people, are desperate for adequate housing, quality health care, and affordable day care.

"But what does Mayor Deborah Kaplan do with your hard earned tax dollars? She turns them over to the boss of her Police State, Commissioner Sean Donahue, to harass the good people of this city who are just trying to go about their business but happen to be the wrong color, or live in the wrong neighborhood, while NYPD cops take expensive vacations and drive around in luxury sports cars..."

Predictable but effective, thought Hudson. Bashing the NYPD was a well-worn path to Gracie Mansion, and Manlius wasn't wandering off it.

Amato clicked the television off, pointedly picked up the morning's copy of the *New York Post* and glared at Hudson, who glared back.

"Captain, we can't react to every political stunt a guy like Manlius pulls."

"Why don't you hold it right there, Lieutenant. What's this 'we' shit? If you think you're going to drag me down with you on this, you better think again, do you hear me?"

"Captain, sir," said Hudson, trying as hard as he could to sound reasonable, "I guess I'm just trying to figure out what's going on here. I know we've had our differences over the years, and maybe we have different styles, but I thought in the end we were both trying to get the same job done."

"Are you implying that I'm not interested in getting the job done, Hudson?"

"Jesus no, sir, I'm just saying..."

"Saying what, Hudson? That this is all my fault? That I was the one driving my fancy sports car up and down Queens Boulevard? That I was the one cruising on a luxury yacht in the Caribbean? That I'm the one rubbing elbows with celebrities at charity galas? That I'm the one making the entire Department look bad?"

"Is that what this is really all about, sir?" said Hudson, but he regretted it immediately. He wasn't ready to walk off this particular cliff, at least not yet.

"What's what all about, Hudson?" said Amato, who clearly was.

"Nothing, sir," said Hudson.

"No, go ahead. Tell me."

"Sir, I just want to do my job, that's all."

"And what would that be, precisely?"

"Right now I'm full time on the Stephanie French murder, sir."

"Oh, you are?"

"Yessir."

"You mean the murder that's been solved as of this morning? What, have you been too busy managing your social calendar to pay attention? It was a mob hit gone bad, that's all. Case closed."

"I don't see it that way, sir."

"Well I do, and the last time I looked I was your boss. Close the case, Hudson, it's over. And if I were you I'd keep my head down and my mouth shut. You're on thin ice, and I for one don't want you hurting this department any more than you already have."

"Sir, I spoke to both Commissioner Donahue and Mayor Kaplan this morning, and they both agree with me. They don't buy this mob hit theory any more than I do. We may have found the shooter, but not the murderer." Fuck him, thought Walter, seeing the stunned look on Amato's face. He hated playing his trump cards, but he couldn't let Amato slow him down.

"This meeting is over, Lieutenant," said Amato in a strained voice, his face reddening. "But remember one thing: Your fairy godparents aren't going to be around forever, and the day they're gone, I'll have your badge, and that's a promise."

"I'll worry about that when the time comes," said Walter.

"Get the fuck out my office, Lieutenant."

"Yessir."

He turned and walked slowly out of Amato's office, not looking back.

18

THE WENDY'S JUST SOUTH OF THE EMPIRE STATE BUILDING wasn't a place that Lieutenant Hudson or Leviticus Welles would normally choose to have a meeting, but Walter badly wanted to get out of the precinct house after his disastrous meeting with Captain Amato, and besides, he knew that it was one of Eduardo's favorite lunch spots.

It was late for lunch, and they were all hungry. Eduardo had ordered his usual Double with bacon and cheese, and a large fries. Walter had ordered a bowl of chili, and, after scanning the menu offerings dubiously, Levi had ordered a chicken salad.

"You know," said Levi, digging into the salad, "this isn't bad."

"I wouldn't know," said Eduardo through a mouthful of burger.

Sanchez filled them both in on his meetings with Barbara Grunewald and April Barstow, after which Walter recounted his meeting with Clay Potter and his subsequent run-in with Amato.

"Walter," said Levi, "you've got to be careful. Depending on which way this election turns out, Amato could give you a lot of trouble. I'd hate to see a great career ruined by the likes of him."

"Depending on which way this election turns out," said Walter, "I'm not sure I'm going to give a damn."

"You know you don't mean that," said Levi. "And remember, mayors come and mayors go. You have a long career ahead of you."

"I know you're right, Levi," said Walter, "but sometimes I just don't know how much more shit I can stand to take from that dickhead." He looked around guiltily, hoping that no children had been within earshot. He also wondered if he would have felt so brave a few short months ago, when his paycheck was the only thing between his family and poverty. Who said it? It's good to be rich.

"How was that chili, sir?" said Eduardo, polishing off the last bite of his Double.

"Pretty good, actually," said Walter.

"I'll be right back," said Eduardo.

"So," said Walter after Eduardo had returned with his own bowl of chili, "where are we?"

"First," said Levi, "I can tell you that what April said about Hollings Harkin is true. I had an email waiting for me this morning from one of my investigators. It listed five separate incidents of women, prostitutes, bringing assault and battery complaints against the man, and that's on top of his shenanigans at work."

"And let me guess," said Walter, "they were all dropped and the records expunged."

"Yes, after a few generous payments to both the victims and the widows and orphans funds of the precincts involved. But, of course, as April said, the NYPD never really forgets anything, and the records weren't that hard to find."

"Did your guys check out Seth Stone while they were at it?"

"Yes, and nothing. He might be miserable and unlikable at work, but at least he doesn't take it out on working girls the way Harkin does. But we did find a couple of other interesting tidbits."

"Oh?" said Walter, swallowing the last bite of his chili at the same time Eduardo finished his.

"First," said Levi, "it seems that the apple doesn't fall far from the tree in the Harkin family. We found similar charges, again, all dropped, against Hollings Harkin IV, Harkin's father."

"Not a lot of charm in that family, huh?" said Eduardo.

"Apparently not," said Levi. "And Barbara Grunewald has had two complaints lodged against her during her career at Brentwood College for sexually harassing students. Of course, all the charges were dropped after the college offered free tuition and expenses for all four years at the school."

"Was either one of those students April Barstow?"

"No, but after doing a little snooping around, chatting with retired faculty and alumnae, it seemed that it was no secret that when April was a student at Brentwood, Professor Grunewald had an embarrassingly obvious crush on her."

"And I can tell you," said Eduardo, "you don't have to do too much reading between the lines to know that she still does."

"And a couple more items," said Levi.

"Your men have been busy," said Walter.

"There are a lot of cops, not just us, who understand the atmospherics surrounding this case, and who know what life will be like if, God help us all, Harold Manlius is ever elected mayor. They don't want this case to fall through the cracks, and everybody's pulling out all the stops."

"Glad to hear it," said Walter.

"Anyway, one of my men chatted up a couple of retired cops out near the Hamptons where the Barstows have their summer 'cottage.'"

"That's where April's mother died, right?" said Eduardo

"Right," said Levi. "It was ruled an accidental death by drowning, but there was always talk of the excessive amounts of barbiturates in her blood at the time of her death."

"So it may have been a suicide?" said Eduardo.

"There's always been talk of that, but what these guys told my investigator was a little different. They said that the autopsy, which was never made public, by the way, indicated that Mrs. Barstow had been in the pool a full half hour before she was pulled out, despite the fact that the EMT team got to the house five minutes after they received the call, and it took them less than two minutes to get the body out of the pool."

"Who called in the emergency?" said Walter, although he suddenly knew what the answer would be.

"Bryce Barstow," said Levi. "He was there the whole time. He claimed he was in his study working and never heard anything, but the EMT guys said that when they got there, their recollection was that he was in his bathing suit."

"Did the EMT guys ever report this to the cops on the scene?" said Walter.

"No, this all came out over beers when the cops and the EMTs were off-duty."

"But why?"

"The EMTs said they were occupied with Mrs. Barstow. They said they really couldn't be sure of their recollections of Mr. Barstow, and they were afraid of pitting their word against his. It didn't sound like a winner to them, and I can't blame them."

"But what about the cops?" said Eduardo.

"By the time the cops got there, Barstow was dressed in dry clothes. Said he hadn't been near the pool all day, and, like I said, nobody was sure enough of their memories to contradict him. Case closed."

"So the man, for all we know," said Walter, "murdered his wife."

"And if you kill once," said Eduardo, "you can always kill again."

"That's right," said Levi.

"Now we're at that point that always drives Commissioner Donahue crazy," said Walter. "He always says that I collect suspects like Jay Leno collects cars."

"Who's on your list, sir?" said Eduardo.

"Well, I've got to think that Hollings Harkin should be on anyone's list," said Walter.

"And now," said Levi, "I imagine we have to add his father."

"But why?" said Eduardo. "I don't see what dog he has in this hunt."

"I can only guess," said Levi, "but he may have wanted to protect his son from some threat, real or imagined, or perhaps he believed his son had a shot at the top job if Stephanie was out of the way."

"Or to protect or help his old buddy, Bryce Barstow," said Walter. "We have to keep in mind that those two have been friends since their school days."

"And of course there's Bryce Barstow himself," said Levi. "I think of all our suspects, he has the most direct motive. The only way he was going to stay in control of his company, and in his mind it is still *his* company, was to get his daughter the top job and control it through her. By the way, Walter, when are you going to talk to him?"

"I've been trying," said Walter, "but he keeps dodging my calls. But I know, Commissioner Donahue would have my head if he knew that I still haven't seen him."

"And we also haven't talked to Seth Stone yet, sir," said Eduardo.

"You're right," said Walter, inwardly wincing at the amount of work he had left to do. It was still only Monday; they'd only been at it a few days, and it's not like they'd been dragging their feet, he told himself. But Donahue had meant it when he'd told Walter and Levi they had no time, and, after his run-in with Amato, every day might be his last in any event. "Stone had just as much of a motive as anyone. Do you know if he was at work when you were there?"

"I'm sorry, sir, I don't know."

"Please track him down."

"And of course," said Levi, "there's Professor Grunewald, who has the dual motive of trying to save her college and apparently being madly in love with April Barstow."

"If I had to choose, it would be the emotional angle that would motivate her more than anything," said Walter.

"I can't disagree," said Levi. "Despite all the money and power struggles involved here, most murders are crimes of passion, and there's no reason this one wouldn't be the same."

"And speaking of crimes of passion, let's not forget April herself," said Eduardo. "I sat there and listened to her for over an hour telling me how much she admired Stephanie French and what a lifelong friend she was and how she couldn't have survived without her. But it's almost impossible for me to believe that she could've been in Stephanie's shadow for so long, and so dependent on her, without some pretty powerful resentments building up."

"And what about Olivia Chase, Walter?" said Levi. "Do you think there might be anything there?"

"I honestly don't see it, Levi. If there was anyone who wanted Stephanie French to succeed, it was Olivia."

"But don't forget, Stephanie had to step over Olivia to get the top job. I don't care what she says, that must've stung."

"I think she was pretty much resigned to her fate at that company long before Stephanie got promoted over her. But you're right, we shouldn't write her off completely."

"Well," said Levi, looking at his watch, "I've got to get back to the office."

"Yeah," said Walter, "and I've got to try and chase down Bryce Barstow."

They all got up to leave.

"Oh, Walter," said Levi, "I almost forgot to tell you. I found your guy."

"Which guy would that be?"

"You know, the manager of the Leopard Lounge back when Stephanie was working there."

"You're kidding me. He still alive?"

"And kicking."

"Where is he?"

"In South Orange, New Jersey, living the good life with his wife and, get this, his ninety-five year old mother-in-law. He owns a small pub and lives in a quiet little residential neighborhood. His name is George Baxter, but he still goes by the nickname Sandy. The name of the pub is 'The Olde Orange.'"

"Geez," said Eduardo, "I bet he spends a lot of time at the pub."

"So, how's your mother-in-law, by the way, Eduardo?" said Walter, unable to resist.

"She's great, I guess. Angelina says she a saint, so I guess she is. She looks like she's gonna live forever, is all I know," said Eduardo, looking scared.

"Okay," said Walter. "Look, Eduardo, I know you've got a lot on your plate, but talk to this guy, will you? I'm not expecting much, but you never know."

"I've never been to South Orange," said Eduardo.

"Don't worry," said Walter, "it's not Mars." Though it could have been, as far as he knew. He'd never been there either.

"Hey," said Eduardo, "you guys want to try out one of those yogurt parfaits they've got here?"

The two older men stared at the young detective in awe.

"Just asking," said Eduardo, heading for the counter.

⎯⎯⎯⎯

Walter had just gotten back to his desk and was about to pick up his phone to call Bryce Barstow when it rang, making him jump. He checked the Caller ID and saw that it was a call from a number with a Long Island area code. At least it wasn't Amato.

"Hudson."

"Hello, Lieutenant," came a familiar sounding voice over the line, "this is Clay Potter, you know, the guy from the Leopard Lounge?"

"Oh, hey, yes. What can I do for you?"

"Oh, nothing, Lieutenant. It's just that I meant to tell you one more thing before I left, but then you got busy on the phone, and I never got the chance."

"I'm sorry about that," said Hudson.

"Hey, we all have bosses. Don't worry about it."

"What did you want to tell me, Mr. Potter?"

"This is kind of embarrassing, Lieutenant, and I hesitated to tell you because I don't want to get anybody else in trouble. But a fine human being was murdered, and we all have to help you find whoever did it."

"Thanks," said Walter, wanting the man to get to the point, but not wanting to push him.

"Anyway," said Potter, "one evening I was having my usual chat with Stephanie between sets, and she said she needed to ask a favor of me."

"What kind of favor?"

"She said that she really wanted to go to college, but she had one problem: she'd never graduated from high school. I asked her if she'd looked at getting her GED, and she said she had. But she wanted to go to Columbia, and she didn't think a GED would get her there."

"She was probably right about that."

"I couldn't disagree with her either, Lieutenant, and I'd spent enough time with her to know that she belonged at Columbia. I figured she could graduate near the top of her class if she could just get in, and a kid like her, I thought she deserved the chance."

"So what did she ask you to do?"

"She asked me if I knew how she could get, you know, a legitimate diploma from a good high school. And she said she needed it in the name of 'Stephanie Marie French.'"

"Was that the first time you ever heard that name?" Walter shouldn't have been surprised that the woman had a plan: First, get the new identity, then, start building her history.

"Yeah, it was. Up till then she was still 'Brittany,' but, like I told you before, I stopped thinking of her as Brittany a long time ago, Lieutenant."

"That must've been awkward. What did you do?" said Walter, remembering with a jolt that, according to her records from Columbia, Stephanie French had been a straight 'A' student at East Island High School, the same Long Island town where Clay Potter and his missus had lived. She'd also gotten, according to Columbia, near perfect SAT scores.

"I'm ashamed to admit it, but one of my buddies in town was a guidance counselor at the high school. I'd been giving the guy free stock tips over beers for years, and he'd done well, so I figured he owed me a favor back."

"So you asked him to forge a high school transcript for Stephanie and stuff it into the school's files."

"It was easy back then, Lieutenant. Everything wasn't computerized yet, you know? And East Island High School is a big school, with a lot of turnover in the staff and faculty. The odds were that no one would ever notice."

"So this guy agreed to forge the transcript."

"It didn't take much convincing, especially after I told him about Stephanie."

"And just like that, Brittany, the underage stripper, became Stephanie

Marie French, honor student from a well-regarded Long Island high school with a clear path to an Ivy League education."

"I'd do it again, Lieutenant."

"And what about the SATs?"

"That was all Stephanie," said Potter. "Like I said, the kid was a genius."

"Well, I certainly can't sit here and blame you for what you did," said Walter, suddenly remembering that he'd failed to pass along a critical detail from his first conversation with this odd man to Levi. "Say, Mr. Potter, the last time we talked, you said you figured Stephanie wasn't from around here because of the way she talked, like people from some radio program or TV show. What was the name of that show again?"

"Oh," said Potter, after taking a few seconds to recall the conversation. "It was 'A Prairie Home Companion,' Lieutenant. It starred a guy named Garrison Keillor, and it was awfully popular for a while."

"Thanks again, Mr. Potter," said Walter, anxious to get off the phone, but not wanting to be rude. He didn't need to worry. Clay Potter was a man who'd spent a lifetime reading people's body language over a telephone line.

"Look, Lieutenant, you must be busy, so I'll let you go. I wish you the best of luck finding the guy who did this."

"Thanks a lot," said Walter, hanging up the phone. He picked it right back up again and dialed the familiar number.

"Hey, Levi," he said. "Have you ever heard of 'A Prairie Home Companion'?"

19

"THAT'S HIM, RIGHT OVER THERE, DETECTIVE," said the assistant rector of Trinity Episcopal Church in lower Manhattan. There had been an Anglican Church on this property on lower Broadway, just across from Wall Street, some of the most valuable real estate in all of Manhattan, since the late 17th century. The current building had been completed in 1846. Some of the wealthiest and most prominent men in American history had served on its vestry, and Alexander Hamilton rested in its graveyard.

Detective Eduardo Sanchez, a devout Catholic, was only vaguely aware of Trinity's distinguished pedigree, but he wasn't there for a history lesson in any event. He was there because of the man seated in the small workshop in the basement of the building, a man he'd had a hard time locating.

"What's he doing?" said Sanchez, speaking quietly. From where he and the rector were standing it would have been difficult for Stone to see them, and Sanchez preferred it that way for the moment.

"Right now," said the rector, "it appears that he's repairing a portion of one of our stained glass windows, but he's a jack of all trades. This is an old building, and the glass, the masonry, and the woodwork are all in constant need of maintenance."

"You can't tell me he does all that by himself," said Sanchez.

"Oh, of course not, Detective. We have a full-time staff of artisans who maintain our properties, but he devotes quite a bit of time to us, and he does outstanding work, so we welcome any effort he wishes to devote."

"Does he come here often?"

"He comes when he can, from what I can gather. Sometimes, like today, he shows up in the middle of the day, but more often it's in the evening or on weekends."

"Is he a member of your church?"

"No, he's not. I'm not sure what his religious affiliation is, or even if he has any."

"How does he get along with everyone around here?"

"I have to tell you, Detective, Seth and I have talked extensively. I know what he does for a living and where he works, and I'm also aware of his reputation. But all I can tell you is that all of us here know him as a sweet, pleasant man who gets along just fine with everyone."

"I guess I don't understand that."

"There's nothing much to understand, Detective. When he's here, he's doing what he loves, what he was born to do. He's content; he's himself, the person he was meant to be."

"But from everything I've heard, he's some, like, genius financial guy at work. I mean, he's being considered for the top job."

"All that means is that he has a rare talent in a highly specialized field. That doesn't mean he likes it. But look," said the rector, casting his gaze over to Seth Stone, who seemed completely absorbed in his slow, patient work, "I've already said too much. As I've told you, Mr. Stone is not a communicant here, but I still consider our conversations to be pastoral in nature and private."

"Kind of like Confession, right?"

"Well, this is no time for theological hairsplitting, Detective, but, basically, yes. So I suggest that whatever else you would like to discuss you should take up directly with Mr. Stone."

"Thank you, Pastor," said Sanchez, and walked toward Seth Stone.

Seth Stone did not look up from his work as Eduardo, a big man who was hard to miss, approached him. He wore a large, heavy apron that looked well used over a white dress shirt and suit pants. He seemed to be soldering a piece of colored glass in place, and he only looked up after spending the few minutes necessary to complete the intricate task. Eduardo saw no reason to disturb him.

"Yes, officer?" said Stone, finally putting down the soldering iron and lifting his massive head.

The man's a peasant, thought Eduardo, staring at him. He's just like me, the first man in his family not to earn his living with his hands.

"How did you know I was a cop?"

"You're kidding, right?"

"It's just that I'm not wearing a uniform, that's all."

"Officer, or Detective, I presume," said Stone with an unaffected smile on his face, "you and I seem to share a common affliction: You can dress us up, but you can't take us out."

Eduardo laughed. "I guess you're right about that."

"I'm guessing you're not here to discuss the fine points of ornamental glasswork repair," said Stone, rising from his seat. He spoke in a polished manner that belied his roughhewn appearance, but Eduardo had already guessed that Seth Stone was a man of contradictions.

"No, sir, I'm afraid not," he said.

"Look, Detective…?"

"Sanchez, sir. Eduardo Sanchez."

"Pleased to meet you, Detective Sanchez," said Stone, holding out a massive hand. Not the hand of a banker, thought Sanchez. He shook it, feeling his own large, strong hand enclosed in a crushing grip. "Look, there's no place to sit down around here, so why don't we go upstairs? There's a small room they use for Bible study, and I'm sure they won't mind if we use it for a little while."

They walked up the stairs and across the sanctuary into a small room whose walls were completely covered by bookshelves that looked like they couldn't bear the weight of another volume. A rectangular wooden table dominated the small space, surrounded by a dozen ancient looking oak chairs.

"I'm sure I can scare up some coffee if you'd care for some," said Stone. Eduardo had been expecting a brawl with this man, and he wasn't sure how to react.

"That's okay sir, I just ate."

"Do you mind if I ask how you found me here? There aren't many people at Barstow & Company who are aware of my little avocation."

"Well, sir, I called your office, and your secretary said that you weren't there, so I called your home."

"Did my wife answer the phone?" said Stone, his facial muscles suddenly tensing.

"No, sir, a maid did. All she said was that she thought you'd gone to work this morning, just like usual. So I called your secretary back, and she finally told me that I could find you here. I told her it was a police matter, so I didn't give her much of a choice."

"Linda is a devoted assistant," said Stone, looking grim, "I'm sorry I put her in an awkward position."

"Sir, I'll try to keep this short, okay?"

"Take your time, Detective."

"Thanks. How long have you been married, Mr. Stone?"

"What an odd question."

"Just for background, sir, that's all."

"My wife, Amanda, and I have been married for twenty-five years. We have raised two children, successfully, I would like to think."

"Would you consider your marriage happy?"

"Define 'happy' for me, Detective, and I'll be glad to answer your question. The marriage has lasted a quarter of a century; we have lived under the same roof for all that time, and we have two happy, successful young adults to show for it. And we have a grandchild on the way. You can define that however you want. Why on earth do you ask?"

"Sir, to be blunt, there have been hints from other people at Barstow & Company that early in your career there you might have had a romantic interest in Stephanie French. Perhaps a strong one."

"And that I was spurned, and that we had a falling out, and so I must have killed her out of personal rage and professional jealousy. Is that the theory?"

"Sir, I'm just asking."

"Stephanie French and I never had an affair," said Stone after a long pause, "and as far as I can tell, she never had anything even resembling a romantic relationship with anyone else; so it's hard to see how we could have had a falling out, isn't it?"

"But, sir, with all due respect, that really doesn't answer my question. A lot of people inside Barstow & Company have made that observation to us. Are you saying they were all wrong?"

"Yes, I am," said Stone, betraying impatience and a fraying temper for the first time. Eduardo didn't believe him, but he also feared that the guy would shut down if he kept on pushing.

"So you and Ms. French were getting along just fine leading up to the time of her death, is that what you're saying?"

"No, that's not what I'm saying."

"Please help me here, Mr. Stone. I'm not trying to be difficult."

"What I'm saying, Detective Sanchez, is that, yes, there was friction between Stephanie and me in the recent past, but it had nothing to do with any romantic interest on my part, past or present, no matter what my colleagues, or anyone else for that matter, would like to believe."

"Was it because you were both competing for the top job?"

"There was no competition for the top job, Detective, and Stephanie and April and I all knew it."

"Then I don't get it, Mr. Stone. Why did the Board go through that whole process if there was never a real competition in the first place? I understand why April was in the running, I guess, but why you?"

Seth Stone looked down at his own hands and then at Eduardo's.

"You're a married man, Detective Sanchez."

"Yes, I am."

"Okay, then let me ask you a question. Assuming that your wife and your children are all in good health, what is the one thing in this world that can make you more miserable than anything else?"

"That's easy," said Eduardo, "having my wife mad at me."

"Bingo, Detective Sanchez. An unhappy wife is the worst misery a man can suffer."

"So, are you saying that you're miserable in your job, but that's better than having your wife mad at you?"

"Something like that," said Stone, raising his massive hands so that his palms were facing Eduardo. "Look at me, Detective. I was born to work with my hands, just as my father, my uncles, and my grandfathers before me did. They were stonemasons, carpenters, and plumbers. My father graduated from high school, but neither of my grandfathers did. My great-grandfather's name was 'Scalpellino.' It means 'stonemason' in Italian. The immigration guy at Ellis Island changed it on him."

"If that's what you wanted to do, why didn't you do it? You wouldn't have gotten rich, but money isn't everything."

"Because my father sat me down one day and told me to go to college. He said, 'Seth, I've worked hard all my life, and I'm damn good at what I do. But at the end of the day, what do I have to show for it? I've always put a roof over our heads and bread on the table, and I've always put clothes on your backs, but that's about it. I don't have two nickels to rub together; I've never been able to give your mother any of the good things in life, and I'm going to have to work until my body gives out.' He told me that I was the first member of the family to have brains, real brains, and that he expected me to use them."

"Okay, but what made you decide on finance? You could've gone to engineering school, or something like that."

"That's exactly what I did, Detective. I went to City College and got a degree in mechanical engineering."

"Then I don't get it. How did an engineering degree wind you up at Barstow & Company?"

"I met Amanda Noordman, that's how. You know how it is. I was a young man. Some of my college classmates and I were at a restaurant we really couldn't afford to celebrate our upcoming graduation. We were all having a great time, and then I looked up from my shrimp cocktail and saw Amanda walk into the room on the arm of some short, skinny, society type."

"The bolt of lightning."

"Damn right. I hadn't even said 'hello' to her yet, but I knew she was the one. She apparently saw something in me, too, and the rest is history."

"But I don't get it. What did meeting your wife have to do with not becoming an engineer?"

"Amanda made it clear to me, almost from our first conversation, that she had no intention of living on an engineer's salary, that she was brought up to expect more from life, much more. She told me that if she were even to consider marrying me, she expected me to make a lot of money, and that the only way to make a lot of money was to be as close as possible to where it all is."

"Wall Street."

"Yes, Wall Street. And for a while it worked. I got myself an MBA from NYU, and it turned out I had a knack for finance. I got myself hired by Barstow & Company, and I moved up the ladder pretty quickly. We had a couple of kids, and things seemed good."

"So what happened?"

"Ah," said Seth, throwing up his hands, "the longer I worked there, the more obvious it was that I was never going to get to the top where the real money, the money that Amanda expected, was. Yeah, I was really good at investing, but I wasn't good at the other stuff, you know? I'm not a sophisticated man, I have no polish, and I stink in social situations. I was always being thrown in with all these rich, Ivy League types, the guys that lived on family trust funds and chatted about the good old days at Morey's. I never knew what I was supposed to say or do, and I hated them."

"And it showed, right?"

"You can only hide that for so long, Detective."

"Yeah, I hear you."

"I tried to talk to Amanda, to explain to her that it wasn't going to work out, but she wasn't having it. Ironically, that's what Stephanie and I had our falling out over."

"What do you mean?"

"About a year ago, she came to me and said, 'Look, Seth, I know we've had our ups and downs, but we've worked together all our lives, and I care about you.' She said she hated seeing me so unhappy. She said, 'Seth, you're a wealthy man now. Sit down and talk to Amanda. I'm sure she'll understand.' I said, 'That's easy for you to say. You're not married to the woman.' Anyway, I reacted all wrong as usual, and I wound up being estranged from the one person who actually cared about my happiness. And then she was killed before I ever had a chance to make things right with her. Smart guy, huh?"

"I'm really sorry, Mr. Stone," said Eduardo, with feeling. Just the thought of that kind of conflict with his wife, or any other woman for that matter, literally made him feel nauseous. "But you stuck it out anyway."

"Yes, I did, and it just kept getting harder and harder, and I just kept getting angrier and angrier."

"And then one day, what? Did you, like, have to apply for the CEO's job?"

"No, it doesn't work like that. The way things work at Barstow, the Board is required to put together a slate of candidates to fill any senior level executive position and then choose one of them. The shareholders technically have the right to review the slate and challenge any decision, but it's never happened."

"Do you know who decided to put you on the slate?"

"It was Owen Morning, from what I understand. Typical Owen. I was a safe choice. Except for Stephanie, I was the best performing investor at the firm, so no one could question the Board's judgment, and everybody knew who was going to get the job anyway, except perhaps my wife."

"Mrs. Stone wasn't happy with the outcome?"

"She was beside herself, Detective. I'd tried to explain to her beforehand what the situation was, but she just wouldn't accept it. When I called her last Friday morning to tell her the outcome, she went berserk. I mean, literally berserk. She wanted me to put together a group of shareholders to challenge the decision, and when I refused, she got even angrier."

"How did she react to the news of Stephanie's death?"

"Let's just say she wasn't exactly heartbroken. She and Stephanie had never gotten along."

"Was it because of those rumors I heard?"

"No, I don't think so. She'd just identified Stephanie as serious career competition from the get-go, that's all." Once again, Eduardo's internal bullshit meter emitted a beep, but he didn't want to send this conversation sideways.

"What did she say?"

"All she said was that I'd been given a second chance now, and, to use her precise words, 'you better not fuck it up.' But no pressure, right, Detective?"

"I'm sorry," said Eduardo, not knowing what else to say.

"I really need to get back to my work now, Detective, if you don't mind," said Stone, suddenly rising from his chair.

"Thank you for being so open with me, sir," said Eduardo, also rising from his chair, and looking around the small room. "A lot of books here, huh? I wonder if anybody reads them?"

"I wouldn't know, Detective, I'm not much of a reader myself."

"I hear you, sir," said Eduardo, "neither am I."

The two men shook hands and went their separate ways, leaving both of them to wonder why Seth Stone had so willingly implicated his wife in the murder of Stephanie French.

DEPUTY COMMISSIONER LEVITICUS WELLES sat in the late afternoon quiet of his office at One Police Plaza in downtown Manhattan.

He rarely thought anymore of the bizarre sequence of accidents and coincidences that had brought him in a few short years from the misery of the unemployment, divorce, and abject failure that the Great Recession had visited upon him to this office. And to Julie Remy. Even when she was away on one of her increasingly frequent diplomatic journeys to the Middle East as part of one or another United Nations delegation, she was never far from his thoughts. The past was fading. Good.

But he was thinking of all that now, as he stared at the high definition video images on the large-screen television that dominated the wall of his office opposite his desk. Because if anyone had followed a more unlikely path to wealth and success than he had, it had been the woman he was watching on the screen, being interviewed by a team of CNBC correspondents. It was the third such recording he'd watched, but it was by far the oldest, going back ten years. She had already established herself as a star in the firmament of Wall Street celebrities by then, already being labeled a "living legend" by the fawning business press who just couldn't get enough of her. And for good reason.

To say that Stephanie French was beautiful and that her beauty had only increased with age missed the point, as did the observation that, beauty aside, she had been one of those women who possessed that ineffable quality of simply having whatever it is that men want. It was all true, but it was all irrelevant.

Because what Stephanie French possessed above all else was that exquisitely rare gift of making every listener feel that she was speaking directly to them, that whatever she was saying was of direct personal importance and profound relevance to them and them alone. Levi, sitting alone in his office watching a decade-old recording of the now dead woman, felt it, felt it in his gut and in his bones, and it lifted his spirit: She was talking directly to him; she saw him; she knew him. The woman was, quite simply, magic. It didn't really matter what she was talking about. In this recording she was chatting about a benefit performance that she and her string quartet would be giving at Carnegie Hall that evening. It had originally been scheduled to be given in the small upstairs recital hall of the venerable old building, but it had been moved to the main concert hall due to the overwhelming public response. And yes, she would be performing her signature piece, Bach's "Air On The G-String." If they only knew, thought Levi, as he looked at the mesmerized moderators, who so plainly didn't want the interview to end.

But Levi wasn't looking at the recording to be charmed. He was listening, listening with that rare inner hearing that he possessed, that allowed him to hear subtle differences in tone, cadence, and pronunciation that few other people in the world could hear. He wasn't listening to what Stephanie French was saying, especially now that he was replaying the interview for the fourth time. He was listening to how she was saying it.

In the more recent recordings it had been there, but much fainter, an echo of an echo. She had clearly worked hard over the years to eradicate her childhood accent. But in this older recording it was plain, at least to Leviticus Welles. Clay Potter's off-hand comment about *A Prairie Home Companion*, passed on to him by Walter Hudson, had piqued Levi's curiosity, but he wouldn't have needed the hint to know, with absolute assurance, where the woman the world knew as Stephanie French had come from. They hadn't once called the neighborhood surrounding the Port Authority terminal the "Minnesota Strip" for nothing. Hordes of miserable young boys and girls, not just from Minnesota but from all over the Midwest, had come to Minneapolis to climb onto the buses headed for the dream of New York City, only to find themselves at the mercy of people even more ruthless than those they had been so desperate to escape. Stephanie French, Levi now knew, came from Minnesota itself, though not from the Minneapolis-St. Paul area. No. Stephanie had come from farther north.

"The Iron Range," Levi whispered to himself. "I found you."

20

"WHAT DO YOU MEAN he went home?" said Walter Hudson, trying not to raise his voice.

"I'm very sorry, Lieutenant," said April Barstow.

"He knew I was coming. I spoke to him directly before I left my office."

They were standing in April's office, where April had just hung up the phone with her father's executive assistant.

"I don't know what to say, Lieutenant, except that I'm sorry and I'm embarrassed."

"Don't apologize," said Walter. "But please tell your father that the next time I come I will have a warrant, and I will search his office, whether he's here or not. And if he's not willing to talk to me voluntarily, I'll be more than happy to give him a tour of the Midtown South precinct house. I'm sure he'll love the coffee." He knew it was all a bluff. He didn't think even a lenient judge would find probable cause for a search, never mind detention of one of the most respected and well-known men on Wall Street. But it felt good to make the threat, and sometimes just the threat would be enough to get cooperation from a potential suspect.

"Don't worry, Lieutenant Hudson," said April, "I'll make sure he doesn't escape next time. I'm as tired of my father's shenanigans as you are. Is there anything more that I can help you with while you're here?"

It was getting late, and Walter was about to say no, when he spied a middle-aged woman sitting outside Stephanie French's former office, which was directly across from April's, looking at him like she wanted to talk. Investigators had thoroughly searched Stephanie's office the morning after her murder. As expected, nothing of relevance had turned up, but there was no record that anyone had spoken to her administrative assistant. Not surprising, he thought, since the investigators had been there on a Saturday morning. He looked at her from across the hall and said, "Good afternoon, Ms…?"

"Oh," said April, "let me introduce you. Detective Hudson, this is

Heather Morton, Stephanie's, ah, former administrative assistant. Heather, this is Detective Lieutenant Walter Hudson of the NYPD."

"Pleased to meet you, Ms. Morton."

"Please to meet you, too, Lieutenant," said Heather in a husky, ex-smoker's kind of voice.

"Has anyone from the NYPD spoken to you yet, Ms. Morton?"

"No, Lieutenant, no one has," said Heather, with an expression that said, "Talk to me."

"Ms. Barstow," said Walter, "I think I'll spend a few minutes with Ms. Morton, if you don't mind."

"I wouldn't mind at all," said April. "Heather, I have some meetings to attend, so perhaps you can escort Lieutenant Hudson out when you've finished."

"Yes, ma'am," Heather said before turning to Walter and saying, "Why don't we sit down in Stephanie's office, Lieutenant, unless you think it should remain untouched."

"No, that would be fine," said Walter, "we've completed our inspection of the office."

"Good. Can I get you some coffee?"

"That would be great, thanks. Black, please."

"I had that much figured out," said Heather, sizing him up and giving him a smile that left him with the feeling that there wasn't much this woman didn't know about men.

It took only a few seconds for Heather to get them both cups of black coffee from a Keurig machine, and soon they were sitting at a round, mahogany table that seated four in the far corner of the spacious office. It was decorated in light pastels and sparsely but tastefully furnished, and, like everything else that Stephanie French had touched, it left him with a strong sense of the woman. Walter scanned the walls of the office and noticed, perhaps to his surprise, that they were filled with reproductions of well-known works of art, mostly Impressionist or contemporary. There were only a very few photos of Stephanie herself, and all of them were taken with fellow musicians at performances.

"Stephanie didn't much like drawing attention to herself, Lieutenant," said Heather, noticing his eyes scanning the walls.

"Neither do I," said Walter, turning his eyes to Heather Morton and taking her in. She was probably somewhere around fifty. Her hair had clearly been dyed blond, but everything else seemed to him to be unretouched Heather. He couldn't detect any signs of surgical enhancement, and frankly, she didn't need it. Her face was plainly that of a middle-aged woman, but her skin was clear and bore only the lines that told of a life well lived, and her hazel eyes were bright and lively. Her body, judging from the quick appraising glance that he allowed himself, was voluptuous without being vulgar, and he bet that she still looked good in a bathing suit, or out of one for that matter. "How long have you worked for Ms. French, Ms. Morton?"

"Please call me 'Heather,' Lieutenant," she said, with a "so you liked what you saw, right?" look on her face. "The only people who call me 'Ms. Morton' are people I don't like. Anyway, I've been Stephanie's admin since she got to a level that rated one, which was about twenty years ago. She moved up the ladder pretty fast."

"Did she choose you, or were you just assigned to her?"

"Actually, Stephanie and I knew each other way before she got her job here."

"Did you go to school together?"

"Oh, heavens no," said Heather, laughing and turning slightly red, "I couldn't have gotten into Columbia on Visitors' Day."

"Then how did you meet her?" said Walter, his interest growing.

"Well, that's kind of what I wanted to talk to you about," said Heather, losing eye contact with Walter for the first time, looking down at her hands.

"Was there some kind of problem, Heather?"

"No, no. It's just that, I don't know, it's just kind of a sensitive subject, that's all."

"Sensitive for you or for her?"

"Oh, not for me, for heaven's sake," said Heather, laughing again.

"Heather," said Walter, "if it helps, we already know about Stephanie's former, uh, career when she was younger. So please don't worry, you won't be betraying any secrets."

"Well, I may or I may not be," said Heather, breathing a sigh of relief, "but that's good to know. How did you find out?"

"An old customer of hers showed up at my desk."

"Oh, my God! You must be talking about that nice Mr. Potter. He was such a harmless old sweetheart. I'm glad to hear he's still alive."

"Does that mean that you worked at the Leopard Lounge, too?"

"Yeah, I did. I was a high school dropout and I had to, you know, use what God gave me to get by," said Heather, spreading her arms and giving Walter a bashful smile. "I was working there when Stephanie showed up, and I was still there when she left. I was a couple of years older than she was."

"Then at least you were legal, right?"

"Yeah, I was, which meant that I was already getting past my prime. Those guys at that place, if you didn't look like their high school prom date, they lost interest pretty fast."

"I imagine you've known Stephanie longer than just about anyone, then."

"I guess I have."

"You said you were at the Leopard Lounge when Stephanie started there. Can you tell me how she got there in the first place?"

"Lieutenant," said Heather, another mirthful smile on her face, "when I said I was there when she showed up, I meant that I was there when she showed up. So, yes."

"Tell me about it."

"There's not much to tell. I'd just walked in the front door of the place one morning – I was working the lunch shift that week – when I noticed this little slip of a girl carrying a small traveling bag and a violin case who'd followed me in. I looked at her and said, 'You're kidding me, right?' She said, 'I'm sorry, ma'am' – she was the first person in my life who ever called me 'ma'am' – 'I don't know where else to go, and you look nice, I guess.' Back then she had this accent that made her sound like she'd just fallen off the turnip truck, and between that accent and the violin case, I guess you'd say she had me won over from the start."

"So what did you do?"

"I asked her what her name was, and she said, 'Alice,' but she hesitated a little, so I figured she'd just made that up, but that was none of my business. I said, 'Come with me,' and I brought her back to the dressing room with me. There were already a lot of other girls there in various stages of, uh, costume, I guess you'd say, but it didn't seem to faze her. I sat her down, got her a cup of coffee, and asked her what her deal was, although, between you and me, Lieutenant, I could've told you."

"What'd she say?"

"She said that she'd just arrived at the Port Authority on a bus an hour ago. Stephanie was a smart young girl, even back then, and it took her about five seconds to figure out what the deal was at that place, so she got out of there as fast as she could. The Leopard was only a couple of blocks from the terminal, and I was the first person she saw. I knew what was waiting for her out on those streets as well as she did, and I knew I didn't want that to happen to her. Me and a couple of the other girls shared an apartment only a few blocks uptown, so I was going to run her back to my place for safekeeping, except we ran into the manager, his name was Sandy something, I don't remember. He took one look at Stephanie and said, 'Are you eighteen?' And Stephanie said, 'Yes,' but I knew she was lying, and so did Sandy. He said, 'Can you prove it?' And she said, 'You can't prove I'm not.' I said, 'Look, Sandy, I'm getting her out of here right now. We can talk about all this later.' Then I took her back to the apartment and got her settled."

"But I'm guessing Sandy didn't just drop it there."

"Oh, no. He recognized a gold mine when he saw one. He kept after me until I finally agreed to talk to Stephanie about it. So I did, and she said, 'sure.'"

"What? And you let her?"

"You know," said Heather, giving Walter a hard stare, "before you go getting judgmental, let me tell you something. There are worse things to do in this world than stripping. It doesn't make you bad, and it doesn't make you immoral. Stephanie had gotten to know us girls, and she knew that, and she wanted to pay her fair share of the household expenses. She also knew by then that, but for the grace of God, and the off chance of running into me, she could've wound up like so many of the other young girls, and boys, who got off those buses at the Port Authority, chained to a bed in a cold water tenement and raped and beaten until she was so doped up on crack that she wouldn't have run away even if she could. The Leopard, with all us girls to look after her, was a safe place for her, Lieutenant."

Walter stared back at Heather for a long time. She was right, and he knew it.

"I guess I'm not in any position to argue with you about that," he finally said.

"No, you're not," said Heather, but the smile was returning to her face.

"So, then, is there anything else that you can tell me that might help with our investigation into her murder?"

"I don't know. Maybe."

"Like what?"

"Well, like about how she helped me and all the other girls."

"What do you mean?"

"Well, you know, Stephanie was pretty good with money right from the start."

"Yeah, that's what Mr. Potter said."

"But let's just say your average stripper isn't. I mean, I'm not saying that we were all stupid, but the only market that any of us knew anything about was, you know, the meat market." She smiled at her own joke, and Walter couldn't help smiling back.

"Are you saying Stephanie helped you to manage your money?"

"Look, Lieutenant, a lot of us girls made good money, and most of it was cash. The Leopard Lounge paid us an hourly wage, but we made most of our money in tips. And then there was the other stuff we did."

"What do you mean, 'other stuff'?"

"Most of us had guys who acted as our managers, I guess you'd call them. They took a cut of what we made at the club, and they also set up outside work for us."

"What kind of outside work?" said Walter, deciding not to get into any fine distinctions between a manager and a pimp.

"You know, private parties. I'd rather not go into the details, but we made a lot of money at those private parties. Our managers took a big cut, but on any given night we went home with a ton of cash in our pockets. The problem was, none of us knew what to do with it. Some of the managers would take the cash and claim they were investing it for the girls, but that money always seemed to disappear whenever the girls wanted it back."

"I'm guessing you weren't reporting any of this income on your tax returns."

Heather gave him a look that said, "duh."

"All I'm saying is you were pretty much limited with what you could do with the money without getting caught up in reporting it."

"That's assuming we had a clue what to do with it in the first place, Lieutenant."

"Okay, so where did Stephanie come in?"

"One day, she invited all us girls to get together before work at a little diner over on 41st Street."

"You're not talking about Hell's Diner, are you?"

"Yeah, that's the place," said Heather, her eyes widening. "You been there?"

"I think I'm the only cop who's ever set foot in it."

"I bet you are too."

"Long story."

"I bet it is. So anyway, Stephanie told us that if we all pooled our money together, we could make a lot of money, and we'd have something put away for when it was time to do, you know, something else. She told us how much money she'd been making for herself, and we were all pretty impressed."

"But Stephanie hadn't even gone to college yet. She couldn't have had a broker's license."

"Lieutenant, we were a bunch of strippers. Maybe half of us had graduated from high school. A lot of the girls were runaways. Do you think we gave a crap about broker's licenses?"

"I hear you," said Hudson, feeling only a little stupid.

"Okay. So, anyway, she explained to us how she was going to pool our money and invest it. She told us that she would keep private records of what everybody had invested, and we could get it back anytime we wanted, or we could leave it in the fund even after we left the Leopard Lounge. She said she was going to call it the 'G-String Fund.' We all kind of liked that."

"Did many of the girls join up?"

"Only a few at first, but then when other girls found out how much money the fund was making, a lot more joined up. And then girls from other clubs heard about it and started to join, and then girls who didn't work at clubs, girls who, you know…"

"I know."

"There was a lot of turnover in the fund, as you could probably guess, but a lot of the girls stuck with it."

"That must've pissed off a lot of the girls' pimps. I mean managers."

"Call them what you want, Lieutenant, it doesn't change what they were. And, yes, a lot of them were really mad. Some of them didn't care, as long as they got their cut, but a lot of them had been making a ton of money from ripping off the girls who gave them their money to manage, and they were pissed. I mean, really pissed."

"But Stephanie didn't work at the Leopard Lounge for very long. What happened when she left?"

"That was the great thing about Stephanie. She quit the Leopard Lounge, but she never quit us, you know? She stayed in touch, and she kept managing the fund, and she did other stuff for us."

"What do you mean?"

"Well, take me, for example, Lieutenant. Stephanie sat me down one day, a couple years after she'd left the club. She told me how much money I had in the fund, and I was shocked. I mean, I got reports from Stephanie; we all did, like clockwork, but I never paid much attention to them. She told me that my stripping days were coming to an end, and I needed to think about my future. She told me I had brains, and I'd stayed away from drugs. With the money I had in the fund I could afford to get my GED and go to secretarial school. It would never earn me the money I got from stripping, but it would be a good living. And she was right. I got my education and a good job afterwards. And then one day she called me and told me was looking for an administrative assistant, at twice the salary I'd been making."

"And you said she did the same thing for other girls?"

"Oh yeah. Lots."

"Heather," said Walter, "I want to take a step back for a minute, to when Stephanie left the Leopard Lounge."

"Okay," said Heather, a little slowly.

"Mr. Potter seemed to think that something bad happened to Stephanie, just before she left, maybe something to do with the tattoo she had on her, uh…"

"On her butt, Lieutenant. I know what you're talking about, that G-Clef."

"Yes. Clay Potter couldn't really tell me much about it. Do you remember anything?"

"You remember, Lieutenant," said Heather, still speaking slowly, "how I told you that some of us would do private parties?"

"Yes."

"Well, Stephanie would never do that. She said she made enough money from her job at the club, and that was all she wanted to do. But one day Sandy came back to the dressing room looking for Stephanie."

"Did he do that often, come back to the dressing room?"

"No, he didn't. Believe it or not, he was a pretty decent guy, and he respected our privacy. So we knew something was up, especially when he asked for Stephanie."

"What did he say?"

"He told Stephanie that he was sending her out for a special private party. When she tried to say no, he said no wasn't an option. To tell you the truth, he seemed kind of scared. Stephanie tried to say no again, but he just wouldn't hear it. He said all she'd have to do was what she did at the club, just for a special audience, which, of course, didn't sound right."

"What do you mean?"

"Do I have to draw you a picture, Lieutenant?"

"Sorry. So what happened?"

"She finally agreed to go."

"Do you think this had anything to do with those managers who were so pissed at her?"

"I'll never know, Lieutenant."

"So, what happened? Did you see her afterwards?"

"I saw her two days later. She didn't show up the next day, even at the apartment. When she got back to the club the day after that, she looked like hell, and when she changed into her outfit I saw, we all saw, that she had bruises all over her body, and the, you know, the tattoo."

"Did she say anything?"

"All she said was that was never going to happen to her again, and that she was never going to forget the three men who did that to her, and that someday they'd pay for it."

"She said 'three'? You're sure?"

"She said 'three.' I'm sure."

"Did she mention any names?"

"No, she didn't."

"What did she say about the tattoo?"

"All she said was that when they were, you know, through with her, they must have given her some kind of drug, because she said the next thing she knew she was waking up and that her butt hurt like hell. When she looked down, there was the tattoo."

"So she never saw whoever gave it to her?"

"No, but she didn't have to. It was good work, and there was only one guy we knew who could've done it."

"Who?" said Walter.

"This guy named Ira. Ira the Inkster. Had a place over on 10th Avenue. He did work for a lot of girls like us, but he also had a lot of high-paying clients. You'd be surprised to know some of the people in this world walking around with tattoos on their asses, or elsewhere, thanks to Ira."

"I probably would be," said Walter, who knew that no matter how long he was a cop, people would never stop surprising him. "What was the name of his place, you remember?"

"'Ira the Inkster.'"

"Do you remember what his full name was?"

"No, I'm sorry, Lieutenant, he was always just 'Ira' to us."

"And she never mentioned the incident again?"

"No. She quit right after that. But I'll tell you something, Lieutenant. Stephanie French was one of the sweetest girls I ever met, but when she said that someday those men would pay for what they did, she meant it. I never found out anything about Stephanie's past, even knowing her for all these years. But being a stripper, you learn a lot about people, and if there was one thing I knew about Stephanie was, when push came to shove, that sweet little girl could be a stone killer."

"I think you could say that about most of us."

"Yes," said Heather, giving the big cop a knowing glance, "I think you could."

"I really appreciate you taking all this time with me, Heather," said Walter, rising from his chair."

"No problem," said Heather, "if you have any more questions, give me a call."

"Just one more question before I leave."

"What's that?" said Heather.

"What ever became of the 'G-String Fund'?"

"I'm glad you asked," said Heather, a smile lighting up her handsome face. "The 'G-String Fund' became the Balboa Fund, and the help she used to give to me and other girls, you know, the counseling stuff, that was the start of SafeWays. Everything Stephanie did kind of flowed into the next thing, you know? She always made it look so easy. There are a lot of women in this world who escaped the sex trade and went on to live happy lives thanks to Stephanie. Some of us got rich to boot. You can't save every puppy in the pound, Lieutenant, but Stephanie French gave it her best shot."

"Yeah, she did," said Walter. And she wound up dead for all her efforts, he thought. He didn't have to say it out loud. Heather Morton, nobody's fool, knew exactly what he was thinking. Her eyes told him.

21

THEY CALL MINNESOTA "THE LAND OF TEN-THOUSAND LAKES," and Leviticus Welles felt like he'd seen at least half of them by the time his twin-prop charter plane landed in Hibbing, in the heart of the Iron Range. The plane, the pilot explained, was normally used for hunting and fishing charters, and by the smell of the tiny cabin, Levi believed him.

The Iron Range itself was not a mountain range, but a vast area covering northern Minnesota and Canada that contained large outcroppings of earth rich in iron ore, outcroppings that the enthusiastic pilot made sure Levi saw through a series of dips and dives made to ensure he got a "genuine bird's-eye view." By the time they landed, any appetite that Levi had developed after a long, very early morning flight from Teterboro airport in New Jersey to Minneapolis, then on to Hibbing, had evaporated.

Hudson and Levi had agreed that Levi should make this trip, for no other reason than that Hudson would have had to get his travel approved by Captain Amato, which would have been tantamount to calling the Manlius campaign and announcing it, if he was guessing right. Given the latest polls, which showed Manlius pulling ahead of Mayor Deborah Kaplan in the Democratic primary race, and his increasingly strident attacks on the NYPD, they'd both agreed that they had to do everything they could to keep this trip under the radar screen. Levi had quietly called his boss, Commissioner Donahue, to inform him of his trip, and had then arranged the flights privately, paying out of his own pocket.

Hibbing, Minnesota was the childhood home of young Robert Zimmerman, later known to the world as Bob Dylan, but that had nothing to do with Levi's visit. It was his unshakable faith in his own ear, which told him that this is where Stephanie French, whoever she was, had come from.

The Hibbing Chief of Police, a big guy with a thick head of blond hair and a wide smile named Arne Jensen, had agreed to pick Levi up at the airport, and he was standing on the tarmac in the bright northern sunshine when Levi gratefully exited the plane. Jensen looked too young for the job, thought Levi, but then again, a lot of people were starting to look too young to him these days. They introduced themselves and hopped into Jensen's patrol car. Levi was puzzled when they drove past the Hibbing Police Station, but his confusion evaporated when they pulled up in front of a place called Caribou Coffee.

"I thought you might be hungry," said Arne, looking over at Levi with an expression that told him that even if he wasn't, Arne was, "or at least you might want a cup of coffee. They make awfully good coffee here."

"Well, I'll tell you," said Levi, "I sure could use the coffee. My flight left New Jersey at 4AM."

"So you were on fisherman's time today."

"Fisherman's time?" said Levi.

"Sure," said Arne as they got out of the car. "I've got a boat and a small cabin on a lake about twenty miles out of town, like a thousand other guys around here. If I'm gonna get any decent fishing in, I gotta be on the road by four at the latest. It's a beautiful time of day this time of year, isn't it?" he said, without any trace of irony.

"Maybe here in Minnesota it is," said Levi as they took a seat in the small but comfortable dining area. "I guess the only thing good about it in New York is there's no traffic. I've never made it through the Lincoln Tunnel so fast in my life."

"Back for more, hey, Arne?" said a large, middle-aged waitress with flaming red hair that just might have been natural.

"I'm just here for coffee, Hedda," said Arne, sounding a little defensive, "but my friend here might want to try out one of your egg sandwiches."

"I'd recommend our Maple Bacon and Gruyere egg sandwich," said Hedda with a friendly smile on her face, and an accent that sounded just like the ghost in Stephanie French's voice.

"That sounds great," said Levi, his stomach starting to grumble amid the warm aromas of the restaurant. "And a cup of your coffee of the day, please."

"Coming right up," said Hedda, heading off for the kitchen.

"Oh, and Hedda?" said Arne.

"Yes?" said Hedda, pausing in mid-step and stretching out the word.

"I'd hate to have our guest Mr. Welles here leave town without trying one of your famous apple fritters."

"That would be a shame, wouldn't it," said Hedda, giving Arne a suspicious look.

"And you know, maybe you could bring me one of those blueberry muffins, just so I have, you know, something to nibble on while we're talking."

"You're always thinking, Arne."

The coffee was served in no time, and the two men made small talk until the food came only a few minutes later.

"This is delicious," said Levi after taking his first bite of the sandwich and washing it down with a gulp of the hot, rich coffee.

"Wait'll you taste that apple fritter," said Arne after swallowing half his muffin in one bite. Young cops are all the same, thought Levi, imagining Arne Jensen and Eduardo Sanchez sitting down to a meal together.

"I'm not sure I'm going to make it to the apple fritter," said Levi. "This sandwich is filling."

"We'll take care of it one way or another," said Arne, giving the fritter a hungry look.

"So, Chief," said Levi, putting down his sandwich, "have you been able to do anything with the information I sent you?"

"Mr. Welles," said Arne, polishing off his muffin, "I'll have you know that you just helped me solve the oldest, coldest case we've ever had in Hibbing. Thank you."

"You're kidding! Already?" said Levi, feeling the excitement rising in the pit of his stomach.

"Dead serious," said Arne.

"Was it the picture I sent?"

"The picture helped, but all the pictures we have of Astrid are pretty old. No, it was the violin that did it. If it hadn't been for the violin, she would've been long forgotten."

"'Astrid,'" said Levi, almost to himself, an emotion far deeper than excitement welling up inside.

"Yes, Astrid Halvorsen. That's the name of the young woman we've all been looking for. At the age of fifteen she won the Minnesota All-State Musical Competition on the violin, and at the age of sixteen she did it again. She was the most famous person in Hibbing for a while. Then, two weeks after she won for the second time, she disappeared without a trace, and no one's seen her since."

"Any idea what caused that?" said Levi.

"We've got a pretty good idea, though nobody's ever been able to prove anything one way or the other. Of course, I don't remember any of this myself; I was maybe two when it all happened; but nobody in this town's stopped talking about it in all the thirty years since, I can tell you that. It's become kind of a legend around here. Little kids tell stories about Astrid's disappearance the way kids from other places tell ghost stories at Halloween."

"Please tell me," said Levi, his half-eaten breakfast long forgotten.

"You done with that sandwich?"

"Yes, I am. It was delicious, but, like I said, it was pretty rich."

"Then I think it would be better if we took a ride, Mr. Welles," said Arne, standing up and throwing a twenty on the table. "This is something I think you should hear from the horse's mouth, so to speak."

"Where are we going?"

"I think it's time for you to meet Greta, Greta Roberts."

"Who's she?"

"Astrid's mother. You're not gonna leave that apple fritter behind, are you?"

GEORGE "SANDY" BAXTER looked like a contented man as he stood behind the empty bar, polishing its gleaming surface. Eduardo guessed him to be in his mid-sixties, but he was trim, his hair was still thick and only gray around the ears, and he looked surprisingly youthful. It was only nine-thirty in the morning, and it would be hours before the first customer showed up, but seeing the placid look on his face, Eduardo didn't think Sandy was polishing the bar in anticipation of any customers.

The Olde Orange Bar And Grille was a small place with a comfortable feel about it, situated on the corner of a busy intersection that gave it good visibility, Eduardo imagined, to thirsty commuters looking for a quick beer before they went home to the lawn and the kids; or the inevitable small core of regulars, looking for company and conversation to ease a lonely existence, and more than a quick beer. He couldn't imagine that it was very profitable, but he was pretty sure Sandy Baxter wasn't in it for the money.

Baxter had been more than willing to talk to Eduardo, but he had insisted they meet at the Olde Orange, not at his house, despite the early hour. It hadn't made any difference to Eduardo; the drive was the same, and he would have gotten lost twice in any event, New Jersey being as foreign to him as Finland.

"Can I get you some coffee, Detective Sanchez?" said Baxter, his voice soft and pleasant, "something to eat? I can toast you up a bagel, or I've got a box of donuts in the back."

"Just coffee would be fine, black please," said Eduardo. He'd picked up an egg sandwich on the way out of the city, and he figured that should tide him over till lunchtime.

"Coming right up," said Sandy, reaching for the coffee pot behind the bar. He poured a cup for Eduardo and warmed up his own. He stayed behind the bar while Eduardo pulled up a barstool.

"Thanks for being willing to talk to me, Mr. Baxter," said Eduardo after taking a sip of the surprisingly good coffee.

"No problem," said Baxter. "I don't know if I'm gonna be much help, though. Like I said on the phone, I haven't seen Stephanie French in thirty years. 'Course, I didn't know her as Stephanie, but that's what they're calling her in the papers. But whatever her name was, she was a sweet kid, so I'll do my best."

"So you haven't seen her since she left the Leopard Lounge?"

"No, I haven't. I know some of the girls used to see her from time to time, but it was never at the Leopard."

"Did they ever talk about her with you?"

"Never a word, and I never asked. In that business, I learned a long time ago not to get nosy."

"How long did you work at the Leopard Lounge, Mr. Baxter?"

"Look, call me Sandy, okay?"

"Sure, Sandy."

"Good. Anyway, I worked there until I bought this place, about ten years ago when the Leopard closed down."

"Do you know why it closed?"

"Sure, but what has that got to do with, y'know, Stephanie's murder?"

"Any background helps, sir."

"I guess. Anyway, business was slowing down. We were still making money, but the owners decided to move on."

"Who were the owners?"

"Never wanted to know. I dealt with a guy named Milt. That's all I knew. Anyway, Milt let on that the owners were moving into the online porn business. By that time about half the clubs in the midtown area had closed down anyway, and they wanted to get out while the getting was still good, I guess."

"Do you know if Stephanie, or any of the other girls, ever had any problems with the owners?"

"As far as I know, the girls didn't have any more contact with the owners than I did. More coffee?"

"Sure, thanks."

"I'm jealous," said Sandy, refilling Eduardo's cup. "I can't drink more than one cup in the morning these days, otherwise I got the yips till lunchtime, y'know? Used to live on the stuff, but not anymore."

"Thanks," said Eduardo, pulling the refilled coffee cup toward him. "One of the reasons I wanted to talk to you, Sandy, is because I've heard from one of the girls who knew Stephanie that the reason she left was because of something that happened to her when you sent her out to a private party."

The air between them grew still. Long seconds passed. Eduardo sipped his coffee.

"Nothing ever really goes away, does it?" said Sandy in a whisper, the placid expression gone from his face as he looked down at the bar. Eduardo knew he'd said it to himself, not to him, so he waited a little longer.

"Why are we talking about this, Detective?" said Sandy, finally looking up, sounding nervous for the first time. "It was thirty years ago."

"Look, Sandy, I'm not looking to get you into any trouble, but I'm going to ask you to bear with me, okay?"

"Okay, okay. I just can't be having any of this getting back to the wife, that's all. Her mother hates me enough as it is. I'd have to move my bed down here to the pub if she ever got word of any of this."

"I'm guessing they didn't like you working at a strip joint, huh?" said Eduardo, trying to keep Sandy talking.

"They never knew. They thought I was managing a restaurant."

"How did you keep that from them?" said Eduardo, his eyes widening. "Didn't they ever go looking for your restaurant when they were in the city?"

"They never went in to the city, Detective. The wife's a Jersey girl, born and raised, and her mother never wanted to be more than a half-mile from St. Anthony's, you know, her church. Neither one of them has left New Jersey for decades."

"Not even for vacations?"

"We go to the Jersey Shore for a week every summer," said Sandy, with a look on his face that said, "Where else would anybody go?"

"Look, don't worry, Sandy. I'm not trying to get you into any trouble here, okay? But we're trying to solve a murder here, right?"

"Right," said Sandy, sounding only a little mollified.

"So, like I was saying, it seems like something happened to Stephanie just before she quit the Leopard. What can you tell me about that?"

"All I know," said Sandy, leaning closer like he was sharing a secret, "is that Milt comes to me one night and says that there's been a special request for Stephanie for a private party. I told Milt that Stephanie didn't do that shit, but he said that 'no' wasn't the answer he was looking for. He told me that it was my job to make sure she showed up, and he wasn't going to talk about it anymore."

"Who was going to be at this party?"

"Milt didn't say, and I didn't ask. He just gave me an address and a time and said she better be there."

"Where did you send her?"

"The Hotel Grenadier over on Seventh Avenue and Thirty-Fourth. I doubt it's there anymore."

"Actually, it is," said Eduardo, recognizing the name immediately.

"You're kidding."

"Nope, still there."

"Well, knock me over with a feather," said Sandy.

"What time was she supposed to be there?"

"At eleven, just after her shift at the club was over."

"And that was the last you heard from anybody?"

"Yeah, it was."

"Until Stephanie came back a couple of days later, right? What did she say to you?"

"She didn't say anything, Detective."

"Then, what did you say to her? She was banged up, and there was the tattoo. You had to say something, right?"

"What the hell was I supposed to say?" said Sandy, giving Eduardo a hard look. "'Did you have a nice time at the prom?'"

"Well, you must've said something."

"I didn't say anything, okay? It wasn't exactly me at my best, but I can't change that now. The next time I talked to her was a couple of days later when she came and told me she was quitting. No notice, no nothing. I never saw her again."

"Alright, alright. What about the tattoo?"

"What about it?"

"Some guy named Ira the Inkster did it?"

"Nobody ever told me that, but, yeah, I knew. It was quality work."

"You know if Ira's still around?"

"I don't know for sure. Right about the time Stephanie quit the Leopard he picked up and moved uptown. I guess he found a market for his work on a higher class of ass."

"You know where?"

"No, just uptown."

"D'you know what his real name was?"

"Yeah, it was Gerald. Gerald Finklestein."

"Okay, Sandy," said Eduardo, standing to leave. "Thank you for your help."

"Well, thanks for nothing, I guess, but you're welcome anyway."

Eduardo wasn't sure how he'd helped, either. But he'd given him the name of Ira the Inkster, and he suspected that Ira might have a tale to tell.

"So, Sandy, you think I could have a couple of those donuts for the road?"

"Take the whole box," said Sandy, his smile returning. He handed Eduardo the donuts and went back to polishing his bar.

━━◄⊪∫⊪►━━

GRETA ROBERTS LOOKED LIKE HER HOUSE: compact, neat, and well kept. She wore woolen slacks and a sweater despite the mild spring air, and she kept her arms folded in front of her, whether out of defensiveness or to ward off a chill, Leviticus couldn't tell. Her silver hair sat atop her head in a bun, but he guessed it would be long and still thick when she let it down.

The small but well-lit living room was spotless, with a braided rug of the sort that Leviticus remembered seeing in his grandmother's house on the floor, and furnished with colonial style furniture which looked ancient but hardly used. Another piece of the puzzle that was Stephanie French fell in place for Levi when he realized that the room was almost identical to the Frenches' living room in faraway Dutch River, New York. People always try to find their way home, he thought.

A man sat silently in one of the chairs with a blanket on his lap. He looked about the same age as Greta. He wore a mild smile on his face, but his expression was vacant.

"Please, sit down, gentlemen," said Greta after Arne had performed brief introductions. He had only said that Levi was "with the New York City Police," a description that widened Greta's eyes but drew no response. "Can I get you some coffee, anything to eat?"

"No, thanks," said Arne, taking, settling in on the sofa while Levi sat down on the love seat, "we don't want to take up too much of your time."

"Time's about the only thing I've got plenty of, Arne," said Greta, with a trace of humor in her voice as she sat in a chair opposite the sofa, "so I wouldn't worry about that. And of course Vern's got all the time in the world."

"How are you Vern?" said Arne in a loud voice, looking at the quiet man in the chair. Levi thought he caught a slight change in the man's smile, but otherwise there was no reaction. Arne shifted his eyes to Greta.

"Vern doesn't change, Arne," she said matter-of-factly. "You know that."

"Did he have a stroke?" said Levi, "or is it Alzheimer's?"

"No, no," said Greta, "nothing like that."

"We'll probably get to that in a little while," said Arne.

"We'll get to that when I say we get to it," said Greta, glaring at Arne. Then, turning to Levi she said, "He took a fall, that's all."

"I'm sorry," said Levi.

Greta's only reply was a small, but unmistakably dismissive wave of her hand. She returned her attention to Arne. "Your phone call got me curious, Arne. What's this visit all about, anyway?"

"We think we might have some news about Astrid, Greta," said Arne. "It's not good news, but at least it's news, something to perhaps give you some, you know, closure."

"Closure," said Greta, her voice flat. "After all these years, I never expected good news, Arne, you know that."

"Mrs. Roberts," said Levi.

"Please, just call me Greta."

"Yes, ma'am. Greta. A woman, a very prominent woman, was murdered in New York City last week. Her name was Stephanie French, but we think she might have been your daughter, Astrid Halvorsen."

"And what would make you think that, Mr. Welles?" said Greta, plainly struggling to keep her expression neutral.

"Well, first of all, from the little we've been able to learn about her in the course of our investigation, the appearance of Stephanie French in New York City seems to coincide with Astrid's disappearance from Hibbing thirty years ago. Secondly, Ms. French, in addition to being a highly successful Wall Street financier, was a virtuoso violinist. And, thirdly, we think there is a strong physical resemblance." He pulled a recent photo of Stephanie French from his pocket and handed it to Greta Roberts. She stared down at it and quickly looked away, her expression suddenly turning stricken. She stared out the window, saying nothing. After a few minutes, she seemed to whisper something. Arne couldn't hear what she said, but Levi did. It was, "Astrid."

Arne started to say something, but Levi quickly raised his hand in a "wait" gesture. After a few more minutes, Greta turned to Levi.

"Tell me," she said.

"It doesn't start out as a very pretty story, I'm afraid," said Levi.

"Tell me. Tell me everything."

So Levi did. He recounted Stephanie's days as a stripper, of the still mysterious incident that caused her to leave the Leopard Lounge. He told Greta of the forged birth certificate and high school diploma, and of Stephanie's education at Columbia and Juilliard. Levi told Greta of Stephanie's brilliant, meteoric rise through the corporate jungles of Wall Street and Barstow & Company. He told Greta of her daughter's musical career and her good work with SafeWays. And, finally, he told her of Stephanie's murder on the sidewalk outside Penn Station. Levi spoke for nearly a half hour, during which Greta's expression remained almost as blank as Vern's.

"Thank you," she said when Levi had finally finished. "It seems that my daughter lived quite a life. I'm glad to hear that, although I'm not surprised. And now I assume you expect me to return the favor."

"If you think it might help us," said Levi.

"I'll let you decide that," said Greta, "but first I'm going to get myself a cup of coffee. Do you boys want some?"

"No, thanks," they both said.

"Well, you're having some anyway. It's not sociable to make someone drink coffee alone," she said, standing up and walking to the kitchen.

"Yes, ma'am," the two men said in unison.

While Greta was in the kitchen, Vern suddenly took the blanket off his lap, stood up, and walked down a hallway, away from the kitchen. Levi stared at Arne, who gave him a palms-up, "Don't look at me" sign. As Vern walked away, Levi couldn't help noticing what appeared to be a large dent in the back of his head. Some fall, he thought. Greta gave the empty chair a quick glance when she came back into the room bearing a coffee tray but said nothing. Just as she was pouring the coffee, the sound of a flushing toilet came from down the hall, and a minute later Vern walked back into the room, sat back down, and put the blanket back on his lap.

"The day he stops being able to do that," said Greta tonelessly, "is the day he goes to a nursing home."

"Can he understand anything we're saying?" said Levi.

"I don't know," said Greta, passing cups of steaming coffee to the two men. The "and I don't care" part didn't have to be said aloud. There was no coffee for Vern. "So, where do you want me to start?"

"Wherever you want," said Levi.

"Then I hope you boys have some time, because I'm going to start at the beginning. I've been waiting for this for a long time."

———◦———

THE SIGN ON THE DOOR simply said, "Finklestein's." And just below that, "By Appointment Only." The address was in the mid-70's on the Upper West Side, not exactly a place where Eduardo would expect to find a tattoo parlor, although what did he know? He wasn't exactly an Upper West Side kind of guy.

He'd rung the doorbell three times and was about to give up when he heard what he thought were footsteps walking toward the door. A few seconds later, a clicking noise came over a small intercom hanging on the doorframe.

"Yes?" came a high-pitched but distinctly male voice.

"I'm Detective Eduardo Sanchez, NYPD, sir. I'd like a word with you."

"Do you have an appointment?"

"No, sir, I do not. I would like to speak to you regarding a murder investigation we are conducting."

"I'm a busy man; maybe you should make an appointment."

"Mr. Finklestein, please."

"Okay, okay. Show me your badge, please. Just hold it up in front of the intercom. There's a camera inside it."

Sanchez held up his badge, and a few seconds later the door opened.

"Come in, come in," said Gerald Finklestein.

"Thank you, sir," said Sanchez as he stepped into a large, brightly painted foyer with a stairway off to the right. A hallway led to what appeared to be a well-furnished kitchen.

The man did not match his voice. He was taller than Eduardo, and he wore a large, un-tucked white shirt that failed to conceal a substantial belly. A pair of worn jeans that somehow clung to his narrow hips and an ancient pair of running shoes completed the outfit. He sported a well-trimmed, graying beard that gave a semblance of a jawline to a jowly face.

"Call me Jerry, Detective," said the man, sounding friendlier than he had over the intercom.

"Okay, Jerry. Is there someplace we could sit?" said Eduardo, looking around.

"If you're looking for my tattoo parlor, it's upstairs. My clients are wealthy people, and a lot of them are famous. You wouldn't believe some of the people walking around with my work on their skin. But they like their privacy, so I work by appointment, only one client at a time, and I keep my parlor out of the way. But you didn't come here for a tat, so let's go into the kitchen. I just put some coffee on. How do you like it?"

"Black, please. Thank you."

"I'm a cream and sugar man, myself," said Finklestein, leading Eduardo back to the kitchen, "as you can probably tell. Please, sit down," he said, pointing to a small kitchen table near the back window. There wasn't much of a view, but it at least let some light in. He took two cups from a cupboard and filled them both with coffee, adding cream and a shocking amount of sugar to one.

"Thank you, sir," said Eduardo, as Finklestein placed the unadulterated cup in front of him. He couldn't help noticing that the man's hands were delicate, well manicured, and immaculate.

"I take it you want to talk about the G-Clef," said Finklestein after taking a large gulp of his coffee.

"Sir?" said Eduardo, caught off guard.

"Let's not beat around the bush, Detective. We're both busy men, and it's not like I don't read the newspapers. And, I'll admit, I just got a call from my old friend Sandy Baxter."

"Okay, then," said Eduardo, "so I guess you know that I'm interested in anything you can tell me about the night you gave Stephanie French her tattoo."

"I can't tell you much, I'm afraid," said Finklestein, standing up to pour himself some more coffee. "Honestly, I would've come to you if I thought I could help. It's a shame what happened to her, you know? You want some more coffee while I'm up?"

"I'm fine," said Eduardo. "Yes, it was a shame. Look, why don't you tell me everything you can remember about that night. You never know what might be helpful, and sometimes you wind up remembering things you thought you forgot, you know?"

"I'll do my best," said Finklestein. His jowls sagged a little as he stared down at his coffee. He was silent for a few moments, but Eduardo didn't interrupt his thoughts.

"I remember I got a phone call at my shop," he finally said. "It was late, maybe ten o'clock, but I was always open till midnight. I got a lot of business late at night back then. A lot of guys would come in after a night of drinking, and women, too; but I always gave 'em good work. I'm a professional, you know?"

"Yessir."

"So, like I said, I got this phone call. The guy on the other end wouldn't tell me who he was. He just said he had an important job for me to do. He told me the tat he wanted, and where he wanted it. He told me to be at the Hotel Grenadier at midnight, and the night clerk would tell me the room number to go to. I said, 'So this tat's not for you?' The guy just laughed and said, 'no.' He said just go to the room number the night clerk would give me. There would be only one person in the room, and she would be my client."

"Didn't this all seem kind of, you know, off to you?"

"Yeah, it did. I'd never had anybody ask me to do anything like that before."

"But you went anyway. Why?"

"Because the guy also told me the night clerk would have an envelope for me, and he told me how much would be in it."

"How much?"

"Enough to get me out of Hell's Kitchen and up to the Upper West Side, was how much."

"So, you went to the hotel."

"Yeah, I did. It was a pretty simple job, so I didn't have to bring a lot of equipment with me. When I got there, the night clerk handed me a key."

"What did he say to you?"

"He didn't say anything. He didn't even look at me, just gave me the key, and I went up to the room."

"And Stephanie was there."

"I didn't know who it was at the time, but yeah. She was just a kid, for chrissakes. She was laying on her stomach, naked, and she was unconscious, I mean out like a light, and, jeez, Detective, this is hard to talk about."

"Take your time."

"Okay," said Finklestein after pausing for a few seconds. "Like I said, she was laying on her stomach, and there were bruises and welts all over her back, and there was, like, blood, you know?"

"You mean from the wounds?"

"No, I don't mean from the wounds," said Finklestein, his coffee forgotten, his eyes glued to the floor.

"Mr. Finklestein, I know this is hard, but you've got to tell me."

"It was coming from her, you know, her rear end," he said, still not looking up.

"Are you telling me that she had been raped?"

"I don't know, but it sure looked like it."

"Didn't it ever occur to you, Mr. Finklestein, to just get the hell out of there and report what you saw to the police?"

"Of course it did, dammit!" said Finklestein, looking up at Eduardo with red eyes. His fat face was mottled, and his jowls were quivering. "What do you think I am?"

"I don't know, sir," said Eduardo, struggling to remain impassive. "Was it the money?"

"No, Detective, no matter what you might think, it wasn't the fucking money."

"Then what?"

"You're too young to remember what Midtown was like in those days. Times Square, Hell's Kitchen, they were bad places, full of people you just didn't want to mess with. And the cops weren't much better back then. For all I knew, if I'd run out of there and reported what I saw, the cop I talked to would've been on the payroll of whoever had done that to that poor girl, and I would've wound up dead."

"Okay, okay," said Eduardo, not wanting to say anything that would silence the man. "So what did you do?"

"I gave her the tattoo."

"Did she ever regain consciousness?"

"No. She'd been pretty drugged up. She never budged. She just laid there with that sweet expression on her face. She was so pretty, Detective, even looking like that. I never forgot that face."

"And then?"

"And then I packed up my stuff and left."

"But not before picking up your money."

"That's right."

"Did you say anything to the night clerk on the way out?"

"No. It was just like when I came in. I left the key on the desk, and the guy handed me an envelope. He never looked at me, and he never said a word."

"You never got the guy's name?"

"Yeah, I did. He saw me staring at his nametag and tried to cover it up, but I saw it."

"You still remember it?"

"Sure I do. His name was Herbert Gray. He was a young guy, like me, at least back then."

"Did you ever see him again?"

"No, I didn't, Detective. But it wasn't like I was looking."

<hr />

"TRIG AND I KNEW from the day she was born she was special," said Greta Roberts, her coffee sitting untouched on a small table beside her chair. "You could just see it in her eyes."

"'Trig,' ma'am?" said Levi.

"Trygve, Trygve Halvorsen, my first husband and Astrid's father. In case you haven't noticed, there are a lot of folks of Scandinavian descent here in Minnesota."

"Not to pry, Greta," said Levi, "but were you divorced? Is he still alive?"

"No, no, nothing like that," said Greta, her expression turning mournful. "He died of lung cancer when he was only thirty-eight. The man never touched tobacco in his life, and he was a teetotaler. Shows what clean living'll do for you. Poor Astrid was only fourteen. But you're making me get ahead of myself."

"Sorry, ma'am. Please, take your time."

"Trig was a high school music teacher, so he always hoped Astrid would take an interest in music. But it turned out we didn't have to worry about that."

"Was he a violinist too?" said Levi.

"No, he played the oboe, of all things; and the piano, too, pretty well actually, him being a music teacher. But there was never any doubt from the beginning that little Astrid loved the violin. We took her to her first high school orchestra concert when she was barely a year and a half old. After the concert, I took her backstage to see her dad, but instead she toddled right up to one of the violin players and kept trying to touch her instrument. The girl finally ran her bow across the strings for Astrid to hear, and Astrid just laughed and laughed."

"When did you start giving her lessons?"

"We bought her first violin for her when she was three. It was a tiny little thing, but it was just the right size for her. She never let go of it. She'd drag it around with her wherever she went, the way most kids drag around stuffed toys. We had to make her put it down at mealtimes."

"Who taught her?" said Levi.

"Well, that was a problem, since there are no major universities around here. Her first teacher was her dad. Like I said, he wasn't a violinist, but high school music teachers have to be jacks-of-all-trades, so he was able to teach her the basics. Then we got lucky and found a wonderful woman over in Grand Rapids, about a half hour away. She was a pediatrician, but she'd double-majored in music in college, and she was an absolutely wonderful violinist."

"And how long did she teach Astrid?"

"Right up until, until, you know. Even after Trig died and we couldn't afford the lessons, she kept giving them for free. But we all knew that we were coming to the end of that soon."

"Why was that?"

"Well, Lavinia – that was her name, Dr. Lavinia Perkins – came to me just before Astrid won her second All-State competition and said that the student had surpassed the teacher, and we had to consider sending her down to Minneapolis to finish high school and study with a real professional coach. But, of course, that never happened."

"Was Astrid a good student in other subjects, too?" said Levi.

"Oh, she was a wonderful student, Mr. Welles. I still have all her report cards from the day she started school. You won't find anything but A's on any of them. And I never saw her study."

"Was she a happy child?"

"Oh, goodness, yes."

"Never any discipline problems at school?"

"Of course not. She was an honors student and the president of her junior class, at least for as long as she was there."

"Then I guess I'm missing something," said Levi. "Why would she have run away? Did it have anything to do with her father's death?"

"I think you need to let me just tell my story, Mr. Welles."

"I'm sorry," said Levi. "Please, go on."

"Like I said, Trig died when Astrid was fourteen. It all seemed to happen so fast, like one day he was here and one day he wasn't. I knew Astrid was devastated; she and her dad were awfully close, but she hardly let it show. I think she felt like she needed to be strong for me. Trig and I were high school sweethearts, and we got married when we were nineteen. I could barely put one foot in front of another at first. And of course, there were the money problems. I'd never worked outside the home, and Trig's teacher's salary was enough to get us by, but just barely. We never had a penny in the bank."

"Did he have any insurance or pension from his job?"

"Some, but not enough. It lasted a few months, but that was about it. I took a job as a cashier at the local grocery store, but that didn't even come close to making ends meet. We were in pretty tough shape, I guess you'd say."

"What did you do?"

"Well, that's when Vern here started coming around," said Greta, nodding impassively in the direction of the silent man.

"Was he local? Did you know him?" said Levi, feeling uneasy talking about the man like he wasn't there, though it certainly didn't seem to bother Vern.

"He wasn't local," said Greta. "He was from some place in Ohio. Circle-something, I can't remember. But yes, I did know him, but only like we all knew him."

"Circleville, Greta," said Arne, "Circleville, Ohio." At the mention of "Circleville" Levi thought he saw another flicker from Vern, but again it evaporated so quickly he couldn't really be sure.

"Anyway," said Greta, "I only knew him because he was the Chief of Police here, about the time you were getting toilet trained, right Arne?"

"About then," said Arne, turning red.

"Well, it was pretty much of a lightning romance, if you want to call it a romance at all. We got married for all the wrong reasons, though I didn't know how wrong until after we were married. Vern's first wife had left him the year before, and he had a son a year ahead of Astrid in high school. I just guessed he missed home cooking, and he wanted someone to be a mother to his son. That was enough for me. I'd loved one man in my life, and I was pretty sure I'd never love another. He admitted to me that his wife had left him because he was an alcoholic, but he said he hadn't had a drink since the divorce, and his drinking days were behind him. He was pretty convincing, and I believed him."

"So Astrid was, what, maybe fifteen when you remarried?" said Levi.

"Yeah, I guess so."

"How long were you and Vern married before Astrid disappeared?"

"It was only about a year and a half, but it was long enough."

"'Long enough'?" said Levi.

Greta stared into her coffee cup like she was staring at tarot cards and not liking what she was seeing. "I need some more coffee." She stood up abruptly, put all the coffee cups on the serving tray, and went back into the kitchen.

"What's this all about?" said Levi in a whisper, glancing at Arne.

"I don't know," said Arne. "There've been rumors ever since I can remember, but I think we're finally going to find out."

"Find out what?"

"Let's just wait for Greta."

Greta came back into the living room, once again bearing a coffee tray. She poured out the coffee and passed the full cups to the two men, who set them down and immediately forgot about them. Greta took a sip from her cup before she also set it down.

"So," she said, "where was I?"

"You said you were married 'long enough,'" said Arne.

"I guess I did, didn't I. This is going to be the hard part," said Greta, her voice suddenly breaking.

"Please, ma'am, take your time," said Levi.

"No," said Greta, her voice suddenly firmer. "No more time."

She went silent for a few moments, but the two men made no attempt to prompt her.

"It wasn't long," she finally said, "before I realized that I'd made a mistake, two actually. I'd been concerned that bringing a teenage boy into the house with my daughter might not be a good idea, and I was right, but not in the way I thought. But I'll get to that. What I didn't count on was Vern." She glared at her husband, who only returned his vacant smile. "Vern didn't marry me because he loved me, and he didn't marry me for my home cooking, either. He did all the right things for a little while, but he never touched me after the first month or two; and he raved about my cooking for a little while, but then he started going out to eat with his buddies on the force rather than come home, leaving me to deal with Kurt, that pervert of a son of his."

"Was Kurt bothering Astrid?" said Levi.

"No, he wasn't bothering Astrid. He was bothering me. At first it was little stuff. I walked into my bedroom one afternoon and found him pawing through my underwear drawer. I mean, it wasn't like he was some pre-pubescent adolescent, he was a big, strong seventeen-year-old."

"Did you say anything to him?" said Arne.

"Of course I did, and I also talked to his father, for all the good it did."

"So Vern didn't talk to his son about it?"

"No, he just laughed it off, said 'boys will be boys.' If it had only been that one time, I guess I would've gone along with that. But then one day, while I was in the shower, I heard the shower curtain rustle, and when I turned around, there was Kurt, staring at me with one hand in his pants."

"What did Vern say about that?" said Levi.

"He didn't say anything, because I didn't tell him."

"But why not?" said Arne.

"Because by that time I realized I had a bigger problem, that's why. I should've seen it sooner, but you know how it is. You can only see something, even if it's plain as day, if you believe it's possible. If you think you see someone walking down the street a foot off the ground, you don't believe your eyes, right? You think your eyes are playing tricks on you, right?"

"Sure," said Arne.

"It took me too long to see what was going on because I couldn't believe my own eyes, and because I didn't want to believe my own eyes. That's the part I blame myself for most."

"I'm sorry, Greta," said Arne, "but I'm afraid I'm not following." He looked over at Levi for support, but Levi said nothing. Levi was following.

"Don't interrupt, Arne," he said. "Go ahead, Greta. Take your time."

"You have to understand," she said, looking at Levi, her eyes pleading,

"I needed the marriage to work. And he was the Chief of Police, for crying out loud! I kept telling myself that I had it all wrong, I had to be imagining it, but I knew I wasn't. And then when he started drinking again, it just got worse, and I couldn't deny it anymore."

"Deny what?" said Arne. He wanted to say more, but he saw Levi glaring at him.

"Don't you see, Arne? Vern didn't marry me because he wanted me. He married me because he wanted Astrid. He only married me so that he could get into her house. While he was sober he could hide it, at least he thought he could. But once he hit that bottle, all bets were off. He'd just stare at her, in that, you know, way, even when I was right there. He started making indecent comments to her, right to her face. I knew things were getting out of hand when, one night, while I was putting dinner on the table, Kurt reached out and grabbed one of my breasts, right in front of Vern. I said, 'Vern, aren't you going to say something?' Of course, he hadn't seen anything because he was too busy ogling Astrid. He just laughed and said, 'Now, come on, son, you just knock it off.' But he was laughing when he said it. By that time, he'd started hitting me. It's hard to believe it now, but he was a big strong man back then, so I just shut up, hoping he wouldn't hurt me."

"What was Astrid doing while all this was going on?" said Levi.

"She did the only thing she could do, Mr. Welles. She hid out in her bedroom and played her violin. She was a bright girl, but she was still a child, and she just couldn't comprehend what was going on. And I think she couldn't understand why I didn't do anything to stop it. She loved me, but she was getting angrier and angrier at me every day, and I couldn't blame her. And then one night, she stopped waiting for me to do something."

Greta looked at her coffee cup and started to reach for it, like she wanted to refill it, but she decided against it. Instead she looked at her silent husband for a long time, an unfathomable expression on her face.

"Vern came home late one night, about nine. He was already drunk, but he headed straight for the whisky bottle anyway and drank a big slug right out of the bottle, half of it ran down his chin and onto his shirt. Astrid had just come out of her room to put her dinner dishes in the sink. By that time she was eating alone in her room almost every night. I saw the look Vern gave her, and I knew that this was it. 'Get over here, you,' he said to her. 'Leave me alone Vern,' Astrid said. I could tell she was afraid, but she didn't flinch. 'It's time you got what you've been looking for, you little bitch,' he said. I begged him to back off, but he hit me so hard he knocked me off my feet, while that creep Kurt just stood there and giggled. Then Vern went over to Astrid and grabbed her by the arm. She tried to fight back, but he was so big, and she was so small. She called out to me, 'Mama, help me!' but I just sat there on the floor in a daze while he grabbed her around the waist, picked her up, and carried her back into our bedroom. I heard her shouting, and I could tell she was fighting back, but there was nothing she could do. Then all of a sudden I heard something that sounded like a crack, and then there was a crash. Then everything was quiet for a minute. Kurt even stopped giggling. Then the bedroom door flew open, and Astrid came out. She had this wild look on her face, and she didn't say a word; she just went straight into her bedroom. I thought she was going to stay there, but she came out just a few minutes later wearing her coat and carrying her violin and a small bag. She said, 'Kurt, you better go check on your father. He fell down and hit his head.' Then she walked out the door without saying a word to me. I never saw her again."

They all sat still for long minutes, no one uttering a word, as if it would be somehow disrespectful.

"Was that fall what left Vern the way he is?" said Levi.

"It wasn't a fall, Mr. Welles," said Greta, staring at him matter-of-factly. "That's been the official story all along. I think everyone knew it was a lie, but it was a convenient lie."

"But Greta," said Levi, "you weren't in the room. How do you know it was a lie?"

"After Astrid ran out, I went into the bedroom. There was Vern, unconscious on the floor with his head caved in. I figured if he wasn't dead, he would be soon. And right next to him was his old nightstick. He never took it to work with him; he just left it in the room, leaning against the dresser. It wasn't hard to tell that the dent in his head was made by that nightstick."

"So what did you do?" said Arne.

"I did what I had to do to protect my daughter. I knew she'd never come back if she was suspected of murdering Vern. So I picked up the nightstick, wiped it down, and put it in the closet. Then I called the police."

"They must have been at least a little suspicious," said Levi.

"Of course they were," said Greta. "That dent in his head sure didn't look like it came from falling against a piece of furniture. But by that time, the police knew about Vern. They knew about his drinking, and I guess he'd made enough comments about Astrid while they were out drinking together that they had their suspicions about that, too. They all knew Astrid, and they didn't want any harm to come to her. And then he didn't die like he was supposed to, so at least there wasn't a murder to investigate."

"So they just went along with the story."

"Well, without any eyewitnesses, there wasn't much else they could do anyway."

"I guess not," said Levi, wondering what Walter Hudson would have done under the same circumstances. "But after all that, why did you keep Vern in the house?"

"What else was I supposed to do? He was harmless after he got out the hospital, just like he is now. If I threw him out, people might suspect it wasn't all just some tragic accident, after all, and I couldn't have that. And besides, I needed his disability checks, didn't I? At least until the other money started coming in."

"What other money?" said Levi.

"Oh, I guess it was about five years after Astrid ran away. Suddenly, money started getting deposited in my bank account once a month, not a lot, but it sure did help."

"Where was that money coming from?"

"I don't have a clue. I always hoped that it was coming from Astrid, that she was still alive somewhere out there and doing well enough to help me out. But that was probably just wishful thinking."

"And what ever became of Kurt?"

"I don't know, and I don't care. He just drifted off and he never came back. It's not like anybody cared to look for him."

Levi had more questions, but he knew they were done. Greta looked exhausted, and she also looked like someone who wanted to be left alone now. "Thank you so much, Greta," said Levi, rising to leave. Arne did the same.

"I don't know how all this is going to help you find out who murdered my daughter, but it was good to get it all off my chest after all these years."

Levi didn't know how it would help, either, but he subscribed to the Walter Hudson theory of murder investigations: Collect all the facts you can. You never knew where they'd lead you.

"Well."

The word was spoken softly, but it made them all jump, and it took them a few seconds to realize that it had come from Vern. They all looked at him, waiting, but it didn't take long to conclude that he wasn't about to say anything more.

"That's the first word he's spoken since that night," said Greta Halvorsen Roberts. "I hope it's his last."

—⧸⧹—

"Arne, do you know where Greta does her banking?" said Levi as they drove away from Greta Roberts's home.

"I know her disability checks go to the Northern Minnesota Bank and Trust. Why?"

"Pull over a minute, will you?" said Levi, typing into his iPhone. "Here," he said, handing the phone to Arne. "Ask to talk to the bank president and tell him who I am and can he please answer a question for me."

"Sure, I guess," said Arne.

A few minutes later, he handed the phone back to Levi and heard him ask the question he knew he was going to ask. It only took a few seconds to get his answer.

"Dammit. Dammit to hell," said Leviticus Welles, a mild man not given to such outbursts.

"What?" said Arne.

"I've got to change my travel plans, that's all," said Levi, already calming down.

22

NOTHING BUT THE BEST FOR
NYPD'S ELITE

The copy of the *New York Times*, with its screaming headline above a photo of Leviticus Welles climbing into a private aircraft, sat on the table staring at Walter Hudson like an angry wife, and the looks on the faces of Commissioner Sean Donahue and Mayor Deborah Kaplan weren't any friendlier. It was seven in the morning, and the ink on the newsprint didn't even look dry. Cups of Irish coffee sat in front of each of them, but they were untouched.

"And that's not the best part," said Donahue. "The lead editorial is demanding that the Mayor withdraw from the primary and for me to resign. Immediately."

"But Levi paid for that plane with his own money!" said Walter.

"A minor detail that the *Times* didn't see fit to include in their article or their editorial," said Mayor Kaplan. She looked exhausted and, for the first time since Walter had known her, completely discouraged. "If I wouldn't be taking you down with me," she said, looking at Donahue, "I'd probably just quit."

"Forget me," said Donahue. "I'm perfectly capable of taking care of myself. But you can't abandon this city to that tin pot terrorist."

"I think it's the other way around, Mike," said Kaplan. "Have you seen the latest polls? I'm behind Manlius seventy percent to thirty in the Democratic primary polls, and I'm even running behind the Republican candidate, which is like running behind 'other.' From where I'm looking, the city is abandoning itself to the guy."

"What do you have to say for yourself, Lieutenant Hudson?" said Donahue. "I'll take the hit for authorizing Levi's trip, but I told you both that you had no time, and I meant it."

Lieutenant Hudson. It hung in the air between them like a bad smell. Both Donahue and Mayor Kaplan had been calling him "Walter" for years. But not today.

"Sir, with all due respect, it hasn't even been a week yet."

"I guess it only seems like a year," said Donahue without a trace of humor in his voice.

"Sir, ma'am, I know how bad this looks, but between what Levi learned in Minnesota and what Detective Sanchez has dug up, we've made a tremendous amount of progress."

"Yes, you've made all kinds of progress learning all kinds of spicy gossip about what happened thirty years ago. So instead of solving Stephanie French's murder, you've succeeded in tainting her memory and making this department look bad. Good job."

"Oh, Mike, I don't think that's fair," said Mayor Kaplan. "Frankly, when all the facts come out about her life, I think Stephanie is going to look like a hero."

"Dammit, sir," said Walter, too angry to want anybody's help, even the mayor's, "I completely disagree. You know how these cases go. Every single fact that we dredge up is helpful to us, and we have a lot of facts now."

"I don't want any more facts," said Donahue, his face bright red, "I want a culprit."

"And you'll have one, sir."

"When?"

"Twenty-four hours, sir." Walter Hudson was as surprised as anyone else to hear himself speak the words; but he also knew that was all the time Commissioner Donahue was going to give him in any event. If I'm going down, he thought, I might as well go down in flames.

"I'm going to hold you to that," said Donahue.

"I don't doubt you for a minute, sir," said Walter. He stood up, took a large swig of his Irish coffee, slammed the cup down on the table, and walked out of the room.

———⚬⚬⚬———

"WELL BEGUN is half done," the saying goes. By that standard, Leviticus Welles's day was not off to a good start.

Levi was tired. He'd landed at the Albany County Airport late the night before, where Officer Bert Steffus had picked him up and driven him back to Dutch River. He'd thought of staying at Walter and Sarah's farmhouse, but he didn't want to rent a car, and he didn't want to rely on a ride in the morning; so he'd decided to stay at one of the new B&Bs that had sprung up in the small village over the past year, just a block down from the law offices of Maas & Maas. He hadn't slept well, and he'd been awakened by a call before the sun rose from a reporter from the *Daily News*, who hadn't seemed overly interested in any facts. He'd gone downstairs at six, only to find out that the B&B didn't start serving breakfast until seven, which was when Jill and Peter Maas had agreed to see him. They'd kept him cooling his heels in their conference room until almost eight, claiming an "emergency." Since almost their entire practice now consisted of real estate closings, he'd been dubious, but he'd decided that this was going to be a tough enough meeting without starting it off by griping about punctuality. Besides, the coffee they served him was hot, and the pastries were fresh from Adam Avery's oven. Things could have been worse.

Jill Maas and her father, Peter, were dressed in almost identical pinstriped, navy blue business suits, though Levi couldn't help observing that Jill filled hers out much more nicely. Her flaming red hair hung over her shoulders, and she looked every inch the prosperous attorney that she now was. Peter, his red hair still full but graying, was affecting vagueness this morning, though Levi wasn't fooled for a second; the man's mind was as sharp as a butcher's knife. They had all refilled their coffee cups and were sitting around the conference table.

"All I can tell you," said Jill, after Levi had told her of his visit to Hibbing while her father stared out the window, "is that most of that is news to me."

"But I'm assuming that you set up the bank accounts and arranged the transfers of funds."

"That was all well before my time," said Jill. She and Levi both looked at Peter Maas, who briefly looked back and smiled before returning his gaze to the window.

"Okay, okay," said Levi. "Then can you tell me when the last time was that you communicated with Stephanie?"

"Why do you ask?"

"Because Stephanie was murdered outside of Penn Station, and I can't think of any other reason that she was there except that she was getting on a train to come up here to visit the Frenches, and you."

Jill gave Levi a long stare. "Okay."

"Okay what?"

"Yes, she had called me the day before. She usually gave us more no-tice than that, so I was a little bit curious. She said that she had some important news that she wanted to share with the Frenches."

"And with you, I assume. What did she tell you?"

"Just that – that she had some important news to share with the Frenches. She told me what train she'd be on so that I could come and pick her up."

"And?"

"'And' what?"

"I think she told you more than that."

"Okay," said Jill after another long pause. "She told me that she expected to be named CEO of Barstow & Company the next day and that she wanted to share the news with the Frenches before it all became public."

"Jill, there had to be more to it than that."

"I don't understand," said Jill. "That was pretty important news. And I thought that your whole theory of the case was that she was murdered because someone else wanted that job."

"It was, and it still may be," said Levi, "but we also know now that Stephanie had a pretty extraordinary life, and we may have been kidding ourselves thinking that this was simply a matter of professional jealousy."

"But it still could be."

"Yes, Jill, it still could be," said Levi, staring at her hard, "but I'm be-ginning to think it wasn't, and I think you know more about all this than you've let on so far."

"Why would you think that?"

"Because I think," said Levi, "that as rare a person as Stephanie was, she was still as human as the rest of us, and she would have wanted some-one to know her story. People don't want to die, but the thing they're most afraid of isn't just dying, but dying alone, without leaving behind people, whether they're family or friends or whatever, who knew who they were, who knew their story. Stephanie French's life was an extraordinary story, and I think she wanted at least someone to know it. All of it."

"And you think perhaps she told the Frenches?"

"I think perhaps she told you."

"Why me?"

"Stop it, Jill. Just stop it. You and your father aren't just Stephanie's attorneys. She has known you and your father most of her adult life, and she has shared the secrets of her life with you, secrets that are her last will and testament. I can't think of anyone else she would have told."

"But, Levi, you've already learned about her life. So what does it matter what she did or didn't share with me or my father?"

"Because there's one thing we still don't know, and I think you know it."

"What could that be?" said Jill, but the expression on her face told Levi that she knew what was coming.

"We still don't know what happened to her at the Hotel Grenadier that night, and I think you do. And I don't think we're going to solve this case until we know."

"But that was all thirty years ago, Levi! What could it possibly matter? Stephanie's dead now. Isn't it the decent thing to do to bury some things with her? You're right, I was her friend as well as her attorney, and I think I have at least some obligation to protect her memory."

"But not her murderer," said Levi.

"Levi, I…"

"Jill," said Peter Maas, making his daughter jump. He looked at her with clear eyes, all trace of vagueness gone.

"What, Dad?"

"Levi's right. The time is over for keeping secrets. Go get the file."

"Dad, are you sure?"

"Yes, Jill. Get the file."

Jill Maas looked at her father. She looked at Leviticus Welles. She looked down at the table for long minutes. "Okay," she finally said. "I'll be right back." She stood and left the room.

"Good," said Peter Maas. "Good."

Jill was only gone a few brief seconds before she returned with the sealed envelope Stephanie French had entrusted her with so many years ago. She placed it on the table in front of Levi.

"I think it might be best if my father and I leave you alone while you read that," said Jill. "Stephanie made me promise that I would only ever open it on her express instructions, and I haven't. She never told me what to do with it in the event of her death, and I have no inkling of its contents. If it contains what you're looking for, good. If it doesn't, I don't know what to tell you."

Levi opened the envelope as soon as the Maases had left the conference room and began to read. It was handwritten in the neat, disciplined cursive script that was no longer taught in schools, and he had no trouble reading it.

"Good Lord in Heaven," he whispered to himself when he was finished. He stared out the window for a few seconds, but he knew that he had no time to waste. "Good Lord in Heaven," he said again, as he pulled his phone out of his pocket and dialed a familiar number.

—⁌⁌⁍⁍—

DETECTIVE LIEUTENANT WALTER HUDSON was sitting in Bryce Barstow's private study with April Barstow when his phone rang.

He'd arrived early, hoping to catch the elusive man before he had a chance to go anywhere. April had met him at the door and said that her father was showering and dressing but should be available soon. In the meantime, she'd escorted Walter to the study and served him coffee from a sideboard against a far wall. Morning coffee in the study was clearly one of Bryce Barstow's rituals.

Walter stared at the walls, covered with framed photographs that told of a life defined by a career spent hobnobbing with the richest and the most powerful in a city full of the rich and the powerful. He wasn't surprised to notice that there were no personal photos, and none that did not feature Bryce Barstow himself.

"Your father has led quite a life," said Walter, in an effort to make polite conversation. April was obviously uncomfortable, possibly fearful that her father would be angered to find that she had allowed a lowly detective into his inner sanctum.

"I guess that's a good way to put it," said April. "I really wouldn't know."

"Have you met many of these people?"

"Some, but not many. Daddy's career was his life, and he led it by himself."

"But you were his heir apparent, at least that's what he thought. Didn't he want you to get to know these people, make your own connections?"

"Honestly, Lieutenant, in his heart of hearts I don't think he ever thought of me or anyone else as his heir apparent. I don't think his ego would let him believe that he wouldn't always be the boss. I know that sounds childish, but I also believe that most people with egos the size of my father's are essentially children."

"Just with more expensive toys, right?"

"Right."

Walter's gaze came to rest on a large, color photo. He was about to ask April about it, but that was when his phone rang, and as soon as he saw the number on his Caller ID, he answered it.

"Hey, Levi," said Walter, "what's up?" The two had already spoken before daybreak, and Walter hadn't expected to hear from his friend until he got back to the city. He listened to what Levi had to say, struggling to keep a neutral expression on his face as April looked on, and hung up without saying another word.

"Is everything all right?" said April.

"Oh, sure," said Walter.

"I saw the *Times* this morning, Lieutenant."

"Well, these things happen," said Hudson distractedly. He pointed to the picture he'd been staring at. "Say, would you mind if I took a picture of this photo with my iPhone?"

"That one?" said April, staring at it. "No, go ahead." She knew her father would be furious if he found out, but she'd deal with him when she had to. Lieutenant Walter Hudson wasn't the only one seeking the truth.

"Thank you," he said, heading for the door after snapping the photo and checking the image, which was bright and clear.

"But aren't you going to wait for my father?" said April.

"Don't worry," said Hudson to the puzzled woman. "I'll be back."

WALTER GUESSED that the Hotel Grenadier hadn't changed much over the last thirty years as his eyes scanned the poorly lit, dingy lobby with its worn carpeting and frayed furniture; and it was probably past its prime even back then. It was still a valuable property, he thought, but the hotel boom that had overtaken Manhattan in the past decade had clearly passed it by.

Herbert Gray, the assistant manager, was past his prime, too, thought Walter, as the man gave him his best hotelier's welcoming smile, but his eyes betrayed his wariness at seeing the big cop again. Lieutenant Hudson's last visit hadn't gone well, and Gray couldn't think of any reason to think this one would go any better.

"What a pleasure to see you again," said Gray, buttoning his gray suit jacket with "Hotel Grenadier" stitched in maroon thread over the pocket, and tightening the knot on the maroon tie around the shirt collar that was too big for his shrunken neck.

"Good to see you again, too, Mr. Gray," said Walter, his eyes wandering to the door that he knew led to Gray's private office.

"Would you like to speak in private?" said Gray, catching the cop's stare, and knowing from experience that Detective Hudson was a man with little patience for pleasantries.

"I think that would be a good idea."

"Dennis," said Gray to a young man with unkempt hair and an indolent expression slouching behind the front desk, wearing a jacket similar to Gray's, "you're in charge."

"Sure thing," said Dennis, responding to the added responsibility by slouching further down behind the front desk.

"What happened to the guy who was here the last time?" said Hudson.

"Oh, you mean Nestor," said Gray after a brief pause. "Funny thing," he said, though his expression said that he didn't think it was funny at all. "While he was ignoring his job here, he developed an online game that he sold to a software company for a small fortune. Last thing I heard, he's living somewhere in the Caribbean with a bathing suit model."

"You never know, do you?" said Hudson, a man who had experienced more than his share of unexpected good fortune.

"No, I guess you don't," said Gray, a man who hadn't. He led them into his small office, which hadn't changed since the last time Hudson had visited: the small, gunmetal gray desk, the bad lighting, and the large photo of Manhattan at night on the wall, the Twin Towers still standing proudly, if only here at the Hotel Grenadier.

"What can I do for you, Lieutenant?" said Gray, sitting down at his desk and waving his arm at the only other chair in the room. "Please, have a seat."

"I'm investigating the murder of Stephanie French, Mr. Gray," said Hudson, sitting down in the small, hard chair, "and I'm hoping you can help me."

"I don't understand," said Gray, "how could I possibly help you?" But Herbert Gray was no poker player, and Walter knew from the expression on his face that he hadn't for a moment forgotten that night thirty years ago.

"As you may recall, I don't tolerate bullshit well, Mr. Gray."

"I do recall that, yessir. Of course, I'll help you in any way I can. Of course."

"Good. I'd like you to tell me about the night thirty years ago when Stephanie French came to your hotel. She wasn't a financial executive back then; she was a stripper, brought in for a private party. But I'm not telling you anything you don't remember, am I, Mr. Gray." He placed a photo of a young Stephanie on the desk. Gray stared at it for long seconds.

"You've got to understand, Lieutenant, I didn't have anything to do with it."

"I'm not saying you did. But I'm not going to sit here and listen to you tell me that you don't remember anything, because that's bullshit, and we both know it."

Herbert Gray stared up at the Twin Towers, perhaps looking for help. He looked back at Lieutenant Hudson, perhaps looking for forgiveness.

"Yes, Lieutenant, I remember the night, and I remember Stephanie, although that wasn't her name back then. It was Brianna, or Brittany, I think, something with a 'B.' I was told she would show up and I was to give her the key to room 501, a corner suite." He stared back down at the photograph. "She was such a pretty girl, and she was so young. You could tell without even knowing her that there was something special about her."

"Who told you she'd be coming?"

"The hotel manager back then, a guy named Harry Marx, but he's long since dead."

"Did you say anything to her when she got here?"

"Please understand, Lieutenant, the Hotel Grenadier was a respectable place when I started working here. It wasn't until it changed owners that it started to go downhill, and it went down fast. All I'm saying is, I didn't know what to do in situations like that, so I just tried to keep my head down. But Brittany, you know, Stephanie, she looked right at me with those bright eyes of hers and said 'hello, how are you' like she was checking in for a weekend on the town. I gave her the key, and she said 'thank you' and got into the elevator."

"And what about the men, were they already there?"

"No, they weren't. They got here just a few minutes after Stephanie did."

"What were they like?"

"There were three of them. Maybe in their late thirties, early forties.

I could tell they were rich by the clothes they were wearing, and, I don't know, rich people act different, you know? They looked sort of like the type of client that used to stay at the Grenadier before it started to change."

"Sort of?"

"Yeah, I mean, they'd all had a lot to drink, but only one of them was what I would have called really plastered. You know how it was, business-men used to drink a lot more back then than they do now, but this one guy, he was drunk by anybody's standards. But that wasn't it."

"Then what was it?"

"There was something scary about these guys, Lieutenant, is all I can say. It wasn't just that they'd all drunk too much. They were the type of guys, you could just tell, who knew how to hurt you if they wanted to, and they'd get a kick out of doing it, especially the one of them that looked like the ringleader to me, but I could've been wrong."

"Then didn't it ever occur to you that you were putting a young girl in danger?"

"Jesus, yes, Lieutenant. I think if the guys had shown up first, I would have told Stephanie to just go away when she showed up. But I don't know. Like I said, I wasn't used to handling situations like that."

"And you were scared."

"And I was a coward, is what I was."

"Don't be too hard on yourself, Mr. Gray. I can't think of too many people who would've known what to do in a situation like that."

"I've tried to tell myself that over the years, Lieutenant, but trust me, it doesn't work."

"What happened next?"

"The next thing I heard was about an hour later. The elevator doors opened, and the three guys came out. Two of them were basically carry-ing the third guy. One of the other guys was kind of quiet, but the other guy – the ringleader, y'know? – he had a big grin on his face and he was, like, laughing. They tossed the keys on the desk and left. I never saw them again."

"Then what?"

"Just a few minutes later, the tattoo guy showed up. He was carrying some stuff, and he looked harmless enough, I guess. I gave him the key that the three guys had just left, and he went upstairs. He came back down about an hour later. He didn't look so hot. He was kind of pale, and he looked kind of shell-shocked, I guess you'd say. I gave him the envelope I was told to give him, and he left, too. I think he saw my nametag, but there was nothing I could do about that."

"And what about Stephanie?"

"Jesus, Lieutenant. It was probably about three in the morning by the time she came down. She looked awful – pale, banged up, her face a mess. She put the key on the counter, and I could see her hands were shaking. I asked her if she needed a ride, and she said, 'no, thanks.' Can you believe that? She actually said 'no, thanks.' And then she gave me a polite little smile and left. I never saw her again until I saw her picture in the paper last Saturday."

"Did you recognize her right away?"

"She had a face that stays with you, Lieutenant."

"Mr. Gray, do you think you would recognize those three men if you saw a picture of them?"

"I'm not sure I'd recognize them now. You know, it was thirty years ago, and sometimes men don't age well. I should know," said Gray, with a stab at self-deprecating humor that fell flat.

"I have a photograph," said Walter, reaching into the inner pocket of his suit coat and withdrawing his cell phone, "which I believe was taken about the same time that all of this took place." He pulled up the picture out of his Photos app, a photo of three prosperous men, holding drinks in their hands and grinning into the camera. He held the phone toward Herbert Gray. To his surprise, Gray smiled.

"What?" said Walter.

Instead of saying anything, Gray reached back into his rear pocket and pulled out his wallet. He opened it and took out a small square of newsprint pressed inside laminated plastic. It was a photograph, small but distinct. He handed it to Walter. It was the same photograph that Walter had just shown him.

"I wanted to make sure I didn't forget," said Gray, "just in case."

"Can you tell me which one of the men you thought was the ringleader?"

"That one," said Gray, pointing immediately to one of the men.

"You're sure?"

"I'm sure."

"I guess you've been waiting for me for a long time."

"I guess I have," said Herbert Gray.

"Do me a favor," said Detective Hudson. "and don't lose that photo, okay?"

"Oh, don't worry, Lieutenant Hudson, I won't," said Herbert Gray, as he put the old photograph, the photograph of Bryce Barstow, Hollings Harkin IV, and their ringleader, Harold Manlius, back into his wallet.

23

LEVITICUS WELLES had wanted to spare himself, Commissioner Donahue, and the NYPD the spectacle of arriving back in New York in a private plane. He also feared that taking any mode of public transportation could lead to a press ambush on his arrival, so he'd decided to drive back to New York. The most nondescript, ubiquitous car he could think of was a Toyota Camry, so he'd rented a blue one from a local agency and avoided the New York State Thruway by taking the Taconic Parkway south. He wasn't hopeful, but it was the best he could do.

The ride down the Taconic was one Levi normally relished, especially on a day like today, with the rich greens and the clear air of the late spring day making the always stunning vistas of the Hudson River Valley resemble a scene out of a Washington Irving tale. But today it was wasted on him as he contemplated the complex life and still mystifying death of Stephanie French.

To Levi, Stephanie French and Astrid Halvorsen were two different people: Astrid, the product of the circumstances of a birth and young life that were beyond her control; and Stephanie, the woman Astrid had willed herself to become. As immersed as he had become in Astrid's young life during his brief visit to Minnesota, he knew he would always think of the remarkable woman as Stephanie.

The ringing of his phone shook Levi out of his reverie as he neared the exit for Hyde Park. He glanced quickly at the Caller ID, which was coded by the NYPD Intelligence staff to override most masking software, but it read merely "Anonymous." This should be interesting, he thought, as he pushed the green "Accept" button on his phone.

"Hello?"

"Hello, Deputy Commissioner Welles."

Levi's sensitive ear recognized the quiet, cultured voice immediately. "Hello, Mr. Fornaio, how are you?"

"Considering what I'm reading in this morning's *Times*, I'm doing better than you are."

"I'm sure you are," said Levi. "What can I do for you?"

"I would like to speak to you on a matter pertinent to the murder of Stephanie French that I think you might find relevant to your investigation. May I ask if you are back in the city yet?"

"Actually, I'm on the Taconic Parkway about halfway between New York City and Albany. I rented a car to avoid the press. I just passed the Hyde Park exit."

"Ah, that's fortunate," said Fornaio. "I'm currently at my private residence in Newburgh, which is only a few miles south of your current location. I know you must be in a hurry to get back to the city, but could you possibly spare some time to stop by?"

Leviticus was, in fact, not in a great hurry to get back to New York City. He'd already given Lieutenant Hudson all the information he'd gathered from his trips to Hibbing and Albany over the phone, and all that was waiting for him there was more grief from Manlius and his operatives, the press, and he feared, his own boss, Commissioner Donahue.

"Sure," he said. "If you give me your address I can punch it into Google Maps."

"That probably wouldn't be wise, Mr. Welles. I doubt it will be long before the intrepid New York press discovers your little ruse of renting a car, and I don't think it would benefit you for them to find it parked in my driveway."

"You're probably right," said Levi. "Do you think we should meet somewhere else?"

"That won't be necessary. Just get off the Newburgh exit. If you turn right at the end of the exit you'll see a small commuter parking lot. Pull into it. There will be a car waiting for you there."

"Thank you," said Levi, "that sounds like a good idea."

"You're welcome," said Tommassino Fornaio.

Di nenti, thought Leviticus Welles. "I'll see you soon," he said.

"GODDAMMIT, HUDSON, I said I want to see you in my office, now." Captain Eugene Amato sounded oddly calmer than the last time they met, which puzzled Walter, but he was beyond caring in any event.

"No can do, Captain," he said. "I'm on my way downtown."

"To do what?"

"To solve a fucking murder, sir."

"Just so you know, Lieutenant, you are now all alone with your little pet theory. I am at this moment preparing a draft press release for Commissioner Donahue to issue in just a few hours."

"And who asked you to do that, your buddy Manlius? Donahue'll just ignore it."

"Donahue requested it, Lieutenant," said Amato, the gloating obvious, even over the phone line.

"I don't believe you," said Walter, trying to keep the shock out of his voice.

"Well, believe it, Hudson. It seems you're not the teacher's pet anymore, and you just got an F on your last test."

Walter was stunned. Only a few hours ago, Donahue had given him twenty-four hours. He knew that Donahue was angry with him, and he also understood the immense pressure he was under, but Sean Michael Patrick Donahue was not a man who went back on his word. Ever.

"What, the cat got your tongue, Hudson?"

"Look, Captain, I'm heading down to the subway station. I'm going to lose my phone signal any second."

"I can't wait to fire your ass, Lieutenant," said Amato. But Walter Hudson didn't hear him. He was still a half block from the subway entrance, but he'd already hung up his phone and turned it off for good measure.

⊷⊶⊷

NEWBURGH, NEW YORK, is a city of contradictions. Located on the banks of the Hudson River, it had once been a prosperous depot for the ships and barges headed for the Erie Canal, and a convenient stopover between New York City and Albany, the state capital, for politicians and their inevitable hangers-on. But the Erie Canal was now an artifact of history, and mass transportation and the New York State Thruway had long since made Newburgh easy to bypass. Like so many of the old river cities, it had seen better days.

But Tommassino Fornaio's home on a well-maintained street on the outskirts of town was an immaculately preserved Gilded Age masterpiece whose fresh paint and impeccable landscaping shone in the midday sun like a well-set stone in an heirloom necklace.

The front door was answered by a stunning woman with honey-colored hair wearing an outfit that quietly but unmistakably said, "Paris." She was probably sixty, Levi guessed, but was doubtlessly routinely mistaken as being in her mid-forties.

"Oh, hello, Deputy Commissioner Welles," said the woman in a soft, unaffected voice, holding out a well-manicured hand. "I'm Christina Fornaio, Tommy's wife."

"Pleased to meet you, ma'am," said Levi, trying not to look too nonplussed.

"Oh, please, call me Christina," she said. "I'm sorry, I'm on my way out, but Tommy's in his study. He's expecting you, of course. Here, let me show you the way."

She led him down a hallway, past a living room decorated in a contemporary style that somehow complemented the old house perfectly, and opened a door on the left.

"Tommy, Mr. Welles is here," she said. "I'm on my way. Don't forget, the cocktail reception at the Waldorf is at five-thirty, not six, and it's black tie. I booked a suite so we can change there."

"Wonderful," said Tommassino Fornaio, coming out from behind his desk and crossing the room to give his wife a light kiss on the cheek. "Don't worry, I'll be there."

"It'll be lovely," said Christina, returning the kiss, "just you see." She gave her husband a subtle, seductive smile and left the room, closing the door behind her.

"I'd rather get my teeth drilled," said Fornaio, in his soft, measured voice, giving Levi a conspiratorial grin.

"I know the feeling," said Levi, returning the grin.

"Please, Mr. Welles, come sit down. I assumed you might have an appetite after your drive, so I've had a light lunch prepared."

"Thank you so much, Mr. Fornaio," he said, taking a seat at a small table situated in a far corner. "You're right, it's been a long morning."

Perhaps he'd watched "The Godfather" too many times, Levi thought, as his eyes scanned the room. He had expected a large, dim room furnished with massive leather furniture, perhaps with a *consigliere* slouching in a corner. He wasn't ready for the light that poured in through the floor-to-ceiling windows that looked out on a garden that reminded him of Giverny, giving the table where they sat and the entire room a warm glow. The room itself was of modest dimensions and simply but tastefully furnished in the same manner as the living room. It had all undoubtedly cost a fortune, but somehow succeeded in conveying the impression that a humble man of simple tastes worked here.

There was an antipasto platter in the center of the table along with a bottle of Pellegrino water. The napkins were linen, and the cutlery was silver. They each put some food on their plates and ate silently for a few minutes. Levi had been hungrier than he realized, and the food was outstanding, but both men ate sparingly.

"Now, Mr. Welles," said Fornaio, putting down his fork and knife, "we are both busy men, so perhaps I should get to the point of this meeting."

"If you gave me a bottle of wine," said Levi, in Sicilian, "I could probably linger over this antipasto all afternoon, but I guess you're right."

"Another time, surely," said Fornaio, nodding his appreciation at the polite gesture.

"I look forward to it."

"Now, Mr. Welles," said Fornaio, reverting to English, "I was as disappointed as you were that Mr. Joe Hanson, the man who shot Stephanie French, met with such a sudden end before anyone had an opportunity to question him properly."

"Yes," said Levi, "that was an enormous setback, especially since we remain convinced that he was just a hired gun."

"I believe so, too," said Fornaio, giving Levi a level gaze. "It had been my hope to locate him and turn him over to the NYPD for questioning, but I'm afraid someone else got to him first. I apologize for not being more helpful."

"You did what you could, and we appreciate your efforts," said Levi. It was hard not to believe the man. "Our current theory is that Mr. Hanson was eliminated by whoever hired him to kill Ms. French," said Levi, "both to eliminate the evidence trail and to make it look like a mob hit gone bad."

"I agree with you Mr. Welles," said Fornaio after taking a small sip of Pellegrino, "and from what I can tell, it seems to be working on both counts."

"I'm afraid you're right."

"Please understand, Mr. Welles," said Fornaio, picking up the linen napkin from his lap and setting it on the table, "that Mr. Hanson was not in my employ, nor was he in the employ of anyone even remotely connected with my businesses. However, at one time, people in my organization had worked with Mr. Hanson, indirectly, of course. So I took the opportunity to have one of my associates speak with some of these people, and an interesting story emerged. It seems that a few months ago, Mr. Hanson, over a few too many beers at a local pub, started bragging that he was now an independent contractor, and that he had, in his words, 'hit it big' on a new job with a wealthy and powerful new client."

"I'm assuming he didn't name the client."

"We're never that lucky, are we, Mr. Welles."

"Not in my experience."

"Interestingly, on the Friday evening of Ms. French's murder, Mr. Hanson showed up at this same pub driving a brand new Audi A6. He claimed that 'his ship had come in' and bought a round of drinks for the house."

"That seems to confirm what we've suspected all along, that he was just the shooter for the person who truly plotted Stephanie's murder."

"Yes, it does," said Fornaio, "except for one thing."

"What's that?"

"One of the people at the pub that night distinctly recalled Mr. Hanson saying that 'revenge is sweet.'"

"That doesn't sound like something a contract killer would say."

"No, it does not, but given the sudden improvement in his financial circumstances, it is very difficult for me to believe that he was acting alone, for his own reasons."

"I agree," said Levi, "but a contract killer simply wouldn't say something like that."

"No, he wouldn't, so I requested some further investigation. After his, let us say, untimely demise, I asked that this Audi of his be located. It was found parked in the driveway of a house in the Bronx that he apparently shared with a girlfriend, one Naomi Barnes. Ms. Barnes initially refused to cooperate, but she eventually came around. She gave us the registration for the car, and, more importantly, she told us where Mr. Hanson did his banking. Interestingly, the car was not registered to Mr. Hanson. There was also no account in Mr. Hanson's name at the bank Ms. Barnes led us to. But there was a bank account in the name of the man to whom the car was registered, and it contained a balance of $97,600. A brief, informal conversation with the bank manager, with whom I have a casual working relationship, revealed that the sum of exactly $150,000 had been deposited the previous Friday. The deposit, by the way, had been made in cash."

"And I've got to assume that any cash that was deposited had already been thoroughly laundered, so that's probably a dead end."

"I fear you are correct, Mr. Welles," said Tommassino Fornaio. "In any event, we wanted to be thorough, so we inquired of Ms. Barnes if she knew anything about the person who apparently owned the car and the bank account."

"And she said that he and Joe Hanson were the same person," said Levi.

"Yes, she did. She said that Joe Hanson was just his working name. His real name was the one listed on the car registration and the bank account."

It struck Levi like a sudden gust of wind. He remained quiet, but Tommassino Fornaio looked at him with his clear, intelligent, blue eyes, and he saw the realization dawning on Levi's face.

"But perhaps I don't have to tell you what that name was," said Fornaio.

"Please, do."

"It's a name that means nothing to me, Mr. Welles. It was Roberts. Kurt Roberts."

⊶⊷

Tommassino Fornaio had arranged for a car and driver to bring Levi back into the city, leaving a flock of chagrined reporters and photographers milling in the commuter parking lot when a nondescript young man in a dark suit came by and drove the rented Camry away.

Levi, in the meantime, tried to order his thoughts as he settled into the rich leather rear seat of the black Mercedes-Benz that was bearing him back to New York City.

Could they have been wrong all along? Could Kurt Roberts have indeed acted alone, extracting vengeance for the terrible injury inflicted on his father a lifetime ago?

No. Levi refused to believe that. He had to believe that Kurt's involvement in Stephanie French's murder was simply one of those bizarre accidents of chance that happen more often than people think. Or if it weren't pure chance, it was at least some confluence of circumstance and purpose that appears to be chance but isn't.

Kurt Roberts, aka Joe Hanson, had obviously lived and plied his trade in New York City for many years. It was entirely possible that he had at some time or another recognized Stephanie French as his long ago stepsister, Astrid Halvorsen. Or maybe not. People come to New York City to leave their pasts behind, to become anonymous, and New York City usually accommodates them. It certainly had in Kurt's case. And Kurt Roberts in all likelihood didn't make a habit of reading the *Wall Street Journal*. And if he had known, why would he have kept that knowledge to himself for so many years? Why hadn't he long ago used that knowledge to destroy Stephanie's reputation and career, or at least tried? From what little Levi knew of him, Kurt Roberts was not a man willing or able to control his impulses.

But he was speculating, and he didn't have time for that. The hard fact was that someone had paid Kurt Roberts what was to him an enormous sum of money to murder Stephanie French. The rest Levi had to ascribe to some degree of circumstance. Perhaps he'd find out the details someday, perhaps he wouldn't. Right now, he couldn't allow himself that distraction. He and Lieutenant Hudson had a murder to solve, and he knew that they were achingly close.

He tried to call Walter as he neared Manhattan, but for the first time in Leviticus Welles's memory, he got no response.

24

"MS. BARSTOW, I'm not sure you want to be here for this," said Detective Lieutenant Walter Hudson, looking hard, not at April Barstow, but at the man who had just entered the room.

April Barstow wasn't at all sure she wanted to be there either. She'd endured a lifetime of her father's antics, and she didn't know if she could bear any more. But as she looked at him, she didn't know if she should leave him alone. In just the past week, he had appeared to shrink and wither. She couldn't help noticing when he entered his study that he was walking with a noticeable limp; and the side of his mouth that drooped was glistening with saliva. Only one eye seemed to be blinking.

But it wasn't just that. In only a few days back at work, it had become painfully obvious to everyone except Bryce Barstow that he simply was no longer even remotely up to the job. He couldn't remember the details of a meeting that he had chaired only two hours before, and in one embarrassing meeting on Wednesday, he had stopped speaking in mid-sentence, unable to remember what he'd been saying, or even the purpose of the meeting.

The Board of Directors had secretly convened the night before and had agreed to meet on Saturday morning, less than forty-eight hours from now, to choose a new interim Chief Executive Officer. April was relieved to hear that she would not even be on the slate. She knew that it would be a horrible blow to her father when he found out, but she was surprised to discover just how little she cared about that.

But even now, while so many long-buried antipathies toward the man were finally maturing in her mind like a late blooming flower, April hesitated to leave him alone with Detective Lieutenant Walter Hudson. Hudson was not a subtle man, and she knew that he was here because, at least in his own mind, he had solved Stephanie French's murder, and that her father was going to help him gain whatever proof he still needed. In his current condition, her father would be no match for the implacable cop.

April had scant experience with Hudson, but she'd had enough to know that violence, both physical and psychological, was one of the foundations of his personality; and even though she had never felt even remotely threatened by him, she had no doubt that he would destroy what was left of her father to get what he needed, and it wouldn't take him long.

"I'm a grown woman, Lieutenant, and I have few illusions left. My father is not a well man, and I think I should stay with him."

"Your choice," said Walter, knowing just by looking at Bryce Barstow that what he was about to do to him would most likely complete his destruction, and that April Barstow, a woman he liked, knew that. He knew he should care, but the devils inside him that made him such a relentlessly good detective had taken over, and the part of him, the very real part, that was a loving father, a faithful husband, and a decent Christian, quietly stepped aside.

As for Bryce Barstow, he'd gotten what he wanted: he'd gotten his company back, if only temporarily. But gazing across the room at Lieutenant Hudson, he felt like an aging boxer looking across the ring at the young contender who would now inevitably conquer him and howl in victory as he, helpless, could no longer prove that he was once the better man. He knew that in the end surrender was inevitable, but that didn't mean that he'd go down without a fight.

"I don't recall inviting you into my home, Lieutenant."

"Dad, please think before you speak," said April, but he dismissed her with a wave of his hand.

"It's your home, Mr. Barstow. If you ask me to leave, I'm out of here," said Hudson.

"I'll keep that in mind. April, will you get us some coffee, please?" said Barstow as he walked slowly over to a chair that was out of the sunlight that poured into the room.

"None for me, thanks," said Hudson, taking a chair opposite Barstow.

"Suit yourself," said Barstow.

April brought her father a cup of coffee and set it on a table that he could reach with his good hand, but he made no attempt to pick it up. She took a seat on a small settee on the other side of the study, in the sunlight.

"Why don't you tell me about that photo, Mr. Barstow," said Walter, pointing to the picture on the wall that he'd shown Herbert Gray.

"What picture?" said Barstow, trying to crane his head to look where Hudson was pointing.

"Here, let me help," said Walter. He stood and took the framed photograph down from the wall and handed it to Barstow.

Bryce Barstow stared at the picture for a few seconds then looked up at Hudson with an expression that was already becoming disoriented and said, "Okay. So what?"

"Who are the men in that photo, Mr. Barstow?"

"Well, there's me, of course. And the other two men are Hollings Harkin IV and Harold Manlius."

"Do you remember anything about the photo? When it was taken? Where? What was the occasion?"

"Oh, I don't remember exactly. It was probably to celebrate some deal we'd just completed, that's all. I don't remember exactly which one."

"So the three of you worked together a lot?" said Hudson, knowing the same thing.

"Of course we did. We'd all gone to school together and made our way in the world together. Harold would come up with a project, usually some big skyscraper; Hollings would do the legal work, and I'd put together the financing. We did it all the time, and we all got rich. Is that some kind of crime, Lieutenant?"

"No, of course it's not," said Walter. He paused a moment and then said, "How else did you celebrate, Mr. Barstow?"

"I don't know what you mean," said Barstow, looking genuinely confused.

"Did you ever celebrate with, say, women?"

"I have no idea what you're talking about," said Barstow, but this time Walter could see his face redden, and a look of dawning recognition on his sagging features.

"Mr. Barstow, let me get to the point. I showed a copy of this picture to a man named Herbert Gray."

"Never heard of him."

"He's the assistant manager at the Hotel Grenadier, just as he was thirty years ago."

"So?"

"So he remembers the night thirty years ago when the three of you raped a young stripper in a suite at the hotel."

"I never raped anybody!" said Barstow, but his eyes were starting to dance, and panic was setting in. Drool ran freely from the corner of his mouth.

"We have a witness who will testify that the young woman was raped, Mr. Barstow." Walter knew he was stretching the truth. Gerald Finklestein hadn't actually witnessed the rape, and Stephanie French was dead. But he wasn't conducting a trial. He'd let the lawyers worry about all that.

"That's impossible!"

"Is it?" said Walter, letting the question hang, watching Bryce Barstow's mind freeze as it tried to reconstruct the ancient memory. It was only a matter of time now.

"Listen to me, Lieutenant, I never raped that young girl, do you hear me?"

Across the room Walter heard April gasp. He looked at her briefly. She'd lost all her color and her lips were quivering, but Detective Hudson didn't have time for her, not now.

"So you remember the night, and you remember the girl," said Hudson, keeping the man's mind locked in the past.

"I'm not saying that," said Barstow, but he'd trapped himself, and he knew it. Dammit! What was wrong with him? How had he allowed himself to get drawn into this discussion?

"Then what are you saying, Mr. Barstow?"

"What?"

"You were just saying that you deny raping that young girl."

"Yes, of course I do," said Barstow, desperately trying to collect his thoughts. "How many times do I have to tell you, Lieutenant? I did not rape that young woman!"

"Then maybe you better tell me who did. Maybe we can help you with the criminal assault and sex with a minor charges if you cooperate."

"Jesus," said Barstow.

"I don't think he had anything to do with this, Mr. Barstow."

"Spare me your pontifications."

"You're running out of time, Mr. Barstow," said Walter, looking impatiently at his watch. He knew how much perpetrators hated that gesture.

"Look, Lieutenant, I was drunk, but I'm telling you, I didn't rape anyone, and no one can prove that I did."

"Good for you. Keep going."

"Okay, okay. You're right. We'd just closed a big deal, and we wanted to celebrate. Hollings Harkin said maybe it was a good time for one of our private parties."

"Then this wasn't the first time you did this. Or even the second or the third."

"We were rich, successful men in our prime, Lieutenant. We took what was ours."

There was a rustling in the far corner of the room, and when Walter turned his head to look, April was standing. Her legs were shaking and her face was bright pink as she stared at her father. She opened her mouth as if to say something, but nothing came out. Suddenly, she fled the room, slamming the door behind her.

"She never had what it took," said Barstow, more to himself than Walter, looking at the closed door. "None of this would've happened if she did."

My God, thought Walter.

"You're stalling," he said. "Tell me."

"Okay, okay. Like I said, I was pretty drunk, and Harkin was plastered. He was already a falling down drunk, even back then. Anyway, Harold said he'd been to a local strip club the week before, and he'd seen this girl, that she was really something, and he'd ordered her up special."

"Did he say which club?"

"Yeah, it was the Leopard Lounge. It was one of his favorites. Anyway, we got to the room, and I've got to say, I was kind of shocked."

"About what?"

"Look, Lieutenant, you've gotta understand," said Barstow, glancing over to the chair his daughter had just vacated, "these girls were usually, well, pro's. A lot of them had drug problems, and all of them had been around the block, you know? They were pretty much okay with anything we did as long as the money was good. It was just business, you know?"

"Sure," said Walter.

"But this girl, she was different."

"What do you mean?"

"Well, first of all, she was so, you know, young."

"You mean she was underage and you knew it."

"I had no way of knowing that, Lieutenant."

"Then what?"

"She just seemed so, I guess, youthful. There was something naïve about her, I guess you'd say."

"What happened next?"

"She did her, you know, routine, her striptease, which was apparently all she thought she was there for."

"How did you know that?"

"Because as soon as she was done, she picked up her clothes and started to head off to the bathroom like she was finished."

"But you guys were expecting more."

"Well, Harold was."

"But you and Harkin weren't?"

"By that point, Lieutenant, Hollings Harkin was just about unconscious, and I was, I guess you could say, hesitant."

"You're not going to try to tell me you were having some sort of moral qualms."

Bryce Barstow stared uncomprehendingly at Walter for long seconds. "I just didn't want to get involved with an underage girl," he finally said, his face blank, "that's all."

"And what about Manlius?"

"When the girl started to head to the bathroom, he said, 'Hey, where the hell do you think you're going? We're just getting started here.' And she said, 'Look, mister, I'm not looking for any trouble, but I was sent here to strip, that's it. If you don't want to pay me, that's fine, but that's all I'm gonna do.'"

"I take it that must have made Manlius pretty angry."

"You don't know Harold Manlius, do you Lieutenant?" said Barstow, an amused grin on his face.

"What do you mean?" said Walter.

"That was music to Harold's ears."

"What was?"

"Realizing that the girl was unwilling, maybe even scared. A lot of times he'd make a girl pretend to be like that. It helped him, you know, get aroused. But this girl didn't have to act, she really didn't want it. Harold's hard-on almost popped his zipper before he could get his pants off." Bryce Barstow, by now completely immersed in his story, smiled at the recollection.

"Then what?" said Walter.

"Well, Harold Manlius is a big guy, and he was awfully strong back then, still is, but this little girl, she fought back like a tiger. Harold said, 'Bryce, get over here, I need some help.' I was pissed that he used my name, you know? But there was nothing I could do about it at that point, so I went over to the bed where he'd managed to get her. He flipped her over so she was face down, as usual, and he told me to hold her down."

"What do you mean, 'as usual'?"

"Oh, that's just the way Harold liked it," said Barstow, once again smiling as though he were recalling an amusing episode from a family picnic. "He used to say that he liked to make them 'take it like a man.' I told him he didn't know what he was missing, especially with that girl. I mean, she was…" He caught himself and stopped, snapping himself back to the present.

"And then?"

"And then, what?" said Barstow, as if suddenly realizing that he wasn't just swapping tales over beers at a bar.

"What happened next?"

"Nothing happened. When Harold was done, we left. We practically had to carry Hollings out of there, but that was nothing unusual."

"What about the girl?"

"What about her?"

"Did you at least make sure that she was okay before you left?"

Bryce Barstow gave Hudson an uncomprehending look, like he'd just been asked if he wanted red wine with his fish at a fine restaurant. "I don't know, she was out like a light when we left. Harold always gave the girls a shot of something while they were down so they wouldn't follow us out of the hotel," he said, as if he were describing a sound business decision.

Hudson decided not to bother Barstow about the tattoo. He didn't have to.

"One more question, Mr. Barstow," said Hudson. Until this moment, he had been absolutely convinced that Bryce Barstow had known who that young woman in the hotel room was, that the episode had been the source of his antipathy, even fear, of Stephanie French for all these years. But now he was no longer sure. He had to find out.

"What?" said Barstow, sagging in his chair.

"Do you have any idea who that young woman in the hotel room was?"

"What do you mean? She was a stripper. How should I know who she was?"

"You never saw her again?"

"Of course not. Why should I?"

"That young stripper, Mr. Barstow, was Stephanie French."

Walter didn't know how Bryce Barstow would react to the revelation, but he certainly didn't expect the one he got.

"It was?"

"Yes, it was."

A genuine grin spread across Bryce Barstow's wasted face.

"Huh," he said, amusement in his eyes, "I wonder if that means Harold Manlius was the last guy to fuck her? That'd be just Harold's luck, you know?"

25

"LET'S NOT GET AHEAD OF OURSELVES HERE," said Leviticus Welles. He was sitting with Lieutenant Hudson and Detective Sanchez in a back booth at the Ninth Avenue Deli, just around the corner from the Midtown South Precinct headquarters. It was late in the afternoon, and they all had coffee cups sitting in front of them, but no one was eating. They would have met in Hudson's cubicle in the detectives' squad room, but, again, Walter didn't want to run the chance of bumping into Captain Amato. He feared that the next time he saw him he'd say or do something that Amato could use as an excuse to fire him, and the last thing he wanted to do was lose his job before he had a chance to solve Stephanie French's murder. And with his support from Commissioner Donahue pulled out from under him, at least as far as he knew, Amato just might be able to get away with it.

"What do you mean, Levi?" said Walter. "We've got Harold Manlius dead to rights on a rape charge, which also makes him the prime suspect for Stephanie French's murder. We're so close I feel like I can almost touch it."

"Walter," said Levi, "take a step back. Let's look at the rape. We have eyewitness testimony from a senile seventy year-old with an active interest in deflecting blame onto someone else, and the written testimony of a dead woman, which may or may not get past the hearsay rules if there's ever a trial."

"But we've got Herbert Gray," said Sanchez.

"Who can place the three men at the scene, but who saw nothing," said Levi. "And of course, we have Gerald Finklestein, who can testify that Stephanie looked like she'd been raped when he got there, but he's not exactly an expert on the subject, so any testimony he'd be allowed to give would be limited, at best."

"And he never saw the three guys, anyway," said Sanchez.

"Right," said Levi. "So what looks to be an open and shut case to any logical, fair-minded person is most likely a dead loser in court. And that's just on the thirty year-old rape. We're nowhere on any murder charge."

"I get it, I get it," said Walter. "But I still feel like we're just one piece of a jigsaw puzzle away from having the whole thing fall in place."

"We may be," said Levi, "but where's that one piece?"

"I have no idea," said Walter, "and we're running out of time. It's almost dinnertime, and my twenty-four hours from Donahue run out early tomorrow morning."

"Assuming you still have your twenty-four hours," said Levi.

"Don't remind me."

"You know," said Sanchez, his eyes suddenly widening, "with all the running around we've been doing, there's something really obvious we've missed."

"I'd love to know what it is," said Walter.

"How did Kurt Roberts know Stephanie was going to Penn Station, and when?" said Eduardo.

"He followed her, I guess," said Walter.

"He couldn't have," said Eduardo. "She was in a limo, so he would've either had to drive himself, take a cab, or take the subway. The odds are pretty slim that he could have found out where she was going, beaten her uptown, and gotten himself into position in time to kill her. He had to have at least a little advance notice."

"I think Eduardo's got a point," said Levi. "If he was just following her around, looking for an opportunity to kill her, he would've been hanging around downtown, either near Barstow & Company or her apartment in the Village."

"But whoever hired him didn't want that," said Walter, catching on.

"That's right," said Levi, "because he didn't want this to look like a targeted hit on Stephanie French. He wanted it to look like the random mob hit that everybody now seems to think it was. 'Nothing to see here, folks, we can all move on.'"

"So they were waiting for her to be somewhere random," said Eduardo, "somewhere where she could've been just an unlucky victim of gang violence."

"And that's tough to do in this city," said Levi, "especially when you're targeting a woman who doesn't walk places or take mass transportation."

"Not impossible, but it can be done," said Walter.

"Sure it can," said Levi, "if you've got all the time in the world."

"But whoever wanted her dead didn't have all the time in the world," said Eduardo.

"If we're right about all this," said Levi, "they'd already run out of time. They'd probably wanted the job done before she was ever named CEO."

"That's only if you believe it was somebody inside Barstow & Company who plotted her murder," said Walter, "and not Harold Manlius."

"Walter," said Levi, "I know why you think Manlius did it. But we have nothing, Walter, nothing, that ties him to Stephanie's murder."

"Look," said Eduardo, "why don't we step back from all that. I'm guessing whoever did this had some help from inside Barstow & Company, somebody who'd know Stephanie's movements and could tip off the shooter so he could be in place."

"Do you think he could've been in cahoots with one of the company limo drivers?" said Walter.

"I don't know how that would've worked," said Eduardo. "The company owns a fleet of limos, and there's a pool of drivers. It's not like there's a driver assigned to each executive. So, if Kurt Roberts wanted to bribe a driver, or even blackmail one, how would he know which one to pick?"

"So what are you saying, Eduardo?" said Walter.

"I'm saying there's gotta be somebody actually inside the company, somebody who was at that Board meeting when Stephanie was elected CEO, who called Kurt Roberts and told him when she was leaving and where she was going."

"I know that kind of blows up your theory about Harold Manlius, Walter," said Levi, "but it seems to make sense."

"I still think it was Manlius," said Walter.

"Walter," said Levi, "don't fall in love with your own theory. You're the best detective in this city, so you know how deadly that can be."

"I know that, Levi. That's Rule Number One. But I honestly don't think I'm doing that."

"Why not?"

"Because Rule Number Two, at least in my book, is 'listen to your gut,' and my gut tells me that even though there are a lot of squirrely people at the top of Barstow & Company, I haven't met one of them who feels like a stone killer to me."

"But lots of people had motives," said Eduardo. "I mean, look at that nut job Hollings Harkin, or Seth Stone, or even April Barstow. I know she looks like Sweet Polly Purebread, but you never know what a kid'll do for a parent."

"Or vice versa," said Levi.

"I hear you guys," said Walter, "I really do, but I think Stephanie French was going to tell her story about the rape. She'd kept quiet for all these years, but she wasn't going to allow Harold Manlius to take over this city, no matter what she had to reveal about herself or what it might have done to her career."

"But Walter," said Levi, "how could Manlius have known that?"

"Because I think Stephanie French told him, that's why," said Walter. He was thinking out loud now, but he felt a curtain being raised in his mind.

"Sir, with all due respect," said Eduardo, "that makes absolutely no sense."

"I've got to agree with Eduardo," said Levi. "And you have absolutely no evidence that any conversation like that ever took place."

"Look guys, I know I'm stretching things, but think about it. The last thing on earth that Stephanie French would have wanted to do is publicly expose Harold Manlius."

"What d'you mean?" said Eduardo. "That was what she was waiting all her life to do."

"That's what I've been thinking, too, Eduardo," said Walter, "but I've been wrong. Think about it. Why the hell would she do that unless she absolutely had to? There was a reason she'd kept quiet all her life. She must have wanted desperately to keep the life she had. She wanted to keep her job at Barstow & Company so she could keep providing financial security to all those young women she was helping through the Balboa Fund. She wanted to keep doing her work at SafeWays without making it controversial by association with her. And she wanted to keep playing her music in her own quiet way. All that would have been at risk if she had made her story public."

"Maybe, maybe not," said Levi. "From everything we've heard, she was a charming, beloved woman. It's possible she could have gone on doing all that."

"But it's also possible that she couldn't have," said Walter, "and I don't think she wanted to take that chance, not unless she had to."

"So what are you thinking?" said Levi.

"I'm thinking that she would have given Harold Manlius fair warning. She would have given him a chance to drop out of the race quietly and retire from public life. He could make up his own reasons why for public consumption."

"What, and let those three guys off the hook for raping her and abusing God knows how many other women?"

"Yes."

"But why?" said Eduardo.

"Because Hollings Harkin IV and Bryce Barstow have already been sentenced to death, Harkin from alcoholism and Barstow probably from another stroke. You should see the man: he's on his last legs."

"And Manlius?" said Levi.

"All she wanted to do was keep him out of Gracie Mansion. If she could make that happen without destroying her own life, I think she would've been more than willing to do it, or at least try. Remember, she's kept her past quiet all these years, I'm guessing because she believed the work she was doing was more important than getting revenge. I think she might have tried to keep it that way."

"I hate to say it," said Eduardo, "but you're starting to convince me."

"But there was only one problem, wasn't there, Walter," said Levi.

"Yes, there was, Levi. One very big one."

"What are you guys talking about?" said Eduardo, but the question was no sooner out of his mouth than he knew. "Oh."

"That's right," said Levi. "If Walter's right, and Stephanie tried to convince Manlius privately to step down, she was also giving him the time and the opportunity to shut her up, permanently."

"Why would she have done that, then?" said Eduardo.

"I don't know, but I think she did," said Walter.

"My guess would be," said Levi, "that she'd figured that, like most men like him, he was basically a coward, and he'd just back off."

"But she was wrong," said Walter. "And it cost her her life."

"Okay," said Eduardo, "so are you saying Manlius had a spy on the Barstow & Company Board of Directors?"

"Let's look at it this way, Eduardo," said Walter, "no matter who's right, there must've been someone inside Barstow, someone willing to sell Stephanie out. If you guys are right, it was the person who wanted Stephanie's job. If I'm right, I think Manlius must have had something on someone," said Walter, "blackmail, or a bribe, or something. But we don't need to know that right now. All we need to know is who did she tell where she was going when she left Barstow & Company last Friday morning?"

"Who d'you think that would be?" said Eduardo.

"I don't know, but I've got a guess," said Walter.

"So do I," said Levi. "The only person with a really close relationship with Stephanie."

"You mean," said Eduardo, "April Bar…"

"Damn!" said Walter, slamming his huge fist down on the table so hard it spilled what was left of the coffee in their cups and made every other customer in the diner jump. "Dammit to hell!" He stood up. "Levi, did you drive your car up here?"

"Yes," said Levi, "it's parked around the corner. Why?"

"I need to borrow it."

"Where are you going?" said Levi and Eduardo in unison.

"Look," said Walter. "I need you guys to do a couple of things for me. Levi, I need you to talk to Commissioner Donahue and give him an update. All I need is for him to live up to his promise to give me twenty-four hours. Eduardo, I need you to get down to Barstow & Company before it closes and talk to April Barstow before she leaves."

"So you think…?" said Eduardo.

"No," said Walter, "that's not what I think." Then he took Levi's keys and ran out of the diner, but not before telling Leviticus Welles and Eduardo Sanchez exactly what he thought.

26

"TALK TO ME, EDUARDO," said Lieutenant Hudson as he roared up the New York State Thruway doing ninety in Levi's Mercedes-Benz 550SL. It was actually Julie's car, though she rarely drove it, intimidated by the little monster's power, but quiet Levi loved it. Levi had called ahead to the New York State Police to give them a heads-up that Walter would be on the road, so the stunned drivers who swerved to get out of the way as he roared by them were all that slowed him down.

"You were right, Lieutenant," said Eduardo, his voice sounding tinny but clear through the tiny Bluetooth device stuck in Walter's ear.

"That'd be the first time in a while. What was I right about?"

"Well, I talked to April Barstow and she said, yeah, Stephanie mentioned to her just before she left the office that morning that she had a train to catch at Penn Station, and that she had to stop off at her apartment first, so she really had to get going."

"Did April know if she told anybody else?"

"She said she couldn't know for sure, but she thinks all Stephanie said to everyone else was that she had a rehearsal for her concerts that she couldn't miss, and that she was really sorry that she couldn't stay for the luncheon they'd planned for her, you know, that kind of thing."

"So Stephanie didn't tell anyone else she was heading to Penn Station?" said Walter, letting the car decelerate. Perhaps he'd been wrong once again.

"No. April said the only other person who would've heard Stephanie say that would've been Barbara Grunewald who was, I guess as usual, standing right next to April the whole time."

Walter stepped on the gas, and the little car leaped ahead.

"Thanks, Eduardo, that's just what I needed to hear."

"And sir?"

"Yeah?" said Walter, only half listening as he concentrated on driving.

"April also told me that Harold Manlius is on the Board of Trustees of Brentwood College. In fact, he's the chairman of the Finance Committee. She said you might want to know that."

SAUGERTIES, NEW YORK, looked like a nice place to live, thought Walter, if you wanted to live in a place like that. But who was he to say? He was New York City born and bred, but he now lived part-time in tiny Dutch River, and loved every minute of it.

Brentwood College sat on a large, leafy tract of rolling countryside on the edge of town that looked out on a spectacular vista of the Hudson River. The gray granite buildings gave the campus the unlikely look of a medieval monastery and probably looked gloomy in poor weather, but the reddening sunlight on this clear spring evening cast a warm glow on the campus, and it looked almost enchanted.

Walter had stopped the car and asked the first student he saw where the president's residence was. The young woman had stared at him like he was an alien from a faraway galaxy but had pointed him in the right direction. She stared after him as he drove off.

The President's Residence, unlike the rest of the campus, was a large, wooden, two-story home of colonial design, clad in a fresh coat of white paint and adorned with green shutters. Walter assumed that it had once been a farmhouse and that the campus had once been a large farm. A late model, white Cadillac SUV and a bright red Volkswagen Jetta sat beside each other in the driveway. Walter pulled up behind the SUV, which he assumed belonged to Barbara Grunewald. He extracted his large frame from the small sports car, slipped on the gray sports jacket that he'd folded and put beside him on the passenger seat, and smoothed his burgundy necktie as he followed a brick walkway that led him up to the front door of the house. He rang the doorbell.

After what he thought had been a solid minute, Hudson was about to ring the doorbell again when Barbara Grunewald answered the front door wearing a bright smile. Her face seemed slightly flushed to him, but it was hard to tell in the fading light.

"Well, isn't this a surprise," she said, as she opened the door to let him in, her smile evaporating, her skin fading to pale. "Please come in."

Soft, classical guitar music filled Walter's ears as he stepped into a large, well-lit foyer. Barbara Grunewald stood before him wearing a raw silk blouse with the three top buttons undone and a pair of charcoal gray slacks that were probably far too tight for a woman her age. Behind her stood the owner of the Jetta, Walter presumed, a twentyish coed with long blond hair wearing a snugly fitting, light cotton sweater with "Brentwood" stitched in a baby blue thread above the left breast and a skirt that was far too short for a woman of any age. Her smile did not evaporate at the sight of Hudson.

"Good evening, Professor Grunewald, Ms…"

"It's Kaylie," said the young woman with a disarmingly frank stare, "Kaylie Talcott."

"Nice to meet you, Ms. Talcott," said Hudson to the young woman without offering a handshake. "I'm Detective Lieutenant Walter Hudson of the New York Police Department."

"You can call me Kaylie," she said, looking Hudson over as if he were a prize stallion.

"Sure," said Walter, turning to Barbara Grunewald. "Professor Grunewald, I apologize for showing up at your home at an awkward hour unannounced, but I need to talk to you on an urgent matter."

"Kaylie and I," said Barbara, looking at Kaylie and avoiding eye contact with Hudson, "were about to share a vegetarian lasagna that I have in the oven along with some fresh artisan bread. I'm sure there's… "

"Professor Grunewald, I really think I should talk to you in private."

"Whatever for?"

"Please, Professor Grunewald."

"Kaylie," said Grunewald turning back to the young woman, "perhaps you should leave for a while so that Lieutenant Hudson and I can chat. Why don't you come back a little later and I can warm up the lasagna?"

Kaylie took her eyes off Hudson and regarded Grunewald with a neutral expression, "Oh, that's okay, Barbara, I mean, Professor Grunewald. I've got a paper to write. I'll see you around." She gave Hudson another long, hard look as she walked out the door. "Nice to meet you," she said.

Barbara Grunewald stared after Kaylie as she left. "Well," she said, after a long pause, "I'd better get that lasagna out of the oven. Please, Lieutenant, take a seat in the living room while I take care of the casserole and change out of these cooking clothes. I've opened a lovely bottle of Soave, would you like a glass?" She stared at the headlights of the Jetta as it backed out of the driveway, an unfathomable expression on her face.

"No, thanks, ma'am," he said, taking a seat in the tastefully but predictably appointed room as Grunewald left.

She returned after a few minutes. Her blouse was buttoned up to the collar and she'd donned a looser fitting pair of slacks. Walter thought she might have freshened her makeup. She held a glass of wine in her hand.

"Are you sure you won't join me?" she said, holding up her glass as she took a seat opposite Hudson.

"No, thank you, ma'am," he said.

"Well, then. How may I help you?"

"I need to ask you a few more questions regarding the murder of Stephanie French, Professor."

"I'm more than happy to cooperate, Lieutenant, but I've already spoken at length with your Detective Sanchez. I really don't know what I can add."

"Yes, I know you have, but I have some further questions to ask."

"What type of questions?"

"In particular, ma'am, I'd like to ask you about your relationship with Harold Manlius."

"Relationship? With Harold Manlius?" said Barbara, affecting a bashful smile. "Lieutenant Hudson, if you're implying that I am somehow romantically involved with Harold Manlius…"

"I'm not implying that at all, ma'am."

"Then what are you implying?"

"Ma'am, we know you spoke to Harold Manlius on the day Stephanie French was murdered, just after she left the building." He knew no such thing, but he knew that he was close enough to the mark to rattle her cage.

"Lieutenant, I have no idea…"

"Ma'am, let me be blunt. I have very little time, and you have very few options. You are in very deep trouble, and I think you know that. We have evidence, strong evidence, that you conspired with Harold Manlius to murder Stephanie French. You are looking at spending the rest of your life in jail, and it won't be some minimum security day camp."

"What on earth are you talking about, Lieutenant Hudson?" said Grunewald, paling. "I never conspired to murder anyone!"

"Perhaps you were coerced, Professor Grunewald. Perhaps you're a victim of blackmail, or bribery. All I'm saying is now is the time to cooperate. If there are mitigating circumstances, the charges against you can perhaps be reduced. You may get a lighter sentence at a more bearable institution. But none of that will happen if you don't cooperate, now."

"This all comes as a shock to me, Lieutenant," said Grunewald, but she was starting to sound tentative. "I hardly know what to say to you. Perhaps I should consult my attorney," she said, fiddling with her wine glass, her face contorted in a grimace that was ruining her mascara.

"Ma'am" said Walter, as calmly as possible, "you have every right to do that, and if that is your wish I will do nothing to prevent you. In fact, I'll get in my car right now and leave If that's what you want But please remember, once you lawyer up, you've burned your bridges, and the first thing any good lawyer will do is tell you to shut up. After that, you're in the system, and there's nothing I or anyone else will be able to do for you. You'll be sitting at the defense table with Harold Manlius, and heaven help you."

Barbara Grunewald sat silently. She took a sip of her wine. She took another sip. The glass was almost empty. Walter sat back in his chair, trying to make his large presence as unimposing as possible. He'd gone way out on a limb, trusting his instincts. This was the moment he'd find out if he was right. If she were truly innocent, she'd fight back right now; she'd throw him out and call her lawyer. But Barbara Grunewald was an intelligent woman, and if she were guilty, she would know that now was her last, best chance to come clean.

"Okay, Lieutenant," she said, sighing, "you win." She rose from her chair. "I'm going to pour myself another glass of wine. Are you sure you won't join me?"

———⚓———

"IF HE'S RIGHT," said Police Commissioner Sean Michael Patrick Donahue, "we could kill a lot of birds with one stone, couldn't we?" He and Levi were alone in Donahue's private hideaway. Donahue, as usual, was standing behind the bar looking for all the world like an amiable neighborhood barkeep. He picked up the highball glass sitting in front of him, his large mitt dwarfing the glass, and took a healthy slug of the Bushmills he'd filled it with.

"Yes, we could, sir," said Levi, who was sitting on the other side of the bar on one of the unfinished oak barstools that had been the final resting place for the careers of countless unprepared detectives who, disarmed by Donahue's amiable demeanor, had never felt the noose go around their necks. He took a small sip of his whiskey.

"But if he's wrong, we're nowhere."

"I don't think he's wrong, sir."

"Neither do I, Levi. When will we know?"

"With any luck, sir, he's talking to Professor Grunewald as we speak."

"I want to know what he finds out as soon as possible. I don't care what time it is. Make sure he knows that, Levi."

"Yessir," said Levi, staring hard at his glass.

"What is it, Levi?"

"Sir, it's my understanding that this morning you met with Walter and gave him twenty-four hours to solve the case."

"I did, and he does. Between us, Levi, he's got more time than that, of course."

"Then why did you tell him that, sir?"

"Because I know my men, and Walter Hudson is a man who needs to feel pressure. He thrives on it. So I gave him some. He ought to be used to that by now."

"I think he understands that, sir. It's just that, there are awkward circumstances this time."

"What do you mean, 'awkward circumstances'?" said Donahue, wiping down the polished bar with a damp towel.

"Well, you know, sir, the letter that you asked Captain Amato to write."

"Ah," said Donahue, refilling both their glasses. It would be a late supper and an early bedtime for Levi tonight. "You must mean the letter that I asked Captain Amato to draft in strictest confidence."

"You may have asked him to do that, sir, but he told Walter about it."

"And you gather I'm shocked to hear that."

"Sir?"

"Deputy Commissioner Welles, when I was talking about how many birds I thought we could kill with one stone, I don't think you were counting as many birds as I was. Now, if my memory serves me, you are my Deputy Commissioner for Intelligence, so I might suggest to you that you find out just who else Captain Amato shared that memo with."

Commissioner Donahue took another large sip of his whiskey. Leviticus Welles took a deep breath and did the same.

"Yessir," he said.

—⁂—

"NOW, WHERE WERE WE?" said Barbara Grunewald, settling herself back in her chair and taking a sip of her wine. Walter couldn't help noticing that she'd freshened her mascara once more while she was out of the room. In an odd way, he understood.

"Harold Manlius."

"Ah, yes."

Walter was willing to be patient, but he also knew that he had to keep her talking.

"Perhaps this all has something to do with his membership on your Board of Trustees, or his role as chairman of the Finance Committee."

"I should've known you'd dig that up," said Grunewald, staring at him hard.

"It wasn't hard, ma'am, once we knew what we were looking for."

"Okay," she said. She sighed and took another long sip of her wine. "You're right." She hesitated again. "I guess I don't know where to start."

"Anywhere you want, ma'am, " said Walter, knowing that they could always patch up the chronology later. At this point, he just wanted her to talk.

"I know you'll find this ridiculous, Lieutenant, but I am a passionate woman."

"Ma'am?"

"I have been a woman of passion all my life, but like many people of my generation, it took me a long time to understand the nature of my passions. In my youth, I concluded that my passion was for the arts, particularly literature, and in a way that was true. I pursued that passion through college and graduate school. I dated a few men along the way, but that always fell flat, though neither I nor the men could ever figure out just why. All I remember is the anger that I inevitably felt afterwards, the same type of anger you feel when you're hungry and you're served the wrong order at a restaurant, I guess you'd say. I always blamed myself because I saw no reason to blame the men, but I couldn't figure out what I was blaming myself for. In any event, I rationalized that I had no time for romantic entanglements at that point in my life, and I tried to put it all out of my mind."

Barbara stared at her wineglass as if contemplating refilling it, but Walter knew she was looking at something else. He sat stock still, waiting. He didn't necessarily want to hear all this, but like so many academics, Barbara Grunewald was a talker. Once she decided to talk, she took the scenic route.

"I came to Brentwood when I was still a young woman in my twenties, right after I'd completed my Ph.D. It was a dream job at a dream college, and I couldn't have been happier. The pay was terrible, but the students were bright, the administration was supportive, and everything was new. There is nothing like teaching a course for the first time, especially when you can see the interest lighting your students' eyes as they look at you.

"Of course, this is a women's college, and I soon learned that the young women who came here, regardless of their true sexual orientation, were inclined to experiment. I was oblivious to all this until I noticed one student in particular who was looking at me with a light in her eyes that I should have known wasn't coming from the Keats poem we were studying. She came up to me one day after class and said that she was struggling with some of the poems we were reading, and perhaps she would benefit from some extra tutoring. Heaven help me, Lieutenant, I honestly believed that tutoring was all she wanted. I was still a young assistant professor then, and I shared a tiny office with another instructor, so I asked her if she would mind coming over to my apartment, where perhaps we could share some tea while we studied. She said that sounded great, so we made an appointment for the following afternoon.

"It all started innocently enough. My apartment was tiny, and all I'd managed to squeeze into my living room was an old chair, a loveseat, and a small table. I sat on the loveseat and the young woman sat on the chair, with our tea on the table between us. At one point, she got up and sat down next to me on the loveseat, so that we could both read from my textbook, she said. I'll never forget the thrill when I felt her shoulder touch mine. I never knew who started what, but all of a sudden we were kissing, and all of a sudden I knew what had been missing all my life. All of a sudden, I knew who I was.

"The next few months were perhaps the most exquisitely contented months of my life. And the lovely thing about being here at Brentwood was there was no secret shame in our relationship; there was no secret at all. We became the 'it' couple on campus, I guess you'd say.

"But then, inevitably, it all changed. My young student came back from spring break with a diamond ring on her finger. She came to my apartment and explained to me that our relationship had been lovely, and that she would always treasure the memory, but that we both knew that it would come to an end someday, and today was that day. She thanked me for all my kindness and wished me all the best. She kissed me on the cheek and left.

"I retained my composure long enough for her to close the front door behind her, and then I crumpled to the floor, sobbing. I didn't know that it would all come to an end someday; I was in love. I lay on the floor for hours, crying, simply because I couldn't get up. Thank God the next day was Saturday, and I at least had the weekend to get myself functioning again, which I absolutely had to do.

"Of course, the news of our breakup spread through the campus like wildfire, and when I walked into the classroom for my first class on Monday morning, every single pair of eyes was on me, not waiting for me to utter my first priceless pearls of wisdom about Robert Browning, but because they didn't want to miss it when I broke. Young women can be cruel, Lieutenant, and these women were like the crowd at a bullfight when first blood is drawn. It's not enough for them to know that the toreador has triumphed, that the contest is finished. That's not what they came to see. They came to see the suffering of the bull, to witness its agony, to see it fall. I couldn't let them see that, because if I did my career at Brentwood would have been finished. I knew that, and they knew that, which is what made it such a blood sport for them.

"But I didn't break. I won, and my career was saved. I kept to myself the rest of the academic year, and I took a long vacation in Italy over the summer that I couldn't afford financially but couldn't afford not to take emotionally. I came back to the campus in September feeling refreshed and rested, like my old self. I was determined not to make the same mistake twice, and I'd promised myself that any future romantic relationships, if any, would have to come from outside the campus community.

"And then I walked into my first class of the semester, a survey of Shakespeare's Tragedies, and there she was."

"April Barstow," said Walter.

"Yes, Lieutenant, April Barstow, and I knew from the moment I set eyes on her that she was the love of my life."

"I know the feeling, Ms. Grunewald."

"I'm sure you do, Lieutenant," said Barbara, turning her gaze to Walter, "but I'm also sure you don't know what it's like to realize that the feeling is not being returned."

"You're right, ma'am, I don't."

"I invited her over to my apartment about a week later, but she declined. She suggested a local coffee shop instead. I said that would be fine. I would have met her in a damp cave if that was what she wanted."

"She never led you on?"

"Not for a moment. April was as refreshingly honest then as she is today. And she wasn't cruel, as so many young women would have been. She understood the environment, and she understood my feelings, but she was very forthright. She explained to me that she simply didn't have feelings or inclinations like that. I asked her if there was a young man in her life, but she said no, she didn't have feelings or inclinations like that at this point in her life, either. Of course, I was so desperately smitten with her that that only encouraged me not to lose hope, that maybe if I was patient she would come around."

"But she never did."

"No, Lieutenant, she never did. She was always kind and friendly. She never pushed me away, but she never gave me any encouragement at all. Of course, I couldn't force myself to let go completely, so I stayed in contact with her, even after she graduated. Then, after I became president of the college, her father suggested that I might be a complementary addition to the Barstow & Company board of directors. I knew not a thing about corporations or finance, but I accepted on the spot, knowing that it would give me an excuse to see April."

"So your feelings for her never really went away?"

"Never, Lieutenant."

"Did that mean that you never had any romantic relationships after that?" said Walter, genuinely curious. He had no idea how he would have reacted if Sarah had rebuffed him. Would he have moved on? Would he have continued to pursue her?

"It depends on how you define 'romantic relationship,' I guess. You might be surprised to learn that women have sexual appetites just like men do, Lieutenant."

"I'm not surprised at all, ma'am," said Walter. Sarah had made sure he understood from the beginning that it was his job to satisfy her appetites every bit as much as it was her job to satisfy his. It was a job he relished.

"No," said Barbara, looking at him with a knowing grin, "I guess not. In any event, then I'm sure you understand that, quite apart from my romantic feelings for April, I still wanted to have some kind of a sex life. So I did what so many people in my position, gay or straight, do. I engaged in a series of short-term relationships over the years that fed the bulldog, so to speak, but that was about it. I guess in some part of my mind I hoped that someday I would meet that special someone who would help me let go of my feelings for April, but that never happened."

"Were these relationships with other students? Faculty?"

"Yes, and yes, sometimes, and sometimes not. Over the years, the administration became stricter about discouraging relationships between students and faculty, but they never took any overt action as long as there were no complaints from the students or their parents. But, that aside, I was growing older so, as you can imagine, the young students found me less and less attractive. I increasingly had to resort to dim lighting and lingerie, but that, too, became a challenge. I will never forget the morning that one of my young conquests walked into the bathroom just as I was getting out of the shower. The look on her face when she stared at my body told me everything I needed to know. It was one of the most humiliating moments of my life."

"So you moved on."

"I should have, Lieutenant. Heaven help me, I should have, but I didn't."

"Then what did you do?"

"I sweetened the pot, so to say."

"How did you do that?"

"Oh, at first it was simply an implicit understanding that they would get a good grade in my courses, that kind of thing. But soon that wasn't enough, either."

"Then what?"

"Lieutenant, this is becoming increasingly painful for me. I hope you won't mind if I refill my wine glass. Are you sure you won't share a glass with me?"

"I really can't, ma'am. I'm on duty, but please, go ahead."

Barbara rose and left the room, leaving Walter desperately hoping that they would get to the point of all this soon. It wasn't that he was an unsympathetic man, but he was running out of time. She returned shortly, and he noticed that she hadn't bothered to freshen her makeup this time, but her glass was filled to the brim. They were getting to the point, he guessed.

"Where were we?" she said. "Oh, yes. A few years back, I bought a timeshare in the Bahamas. I would invite the current object of my affections to stay with me over spring break as an enticement. But I was forced to realize that even that was no longer working when I stumbled upon one of the young women in bed, my bed, with a young man she'd met on the beach."

"I'm sorry, ma'am."

"So was I, Lieutenant. But at least it forced me to realize how humiliating all this had become, and I told myself to stop."

"Did you?"

"Yes, I did, for many years. But then, last January, I walked into my first class of the spring semester."

"But you were the president of the college by then. You mean you kept teaching?"

"Only one course a semester. I thought it was important not to let my teaching skills get rusty, and it was a good way to stay in touch with the students. And besides, I love teaching. But this was one course I should never have taught."

"Why not?"

"Because there, sitting in the front row, was April Barstow."

"*What?*"

"Oh, no, Lieutenant, not the real April Barstow, but a young woman who could have been April Barstow, the young April who had so captivated me all those years ago. I took one look at her and my knees almost buckled. She noticed, of course, and gave me what I recall was a seductive smile right there in the classroom."

"So what did you do?"

"I didn't do anything. I didn't have to. Unlike the real April, this young woman wasn't shy at all. She came up to me after that first class and invited herself over to my house that afternoon. I knew what was coming, and I told myself I would not allow myself to be drawn in, but I simply couldn't resist. Before I knew it, we were involved in a full-blown affair."

"Did you invite her to your timeshare over spring break?"

"Once again, there was no need. She just invited herself down and that was that. Somewhere deep down I knew this was all a big mistake, that nothing good would come of it. I even recognized, at least on some level, that there was possibly an ulterior motive, an agenda. But I'm ashamed to say that I couldn't force myself to break it off. And, of course, I was right. On our second night at the timeshare, she sat me down and told me that she was having problems."

"Did she say what kind of problems?"

"Money problems."

"What did she do, ask you for a loan?"

"No, no loans. She said she needed a $25,000 unrestricted grant in order to continue her education, and she wanted me to arrange it for her. I knew it was a lie. Her parents were extremely wealthy. She was receiving no financial aid at all. The checks for the full amount of tuition, room, and board arrived like clockwork, and they all cleared."

"I'm sorry, what's an 'unrestricted grant'? Is it like a scholarship?"

"No, it's not. Scholarships are awards that are simply deducted from one's academic bills. Money is never actually given to the student. Grants are payments made directly to the recipient and often do not require the funds to be used to offset tuition and fees. And they are never, ever, awarded to undergraduates. They are mostly given to faculty to pursue important research, or, rarely, to extremely gifted graduate students."

"What did you tell her?"

"I told her that it would be impossible, but of course she didn't accept that answer. I told her that perhaps I could nominate her for a scholarship, but she scoffed at that."

"So she was shaking you down."

"Crudely put, but accurate. She apparently wanted money to spend on activities she wanted to keep from her parents. I never knew exactly what."

"Couldn't you have paid her out of your own pocket?"

"I am the president of a small, impoverished college, Lieutenant. My compensation comes to me mostly in the form of prestige. You would be surprised at how little I am paid. I live in this house for free, but I have to furnish it and maintain it myself even though the college owns it. Of course that means I have no equity in it. I have exclusive use of the SUV, but, like the house, it belongs to the school. Every penny I earned was sunk into my timeshare and this home. I live, literally, from paycheck to paycheck. The only thing that keeps me afloat is my stipend for serving on the Board of Barstow & Company."

"Did you ever consider reporting her?"

"Lieutenant, I'm sure you read the newspapers. College campuses are surreal places these days. This is the age of micro-aggressions and safe-speech zones. There is no due process of law on college campuses. If a young woman makes an accusation of sexual trespass against a young man, that man is presumed guilty unless he can categorically prove himself innocent, and his life can be destroyed without ever being granted an actual trial."

"And I suppose that goes for college presidents, too, regardless of gender."

"Oh, yes, it does. And my young lover made it perfectly clear that if I did not come through with her 'grant,' she would report me to the administration the minute she returned to campus. And I, Lieutenant Hudson, would be ruined."

"What did you do?"

"I told her I understood and that the check would be waiting for her when we returned to campus. She said 'thank you so much' and gave me one of her lovely smiles. And then she took me by the hand and led me to the bedroom. And yes, Lieutenant, of course I did. The video, of course, showed up in my email the next day."

"I'm sorry," said Hudson, inwardly wincing. What would he have done? "Do you know if she shared the video with anyone else?"

"No, I do not, and I doubt I ever will."

"So then what? I assume that grants have to go through an approval process."

"Yes, they do. But I'm the president of the college, and I have what the lawyers would call a lot of 'apparent authority.' So I typed up an official-looking request for payment and brought it directly to a young staff member in the bursar's office. I could tell she was skeptical, but she had a very difficult time refusing me while I was standing right there, and I walked out with the check in my hands. My lover was waiting for me at my home when I returned. She took the check from me without saying 'thank you' and left. I haven't seen her since."

"Then she wasn't the young woman I met when I got here."

"No, she wasn't," said Barbara, giving Walter a neutral stare.

"I'm guessing," said Walter, "that you wouldn't have told me all this if that was the end of it. What happened?"

"For a couple of weeks I thought I'd actually gotten away with it. No one said anything, and life went on. Of course, I was cured of my young lover for good, and the only thing I felt was relief. But then one day I received a phone call from Harold Manlius. Apparently that young woman in the bursar's office had experienced a fit of conscience and had reported the $25,000 payment to her boss, who in turn, because it involved the president of the college, decided to take it directly to the chairman of the Finance Committee himself. I tried a couple of lame explanations, but they didn't work with a man as sophisticated as Manlius. I wound up begging him for a chance to make it right."

"And that's when the blackmail began."

"I wouldn't call it 'blackmail,' Lieutenant."

"Then what was it?"

"It was a way out. He told me that my admirably generous nature had led me to an ill-considered decision, a decision that he knew I regretted and that in no way should threaten my career. He said he was sure that he could find a way to make it right. I told him that I was in no position to return the money, but he said that wouldn't be necessary."

"Because he volunteered to return the money out of his own pocket and massage the whole thing with the bursar's office, right?"

"That, and much more."

"How much more?"

"He said he understood that the college was on the verge of insolvency. He'd always been a strong supporter of women's rights, he said, and it would be a shame if an all-women's institution like Brentwood College were allowed to fail. He offered to help, if I were willing to cooperate with him."

"Help how?" said Walter. He had to admit that Harold Manlius had brass.

"He promised an unrestricted $50 million dollar donation to our endowment, that's how. He promised to save my college."

And there it was, thought Walter. Only a few months ago, he would have been shocked. But the *Dutch River* and *Placid Hollow* cases had opened his eyes to the world of immense wealth, wealth inconceivable to most people, especially NYPD cops. He now knew that the extraordinary sum of $50 million was a mere trifle to the Harold Manliuses of this world, especially since he knew that in return he'd be getting Stephanie French handed to him on a platter. The only question left was the extent of Barbara Grunewald's complicity.

"And what did he want in return?"

"He told me that he had been Barstow & Company's largest client for forty years and that he was concerned about rumors he was hearing that Stephanie French would be named CEO when Bryce Barstow stepped down, which he assumed would be soon due to Barstow's 'recent illness,' as he called it. He said he was convinced that she was the wrong choice for the job."

"What did he do, demand that you lobby against her promotion?" said Walter, knowing that it didn't make sense. Manlius didn't give a damn if Stephanie became CEO. He only cared about what she was about to make public, and he wanted her dead.

"That was the funny thing," said Barbara, a genuinely perplexed expression on her face, "he didn't ask for anything of the sort."

"Then what did he ask for?"

"All he asked was that I keep track of her, that if I knew she had an appointment, or a dinner, or a recital, that I just give him a call and let him know. I reminded him that I didn't work at Barstow & Company, so my opportunities would be limited."

"What did he say?"

"He said that he was pretty sure that there would be plenty of Board meetings in the near future and I would have plenty of contact with Stephanie."

"What did you think about that?"

"What I was supposed to think, I guess. I thought that he was looking to find her in compromising situations, personal or professional, that could be used to discredit her as a candidate for the top job at Barstow & Company."

"And you were okay if he did that?"

"Of course I wasn't okay with it, Lieutenant! But it was what I had to do if I wanted to save my school, and, yes, my job and my reputation as well. I didn't support Stephanie for the CEO job anyway, so I have to admit I didn't see it as much of a price to pay. And it was a way for me to help April."

"And it never occurred to you that Manlius wanted to keep track of Stephanie's whereabouts in order to set her up to be murdered?"

Barbara impulsively reached for her almost empty wineglass. "Jesus, Lieutenant…"

But Walter Hudson never got to hear her response, as the first shot rang out and Barbara Grunewald and her wineglass fell to the floor, both shattered.

27

"**G**OOD EVENING, Deputy Commissioner Welles," came the calm, distinct voice over the line. But for the first time, Levi heard a sense of urgency in it.

"Good evening, Mr. Fornaio," said Levi, sitting in his office in One Police Plaza. He could hear the sounds of clinking glass and loud, politely inebriated voices in the background. He recalled that Fornaio and his wife were attending some kind of social event at the Waldorf. "To what do I owe the honor?"

"Pardon me if I skip the pleasantries," said Fornaio, "but I just received some disturbing information from extremely reliable sources that you need to know if you don't already."

"What would that be?" said Levi, sitting straighter in his chair.

"You apparently have a mole in the NYPD, Mr. Welles, a mole that is funneling information directly to the Manlius organization."

"I guess I shouldn't be surprised," said Levi, thinking back to the embarrassing photos of himself and Lieutenant Hudson that had popped up in the newspapers.

"Specifically, it looks like this mole has information regarding the whereabouts of your colleague, Detective Lieutenant Hudson. He seems to have access to the GPS tracking device on his cell phone. Do you know where Detective Hudson is right now, Mr. Welles?"

"Yes," he said, trying to keep the rising panic out of his voice.

"I'm sorry to tell you this, but so do I, and so does Harold Manlius. Detective Lieutenant Hudson was followed to his current location, Mr. Welles, and I believe he and the person he is visiting are possibly in danger."

"Thank you so much for calling me, Mr. Fornaio, but I think you'll understand if I hang up now. Again, thank you."

"*Di nenti*, Mr. Welles."

WALTER'S PHONE WAS RINGING, but he didn't answer it. It was either someone warning him that he was about to be ambushed, which was now old information, or the people attacking him, which he doubted, since it was apparent that polite negotiation wasn't on their agenda.

He crawled over to Barbara Grunewald, staying close to the floor, trying to avoid the broken glass and the blood.

"What happened?" she said, her face white, her eyes glassy. She was clearly in shock.

"You've been shot," said Walter. "Stay down and don't move." She has no idea what just happened, he thought, and it's just as well.

"Oh, okay."

Hudson had seen a lot of bullet wounds in his life, and it took him only seconds to determine that it was a through-and–through wound to Barbara's lower left abdomen that, despite all the blood, hadn't pierced any arteries or major organs. Good. He didn't have the means or the time to deal with anything else, and at least whomever he was dealing with wasn't much of a sharpshooter. Staying on the floor and avoiding the broken glass as much as possible, he grabbed her by one arm and dragged her into the hallway. He thought of getting her to the kitchen, but there were large windows in the kitchen, and Hudson didn't know how many attackers there were or if they'd surrounded the house. There was a large coat closet in the hallway that was mercifully uncluttered. He stuffed Barbara in. The vintage home had hard plaster walls, and she was probably safer there than anywhere in the house.

But getting Barbara Grunewald to a safe place wasn't Walter's biggest problem. His biggest problem was that in his haste to leave New York, he'd left his service revolver behind. He knew that if there was more than one attacker, and if they were any good, he was a dead man. But Walter had that rare capacity not to dwell on that. He put Sarah and the kids, and the possibility that he may never see them again, out of his mind and concentrated on only one thing: what to do next.

His one advantage was that he'd been in the house and knew its layout, and the attackers didn't. But it would only be an advantage if the house was dark. He spied a light switch on the corner of the hallway wall adjacent to the living room. He'd have only one chance, and he hoped he was lucky. He reached up and flipped the switch. Shots rang out, but they were far off the mark. The house went dark.

He crawled quickly to the front door, keeping his body below the level of the windowsills. If the attacker was a pro who knew how to enter a house, Walter didn't stand much of a chance, but if the attacker was a petty thug, Walter might get the guy by surprise. But as he listened, his heart sank. He heard multiple distinct voices out in the front yard. That was the bad news. The good news was that the attackers didn't have the discipline to keep their mouths shut, so they weren't pro's. But at best it was still multiple armed thugs against one unarmed cop. Hudson was good, but not that good.

Walter heard footsteps just outside the door. Shit. He hadn't had a chance to lock the door, which might have given him a couple of precious extra seconds. He heard the doorknob rattle. He tensed himself. The door opened a few inches. The guy was tentative, not a pro. A toe of a shoe edged its way across the threshold of the door. Now was Walter's chance, probably his only chance. He grabbed the man's ankle and pulled hard as he stood himself up. The invader fell flat on his back, and Walter could hear the air explode out of his lungs as he hit the floor. A gun went off, but it was a frantic shot that went straight through the ceiling. Walter grabbed the gun and twisted until it came loose, and he took control of it. He heard loud cracks come from the man's arm, and he knew that he'd not only broken the man's wrist but probably both bones in his forearm as well. It felt good. The man writhed on the floor, both from pain and lack of air. Walter brought his fist down on the man's face. He heard a thud as the back of the man's head hit the hardwood floor. Blood spurted from his shattered nose. The man was still. Walter hoped he hadn't killed him, though not out of any concern for his immortal soul. He just didn't want to bother with the paperwork.

Walter looked down at the gun in his hand, a Smith & Wesson .38. He would've preferred his .45 caliber service revolver, but it would do, especially at close range. He also knew that if it had been a .45, Barbara Grunewald would probably be dead. He checked the magazine. Eight rounds. The only shot fired had come from the chamber. Good, more than he needed. Look who's in charge now, he thought.

He crab-crawled over to a side window and waited for more gunshots to send bullets crashing through the front windows, shots that would tell him where the other attackers were. His blood was up now, and he couldn't wait.

And then, nothing. Walter heard what he thought was a muffled "hmpff," and perhaps some quiet footsteps from soft-soled shoes. He waited a minute. He waited another minute. Then he heard the sound of car engines firing up from down the street. He slowly raised his head.

Nobody. Nobody in the yard. Nobody on the street. The only cars in the driveway were Barbara's and his. Walter put the safety on the .38 and stuffed it in his waistband, more than a little disappointed. He went over and looked down at the unconscious man lying in the front hallway. He was completely inert, but he was at least breathing. Walter would worry about him in a minute. He raced over to the closet, turning on the lights as he went, and opened the door. Barbara Grunewald had managed to get herself into a sitting position. Her eyes were open, and the bleeding seemed to have slowed to a seep. She stared at him, and he stared back.

"Could you please give me a hand, Lieutenant?" she said. "I think I may have drunk a little too much wine."

⊸⊸∙⊸∙⊸

"WHY AM I not surprised?" said Walter, as he stepped into Commissioner Donahue's private pub. For once, the door had been left ajar, the hour too late for even Donahue's long-suffering assistant.

"Close the door behind you, Walter," said Donahue. "You're the last one to the party."

"But not the least," said Mayor Deborah Kaplan.

"Hey, Levi," said Walter, tossing him back his car keys.

"Is there anything left of it?" said Levi, pocketing the keys.

"There's nothing I can do to hurt that little monster," said Walter, turning to the only person he hadn't expected to see. "Good evening, Mr. Fornaio."

"I imagine my presence may answer some of your questions, Lieutenant," said Tommassino Fornaio, a rare smile on his face. They were all sitting at the bar except Donahue who, as usual, was reveling in his role as bartender. He slid two fingers of Bushmills, neat, over to Walter without being asked. Walter couldn't help noticing that Fornaio, still dressed in black-tie, did not have a glass of whisky in front of him. Instead, there was a tiny glass of what Walter guessed to be anisette, and an equally tiny cup of espresso. It was the first time Walter had ever seen someone drink anything but Irish Whisky in this room, but he wasn't surprised. Tommassino Fornaio was the kind of man who always got what he asked for, and he never had to ask twice.

"Yes, I guess it does," said Walter, "but first, does anyone know how Barbara Grunewald is doing?"

"She is resting comfortably in the Albany County Hospital intensive care unit," said Mayor Kaplan. "She still isn't quite sure what happened, but perhaps that's all for the best for now."

"The thug you cold-cocked, however," said Donahue, "is not faring quite so well. He's still unconscious and in critical condition, but the docs think he'll survive. The trauma doc asked if someone had dropped a piano on his head."

"I only hit him once, sir," said Walter.

"I'm sure you did," said Donahue.

"Can somebody fill me in on what happened?" said Walter, taking an un-reluctant sip of his whisky.

"I guess we owe you that, don't we," said Donahue. "Levi?"

"Three men were sent to Saugerties to kill you and Barbara Grunewald," said Levi.

"Hold it," said Walter. "How did they even know I was going there? And who sent them?"

"Let Levi talk, Walter," said Mayor Kaplan. "It'll all come out."

"You probably figured out pretty quickly," said Levi, "that these guys weren't exactly skilled assassins, but we guess on short notice you have to take what you can get."

"Yeah, that was a piece of luck," said Walter.

"I'd never bet against you under any circumstances, son," said Donahue, "but it probably was."

"I figured that's why the other two ran," said Walter.

"They didn't run, Walter," said Levi. "They were captured and turned in to the NYPD. They are currently in custody and have confessed and named names."

"I'm sorry," said Walter, "I'm probably tired, but I'm confused. How did you get cops up there so fast?"

"They weren't cops, Walter," said Levi. "About an hour after you left the city, I got a call from Mr. Fornaio. He told me that he'd learned through back channels that you and Ms. Grunewald were in grave danger. Of course, we didn't have any time to send NYPD cops to help, but Tommassino said he'd already sent some, uh, professional operatives known to some associates of associates of his. They didn't get there quite in time to prevent the shot that injured Barbara Grunewald, but they secured the two assassins who were still outside the house. Then, while you were in the hallway tending to Ms. Grunewald, one of the operatives snuck back and briefly entered the house. He was going to remove the man you took down but he didn't dare move him in his condition. He heard you and Ms. Grunewald speaking in the closet, so he knew you were both okay for the time being. Then he called 911 and left. He would have stayed, but as you can imagine, anonymity is important to these men. By the time the other two were placed in the custody of the NYPD, they were already singing like nightingales in Berkeley Square."

"So?" said Walter.

"So they pointed the finger right at Harold Manlius," said Levi. "He was apparently so panicked about what Barbara Grunewald was going to say to you that he contacted these guys directly, not wasting the time to use an intermediary."

"We would've cracked through any intermediaries in about five seconds in any event," said Donahue, refilling everyone's glasses, including his own.

"My God," said Walter, "that's great. When do you plan to arrest him?"

"Already done," said Donahue. "I wanted to wait until tomorrow when we could have given you the pleasure of putting him in cuffs in the middle of one of his campaign rallies, but the man was a flight risk, so we arrested him as soon as we could."

"Where is he now?"

"He's just down the street in the Tombs," said Donahue, "facing charges of first degree murder, conspiracy to commit murder and, yes, rape. The judge denied bail. He'll be moved to Rikers Island in the morning. We promised him a change of underwear."

"And based on what I'm seeing on my iPhone," said Levi, "his campaign manager has already announced that his campaign is being 'temporarily suspended pending further developments.'"

"Now," said Fornaio, "if you folks would please excuse me, I left a very unhappy wife by herself at the Waldorf. I think it would be wise of me to get back to her." He rose to leave.

"Please give Christina a hug for me," said Mayor Kaplan.

"And give her one for me, too," said Donahue. "And, Tommy, thank you."

"*Di nenti*," said Fornaio. He quietly slipped out the door.

"Sometimes I just don't get it," said Walter, staring at the closed door and shaking his head.

"Sometimes you don't have to," said Donahue, taking a sip from his glass that nearly drained it. "Take that as a lesson."

"With all due respect," said Walter, "there's still something you haven't explained to me, sir." He drained his own glass in one gulp, something he rarely did. He was in a mood. Donahue refilled both their glasses, and Walter didn't protest.

"I know, I know," said Donahue, "Captain Amato and the letter, right?"

"Yessir."

"You have to understand, son, that I couldn't do anything to lead Amato to suspect anything."

"Suspect what?"

"That I knew he was a mole for the Manlius organization, of course. He wasn't the only one, but he was the one that tipped Manlius off that you were on your way to Saugerties to talk to Barbara Grunewald, thereby putting your life at risk."

"Son of a bitch! It was my phone, wasn't it."

"Sure. They're NYPD phones, and the GPS tracking usually serves to protect you, but he could also track you real time right from the computer on his desk. He was smart enough to use multiple throwaway phones to communicate with Manlius, which caused us a problem, but we were catching up with him. Thank God Tommy Fornaio was one step ahead of us. But in the meantime, I had to play meek with Amato and let you storm out of my office angry."

"You said there were others?"

"Yes. Only four, but it was enough to give Manlius a pretty effective spy network right under our noses."

"But why?"

"Oh, I don't think I need to explain that. I'm sure you already know. They were all ambitious, greedy young men, and Manlius offered them all the same bait: big promotions, a clear path to my job once he'd fired me, or maybe a fat job in his private company, that kind of thing."

"Where are they all now?"

"Well, if I had my way they'd all be in jail, but of course we've got the union to deal with, so right now they've all been placed on administrative leave pending an investigation. All, that is, except Amato. He's been charged with conspiracy to commit murder, and the union can't do a damn thing about that. So he's Manlius's next door neighbor in the Tombs right now."

"You can't send him to Rikers, Mike," said Mayor Kaplan. "He might be a dirty cop, but he's a cop all the same. He won't last a day there. It would be a death sentence."

"It wouldn't be the first," said Donahue, a hard edge to his voice.

"Mike."

"Oh, don't worry, Deborah," said Donahue, "I'll order him to be kept at the Tombs. But once he's convicted, and he will be convicted, there won't be anything I can do for him."

"I understand that," she said. She paused a few seconds, and then she held out her glass to Donahue. "Pour," she said.

"Yes, ma'am," said Donahue, obliging.

When it was full, she said, "Now, since we're all here, and since Commissioner Donahue seems to have an endless supply of whisky, maybe we should toast another fine job by the NYPD. You didn't just solve a crime this time, men. You saved this city from what I'm convinced would've been chaos, though that may sound self-serving coming from me. Thank you so much."

"Hear, hear," said Commissioner Donahue. "Here's to you, Levi, and here's to you, Walter. You're two of the finest of New York's finest, and I don't know what I'd do without you."

"And here's to you, Mayor Kaplan," said Levi, "and here's to wishing you a long residence at Gracie Mansion." They all drank, and the glow in the room wasn't just from the whisky.

"And now," said Walter, "I'm going home to my wife, who will promptly beat me about the head and ears for showing up on her doorstep drunk yet again."

"If that's the only thing she's mad at you about, Walter," said the mayor, with a smile on her face, "you're a lucky man."

28

THE FOLKS IN DUTCH RIVER were talking about the heat on this Fourth of July. They didn't know what heat was, thought Sarah Hudson as she sat on the back porch of their farmhouse in the early evening sunshine, not until they spent a Fourth in New York City. Sarah was glad to be out of the city and on the farm, and she was glad to be there with friends.

Levi and Julie had come up with them the weekend before, and the old farmhouse, so often empty but kept well stocked and immaculate by their good friend and neighbor, Fred Benecke, felt alive, as if it had its own intelligence. Maybe it did, thought Sarah.

Walter and Sarah had brought their three kids along, of course, though in the ten days they'd been at the farm they'd barely seen them except at mealtimes. And that was only when they hadn't been over at the Averys's house horsing around with Adam and Sally's kids and eating Adam's incredible home cooking. Sarah had wanted to be put out, but the four adults had also spent the week downing as much of Adam's mouthwatering cuisine as possible, so it was hard to argue with them. So the adults had been able to spend quality time together, and apparently apart, if you were inclined to take Julie Remy's announcement seriously that she and Levi had enjoyed not one but two genuine rolls in the hay since they'd arrived.

Of course, Fred Benecke and his son, Arthur, the neighbor farmers who farmed Walter and Sarah's fifty acres rent-free in return for maintenance of the property, had put Walter and Levi to work as soon as they'd arrived. Fred, now in his seventies but still possessing the strength and stamina of most men half his age, had joked that having Walter on the farm was like having an extra horse in the stable, and he cost less to feed. But it was Levi who astonished them. The bookish, physically unprepossessing man displayed a capacity for hard labor and a level of physical stamina that astounded everyone but his wife, who just smiled as he came in from the fields every evening looking refreshed and, most importantly, ready for a roll in the hay.

After receiving permission from the State of New York and Columbia County, they had quietly laid Stephanie French to rest next to her namesake in the old French family burial plot. Sadly, Greta Roberts had chosen not to attend, but Bernard French had played his violin over the grave, and he and Lydia had wept as if they were burying their own child all over again. It had given them some closure, thought Sarah, and they both looked at peace as they sat together on the porch sipping iced tea.

Sarah shifted her gaze to her big husband as he stood over the gas grill, cooking meat and sipping a beer as he chatted with Jill Maas, his enormous hand making the spatula he held look like a child's toy. He looked good: his skin brown, his eyes lively, his enormous frame lean and hard. Good, she thought. She'd been worried about him ever since he'd closed the Stephanie French case more than a month ago now.

It normally took Walter a couple of weeks to decompress from a difficult case, but he always bounced back. But this time that hadn't happened, and by the time they'd arrived at the farm, he was still in a funk. He tried to hide it, and perhaps to most people he had, but he hadn't been able to fool her, nor had he been able to fool Levi and Julie, perceptive people who perhaps knew him better than anyone but her.

When they'd gotten to the farm, the kids had immediately disappeared and come back just in time for dinner, exhausted. The children were all in bed by nine, and the adults had had the lovely home, the walls covered with Sarah's Uncle Armin's extraordinary collection of Hudson River School art, the collection that had made them rich, to themselves.

Julie, a lover and connoisseur of French wine, had brought with her a dozen bottles from her private cellar, and after coffee and dessert she had proposed to crack one open, maybe two, she'd said. They had all instantly agreed, including Walter, which had surprised Sarah, since he hadn't touched a drop of alcohol since the case had been solved, claiming that Commissioner Donahue had poured enough Bushmills down his throat during the investigation to last him the rest of the year.

The others had grown more voluble as the wine had been consumed, but Walter had only grown quieter. It was Leviticus who had broken the ice.

"Walter," he'd said, "you seem a little subdued. Is everything okay?"

"Oh," said Walter, with a laugh, "don't worry, I'm fine. I'm still decompressing from the Stephanie French case, that's all."

"You can't fool Levi and me any more than you can fool Sarah,

Walter," said Julie. "Usually after a case, even a tough one, you're your old self after a week. So out with it, you're among friends here."

Walter hadn't wanted to talk about it. He was a private man doing a difficult job, and he would have preferred to deal with the fallout himself. Murder was an ugly business, and he'd never wanted to infect his family life and his friendships with what he had to witness and endure to solve his cases. He'd get over it; he always did. But they'd all seen the struggle on his face, and they knew as well as he did that this one had been different. Whether it had been because of the bizarre circumstances surrounding it, or because of the extraordinary woman he'd come to know so intimately in order to solve her murder, he may never know. But they all knew that he needed their help in order to come to terms with it, and he knew it too.

"Look, I'm a homicide cop," Walter had said, after a long silence. "I love my job, and I never wanted to do anything else. I still don't. But I fail on every single case I take. I fail before I even start, and I guess the older I get the more it starts to wear on me, that's all."

"Walter," said Levi, "you close your cases."

"You're right, Levi, I do. And I closed this one. I solved the crime. Good for me. I solved another murder. And good for you, and good for Eduardo. We all solved it together. But you know what? My victim, my client, is still dead. Stephanie French is still dead, and there's nothing I can do about it. There's no restitution, no putting things back together again in a murder case. She'll never have the chance to run Barstow & Company. No one will ever hear her play the violin again. SafeWays will have to get along without her. I'm like a doctor who loses every single patient he has, or a lawyer whose clients are all sentenced to death, even though they're all innocent. The doctor can explain why every one of his patients died, and the lawyer can prove that he performed his job perfectly, but so what? They're all still dead."

"I hate to sound harsh, Walter," said Sarah, "but everybody dies."

"Of course they do, but…"

"Listen to your wife, Walter," said Julie, "she's right. Everybody dies, and it's always a tragedy to someone. There's hardly a person in this world who hasn't experienced it, and it's never fair. Look at you. You lost your father when he was far younger than Stephanie was when she died. Levi and Sarah both lost their mothers when they were still in high school. These tragedies happen every day, and we almost never notice any of them, except the ones that happen to us. It doesn't make them fair or any less tragic, Walter, but it's just the world the way it is. The tough thing about being a homicide cop is you have to experience it every day, and it's not just nature taking its course. I understand that, and I can't imagine how tough it is. But keeping everyone alive isn't your job, Walter. We have to put that in God's hands and move on."

Walter had gone quiet after that, but Sarah could tell that Julie's words had found their mark. They'd changed the subject and enjoyed their wine before going to bed with their windows open to the mild country air.

The next morning Sarah could tell that Walter had awakened a different man, ready to heal. And heal he had.

"Meat's ready!" Walter shouted, snapping Sarah out of her reverie. Jill said something to him that made him laugh as he heaped steaks, sausages, and burgers onto a huge platter she held. Sarah liked his laugh, a laugh that made him sound like a boy again.

Walter Hudson was a cop, a cop's cop. That was his job, a job he did well, and she was proud of him.

But it was the boy she loved.

THE END

ALSO BY CHARLES AYER

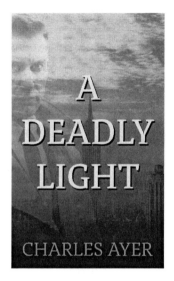

A DEADLY LIGHT

Why did two apparently unrelated murder victims, a young prostitute and an unidentified Korean man, die on the streets of New York City with the same cryptic words, "A thousand points of light," on their lips? NYPD Detective Sergeant Walter Hudson's efforts to find out unexpectedly but inexorably lure him into the treacherous worlds of political intrigue, unchecked power, and limitless wealth—worlds that he is ill-equipped to understand. But he has to learn fast as he begins to peel back the layers of a monstrous plot that threatens not only the city he loves, but his country as well. It's a race against time, and Detective Hudson has less time than he thinks.

Learn more at: www.outskirtspress.com/adeadlylight

ALSO BY CHARLES AYER

PLACID HOLLOW

Federal Judge T. Franklin "Teddy" Braxton was beloved by his family and admired by his peers. His immense wealth had put him at the pinnacle of New York City's elite political and social worlds. So who murdered him in cold blood? Perhaps it was the nearly naked young woman found standing over his body with a .45 caliber pistol in her hand. Or perhaps not.... Detective Lieutenant Walter Hudson is in over his head, and he knows it, as he immediately begins to receive intense pressure to solve the case from both Mayor Deborah Kaplan and Police Commissioner Sean Donahue, both personal friends of the Judge. And he may be getting in over his head personally as well, as the judge's beautiful daughter, Virginia, starts giving him more help than he's looking for. He'll need all the help he can get from Leviticus Welles, now a rising star in the NYPD's Intelligence Division, to guide him through the maze of Teddy Braxton's life as well as the tangle of his own emotions. But one thing Walter knows from the start is that there's nothing placid at all about Placid Hollow.

Learn more at: www.outskirtspress.com/placidhollow

ALSO BY CHARLES AYER

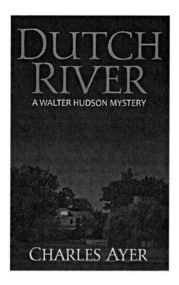

DUTCH RIVER

When NYPD Detective Lieutenant Walter Hudson's wife, Sarah, unexpectedly inherits a family farm in the tiny upstate village of Dutch River, New York, their first thought is to sell it as soon as possible. But they are immediately charmed by the village and its residents, and Sarah's great-uncle, Armin Jaeger, leaves them a letter too puzzling to ignore. They are soon stunned to find that Sarah has been left more than a simple farmhouse in a quaint village; and matters turn even more intriguing when Walter discovers a mysterious connection between Dutch River and the murder of a prominent Boston philanthropist, Charles Martin Sewall. And matters take an even more deadly turn when Walter's family is threatened. Walter will need all his skills and all the help he can get from his good friend, Leviticus Welles, as he desperately races against time not just to solve a hideous crime but to save his family as well. It's a race he can't afford to lose.

Learn more at: www.outskirtspress.com/dutchriver

CPSIA information can be obtained
at www.ICGtesting.com
Printed in the USA
FSOW01n1053200717
36550FS